Behind the Sun, Above the Moon

A Queer anthology inspired by magic and the cosmos, a vast and beautiful place where planets, stars, comets— entire galaxies, even—live without borders, specifications or binaries. Stories span science fiction, science fantasy, contemporary, fabulism and magical realism, and celebrate Non-binary and Transgender characters.

twice-spent comet by Ziggy Schutz

On an isolated asteroid, Fer serves out their sentence with a found family of ramshackle criminals. Life takes an exciting turn when they befriend Ophelia, a beautiful humanoid creature with a tail like a comet.

From Dusk to Dying Sun by Paige S. Allen

Jay Morrison almost believes the rumors of magic and mischief haunting the US-50. But their partner, Luis Inoa, has made a career guarding the dusty Nevada trails. According to him, the only scary things on the highway are the silences, until a group of tourists break open the sun and disappear into a fiery blaze.

Lost/Found by Brooklyn Ray

When Hollis Griffin, a lonely sex worker living in Venice Beach, forms an unlikely friendship with a fallen star, she begins to face the truth about her life, her past, and what the future holds.

Awry with Dandelions by J.S. Fields

For thirty seconds every night, a disembodied specter named Mette visits with Orin who has long since written the ghost woman off as a recurring dream. But when Mette suggests meeting in real life, Orin's inner world turns out to be more substantial than imaginary, and xie embarks on a journey to discover the truth of Mette and their strange connection.

The Far Touch by S.R. Jones

A long-standing coven of witches trek to their sacred space and accidentally discover life on another planet when their Solstice celebration interferes with a lone practitioner.

Ink and Stars by Alex Harrow

Locked in a contract to steal their ex-lovers ship, Chaz Neoma comes face to face with consequences, lost partnership, and the chance at a future, after discovering they aren't the last Weaver in the universe.

Horologium by Emmett Nahil

In the far reaches of the Horologium Supercluster, an astronaux is stranded alone on a long-distance astral ship where they're visited by three apparitions, telling stories of ancestors who traveled space before them. Coeie must decide whether to follow the ghosts of the past, or forge their own path through the cosmos.

Death Marked by Sara Codair

As chief security officer in the Lunar Guard, Enzi is in charge of the security for their sister's coming of age ceremony. A fragile relationship with their family doesn't make keeping Ulsa safe any easier, and neither does a group of pesky drones or a hidden plot to overthrow their sister's place in the family.

Weave the Dark, Weave the Light by Anna Zabo

On a crisp night, Ari, a supposed elemental witch, meets Jonathan Aster, a powerful being they desperately want to understand. As they explore an intense, intimate and passionate relationship, Ari unearths long-hidden mysteries about themself and their magic.

BEHIND THE SUN,

ABOVE THE MOON

Ziggy Schutz
Paige S. Allen
Brooklyn Ray
J.S. Fields
S.R. Jones
Alex Harrow
Emmett Nahil
Sara Codair
Anna Zabo

A NineStar Press Publication

Published by NineStar Press
P.O. Box 91792,
Albuquerque, New Mexico, 87199 USA.
www.ninestarpress.com

Behind the Sun, Above the Moon

Printed in the USA
First Edition
January, 2020

Print ISBN: 978-1-951880-19-4

Also available in eBook, ISBN: 978-1-951880-18-7

Warning: This book contains sexually explicit content, which may only be suitable for mature readers, mention of body horror (organ donation), mention of murder, brief mention of sexual harassment, violence, BDSM, consensual D/s play, and pain play.

Table of Contents

TWICE-SPENT

COMET

Ziggy Schutz

Warning: mention of body horror (organ donation),
mention of murder

In the beginning, before Humans had claimed the stars as their own, they held hands as they watched lights streak across the sky and called it Magic.

Magic, as everyone knows, must be Spoken and Heard and Believed, and so it was so, that stars were Magic, and those that fell especially so.

Sometimes, the beginning of stories are just as simple as that.

*

Waking up is always the hardest part.

Fer's been on this rock long enough that they've gotten used to it. Even grown to almost like it in true Earth Syndrome fashion. They like how easy the work has gotten, when early on they'd barely been able to make it through the day. They like their new muscles, filling out fabric that had hung loose before. They're fed better here than they were in the prison or the transfer ship, and the companionship is a huge upgrade.

Waking up, though. Waking up has always been a slow process for Fer, and there's always a moment where they forget they ever got caught at all. Where they open their eyes and expect to see the cluttered walls of their last hideout—dangerously close to being a *home*. Back before Adrastea happened, and everything went tits-up.

Then they open their eyes to the soft curves of their small cell, and they remember they're here. Officially occupying the middle of nowhere, six months into a fifteen year sentence they're not expected to survive.

But, hey. Food's all right.

Fer reaches over, taps the speaker set into the wall so that it'll stop telling them to wake up. They step into their orange jumpsuit, garishly bright against the soft blues of the grown-metal walls with an underlayer that would glow even brighter in the event of a loss of light. The suit was the height of prisoner-safety technology, according to the worker who had issued it to Fer, as if Fer wouldn't notice the fraying seams or dried blood staining the cuff of one of the five otherwise-identical suits.

They saved that one for days when they felt especially lucky. Or bitter.

Today, they're mostly feeling hungry.

They duck through their empty doorway—no doors here, no barricading yourself away, just a thin audio divider that always feels slimy when stepped through—and into the common room, letting the noise of the only other occupants on this asteroid roll over them.

The best thing about prison is other people. Who knew?

"Looks like it's going to be another hot one," calls Moll. Her booming voice carries easily in the dome-covered area connecting their rooms as a common space. The storage unit is tucked against one wall as best it can be, being a large rectangular container in a round room.

"Not all of us grew up in weather too hot to breathe in, Moll. Would it kill ya to turn it down a notch or two?"

Benat's grumble goes cheerfully ignored.

Moll, as the tallest of the four, has claimed dominion over the temperature control—both inside and outside—for as long as Fer's been here. She keeps it just a little too hot for comfort, and they all complain like they're working off a script. But Fer also knows that Moll checks all of their outputs during their lunch break, and when they're in the red, she turns the heat down, gives them that extra boost. Moll's the reason so few of them ever end the day with a deficit.

Moll had winked, the only time Fer had caught her at it. "Conditioning, love. Always nice to have an ace in the sleeve, right?"

Moll's got two—permanent aces traced in white ink against each dark forearm. Because she makes her own luck, whether with her large, surprisingly nimble fingers or the permanent buzz of a contraband tattoo gun, which she slides out of a hidden chamber in her prosthetic leg and can reassemble in under thirty seconds.

They're all a little in love with her, and she knows it. Fer would bet another ten years on their sentence that Moll's never met a person who didn't fall for her in some way or another. She's just that kind of lady.

Benat groans again, slumped facedown on the table, breakfast ration turning less and less edible with each moment she leaves it untouched. The drawl that marks her as a moony brat is even more pronounced when she's just waking up, almost incomprehensible if you're not used to picking the words apart from where they slur into each other.

Benat has the dubious honour of being the most high-risk of them all. The metal cuffs they all wear variations of proclaim her a murderer with their bright red sheen.

(The rumor is: cuffs came from an Earth tradition, cutting the hands off of criminals. People say they can sever a wrist as easily as they can snap together and restrain. Fer's never seen it happen, but they believe it all the same.)

Benat doesn't look dangerous, though. Most of the time she just looks tired, like her body's never adjusted to the pull of the prison's gravity, artificially altered to match the Earth's stronger weight rather than her own home. Her shock-blonde hair hasn't grown out from when they shaved it during her transfer, and it sticks up unevenly, always betraying her on the days she tossed and turned instead of sleeping, and her eyebrows are almost invisible against pale, freckled skin.

She looks young. *Too young for a life sentence*, Moll had muttered to Fer. Like they're much older than her. Like anyone deserves this.

Fer's wanted to ask Benat, in the quiet moments after a long day where the barriers between them all feel paper-thin, what she'd done to earn a murderer's mark. But it's hard to talk about why they were here when Mark is so fresh in all of their minds. He'd been a spitfire, chatterbox, talking too much and too loudly, until he'd paid for it with a cut safety line and a room that still sits empty.

It's best to talk about lighter things.

*

Magic has many forms, passed from hand to hand until smooth. Magic can be wonder, breathed from one mouth to another. Magic can be a spark that feels like home in the eyes of a stranger. Magic can be the breeze reminding the lonely that the world is bigger than they know.

Magic is connection, common ground, two voices telling the same story.

Magic is the space between.

*

"Can I eat yours, then?"

Benat's palm comes down, surprisingly fast, and smacks the hand reaching for her food. Even at her most wide-awake, she'd be lucky to catch Rack, a foot shorter than Benat and faster than anyone Fer's ever seen. He swears he's famous in at least three systems, although Fer's never heard of him. His cuffs are dark green—*thief*—and when he breathes there's a faint whirring sound, like something inside him is more metal than flesh.

He's fond of saying his best heist was stealing himself a new set of lungs. This, Fer can believe.

And that's them. Worn bodies around a small table, breaking metaphorical bread before the day's labours begin. Their prison is built to hold eight, but right now there's only the four of them. The four of them on their own little asteroid, completely indistinguishable from all the other asteroids in this belt except for the fact that this one was owned by a rich developer.

Back on the holding ship, before their trial, and then on the transport, there'd been all sorts of folk. But there's certain prisons you can only be sent to if you're human.

Other races have rules about isolation. The word they use would translate to 'inhumane' except that other species' words for cruelty often sound like 'human.'

There's still a year left of groundbreaking to do, as long as their little team's numbers stay steady. Then they'll send in the experts, get to building the luxury retreat homes, and their little pod with its eight tiny bedroom-cells and its rickety chairs will fold up and take off for the next asteroid, the next quota, until all of their bones break or until the timers on their cuffs run out and fall off and their time is served.

But for now, Benat has pulled herself up enough to eat her food, shoving the congealed meal into her mouth without breaking eye contact with Rack. It's not especially funny, but Fer catches Moll's fond eye roll and laughs anyway.

If Fer shrinks their world to just this, the years ahead don't feel impossible.

Unfortunately, it's not long before the alarm sounds, and then they're grabbing their kits and heading out. The screens attached to their shovels project the grid, dictating which of them is working where today, who is planting atmosphere-establishing seeds and who is digging holes for swimming pools and survival bunkers or whatever else rich people put in their space-mansions. The assignments always feel just this side of arbitrary, and they're always spread out enough to be just out of sight of each other.

Out here, all Fer can hear is their own breathing, echoed back at them by the edge of their artificial atmosphere. It sits well above their head, pressing down on them, a constant reminder that it can disappear with the push of a button in a watchtower thousands of stars away.

Fer ducks their head, pushes those thoughts away like so much collected dust, and lets their shovel bite into the rock beneath them.

*

If Life comes from light, and stars from dust, then every blessed thing that exists is made of stardust, lit by its own existence.

However, there are some beings who are more star than most.

Tails made of the sky, held up by magic—some of these beings swim between worlds. They were others once, small crawling creatures with names and curiosity too big for their fragile bones.

Many stories start with an ending, and theirs ended in an explosion, every moment of them suddenly everywhere. Ages passed before they could pull themselves together again, and when they did, their bodies were no longer large enough to hold all that they Knew.

So they left them behind.

*

Before, when Fer first arrived, they kept one eye on the sky. For debris from the asteroid field around them. For rescue, something their old friends had often hinted at and half planned, but never something they dared put down in writing. More prayer than anything concrete.

It should be strange, how quickly the movement above their head faded into the background, like noise in the heart of a city. But Fer knows the rules now. No errant rocks will hit them—the bubble that keeps their atmosphere stable sees to that, built for future rich residents. And no rescue will reach them, because even if any of their people were as lucky as Fer to avoid a traitor's sentence, they'd be scattered like smoke off a gun—too far away to ever find each other again.

So, Fer keeps their head down, most days, lets space bear down on the back of their neck as much as it likes. It's why they miss the creatures when they first fly by.

It's only when they feel the weight of eyes on them that they freeze, shovel half-buried in the rock, and look up.

The first sense Fer gets is *vast*.

The objects are large, like ships, but also stretch beyond what a space vessel encompasses—like they expand past what Fer can comprehend. Streaking across the horizon like comets, trails sparkling and alive with much more than dust.

Fer should have been terrified. But.

They had lived the first part of their life so unbearably grounded. They remember what it felt like, when they first saw the ship that would carry them away from the bits of life they'd managed to cling to. More than bolts and sails and thrust, it was freedom, and they knew no matter what the stars brought them, they would never see anything as beautiful as that.

And that had held true. Until this moment.

If Fer carried any religion in their heart, they might have thought they were angels. Humanoid but not, limbs stretched out like wings or judgement.

Fer should have been terrified, *but*.

Fer had grown up a dreamer, had relied on stories to fill their soul when there was nothing to fill their stomach, devoured each scrap of fable they could get their greedy hungry hands on. Beneath the shell of boredom and routine is someone who secretly hoped for *more*. It's how they got into the rebellion in the first place, a sense of wonder well-hidden and hard-won.

It's blooming now, deep between their ribs, because they recognize a myth when they see one.

"Mermaid," slips from their lips, like a penny in a wishing well, and the closest creature turns toward Fer, eyes twin moons against skin dark enough to have its own stars.

Once named, one could perhaps see where Fer is coming from. The creatures' bodies trail off like ellipses of stardust, unsubstantial and undulating them forward through space all the same. Certainly, with hair that shines like nebulas as it bounces around their heads, 'mermaid' feels just as impossible as 'angel' and just as true.

But this is not why Fer names them mermaids.

*

And so they swam through the stars, and knew of humans but knew none, until they happened upon a ring of space rock and bright eyes spotted them.

And the bright eyes, the scurrying creature, they knew nothing of space except how to live in it, and they knew nothing of tales but their endings, but they let the large bodies and the stardust caught up in their fins sweep them away for just a moment, and although they had lived two decades they opened their mouth and a child's voice spilled out to call these celestial bodies mermaids.

And the Mermaids (for so as they were called, so then they were) paused, for the scurrying creature was as small as they were vast, and yet with a word had Named them, and therefore Changed them.

And the Leader, who swam at the front because she was most Curious of the lot, she looked down at the creature, and saw them to be Human, and in this seeing saw that she was No Longer the same. And that scared her, and delighted her, and in that moment she was both Named and Found.

And the Human (for that is what they were), who had always been Lost through their own design, looked into the Mermaid's eyes and saw themselves, and saw the stars, and saw a story.

This story, they did not know the ending to. And that made them Curious, too.

*

Fer stares at the creature, and she stares back.

And everything in Fer's head, every doubt and every hard truth and every bit of lost hope, goes quiet.

They breathe in, and think of a storm on a distant moon, one that disrupted their sensors enough that when the raid came, no one was ready. Their little rebel crew, dashed on the rocks of a government that only wants one narrative told, paints and paper floating weightless like flotsam.

Since that moment, Fer's been living underwater, unable to shake the pressure in their chest.

They breathe out, and no bubbles escape, leading them to a distant surface. They breathe out, and nothing terrible happens at all.

So they take it one step further.

"H'llo," says Fer. Not the most inspiring of greetings, but words come slow to them even when not addressing an impossible thing.

The being stares, leans close enough that Fer could reach out and touch the creature's bare shoulder if they wanted to. For a moment, Fer feels a weight push down on them, and they lock their knees, stubborn until the end. They've never kneeled for anyone, never begged, never asked for an inch they hadn't fought to earn. They're not about to start now, even with such an auspicious audience as this.

And then the whole sky seems to pulse. Fer flinches, closes their eyes, and when they open them the pressure is gone, and the mermaid floats in front of them, shrunk down to Fer's height with proportions to match.

"Oh," the mermaid says, voice a soft rasp. "Talking out loud. Of course. Hello."

*

Sometimes, the beginnings of stories are just as simple as that.

*

The other mermaids linger just long enough for the one in front to gesture at them, fingers moving almost too fast to follow, delicate and firm. Fer's seen similar signs from some of the gangs they grew up around, kids speaking in a language no authority could parse, usual methods of silencing with sound dampeners or pinned tongues having no impact at all. Fer's own group of rebels had a dialect of their own, although it was scraped together from across Earth and three moons, each of them bringing a few words to the table from what they'd picked up from their respective childhoods. Theirs was by no means a large vocabulary, which the mermaids' obviously is.

Complete and strangely familiar—Fer doesn't know why these space beings would be using signs that resemble ones they saw back at home, but can pick out a few they recognize. It makes them homesick in a way that always sneaks up on them. Not for the planet but for the press of people, for the feeling of being another face in a crowd, of not knowing the names of your neighbours but knowing they'll fight for you if the uniforms come a-calling.

Their own fingers are clumsy, but they still remember how to say hello.

The creature beams, smile stretching her face into something almost human. The signs flow from her hands like a riptide, pulling Fer in over their head.

"Sorry," says Fer out loud. "I don't know enough to follow."

The others are swimming away, blending in with the stars as they do, but her only movement is to reach out, rest strange, cold hands against Fer's half-signed second apology.

"You don't need to say sorry," she says. "I am the one who has come a-calling. It's rare we spend time anywhere with enough air to speak out loud, that's all."

Fer's closed fist rests somewhere above their heart, and surely she can feel how hard it's hammering, because for all their comradery, the others don't touch Fer.

It's not something they always feared. It's just that since they got caught, any brush of skin reminds them of what it feels like to have the family they built be torn away, even as desperate nails cling.

The authorities had found them last, Fer and their closest friend, tucked into a supply cabinet. Quarter Jones curled around the printing press and Fer curled around her, scared breathing bouncing between them as they played at invisibility. Quarter Jones had grabbed Fer's arms with his long artist hands, nails drawing blood as they ripped them apart.

Fer wishes they had left scars, but no such luck.

Somewhere between Moll's welcoming embrace and Benat's offered handshake, they must have done something—something to show that touch was not a thing they liked, not anymore. So, the other three filled the space around them with words of encouragement instead, enough to tether Fer to them without putting fear in their eyes again.

The mermaid doesn't know any of that, and she gives contact with ease, without expectation. When she pulls back her hand, Fer almost chases it with their own. They hadn't known. Hadn't known a simple touch could be so grounding.

"I'm Ophelia," says the mermaid, and again, Fer is thrown by how human the name is.

"Like the drowned girl?" they ask.

"Like the moon," Ophelia responds.

Fer has never met a celestial body with a gravity quite like Ophelia's.

*

Curiosity has its own current, its own pull, has been tugging at the hearts of those trapped on the ground since they learned to look up. Curiosity led metal into space and lent bravery to those who wanted to follow.

Curiosity burned bright in a human who dreamed of stars and mapped routes to them with numbers and years. And when it went wrong, and her and her companions were undone by overreaching, sent into the sky in pieces too scattered to count, curiosity is what brought her back together again, waking up among moons named after others almost-human.

It takes them a long time, to pull themselves together again, to find each other against this new backdrop of theirs, further than most had dreamed. But not her, no.

They find each other in the end, though. Because that's what happens to family, in stories like these.

*

Ophelia echoes Fer's name back at them like it's something delightful, a new toy just for her. She floats around Fer as Fer gets back to work, because not even meeting a myth will get them out of their quota. She peppers them with questions on where they're from, what they did to get here, and Fer...tells her.

Not all at once, but in stuttered stops and stars, because Ophelia's eyes literally sparkle when Fer describes the simplest things.

"I've never been to the night markets of Pluto... What did it all smell like?"

"And what did his face look like when you said *that?*"

"Do you think you'll ever see them again? When you get out of here?"

Fer winces at that, their strike at a particularly stubborn rock skidding off and narrowly missing their foot instead. It's easier to accept a slow death sentence when you don't have to say it out loud.

"Even if I manage to live through my sentence, and they all do the same, I would have no idea where to start looking." Ophelia has been floating on her back a few feet above Fer's head, tail occasionally swishing to keep her there, her arm dangling almost low enough to brush at Fer's close-cropped hair.

(Of all of them, only Moll had managed to avoid a shaved head before being sent here. Benat was still sensitive over her loss, but Fer thinks they would like the shaved-head look if they ever got the chance to choose it for themselves.)

At this though, she sits up.

"How long is your sentence here?"

"Fifteen years, at least," Fer says.

The air around Ophelia seems to stutter. Her form stretches large again for just a second before she pulls it back.

"Fifteen years? For drawing some pictures?"

"For propaganda," Fer reminds her softly. Ophelia appears to be ageless, but she looks very young in this moment, outrage over something so obviously illegal betraying naivety or a disconnect with the times.

All at once Fer is exhausted. They don't want to explain the state of the worlds to this woman, mermaid though she may be. Doesn't want the pity, or the anger that is sure to boil over in her.

Fer's been there, let themselves be pulled to fury and action. And it lost them everything.

(They wouldn't change it for all the stars, those too-brief months. They had already known fear, known it their whole life. Being part of something bigger didn't mean more fear. It meant finally finding something that made the fear feel earned.)

"I should go back," Fer says, and doesn't look up, doesn't want to see the look Ophelia is giving them. "It's almost lunch."

They don't ask Ophelia if she'll be there when they get back, but they do take one last peek right before the curve of the asteroid puts her out of view.

She's on her back again, signing up at the sky. If there's anyone there to answer, Fer cannot see them.

*

Once upon a time, a boy was born in the cargo hold of a courier ship.

He hasn't slowed down since.

*

Fer walks into the common room and into the middle of a discussion. It's a relief, because Fer doesn't know how they're going to open their mouth and talk about anything but the mermaid they met this morning. Maybe a pre-established topic will help.

"Hey, Fer! What do you think? Love at first sight—real or nah?"

"With a face like yours, you'd better hope it is. No one's gonna want to look at your face twice."

Moll laughs hard enough to almost completely drown out Rack's indignant shout.

"Now, now, kids," Moll chastises. "No fighting during mealtimes." It would almost be convincing, if not for her face-splitting grin.

Rack sticks his tongue out at Benat, who reaches over to shove at him playfully before freezing. Instead, she drops her hands quickly out of sight underneath the table, and stares angrily at her plate.

There's an awkward beat. If the cuffs think they're being violent towards each other, they can deliver a nasty shock, and Benat's, in particular, are notoriously trigger happy.

Moll steamrolls over the silence before it gets stifling.

"Anyway, I can put this whole thing to bed." She winks at Fer, which means she's either about to tell an outrageous lie or an even more unbelievable truth. "Love at first sight is definitely real. I know, because I've felt it."

This is enough to get even Benat's eyes off of the table and on Moll.

"Well?" says Rack, practically crawling over the table at Moll. " You can't just say that and not tell us the story, Moll."

Moll shrugs, doles out their rations for the meal like love ain't no thing.

"I was around your age, Fer. Got myself in a bit of bad news, ended up crash landing on this farm..."

"You fell in love with a farmer?" Benat asks with breathless awe. Farmers are the richest of the rich, on her moon, if Fer is remembering right.

"Not your kind of farmers, Benat. Just the two of them, the land had been a wedding gift from someone's second uncle..."

"The two of them?" Rack squeaks.

Moll looks pointedly at his chair, and he climbs back into it, mutters thanks as she tosses a bowl his way.

"Yeah, give me a moment. Trying to tell this in order."

Fer snorts, because it had been something they'd complained about, last time Moll had decided it was storytime. Sequence of events.

"So, there I am, staring up at the red sky through the giant hole in my little ship's roof, and then two hands reach down and grab both of mine. And even before I see them, I'm thinking, man, I've never felt as safe as I feel in this moment. And then I see them both, and...wow."

This isn't a lie, Fer realizes, watching their friend's face go soft. This is the truth, and it's something she obviously thinks about a lot, even with it being twenty years past.

"Her name is Hadra, and their name is Tammy. Neither of them had ever been off-planet, and here I was, with my tattoos and my leg and my broken ship. I thought, of course they're interested in me, they've never seen anything like me. That's all this is. They just want to hear some good stories. Took a few months for it to really sink in, that what I'd felt in that first moment was something mutual.

"They called me their little fallen star; isn't that just the cutest thing? There I was, prickly and young and not sure if I believed in love at all, and then falling for two people at once. It was like some kid's bedtime story."

"So...what happened?" Benat's voice has gone watery, and Fer wonders who she's thinking of, and where they are now.

"We got married, obviously. Lived with them for a couple years, still visit as much as I can."

"What?" Rack's shouting again. "You're married?"

Moll shoots him a look, and holds up her hands. "What do you think these are all for?"

One of the first things anyone looking at Moll will notice is the tattoos. Covering both arms, crawling up her neck to caress the left side of her face, all steady black lines that Fer knew she'd done herself, even though some of the angles seem almost impossible.

The pattern on Moll's fingers had always looked like just that—some abstract pattern. But as Moll wiggles her fingers with a purpose, the lines take on new meaning.

They're all rings, each one unique. There's at least one on every finger.

"Am I married, he asks," teases Moll, and Rack grabs at her hand to get a closer look.

Benat's staring again, and it takes a moment for Fer to identify the emotion in them. It's hunger.

"You're married sixteen times?" Rack is impressed.

"Do they all know?" Fer asks. "Do they know you're here?"

"Can you give me one?" Benat's voice is soft steel, cutting through the comfortable atmosphere like she really is the deadliest thing in the room.

*

There are many ways to be a wife.

Once upon a time there was a girl who wanted to try every one, who loved the world and whom the universe loved in return. But the law ain't the universe, sweetheart. And the law caught her, and she laughed as she ran away.

Only, legs get tired after years of playing hide and seek. No matter how many times one oils the joints.

She marks her story on her own skin and counts the days until it's time to run again. A wife's got promises to keep, after all.

*

Benat doesn't look away as Moll brings the needle to her skin, just bites her lip against the pain.

Moll doesn't question Benat's request. She'd pulled out her gun as soon as the younger girl had asked. Wondered aloud at a general shape until Benat had nodded sharply at one of the suggestions, and gotten to work. Now, she chatters, letting Benat's silence hide underneath her own cheer.

"I'm always open with them. It's an old Earth thing, even. A girl in every port, they used to say. And it's not like I love any of them less." She gets dreamy when she talks about them. Moll's always the most eye-catching thing in the room, but now she's positively stunning, love softening her edges and blurring her lines into something larger than life.

"I think I love them all better, the more people I fall for. And every single love feels different, exciting but also like coming home, every time."

"What if you don't?" Benat swallows, her voice shaking but her hand perfectly still. "Come home, I mean."

"It's always a risk. But they all know what I do for a living."

None of them actually know what that is. Her cuffs are black, which could mean a multitude of petty crimes. They would probably be blue, like Fer's, if she were here because of the ink. Sometimes Rack liked to guess, but Moll had never given so much as a hint.

"Anyway, we don't get to choose whether or not danger finds us. We're all just holding tight to rocks speeding through space, in the end." Moll pulls back, taps her gun against a part of her leg, comes away with fresh ink on the tip. "Ain't that right, Benat?"

Benat flinches, but Moll's solid grip holds the younger girl's hand steady.

"What's that supposed to mean?"

It's easy to relax around Moll. She's good with people.

Fer didn't know she could wield that like a weapon until this moment, and now Benat is trapped, unable to dodge away from hard questions. Rack's eyes flicker to Fer's.

Should we stop this?

Fer shrugs. *If it gets out of hand.*

They're curious, too.

Moll continues like she's too focused on the tattoo to notice anything else. "I've seen your sentence. It's a hefty one. You don't strike me as someone who went out planning to be a mass murderer, and yet, here we are."

Benat ducks her head, like she's embarrassed. Not ashamed, not regretful. Just embarrassed, like she's been caught in a lie.

"And yet here we are," she echoes.

"Oh," says Fer, staring at the gun, as the buzz of it worms its way into their teeth. "I know that noise."

They had a little oven in the corner of their common room. Turned it on when they were planning their more serious moves, ones that had to include dates, times, and locations. Just in case.

Moll's smiling, but her voice is soft and so, so gentle.

"They can't hear us, Benat. You can tell us."

Benat's shoulders are caving in, curling in on herself like the only things holding her up are secrets.

"I didn't plan it, or anything. It wasn't premeditated. But I wasn't just some victim in it either. I knew what I was doing."

"And what was that?" Fer speaks in a whisper out of habit.

"They were taking people. Taking people apart, so people who could afford to would buy the parts they needed to live longer." Benat looks up, and is suddenly, startlingly present. "Did you know when you kill an organ thief, they charge you for the people their 'stock' could have saved too?"

*

Once upon a time, there was a messenger. 'The fastest in the city,' she would say, not a brag but a challenge she met every time.

Some might try to call what happened to her fate. She calls it bad luck, and tries to resist the instinct to reach for the talisman she used to wear, protection offered by a half-forgotten goddess.

She crashes, somewhere between one point and another, where she's not really anywhere at all. When she wakes up, it's to a man attempting to remove her arm.

Benat is the fastest, though. He's unconscious before he even knows she's awake.

The papers call it a vendetta. The police call it a murder spree.

Benat calls it a routing, a cleansing fire, like the lady in red she would pray to when no one was looking. She leaves a trail of dead organ dealers in her wake, and when the authorities finally catch up to her she pleads guilty to every charge.

She expects to die when she's sent to the high risk prison. Instead...

Instead, she falls for an artist with a laugh like the future, and a sentence almost as long as her own.

*

"She was the best thing in the entire system," Benat says, staring at the finished ring with something like longing. Rack is under the needle now, a starburst just starting to burn across his collarbone as Moll works. Really, they should be getting some sleep, because as much as they try to pretend this is a break for lunch, it's really a few hours between one shift and another. Their schedule is perfectly designed to make them never feel quite rested, slowly wearing them down.

"Is that why they moved you?"

Fer is off to the side, watching the horizon outside their doorway out of the corner of their eye.

Rack groans. "Man, if you're about to tell me the only thing I had to do to get away from y'all was pretend to fall in love with one of you, I woulda been out of here ages ago."

This pulls the laugh out of Benat, which makes Rack grin for all of ten seconds, until Moll's needle hits a particularly sensitive patch.

"No, no... We caught on to a murder plot some of the other prisoners had hatched. Um, for the two of us. So, we snitched. Think we even got a few years taken off of our sentences for it. I don't know. By the time I finished with the investigators, he was already gone, and I was sent here."

"What was their name?"

"Just he or she is fine," Benat corrects, and Moll nods, committing the set to memory. Fer, who has only met one person who uses those particular pronouns, feels their heart clench. They're not uncommon sets, together or apart. Fer can't feel winded just by some preferred pronouns that rest a little close to home.

"And...this is going to sound silly, but I'd rather not say her name?"

"Even though they can't hear you right now?" Rack asks.

Benat pulls herself in, as small as her frame will allow, and stares at her new ring.

"I wished on a star for him to find his way back to me. I don't... If you say a wish out loud, it doesn't come true. And I used her name."

Rack laughs. "Is this more moony superstitions?"

"No," says Fer. "It's the same on Earth."

"And on a lot of planets I've visited too," Moll adds, and pulls the gun away from his skin so she can flick his ear. "Not all of us are purely ship brats like you."

"I prefer untethered from all groundish wishwashery." Rack winks as he says it, which earns him another flick.

"It's beautiful," Fer says. Moll uses the gun as an excuse to shut Rack up. "The ring. She's going to love it when she sees it."

Benat stands up, stretching as she reaches for her shovel. It's nearing the start of the second shift.

"Oh, he's never going to see it. It's for me, mostly."

The walls are coming back now, and they may be shorter but they've got twice as many spikes as before.

"You didn't wish for her to...find you, then?"

"No. No, I was lucky enough to meet him the one time. Finding her again would be like wishing on the same shooting star twice. That's no good."

"What's that supposed to mean?" Fer tries to keep the defensiveness out of their voice and doesn't quite succeed.

"You've never heard that? 'Don't waste a wish on a twice-spent comet'? It's why me and my siblings would always call dibs on the comets we saw."

Fer thinks back to when they were smaller, climbing onto the roof of their apartment building just to get some breathing room, sending up wishes as fast as they could at any blur in the sky.

"Guess that one is a moony thing," they say, and something twists in their chest, all the words they idly tied to stars as they worked, hardly daring to hope it would speed them toward an impossible reunion.

They walk out before the alarm signals they have to. They don't even care.

*

Once upon a time, there was a kid who dreamed of leaving the world behind.

They dreamed of many things, but they always come back to this—wishing the ground underneath them was less solid, wishing to be somewhere far, far away.

*

The mermaid is still there when Fer gets back, and she's still the most beautiful thing Fer's ever seen.

"Do you know any stories?" Fer asks, because they're tired of thinking about real people, of things they can't reach.

"I know a few," says Ophelia. "I was a scientist, not a storyteller, but we all grow up with a few, don't we?"

Fer fought for every one they could find, and now here is this myth, offering them freely.

If they stare at Ophelia, they can see their own face reflected in her eyes, so they don't do that, because they're not sure if they believe in love at first sight, and they're not ready to change that right now.

"I'd love to hear them," Fer whispers, but Ophelia is close enough to catch each word.

"Of course," she hums, and this time she does reach out, runs her fingers across Fer's scalp, smiling at the sensation of their short-cropped hair. "Most of them start with 'Once upon a time...'"

Everything feels possible when a story starts like that. Impossible rescues, love in every colour, even happy endings.

Fer knows those are the most unlikely things of all. They'd collected endings like loose buttons when they were young. Remembers the girls drowning, turning to foam, growing old. Happy endings are just choosing to stop the story at the right time, Fer thinks.

Ophelia is very good at that.

*

Once upon a time, there was a person who took to the stars like they took to the roofs of their city, who could run but never far enough to feel truly free, and so turned around and dug their heels into the proverbial sand (they've never felt real sand) and linked arms with a family found (they've never known any other kind) and they even held their ground. For a little while.

*

"How will you find them again?"

It's been three weeks since Ophelia first floated down into Fer's life, although it feels like it's been longer. Something is untangling in Fer, words that used to catch fall off their tongue freely now, sometimes spelt out by quick fingers as their vocabulary expands.

"Who, my friends?" Ophelia smiles, and Fer smiles back. Sometimes, they think they will be found out by their bunkmates simply because of the new lines their face must have—all the smiling they seem to be doing.

"Yes, your friends." Fer says it out loud, but also signs it, because 'friends' out loud doesn't quite encompass everything the other mermaids mean to Ophelia, friends and family and a flock all fitting into something different altogether. "How do you find each other, when one of you decides to stick around somewhere for a while?"

Ophelia hums, and it makes Fer's bones vibrate, like even their building blocks resonate with her voice.

"Well, no matter how far apart we are from each other, we'll never be as far as when we first got scattered. And we found each other then." She flicks her tail, and sparks shoot up. She gathers them in her hands like it's nothing, holding space between your fingers. "Obe thinks it's because when we pulled ourselves together again, we all got a bit mixed up in each other. And it's hard to lose track of someone who is also a part of you."

"Wish that's how it worked for us normal folks too," Fer says.

Ophelia laughs, runs fingers still streaked in light along the planes of Fer's face.

"Nothing about you is normal," she whispers, so that even if someone were listening they would not hear her. "If you sent your people a letter, I'm sure it would find them."

"A letter?" Fer asks, and Ophelia pulls them closer, snakes around them so that their back is flush against her front, and Fer can't recall ever feeling so safe.

"Like this," she says, fingers wound with theirs. She brings their tangled hands toward Fer's face, and when she blows on them, her breath tickles Fer's ear.

"How will he know what I'm saying?"

"Say it. Spell it out if you have to." And Ophelia pulls their hands through a simple message, one more full of truths than Fer usually lets themself indulge in.

I miss you. I'm okay but I'm far away. Follow this, if you can.

"Like a message in a bottle," Ophelia says, and Fer stares as sparks make each word linger in the sky for a moment before disappearing, and lets themself believe that somewhere, somehow, Quarter Jones will hear it.

Fer doesn't want Ophelia to let go.

"Show me again?" they ask, and Ophelia does.

*

The trouble with only knowing endings is you don't always fight like you should, when you see your own coming.

*

"I wish I could see my file," Rack says, fidgeting as he tries to keep from scratching at the new ink spilling across his chest, joining with the healed lines of his shoulder. Only Moll's sharp eyes stop him from picking at the stark lines. "I'm not even sure what I ended up getting charged with. Wasn't allowed at my own trial."

"Well, that tracks," Benat says. She hasn't embraced Moll's inks with quite the fervour that Rack has, but there's the beginnings of a sleeve stretching over one arm. With ink breaking skin, it's hard to tell it apart from the slightly different colour of her other arm, lingering evidence of when she almost lost it.

"They musta taken one look at you and known you wouldn't be able to keep your mouth shut," Moll teases, and Rack shrugs, not denying it.

The loss of Mark is distant, softened by months of growing closer and, in Fer's case, growing in love. They're comfortable in each other's presence and this tiny fake kingdom, where they're not free but they're also not struggling to eat each day.

None of them would go so far as to say they're happy to be here, but they're content. For now.

That in and of itself is dangerous, but no one is thinking about that right now.

"They let me see my file," Fer says. They're using their nail to doodle designs on the table, planning for when they finally get their own Moll original. They're no artist, but they have an idea, shapes against an open sky. It's a work in progress. "I asked. I think they were hoping I'd fill in some gaps."

"And what did the good old authorities have to say about you, Fer?" Moll retraces a line, and Fer smiles at the suggestion.

"Not a lot. I was... I was hoping it would fill some gaps in for me, honestly. No luck."

"What kind of gaps?" Benat wants to know. They've all gotten better at asking, this last little while.

Fer bites back the instinct to change the subject, retreat, refuse to answer. Sometimes, change is an intentional effort.

"I don't know anything about my parents," they hear themself say, as if from far away. The distance here is intentional, too. They can't own this, can't be inside themself while they talk about it. It will feel too real, like a second skin made of someone they no longer want to know. "I was hoping for a...birth certificate, a name. Something."

They don't meet anyone's gaze when they say it. It's somewhere between childish and selfish, and rolled eyes will hurt just as much as pity. But it builds all the same, the expectation that there's more to it, and the words trying to explain just spill out.

"It's more about roots. Belonging? I didn't really want to belong to Earth, but knowing there was at least some record of me existing, or of me coming from somewhere or someone... But it turns out that was one of the gaps they were hoping I would fill in, so. Well."

"It's not worth much," Benat says, going for comfort but falling a little short. "Roots like that usually just mean more people can hurt you."

Benat has siblings and mothers that cried when she left. She's not a great liar.

"Lotta people pay a lotta money to make those go away," says Rack. That's a fact, and Fer knows it, because Quarter Jones talked about rebirth and records going up in flames more than once.

Moll, as always, cuts right to the point, down to the bone.

"Some old piece of paper—or some file with your mugshot on the front—none of those things tell you who you are. You don't get any help figuring that one out, Fer. You gotta do it on your own."

Fer grimaces. "I know it's about what your parent hopes for you more than anything that's supposed to last," they whisper, voice thin. "Just wanted a piece of a parent, I suppose. Something."

Moll snorts. "Parental hopes or not, that paper can get awful hard to change. Lots of people would've loved an opportunity to not have to bother."

Moll's not going to let this go. She does this, picks at what hurts until they're forced to confront them. Fer has watched her do this to Rack and Benat both, but this is the first time the focus has been on them.

"I know that, Moll," Fer snaps, feeling worn, weaker than they have in a long time.

"I'm one of those people," Moll says, and her tone is solid ground. "I grew up with nothing much too, and when I found out who I thought I was supposed to be, I clung to it with everything I had. But a piece of paper and a want to do right by strangers who named me couldn't make me a good man. Or a man at all. The boy in those records never existed, as much as I wanted him to. The day I let him go was the first day I felt steady. What-ifs, doubts like that...they're prisons, Fer. They'll trap you as well as any isolated asteroid. Only rescue from them is a lot harder."

If they'd been paying attention, they might have seen Benat's eyes shift to Rack's at the word *rescue,* or how the air in the room got a little thicker with nerves. But they were busy collapsing in on themselves, and they missed it all.

"Moll," they say, and they won't cry. They won't. "I didn't mean... I don't know. I don't know what I meant."

Moll pulls up a chair, sitting beside them and not saying anything at all. Fer slowly, so slowly, lets themself lean against her.

"For the record," she says, after enough time has passed for Fer's breathing to steady again. "I'm glad I'm trapped on this rock with you, Fer. If I had to be here, I'm glad it's you."

The way she puts emphasis on Fer's name does not go unnoticed, and Fer is so in love with this woman, this older, sister figure, and it makes them so angry, angrier than they've been in a long, long time. Because someone as large as Moll shouldn't be stuck somewhere as small as this.

"I'm going to bed," Fer says, and hopes Moll can hear the *thank you.*

"Sit here a bit longer," she says, and it sounds like *you're welcome.* It sounds like *anytime.* It sounds like *love you, too.*

*

For the first time since the sentence came down to hang around their wrists, they doubt it. They want to kick and scream and fight and wish, only they're not sure they remember how.

Once upon a time, there was someone who always knew this is where they would end up. Who knew each free step was borrowed time.

And now, the clock has struck midnight and then some, and they are finally realizing they want something else entirely.

*

"It's not fair," they growl, fists clenched. They've already gone and thrown their shovel. They could pick it up, but if they do they know they're just going to throw it again, or find a particularly sharp-looking rock and bring the shovel down over and over until the screen shatters and the metal warps.

And then they'll be in trouble, and for what? For nothing.

It's all for nothing.

"It isn't," Ophelia agrees, and if she were soft and calming, Fer would storm away from her too. But she's lit up like a city under siege, like moonlight against the sea, and Fer has never seen an ocean properly, but they know what it feels like—to be a siege engine to survive.

Ophelia is angry too. That's what makes Fer stay.

"They're just...they're so much bigger than this, Ophelia." Her name rolls off their tongue, and they wish they'd said it more, because when they say it Ophelia's star-kissed cheeks sparkle with comet trails. Blushing seems all too human for someone as magical as Ophelia, and it just makes Fer ache for her more.

"Tell me about it," she says, and Fer does. Fer's told her everything, and taken every word Ophelia has told her in return like a gift. Every story is something to treasure, and Fer's life is pale in comparison. They share it anyway.

Fer never thought this asteroid could make them feel like they could love again, but they can, they have been, they are.

"Benat really believes things can be good, she didn't have to fight but she did, and she's here as a murderer... But she saved so many lives, doing what she did, and she misses her partner so much, and she deserves the chance to find him. And Rack is so young and clever and he's stuck here running himself into the ground, and Moll is..." Fer brings their fists to their face, pressing knuckles against their eyes until their vision goes past black. "Moll is carrying us all, she really is, and she doesn't even mind, because she's just that good, and she's absolutely stunning and strong and...and she deserves better than this. They all do."

Gentle hands pull their fists away, and Ophelia's thumb brushes at their pulse point, right above their cuff. The intimacy shoves all the air from Fer's lungs.

"You love them all a lot," she says, and there's something wry in her voice, something unfinished and raw. "Are you gonna tell her? Moll?"

"Tell Moll what?" Fer manages to get out, trying to breathe to the tempo of Ophelia's metronome touch.

"That you're in love with her."

"What?" Fer opens their eyes to Ophelia's face, gorgeous and hesitant. "I don't... I mean, I do. Love her. But not the kind that needs a confession."

And now hesitation melts into something hopeful. "You're not?"

"No." And the shock at the misunderstanding is enough to spur them forward. "No, of course not. I'm in love with you."

Ophelia's soft grip goes tight around Fer's wrist, and her eyes blow wide.

"I thought..." Fer bites their lip, but it's too late to take back the words, so they keep moving forward. "I thought it was obvious."

For the first time since Ophelia arrived, she loses herself for a moment, her presence spinning off in every direction. She's not merely bigger; she's an explosion, she's a star being born, and for a moment, Fer is surrounded by a constellation of a girl, and every bright point is Ophelia, and every point is overflowing with love for them.

Fer blinks, overwhelmed, and when they open their eyes again, Ophelia is smiling at them, their hands cradled by her own.

"I guess I'd forgotten what a human's love could look like." She leans in, rests her forehead against Fer's. "You shine so bright already, I hadn't noticed you were shining in my direction."

Fer wants to kiss her, but that's against the rules. Everyone knows that. People fool around in prison, but no kissing. Kissing gets you killed.

So, instead they lean into her, savour the feel of her against them, and they get so lost in the moment that they don't realize they've left the ground until they think to look down.

The ground is several feet below them, and Ophelia's blushing again.

"I'm sorry. I'm just really happy," she says, like that's something to apologize for.

"It's okay," Fer says, voice full of wonder. "You're okay."

Ophelia laughs, and her tail flashes, sending them spinning.

"May I have this dance?" she asks, and Fer nods, holds her tight as she leads them through the stars, a few feet and a thousand miles off the ground.

Fer has no idea how much time has passed when something tickles the back of their neck, and Ophelia pauses. She looks up, lets go of Fer with one hand so she can trace something in the air.

"A message?"

She nods. "I... I have to go. But it will only be for a little while, okay? I'll come back." And then she scowls, and Fer is reminded again how strangely human she can appear, even when flying. "Obe's timing is always terribly inconvenient. But I'll be back as soon as I can. I promise."

And Fer, forgetting for just a moment what kind of story they're a part of, believes her.

*

All they wanted, all they'd wished for, for so long, was to be someone.

And they were someone, oh they were Someone.

Someone who could be loved, who could be wanted.

Someone who could be noticed.

*

Here's the thing about this particular kind of imprisonment—it's all well and good to have your own space. To take a piss when you want to, to track your numbers and get fed and do your time.

To occasionally spend an afternoon dancing, instead of working. To fall in love.

But there's no one to argue your case with, no grey area, no pushing the line.

They had let themself get carried away. They'd fought for every one of their twenty-something years, and then they'd let themself have a moment where they'd let go. Where they'd relaxed. Just for a moment.

The cuffs did not know they'd been too busy dancing to think of flying as an escape. The cuffs didn't care. All they registered was that Fer had been somewhere they should not have been.

It takes three days. Three days of Fer adjusting to Ophelia being gone, of counting down until she was back. They're coming off a shift, picking at a callous on their hand as they follow Moll into the common room.

The invisible barrier that separates the inside from the outside doesn't let them through. And as soon as they feel resistance, they know.

Moll turns, sensing something's wrong in that way she always does. It's why she might live to see fifty.

"Fer?" she says, and then sees them, hand pressed against what was, to her, just an empty doorway.

"No," she breathes, and Fer can't remember ever hearing her so quiet. "No, stop playing and get in here, Fer."

"I can't," they say, even though Moll already knows that.

"You can," she argues, and reaches through, grabbing Fer's wrist and giving it a tug. It doesn't work, of course— the same thing in Moll's cuffs that lets her pass through the invisible force field is what prevents Fer from following.

"But you didn't do anything," Rack says, eyes wide with panic. "You...you never do anything!"

"Doesn't really matter, does it." Fer doesn't let their voice crack with the fear they can feel tearing through their breastbone. They should have told them about Ophelia. About it all. "It's all automated. You know that."

Moll's grip tightens. "I'll hold on, then."

"Don't be stupid." Benat flinches, and Fer feels like they're already floating, no atmosphere already, gravity letting them go early. "All you'll do is freeze your fingers off."

"Shout, then." Moll's eyes are steel, not letting Fer look away. "Yell for whoever you've been meeting with these past few months."

Of course, Moll knew. Fer doesn't know how she does it, but can't muster the energy to be surprised.

"She's gone." Fer should have kissed her, probably. They'd been cautious about all the wrong things.

Moll shakes their hand, reminds them they still have limbs. "Do something, at least! Don't let them kill you without a fight."

And Fer gets it. Can see the fear in Moll's eyes. Moll needs them to fight, knows it won't change a thing but needs to see them do it anyway.

Fer can't remember the last time they did something entirely for someone else. It's a nice final act, as far as final acts go.

"You're right, Moll." Fer tries for a smile. Somewhere, a light is flashing, counting down. "You always are."

Moll nods once, and then lets go. Rack is crying, and behind them both, Benat offers a single wave before turning away.

Fer doesn't blame her one bit.

They fill their lungs, trying not to number their breaths as they do it—*how many do I have left? Ten? Less?*—and cup their hands around their mouth, shouting for Ophelia, fingers tracing the words. As they do, they imagine their message like letters in a bottle, floating between the asteroids without a care, washing up on some distant, undiscovered planet.

Sorry, say the letters. *I was a criminal and a coward, and now we're both stardust, only I've gone and left myself behind.*

Fer doesn't get a chance to listen for any reply.

For the first nineteen years of their life, Fer lived in a city stuffed into a postage stamp. They sat on rooftops and reached for a sky that promised them room to stretch their legs, to spread wings they knew they could build if just given the chance. They cheated and stole and ran every inch of that city ragged until their bones felt as worn as the streets they knew too well.

And it had worked. The first time they'd left the surface, smuggled away in a box smaller than their bed but bigger than any space they'd ever slept in before. They'd felt gravity let go. It felt like finally breathing deep, like a high they hadn't known they'd been chasing until they caught it.

And now... They feel gravity loosening her grip on them, and for all the fear and all the dread, they can't help but feel stirring excitement too, because at least it's like this. At least they won't die with their feet on the ground.

They always knew how their story was going to end.

Their vision blurs as their body rises up, and the last thing they see are stars, stretching from horizon to horizon, as far as they can see.

*

Every loving thing is made of Stardust.

Even humans, far from home.

Even messages, caught by Curious hands.

The Mermaid sees her Human's message, and thinks of the stories she learned, back when she too was human, and believed in endings. Remembers a young girl in her bed, begging her mother to read the story again, because maybe this time, everyone would get to live.

What use are comets, if one can't wish on them?

What use are comets, if they cannot fly?

The Mermaid shoots across the sky, faster than she's ever imagined, and she feels her fellows giving her bits of themselves so that she can push even faster, and it may take years for them to collect all the parts of themselves, but they love her, and she loves them, and she loves a Human, who is delicate and dying.

The Mermaid reaches down, hands catching a body that is still home to a soul she knows, although only just. The Mermaid reaches down, presses lips to lips and heart to heart, and she breathes all the space she knows into her Human's small form.

Every loving thing is made of stars. Nothing can change that. The Human is still Human; the Mermaid is not.

But now, the Human is also a little bit More. A little more space. Constellations a little more clear.

The Human breathes, and the Mermaid breathes with them, and the Universe breathes with them all.

*

Fer wakes up.

It's always the hardest part.

They wake up, and they don't want to open their eyes. Because until they open their eyes, they can be anywhere they want to be. They can be tucked away in the small room they shared with Quarter Jones, writing captions for her political cartoons, which in the dream are still circulating around the solar system but haven't led back to them yet—a voice of the revolution put to paper by a crew of clever hands who felt invincible. They can be dancing with Ophelia again. This time there's no cuffs around their wrists when they lean in to kiss her.

They can be wherever they want to be, but only for a little while. So, they open their eyes to the grey curved walls of their bunk, of their cell, and they try to not let it get to them.

And then the memories of where they had been when they had closed their eyes come rushing back, and they shoot up in bed, gasping.

"Woah there, careful!"

Moll is there to catch them when their body, weak from their brush with death, sways to the left as the world tilts. Her hands are familiar and very real, which must mean this is real.

"You gave us quite a scare there, Fer." Moll is grinning. The telling off doesn't feel as sharp. "Lucky for you, you fell for the fastest girl in the universe."

Fer blinks at Moll. Vertigo makes it impossible to focus.

"What?"

"Your girl. Ophelia. She caught you. She's outside." Moll's ready for Fer's lunge, hands pushing them back down before they really register their decision to try to move. "And you can see her soon, don't worry. But give your body some time. It's been through a lot."

Fer wants to protest, but their words come to them slowly. "I don't understand?"

Moll pulls back Fer's eyelids, checking their vision for...something.

"Listen, I've worn a lot of hats, Fer. Lived a lot of lives. Used to be a field medic before everything else. I know what I'm doing."

"...Doc Moll?"

She chuckles, and Fer feels themself relaxing, still not sure exactly what happened but willing to trust in Moll's laughter.

"Sure. Doc Moll."

"Oh." Fer waves a hand weakly at her cuffs. "Black for deserter."

That earns them a wink.

"Among other things."

"...Tattoos?"

"Tell me, do you know what happens to doctors who are told the way they've been helping people ain't allowed no more?"

Fer manages a slow-motion shrug.

Moll grins. "They become tattoo artists. No one notices a tattoo shop that's got scalpels and a surgery in the back room." She pats Fer's cheek gently. "Also, they're a lot of fun. Anyway, sleep. Dream of weird space girls."

"Mermaids," Fer mutters, already drifting away.

"Damn. You're not wrong there. Wish you'd mentioned her earlier, honestly. Took me ages to sweet-talk her friend, and there you were on the other side of the asteroid, confessing your love already." As she talks, she's fussing with Fer's blankets, and they have so many questions. But the cheap mattress beneath them has never felt so comfortable. Moll's voice sounds like it's coming from three rooms away.

"Although, I suppose I could have said something too. It was my fault she wasn't here when you got floated, in a way. Hopefully the ship will make up for it."

"The ship?"

But already Fer is sinking down, back into the dark.

*

Once upon a time, there was an artist with a laugh like the future and an eye for getting there, and she waited for no ending, told her own story with each strike of her pencil, like every piece was a fire that could burn away all of the injustice in the world.

Some say artists are dreamers. Some say they make dreams.

When the Mermaids came a-calling, he pointed his stolen ship at their trail and followed.

This artist is a dreamer, and she trusts in her hands, firm on the wheel, to see those dreams through to truth.

*

When Fer wakes up again, there is no confusion.

They remember gravity letting go. They remember closing their eyes and opening them to air in their lungs and stars in their eyes.

They remember Moll, tucking them in.

They remember not ending.

"You awake, then?"

Rack is by their bed, trying to look bored instead of excited. A thief he may be, but he's no good as a liar.

"I think so," Fer says, and gets a huge grin for their troubles.

"Excellent. I'm supposed to bring you outside, so I sure hope you can walk, because I ain't gonna carry you."

Fer can walk, although their legs feel too long to properly control. They lean on Rack as little as they can, but Rack is surprisingly strong for his size, and he gets them through the empty common room and outside.

Moll and Benat are there, waiting for them.

Before Fer can say anything, Benat is moving, wrapping her arms around them tight enough to make their chest ache. Rack joins in, and then Moll, and Fer's eyes sting.

They didn't think feeling this safe was possible for people like them.

"Your lady will be here soon, don't worry. She's just gone to meet the rest of them." That's Moll, answering questions Fer hasn't found the words to ask yet. "The field wouldn't let her inside, so she's mostly been hovering by the door and badgering us every five seconds to see how you were doing."

"It was cute," Benat assures them.

"We all like her, don't worry," Rack adds.

Fer nods, tries to wipe their tears on Benat's shoulder without anyone noticing.

"...meet the rest of them?"

Moll pulls away. "You probably don't remember; you were pretty out of it. But while you and your Ophelia were dancing, I met Obe, another...mermaid." She reaches out, ruffling Fer's hair. "Ever since you called them that, it's impossible to think of them as anything else. Anyway, Ophelia had sent him to scout for a ship, and came back to let us know they'd found one." Fer can hear the teasing in Moll's voice without looking up. "He hadn't wanted to interrupt you two, so he reported to me instead."

Fer remembers Ophelia signing as the other mermaids floated away. Had she already been asking for a way to save them? How had she known?

Maybe love at first sight was something she believed in too.

There's a burst of movement beside them—it's Rack, waving his arms like he's bringing someone home.

"Look! They did it, they fucking did it!"

Above their heads, the asteroids are blotted out by the whole school of mermaids, all of their tails shooting off little sparkles of excitement. They're chattering, and Fer could probably follow along if they were trying, but they're too busy looking for Ophelia. It takes them a moment to find her, because her smaller body is easily lost amongst the larger mermaids, but she comes darting down to meet Fer with a speed that takes Fer's breath away, spinning as she curls her tail around them. Fer was as good as dead not too long ago, but they can't remember ever having felt this safe.

"I'm so sorry" is the first thing Ophelia says. Her eyes are wide. Now that Fer knows what drowning is like, they wouldn't mind if they fell into Ophelia's eyes and never breached for air.

"For what?" Fer says, genuinely confused as to what in the universe she could be apologizing for.

"For leaving you," Ophelia whispers, and oh. No one's ever apologized for leaving before.

"But you came back." Before they can overthink it, they lean in, killing the distance between them to press their lips to Ophelia's cheek. "You came back."

Beside them, another myth is chatting with Moll, one hand lingering on her arm, and Fer would tease her about needing a new ring but they know Moll will just turn it back around on them, and they're not ready to admit out loud that if they could they would marry Ophelia right here and now.

"I brought you a ship," Ophelia whispers against Fer's cheek. "And someone who can get the cuffs off too." Her voice goes soft, shy. "You don't owe me anything, but I'd like to come with you, if you want. Even if you don't, I don't regret asking them to find you one. You're the brightest thing I've seen in a long time. I couldn't leave you here."

Fer isn't the best with words. They'll have to find the right ones to thank Ophelia eventually, but they hope this will fill the gaps until they do, as they cup her face in their hands and kiss her, the way they've been wanting to for months.

By the little gasp and the way Ophelia leans in, she understands.

Above their heads, the sky opens, the mermaids all flipping their tails and signing their excitement. And through the gap in their wake flies their salvation—a vessel like a ship graveyard come to life, parts mixed and matched to find poetry in the construction.

"Benat," says Rack, tugging on the taller girl's sleeve. "Is that...you?"

Painted across one of the sides, like the plane skeleton Fer found once in the junkyard, is a pinup of a girl. She's got cropped shock-white hair and a smile that won't stop, and she is unmistakably Benat.

Benat sucks in a deep, shuddering breath, and Fer recognizes the sound. It's the sound of someone whose lungs haven't been full for far too long.

"It's her," she says, not a drop of doubt in her tone. "It's...that's my partner's ship. It's gotta be."

And the universe is surely a strange one, because Fer knows this art. Knows it as well as they know their own handwriting, built a revolution with this art as the face.

All this time, Fer has let themselves believe their life is a tragedy. It isn't until the ship touches down that they realize this simply isn't true.

The door opens, and Quarter Jones steps out.

He tilts his head, and it's like the first time they met, Fer a stowaway, her the captain who took one look at the ragged person in front of him, and offered Fer a hand and a family and a cause, all at once.

Benat is already moving, hands outstretched like she's in a trance, and Quarter Jones' hands come out to catch her and Fer knows exactly what that feels like. To need touch to believe, because Quarter Jones is made of impossible things.

"Hey, Fer." Her voice is clear and cutting and warm like home. "Hey, babe. See you've met the in-laws already. Always knew you two would get along."

Once upon a time, in a closet on a ship being boarded by an enemy too big to fight, an artist had taken out a knife and cut across his palm, her voice whispering a promise. Fer had copied the line across their own skin, clasped their hands together with the closest thing to blood they had ever known.

"We're siblings, Fer," said Quarter. "They can't take that away from us."

And Fer, Fer knows endings. Knew endings. Had learned, through the months of adding pointed words to Quarter Jones' art, that a few words could make something true when said at the right time.

"We'll find each other again," they said.

Quarter Jones hadn't believed them then, but Fer can see the gratitude in his eyes now, like this was all somehow Fer's doing, this chance meeting, this fairy-tale rescue.

They hold Ophelia's hand tight, and reach out with the other, letting their sibling pull them onto the ship and into another story altogether.

*

Magic has a way of making everything feel closer.

Magic is what makes the sky close enough to touch, if you reach out often enough. Magic is connection out of nothing, tying strangers into a family tree. Magic is making space feel vast and at the same time so, so small.

And sometimes, just sometimes, Magic is wishing twice on a falling star.

From Dusk to Dying Sun

Paige S. Allen

Warning: mild body horror

Tradition found a new home in your mother's grave decades ago, and even still, you sometimes catch yourself wandering through its old stomping grounds.

The lapses happened more when you were young. An itch of disappointment crawls into your throat when you think about it now, but in hindsight it makes sense. Things were foggy back then. Your body shuffled through an indistinguishable smear of suburban foster homes while your mind remained in the smoky backroom of your mother's apartment, holding her withering hand while she died. The thin boundaries of Before and After became easily intertwined, and you only awoke when the particulars of those realities merged with difficulty.

It would be a sticky Louisiana Sunday in the house of Mr. and Mrs. Shreveport, and you would be standing on your tippy-toes in front of the kitchen stove, a chipped cup cradled gently in your tiny hands. You would be waiting for the kettle to hum, so you could be helpful and make the special turmeric with a splash of honey to give to—no one, now.

You don't remember much of your formative years in elementary and middle school in the After of your life. But you do remember that at the beginning of every school year you would sit alone in the parent drop-off courtyard before first bell, rummaging in your messy backpack. First days always made you nervous back then. But you had a good luck charm to calm you down. Your mother always made sure of that. It took some digging, but you knew that with a little perseverance you would find that, plucked from the community garden and bound together in one of her silk ribbons, was—nothing, now.

Sometimes the young Ms. North of Dallas would light candles around the house to compensate for the lights being turned off again. You would steal a candle anywhere you could: the busy hardware store or that brand-name pharmacy or the bustling liquor store, places where you sometimes worked at night and knew for a fact wouldn't hurt for much with it gone. You'd drive the waxy stems into the backyard concrete late at night and close your eyes, slow your breathing, and recite the words your mother always tried to teach you when you did this trick at home...only for you to jumble them, struggle to taste the shape of them around your mouth, until they disappeared completely in wisps of smoke and heat. Their shadow does not even exist in your mind now.

And despite the name, living in Carefree, Arizona, was a hell that you never experienced before—and you had already figured high school was going to be rough for you. Hostility and mistrust seemed to follow you wherever you roamed, but these dual sentiments became especially prevalent whenever your actions clashed against the confines of normalcy. Too many instances spring to mind now, but the last remembered straw had to do with, of all things, your shoes. You received so many strange looks in the orphanage every time you placed your shoes in the opposite direction, facing toward the door instead of away. By eighteen you didn't even need to remember the *whos* and *whys* about this specific tradition to realize its value for self-preservation—perhaps the only value it had left for you. When it looks like you're always two steps away from running out the door, never to return, no one even realizes when you finally decide to do it for real.

All the ways you couldn't cope before don't matter now. You're older; older, wiser, and purposefully alone. You make your own traditions from all the little pieces of a whole new life you've managed to cobble together. And they're mostly normal and boring like they're supposed to be, to prove just how well-adjusted you've become.

But you're the first to admit that you're a bit peculiar, even without your mother's influence. So, while most of your new traditions are normal and boring, there are one or two strangely lingering traditions that usually begin and end with—

"Shit, Morrison!"

A husky voice calling your name too close and too loud against your ear, a screeching swerve in the middle of the road, and an explosion of pitch-black exhaust smoke that blocks out the very sun from the horizon. These are your traditions now.

But you've gotten used to it. You don't even spill your morning cup of coffee as your entire body jolts to the side.

The patrol car just manages to avoid nosediving headfirst into a ditch at the side of the road. You'd give your compliments to the chef for that save, but the man beside you looks a bit worse for wear. His breath labors through his barrel-wide chest. His dark-brown eyes are bulging off into the distance. The death grip he has on the steering wheel forces every veiny muscle in his arms to strain against his close-fitting uniform. His legs are shaking a little, two thick planes rubbing against each other with enough nervous energy to kindle firewood.

You hesitate for a moment and put your coffee down. And then you set your hand on him, brushing your fingers on top of his closest thigh. You catch at the contrast of your black hand against the light color of his pant leg, just for a split second, before you look him in the eye.

"Do you think I should use the radar gun?" you ask. You even pull it from your lap, where it's been shut off for the entire shift, and give it a little jingle. "You know, to figure out if they were going faster than the speed limit when they almost knocked us off the road?"

Inoa turns just enough to give you a devastatingly withering side-eye. But a smile pulls at the corner of his lips too, just a little bit. "Morrison," he breathes. "You asshole. I could just about leave you on the side of the road right now."

"You wouldn't, Inoa. You know I have abandonment issues."

"As if *that* justifies your bad behavior. Or your shitty jokes."

You laugh, and give him a good squeeze before leaning back in your seat. It's a quick squeeze, though. More of an accidental reflex, really. "Quit your bellyaching, partner. We've got a speed demon to catch."

Fortunately, Inoa's not the type of man who needs a twice-telling of instructions. The patrol car shudders forward as soon as he upshifts the gears, and he adjusts himself in his seat for better control. You're back on the road proper now, following the smoke trail left behind.

For your part, you decide to put down the radar and actually be helpful. Not much you can do in the passenger seat right now, but you can get on the scanner and see if there's something up ahead.

You've always had a particularly complicated relationship with fast divers on the US 50. On one hand, you *get* the impulse: the highway offers a nice stretch of straight, relatively uncongested land as a venue. And who knows; that could have very well been *you* cruising in those cars a few years ago, head in the clouds, beer in hand, safety be damned.

But safety *is* a concern for you now, especially since this is the fifth time something like this has happened in the last two and a half months. Honestly, though, these constant near-death experiences are starting to piss you off. Just a little.

The speed demon you're trailing almost derailed you a stone's throw away from Dayton, which makes this situation a burden on the entire Lyon County. Which is a shame, because you'd rather call into Fallon for the assist. It's a bigger crew, friendlier too, and they employ the type of people you imagine *other* people envision—someone who never grew up after college. But like, a liberal college, so they're really supportive of, for example, the lives of black and brown people and extremely progressive social ideas and the universal decriminalization of weed, and...well, you get it.

The other side of the never-grew-up-from-college spectrum are the guys over in Fernley, unfortunately. But they'll have to do.

Meanwhile, Inoa's excellent driving has finally gotten you close enough to your target...which, as you get closer, is admittedly not the kind of target you thought you'd be dealing with at the start of this shift. A beat-up Toyota Corolla is zigzagging its way along the median of the highway's four lanes. Its fading grey bumper is covered in stickers of various bright hues and insignias. The back window is tinted, so you can't exactly see who's inside, but you can make out the shadowy silhouettes of at least three people.

Inoa flicks the siren on, but it's of no use: precious minutes pass you by like this, with no signs of the Corolla slowing down. In fact, the vehicle seems to be gaining speed from somewhere in its ancient engine. Whenever Inoa gets close enough to start hitting the bumper, the car jolts forward violently, gaining at least ten inches in front of you when it lands back on the road.

Not to be outdone, Inoa curves the patrol car sharply to the left, trying to gain purchase. The driver-side window is tinted like the back. You can't see anything at all.

Music drones out that window, but you still try to get your message across. "This is the Nevada Highway Patrol. You need to slow your car down and pull over!"

No response. You push your upper body out of the window entirely. If you stretched just a little more, you could smash your fist against the Corolla's window. Shatter the glass and pierce the driver with the shards. Drive those sharpers deep into their skin with the force of your blows. The possibilities were endless, and would be effective; but even the thought of them makes your hands twitch and painfully constrain. Despite the training, the uniform, the expectations of the job etched so deeply into your bones they ache when under pressure...you've never been comfortable with violence.

"I'm not playing with you; slow down," you shout again. "You're going to kill someone out here!"

As if taking your words as a cue, the Corolla shudders to the side. Inoa anticipates it and swerves to give them more room, but now the patrol car is edging toward the ditch again. You've been burning a lot of fuel, flying by multiple miles in all four lanes. Luckily, there hasn't been anyone on the road besides you and them, but you're not too sure that luck will last for much longer.

"I said slow the car down. *Now!*"

Seeing no other option, you whip out the radar gun and point it at the window.

From this speed and the angle you're holding it, there's no way the Corolla driver can tell it's not a real gun. You really hope. It's a stupid move to pull, stupid and *dangerous*, especially when you have a real strap at your side. But you don't want to shoot anyone, never have. You just need to get this driver's attention somehow. You need to be a distraction, so no one notices—

It's a heart-stopping second before the window rolls down, the slow crawl of a manual window crank rather than an automatic system. It rolls down far enough for the driver to shove their fingers through the crack, waving them at you, as if it's the start of a—

"*Watch out!*" someone screams from within the Corolla.

Inoa pulls you back inside the car and hits the brakes hard. The Corolla careens forward right into the spike strip laid out by the Fernley police, who are stationed up the road in a line, ready to continue the chase on their end. Not that the extra step is necessary, of course. Not with how badly those tires shredded at the impact, leaving metal frames to crash into the asphalt and immobilize the car.

You're breathing hard, back in your seat. Your heart feels like it's about to burst out of your body, and it's doing a pretty good job considering how hard it's slamming against your binder. Inoa's doubled over the steering wheel at your side, groaning and nursing what's sure to be a harsh adrenaline headache with his hands.

While you're getting your bearings, the Fernley crew is quick to get to work. Out of their patrol car comes Officers Anderson and Cooper, because of course *those* are the two who would jump at your distress signal. You're pretty sure you see them exchange a smirk as they stroll over to the front of the smoking Corolla, real guns drawn for a fight. They don't have to shout. The front and back doors fly open. Three white kids tumble out, hands in the air, tears streaming down their faces.

Christ Almighty. They barely look eighteen years old.

The fallout happens quickly. Anderson and Cooper place the trio in handcuffs and drag them over to their car for questioning. You and Inoa do a sweep of the Corolla itself. It's beaten up pretty badly outside *and in*. Fast food bags and soda cans overwhelm the floor. The car seats are torn dirty tendrils of leather and padding. Tacky charms hang from the rearview mirror: dice, a dream catcher, a couple of fuzzy peace signs. A heavy perfume of incense wafts through the air.

You kind of want to gag. It takes all your strength to keep your composure as you and Inoa walk over to Anderson and Cooper's car. The trio are together in the backseat, while the Fernley crew pours over a police report on the hood.

"You're sweating like a sinner in church, Anderson." You notice as soon as they get too close. "And you didn't even do any of the heavy lifting back there."

"It's hot today," Anderson grumbles. "We live in the desert. Big surprise."

"What did you find out from those kids? Did they explain what in God's name they were doing driving out here like that?" Inoa steps in, like an actual professional.

Cooper, the marginally nicer one, straightens up just to shrug. "Some crazy shit about 'chasing the sun' and 'following their dreams' or something. None of it makes much sense, so we're thinking they're under the influence."

You're not convinced. "How do we know they're not just some kids with incredibly poor impulse control?" God forbid these two start throwing charges around where they didn't belong...

Anderson glowers up at you, but Cooper replies breezily, "Sure, we didn't smell any alcohol on them. But we're still gonna give them a drug test when we get back to the station and hold them until the judge is in tomorrow. They're not right in the head, Morrison. And, if you didn't notice, they're obviously a danger to anyone else in a vehicle."

"Do you have any more information that we can use in our report?" Anderson bellows at no one at all, which means he's asking you and Inoa a question, and very specifically wants Inoa to supply the answer.

Inoa shakes his head shortly. "Not really, no."

"Along with being menaces to our fair society," you interject, "I'm pretty sure their car is a biohazard. I'd be careful about where I'm sticking my fingers, if I were you."

Anderson ignores you. "Well, how about when you found them? What happened there?"

"They came out of nowhere and blindsided us right off of Dayton. If you're looking for anything else, I'd start there."

Anderson and Cooper exchange a look, deeply unsatisfied with your responses. Cooper quickly hops around the side of the car to get into the driver's seat, while Anderson takes his sweet time getting into the passenger's seat—giving one of the kids in the back enough time to surge forward and start screaming.

A girl snarls at you. "This isn't over, do you hear me?" Her hair is bleached tawdry red and blonde. She's throws herself against the seat so violently that greasy strands whip around her face. "The sun is waking up again! And it's because of *us*! *We* will be the ones to restore this realm to its rightful, beautiful glory of ma—"

Despite the day's humidity, a chill runs up your spine and freezes your limbs in place. A shaky inhale shudders through your body, and you feel your face twisting into shapes your mind struggles to identify. For once, thankfully, everyone around you is too distracted to notice.

"Hush the *fuck* up back there." Anderson swats her away like a fly as he clamors for his seat. He's about to slam the door, but stops short to look back at you. "We'll send a tow to come collect their car, and we'll send our report over to the Carson headquarters."

"Wait," Inoa says. "Why don't you just send your notes our way? We can write up the report for headquarters ourselves."

"Not necessary," Anderson assures. "Our report will be more helpful in the long run."

"Hope you don't mind clearing those spikes on your way out. Since it's your shift, and all." Cooper calls. The engine roars to life. "Have a nice day out there!"

With the extent of their sociability finally extinguished, Anderson and Cooper turn their patrol car around. You and Inoa stand in the middle of the road for a moment, watching them ride off casually into the sunset like the pricks they are.

Then, Inoa nudges you with a sigh. "Come on," he says. "We'll have hell to pay if we don't clean this up. Those two are always looking for some excuse to rat us out to headquarters."

"Right," you say. It's maybe a little curter than you wanted to convey.

Inoa eyes you at that, but he doesn't push. Instead, innocently enough, he asks, "What do you figure she meant by that?"

"I have absolutely no idea." Your shrug is nonchalant. But you turn anyway, just to make sure Inoa doesn't see what's creeping across your face. It isn't indignation at Copper and Anderson's latest round of bullshit. It isn't agitation at the tedious task now at hand. It isn't even exhaustion, justified as it would be after coming down so haphazardly from today's chase.

It's fear.

*

As professions go, highway patrol isn't the strangest job you've ever had. It's definitely the most legal, and probably the most respectable out of the patchwork list of things you've done for money that could theoretically be woven into a job history.

For the past six years, you haunted the West Coast with no cash to your name, no proper identification, no relatives you could call on, no skills to utilize. Hell, you didn't even know how to *drive* back then.

But you could keep your head down. You could keep your mouth shut too and let your boss do all the talking, unless your boss was the type who wanted to pretend to care about their employees' *professional* development. For those bosses, you asked all the stupid questions you could muster; not *too* stupid, but stupid enough to correlate your curiosity with a willingness to learn. Or, more accurately, a willingness to be taught by someone—a much older man, more often than not.

The former weren't bad overall. But the latter...let's just say you had a lot of bosses like them. And let's just say you never lasted too long at those. So, you more or less grifted, and you survived just fine on your own.

Like all your other gigs, the opportunity to join the Nevada Highway Patrol fell unexpectedly in your lap. At the time, you'd been working at a casino in Reno, helping coordinate one of the many shady financial activities that a class-act joint needed to keep the lights on. You were embarrassed when you realized the plainclothes cop you were trying to deliver protection money to behind the kitchen was just a highway patrol officer heading out to California for a new assignment. Well, embarrassed and disgusted; it's not like you enjoyed helping cops under normal circumstances.

But she was nice enough. She was almost as dark as you, and she didn't report you to anyone—she was out of her jurisdiction anyway. Plus, she let you pocket the money and bum a smoke, enthralling you with stories of her nephew, how he was finding himself in a clumsy, youthful way you've always read about over at Howard University.

Somewhere along the way, she planted the crazy idea in your mind that *you* could join the highway patrol. The application was easy, she promised, the paychecks steady, the health insurance reliable. It would just be you and the open road every day and night, alone, for as long as you wanted to be there.

You were on a one-way bus to Carson City the next afternoon, as destitute and alone and hopeful as you were when you first ran away.

What greeted you in Carson was unremarkable mundanity, something you also hadn't experienced much since leaving Arizona. Towns like these were all the same: quaint little homes, office buildings that never surpassed two floors, the scrawl of suburban strip malls endlessly chasing the mountains on the horizon. But it also had real trees and cheap apartments within walking distance of the highway patrol headquarters. That's all you really needed to be happy; you're not one to look a gift horse in the mouth and beg for seconds.

So, imagine your surprise when, on the first day of training at the police academy, this burly, smiling, giant man raps his knuckles against the window of the patrol car you're pretending you know how to turn on. Imagine your surprise when you're expected to have a *partner* out on the road all of a sudden. Imagine your surprise that, based on your aptitude test scores and the semester's low enrollment, *this* man is going to be your alleged new partner from here on out. Six foot tall and gorgeous, with sun-kissed brown skin almost as dark as yours and inky black curls everywhere. Too loud and too open and too comfortable around you. Even has a name that swan dives headfirst down your throat whenever you say it out loud— *Luis Martínez Inoa,* he's your partner now. Imagine that.

And somewhere along the way—after months of working together on the loneliest, most boring, and shittiest route for green officers—imagine your surprise when one day you sneak a glance at him and realize you actually might need him too. You looked that gift horse in the mouth and ripped out its damn tongue.

So, you know, you're fucked now. Pretending this situation is fine is one of your most sacred and noble traditions.

Slowly but surely, the night patrol of the US 50 has become another. Within Nevada state lines it's about a five-hour drive from one end to the other, which doubles to just over ten hours during a typical shift with a two-hour break. Inoa lives near the lake in the nicer part of Minden, so three times a week he picks you up from the Carson headquarters in the late afternoon at the start of the work night. From then on, Inoa drives all the way to Ely for the first leg of the trip.

Meanwhile, your job is to be the state's eyes and ears on this wide, open highway—you're a natural at it. Barring any *serious* issues, your major job responsibilities include saving tourists whose own travel ineptitude has stranded them next to one of Nevada's fun and dangerous roadside attractions; subsequently helping those tourists take great selfies next to those aforementioned attractions; and trying to stop drivers blatantly breaking the law.

Before, that used to mean stopping drunk drivers and throwing condoms at couples trying to have sex next to a Pony Express Station. Now, apparently, it means risking your precious life to catch a couple of thrill-seeking teenagers. So it goes.

Traffic actually starts to pick up once you pass Fernley. By then, the pink beginnings of dusk have settled into a ruddy blush, streaking across the sky. You're a little off schedule for this shift, so you and Inoa decide to make your next major pit stop in Fallon instead, an hour away.

Throughout the ride, you and Inoa are silent partners. Truth be told, you two don't talk too much while out on the road. Over the last few months, all the nervous chitchat you'd sling over yourselves like body armor has melted into quiet familiarity as warm and comforting as the desert air. At most, you'll lazily trade quips or share them with other travelers along the highway. You save the silences for each other.

Fallon greets you two with proper nighttime. It's no Reno by any means, but there's a nice hum of evening activity in this town. You're pumping gas, flush against a street bleeding out more people than it's welcoming. The last of the corporate commuters have gone home, and now it's the second shifters trekking into the darkness, the fluorescent blur of their cars rivaling the starry night sky. The gentle hum of their engines and the half-snatched noise of their radios as they drive past is almost enough to keep you engaged while you wait for Inoa to finish his business in the bathroom.

It almost makes you laugh, thinking about it. You're the one that needs a good ten minutes to make sure you're, well, *situated* properly in your clothes, and yet it's Inoa who spends precious moonlight mulling around in front of a dirty gas station mirror. As if there's anything about him that needs to be fixed at all.

It isn't much longer until Inoa is sauntering back to the car, exaggerating a yawn and stretch that lifts the hem of his shirt right out from under his belt.

You call out, "Finish making yourself pretty in there?" Mount the gas handle back into place, then lean, all cool and casually, against the car.

He smirks, not out of unkindness. "Not really," he says. "It's so muggy out here I can't get my hair to look right. But I got distracted." Once he gets closer, he leans into your space and whispers, "Do you hear that?"

You do not, in fact, hear *that*. You wager a guess anyway. "The sound of your brain leaking out of your ears?"

"I'm serious!" He pouts at you. "Don't you *hear* it?"

"I hear a lot of things, Inoa. My answer depends on what you're wanting out of me based on what I say."

"I don't want anything in particular *from* you. I just want to know if you *hear* something."

"No, man, I *know* you want something specific out of me." Fine, fuck him, you can play along. You cross your arms and cock your head, as if you're trying to get a better listen. "You want me to guess it's the two cats fighting so we can throw water on them? You want me to guess it's that pop song that someone was playing, because you want me to find the station while you drive? You want me to guess it's the people I'm pretty sure are having sex in one of the buildings across the street, so that we can..."

Um.

Your mind goes blank at wherever the *fuck* you were trying to go with that one.

"So, we can...should probably write them a—a ticket for the noise. It would be a complaint. A noise complaint ticket. Maybe."

He laughs at you. He just laughs. "No! I mean, *yes*—" Oh dear God. "—there actually is a cat brawl going on in that alleyway over there—" Oh. Right. "—but I already threw some water from the bathroom sink to break them up. What I'm *really* hearing is our stomachs. I can hear mine; can't you hear yours?"

You can't, in fact, hear your stomach, because you're always smart enough to bring snacks on your shifts. But Inoa's not expecting a real answer from you. He's jutting his plump bottom lip and sulking. He's letting his eyes go all big and glassy. He's lifted up his shirt even more than before to pitifully rub circles over his tanned, rock-hard abs. He just wanted an *excuse* for this.

You'd be outright drooling like the fool you *clearly* are if you weren't fighting the urge to roll your eyes and throw yourself back against the car. And Inoa knew you were going to put up a fight over this; hence all his silly, stupid, unintentionally sexy theatrics.

And look, it's like you're *his* mother or anything. When it comes to responsibilities, he's the one pulling you along on a leash. You're more of a Pretty Cool Dude, ready for anything, always have been. It's just that, in the grand scheme of things—like time, and efficiency, and thinking about the easiest ways to do the least amount of work as possible to earn your paycheck—what Inoa *wants* is not a necessity. It's not really close enough to your route to justify stopping. It's not even that *good*, really.

And yet...

You simply cannot give Inoa the satisfaction of seeing you give in. Instead, you primly stick your nose in the air and put your back to him to get in the car. The passenger window is rolled up, so you catch the exact moment Inoa's face illuminates like a Christmas tree.

He whoops in place before sprinting to the other side of the car, grinning like a fool. You turn your bashful smile away from him when he gets in and peels back out onto the road.

*

There is a certain reverence about Middlegate Station around these parts. It's known as something of a haven, the central hub for the lost and weary travelers of the US 50. The draw of its location was certainly more relevant back in the olden days, sure, but the legacy of safety and civility against a backdrop of dangerous wilderness was something not even modern technology could wash away.

It was the first place Inoa took you on your first shift together. Spring was just starting to peek out from under the heavy desert clouds. You had the windows rolled down, so the chilly air could pass over your skin. Inoa spent the entire drive combing his hand through his curls and wrapping your mind in wonderful tales about that place: delicious burgers bigger than your head, a canopy of hundred-dollar bills that created its ceiling, the true unmarked gravesites of Elvis *and* Dawn Wells, and shoe trees that somehow offered promises of true love.

After all the times you've been here, you can confidently say the Middlegate has only delivered on two of its longstanding mythologies.

In *reality*, it's more like your typical roadside rest area—gas station—bar—barn combo, with the added flavor of historical significance to keep its wooden floorboards oiled and its cash flow steady—tourists were always looking for authentic Nevadan experience. It's nowhere near the middle of the highway; that coveted designation would be Austin. The burgers are bigger than your head, but do they pack as much of a deliciously jumbo punch? Debatable. No comment on Dawn Wells' grave, of course, though the Elvis rumor might have some legitimacy. And you've never tried to actually see if the shoe tree could make good on any specific promises...but you've gotten lucky with a few dollar bills gently floating down from the ceiling.

However, like you said, the belief in all these tall tales is more important than the truth, and Middlegate has never suffered for much because of it. Even now there are a few stragglers of the tourist kind still inside by the time you arrive, about half an hour before closing time. It's almost funny, how they're the only ones still helplessly enamored with this place. They stare, transfixed at gaudy walls filled with military patches and Gold Rush memorabilia. They *always* want a Monster burger, and they giggle at their struggles to finish it. Their souls have not yet been crushed by the distinct way living in the desert changes you, and that must fuel enough happy memories to keep convincing people to come out here.

Inoa also remains helplessly enamored with this place, but he doesn't count. He's just a sap.

You see three separate tourist groups seated at round tables. Locals hover around the bar, a much older crowd of grizzly men and women. To respect their search for peace, and to preserve your own mental sanity, you and Inoa choose one of the tables wedged in a corner next to the window by the bar.

The freckly man they've got serving tonight appears before you've barely fixed your ass in the seat. He's got a tired but friendly smile on his face and a notepad fixed in the air for your order. Inoa goes sloppy with a bacon cheeseburger, while you settle for a sourdough melt with extra fixings. You two share the fries, of course, like respectable gentlemen do.

The first few minutes are nice. You're watching him pick the bacon out of his sandwich to munch on first, he's watching you lick your fingers clean after every bite—because they gave you a lot of ketchup on your order, that's all—and you use fries to sword fight to the death over the little cups of the house-made condiments. There's a reason you try not to stop at Middlegate; you don't like it, and yet if you had it your way, you'd stay here forever. With him.

So of course, as if someone felt the disturbance of your happiness in this otherwise depressing hellscape, your phones jingle with a ping specifically designated for work e-mails. Inoa's hands are cleaner. He pulls his out of his back pocket first and groans *real* loud.

"Who do I have to kill?" you ask around another bite.

"You might want to make it a murder-suicide," Inoa replies, and turns his phone for you to read from across the table. "Because the report Anderson just filed makes us look like *jackasses*."

Once you start reading, you can't help but groan too. In his highly sterile and economical writing, Anderson describes an otherwise quiet day down in Fernley and the great disruption by a desperate distress signal from one of Carson City's own patrol officers: you, of course. While Inoa was subsequently able to engage the speed racer in earnest, somehow the very recent strategic driving training he received was no match for the horsepower of a 1996 Toyota Corolla. Several times during the chase, the Carson City patrol officers gravely feared for your lives, but had no idea how to properly deal with this situation.

So, the report goes on, longtime employees of the Fernley Police Department, Anderson and Cooper, set out to offer their assistance. In arresting the three culprits— WHITE, 1 MALE AND 2 FEMALE, AGES 19-20—no drugs or alcohol were found on their person or in the Corolla, which has been confiscated and placed in the Fernley junkyard. As the Carson City patrol officers had no part in the arrest or the subsequent interrogation of the culprits, they most generously offered to clean what they could from the highway confrontation, as is part of the basic job description of their profession.

You know the appropriate response to this report is outrage. And like, it's definitely *there* in the pit of your stomach, churning in a seriously uncomfortable way. But you can only laugh and lean back in your seat.

"Chief is going to have our whole asses when we get back," you say, before taking a big bite of your food. You don't bother wiping the ketchup off your mouth with your fingers. You just let it roll down your chin as you take another bite. The mess doesn't matter. None of *anything* about his job really matters.

This is probably what despair feels like.

Inoa shoves his phone back in his pocket and throws his hands in the air, because he's able to express his emotions like a normal human being. "This is such bullshit," he says. "And incredibly *inaccurate*, based on what we saw out there."

"Oh, so you don't agree that Anderson's assessment that your poor training and my girlish squeals almost got us killed?"

"What I don't *agree* with is the omission of the perpetrator's statements at the time of arrest. That girl was talking like she just walked out of a cult or something!"

"What does *that* have to do with anything?" You finally put your food down and stare at him incredulously. You don't want to feel offended—and you really, *really* shouldn't be—but fuck, here you are. Being offended about things that Inoa doesn't know, and can't even begin to understand.

"What do you mean?" Inoa says, raising an eyebrow.

"I mean—" What *did* you mean, genius? You change course quicker than you ever have in your life. "I *mean* we're probably going to be fired tomorrow morning, and all you care about is the nonsense of someone very clearly off her rocker?"

Now it's Inoa's turn to give you a look. "Morrison," he says slowly, trying to be convincing. "This is the fifth time something like this has happened around here. Don't you think it's a little suspicious?"

"It's the middle of summer, Inoa." You sound out each word, just to be a patronizing asshole. "Those kids looked like they just graduated high school. This could all be some, like, fucking stupid senior dare they have to do together to celebrate their friendship before they all go to different colleges. Like some *Ya-Ya Sisterhood of the Traveling Pants* or something."

"Do you seriously believe that?" he asks, leaning forward.

"Do you seriously believe it's a *cult*?" You follow his lead.

You're glaring at each other from either side of the table. It feels like you're punching yourself in the throat. But your pride is taking over. Fear might drive this conversation over the edge of a cliff.

Finally, *finally,* Inoa is the one to cave first, because he's a good person. Because he's trying to solve a case. Because he's not a fucking liar. He sits back, running his hands through his hair, frustrated. "Just walk through this thing with me for a second, okay?"

You hold on to that glare. It's a very long second, but he's giving you an out here, and so you take it. You uncurl your body and lean back in your seat, crossing your arms.

You nod.

"Okay," he says through a sigh. "Listen. In the last couple of months, we've had a string of these speed-racing incidents along the US 50. All different kinds of cars with what I'm assuming are different people in each. This is the first time we've caught one of them, and they immediately go on this rehearsed rant about saving the Earth from evil and shit?"

He leans in closer to look at you again. He even puts his palms on the table, like you're supposed to hold his hands and gaze back at him. "Don't you think it could be some kind of collective effort? Maybe not a *cult—*" he clarifies, since he probably picked up on how much that specific word upset you. "—but something a group of people all came together and decided to do on their own one day? We have tourists who come to Middlegate because they hear about the damn Monster burger. Who's to say this isn't an example of *that*?"

It's a smart angle. Real pretty too, the kind of X-to-Y correlation the chief can slap a bow on and present to the press without a lot of questions about the real investigation. You want it to feel right, what Inoa's suggesting. You want to agree with everything and drop the whole thing, right now.

But you can't. You just *can't*. And the way he's looking at you, he knows you can't either.

"It's not the worst idea in the world," Inoa says. He leans even closer. "But it's not right, is it? What else could it be? I know you have an idea, Morrison."

"I don't know, Inoa," you whisper. You're so damn tired all of a sudden. Your arms just fall to the table, and you plant your chin in your hands.

"Yeah, you do. Just try to tell me..." He reaches until it's his fingertips ghosting over the exposed part of your forearm. "It's okay."

"My mother..." you begin and end.

You feel more than you hear Inoa take in a shaky inhale, from his fingertips right to your arm.

"Excuse me," a voice calls out suddenly. "You two aren't from around here, are you?"

Compared to how quiet things are between you two, hearing that voice feels like you've been shot. You and Inoa both whip around and come face-to-face with an old man sitting at the nearest corner of the bar, staring at you over the rim of his glass.

Neither you nor Inoa respond, but your expressions seem to be enough for him to continue. "I'm saying you two haven't lived here too long. It's not a family thing for you here, am I right?" A pause while he takes a sip and slaps the taste against his lips. "Course I am. Because if you *had* lived here long, you'd know stuff like this happens all the time."

Inoa regains his senses faster than you do. "This has happened before?"

"Oh, sure," the man replies. "For at *least* the past thirty years or so. I mean, it happens closer to Austin, but we've always gotten some stragglers of the race down here too."

"Come on, Inoa," you mumble weakly. "This is stupid‘ don't listen to him."

"But this is important," he says. "What do you mean by 'race'? There's a competition out there or something?"

The old man shrugs. "I guess you could put it in those terms, but it's not for money or anything. They just want to be the first to... I mean, they've mention something 'bout the sun to you, right?"

"Yes! Yes, they did!"

Fuck, he's getting excited now. The dread in your stomach feels like it's going to crawl out of your throat. You start to say, "But it doesn't matter—"

"It *does* matter—" Inoa interrupts.

"It matters to them," the old man compromises. "But it's not going to work. Every time I see them, I tell them it's not gonna happen, especially how they're doing it."

"What's not going to work? How are they doing it wrong?"

You tense. "Sir, please, can you just drop this?"

"It's mostly because they're young and dumb. They don't know the traditions behind it, not really."

"What do you mean, what are they trying to do out here—"

"Inoa, stop—"

"Well, if I can use a word you might understand, what they're trying to do is, well, in metaphysical sense, more like a summoning—"

"*Shut up!*" It happens fast. First you're panicking; then you're screaming. "You don't know what you're *talking* about!"

You're standing in front of the entire restaurant, panting. Dozens of eyes stare at you, shocked. The old man looks a little angry, but mostly hurt, and so very small. Inoa's looking at you like he doesn't recognize you.

It's all too much. You run.

The air outside of Middlegate is as hot as it's ever been, or maybe that's just you. Either way, a cold sweat causes your uniform to cling angrily to your body as you walk across the gravel parking lot, and the patrol car's AC does nothing to make you feel better.

It's a three-hour shot to Ely from here. You and Inoa will switch places once you get there. Usually he encourages you to sleep until it's time for you to make the trek back to Carson City. You recline your seat back and close your eyes, trying to get comfortable as you tilt your body to face the passenger door and nothing—no one— else.

You keep your eyes closed when, sooner than you thought, the driver's side door opens. It's quiet, and you think Inoa's might reach out and touch you again. To...you don't know. Try to talk to you or maybe hit you. He won't be wrong either way.

But he doesn't do anything. He doesn't *say* anything. All he does is turn on the engine and pull the car out of the lot.

You keep pretending to be asleep. Eventually, you actually are.

*

It's hours past midnight. The rocky roads of White Pine County had been rough enough to almost rock you back to consciousness, but it takes Inoa nudging you to get the job done.

He's up and out of the car before you're able to look at him. Which is fine. You're still feeling lazy from your nap, and annoyed about before. You thank your lucky stars and the genetics that blessed you with your short-ass body as you shimmy across the console into the driver's seat.

Inoa gets in the passenger's side. He lies down on the seat, but doesn't bother rolling over like you did because he's not a child. Neither of you say anything as you drive into the desolate night.

You're probably not going to say anything for the rest of this shift, and not when you get back to the station, and not when you leave to go back to your respective homes. Who knows if you'll get to talk to him before the next shift starts? Is this going to be your next adult tradition? Distance and secrets and eventual loathing between you and the person you care about the most?

It's...fine. It will be fine. You've survived just fine on your own before.

You have, and you will again if you have to.

But God, you don't really want to.

It happens at the same time. You inch your right hand off the steering wheel and reach into the darkness of the patrol car, and something warm and soft hits your fingertips. Inoa's hands are in the air too, reaching for you.

The touch is shocking—it feels like it burns, and you try to pull your hand away. But Inoa has a solid grip on you now, and he tugs you closer. You really shouldn't, but you can't help it. You look.

Your eyes meet. You're not 100 percent sure you didn't crash the car a mile up the road and you're now having some sad, delusional, dying dream. You could be.

"Morrison..." Inoa breathes. He holds your hand in his own, right over his heart. "Morrison, what aren't you telling me? What's all this have to do with your mom?"

This is uncharted territory for the both of you. Inoa knows as much about your mother as anyone could find on an online obituary, skeletal remains about an entire life once lived. Personally, you've said even less about her to him, and yet more than you've ever told anyone else. It's all too private, too personal, too... strange. You don't know where to begin.

But here he is, prying that hidden part of your past out with the lightest coaxing and those wide eyes. Nothing you say will make any kind of sense, and he seems like he knows it...yet here he is, genuinely curious to hear your ideas. Hear your thoughts. Learn more about you.

He's trying. And fuck, at the very least, you can try too.

You have to.

"My mother..." you begin again. "She had all sorts of superstitions from Jamaica. She made up a lot of these really ornate traditions out of them when I was growing up—I was a kid, and it's not like I had any other family, so of course I went along with it."

"Like what?" Inoa asks.

"Um..." You falter a bit, struggling to keep your eyes on the road. "Well, a lot of it was ridiculous. Making potions to cure sicknesses, and blessing certain plants for luck. Little incantations like that."

"What, like you were doing this stuff all the time?" Inoa asks *again*.

"Not really, no. Funny thing was there were some things you could only do at night, and some things you were supposed to save for the day. You know, so the...tradition would work properly."

"What was the difference between the two?" Inoa *keeps asking*.

You huff out a laugh to mask how much heat spreads into your cheeks. "Man, you're really pulling my leg with this one."

"I'm serious." Inoa squeezes your hand for good measure. "Keep going."

"Right. Okay. It was a lot of healing stuff, mostly. Finding lost things. All of it done at night. Things to clean up the house. The things we could do in the daytime were much bigger and bolder, because that's the very nature of the sun, you know? Bring things to light and show your true self...shit like that. Basically, if you're doing something in the daytime, it's because you want to celebrate it. You want people to see it."

"So, do you agree with the old man from the bar? Do you think what's going on is some...what, some extremely cultural shit? Like what your mother used to do?" Inoa asks, again, wondrously.

You sigh. "Yes. I mean, I think so... What my mother did was never like this, but it does remind me of it." Of her: her love, her labor, her life. All the things she tried passing onto you before she was gone. All the things you didn't understand, couldn't get right, felt shame over how different and alone it made you. All the things you tried to run away from because of shame. So many contours of meaning and history and pain conjured up even by the *mention* of her magic.

Inoa turns onto his side now. One hand cradles his head so he can look at you better. You're still holding hands. You wonder, distantly, deliriously, if he notices how this contact is making your hand damp. "The old man said they were summoning something, right? Is that you're thinking too?"

And *fuck* that old man, but he's definitely got you thinking now. Memories are speeding through pathways in your mind you had long thought dead, coming back to life in a bright, burning haze of light. It's making your head hurt, but the act in and of itself reminds you of something else too.

"Honestly? With the way they're going at it, I'm thinking it's more like..." You hesitate, but there's no other way to put this. "More like a revival. Maybe something's going on with the sun that we don't know about."

"Something that they're willing to kill someone over? That doesn't sound like any kind of revival to me."

"Well, it is if they need a sacrifice."

You and Inoa are quiet again, just taking...all of that in, you guess. Letting all these outlandish ideas and theories, and all your vulnerabilities surrounding them, just hang in the air.

Eventually, Inoa plops into the seat. He's *still* holding your outreached arm, your hand in his. "Jesus, Morrison."

"I told you it was ridiculous."

"Listen, I'm not one to judge," Inoa says solemnly. "My mom curses out five different gods when she loses her car keys. My abuelita used to demand a strand of hair from my middle school bullies. I know quirky family shit."

Delving into the true extent of your *quirky family shit* would definitely convince Inoa to abandon you in the middle of the road. Best not to bring it all up now.

But...this is a good start.

"Besides," Inoa goes on with a little handwave, "it does explain some things."

At that, you can't help but raise an eyebrow. "Explains what?

"You know, how you're so naturally cool with things." He says it casually, like it's obvious. "I don't know, kind of sounds like you're seen it all before."

"Probably not, but I guess I have a high tolerance for bullshit."

He looks at you and asks, "But you've seen some shit, right?" And you can practically hear the smile sliding back to his face. "Like, shit you'd only see in a movie. You ever meet any mythological creatures?"

"Why?" you tease. "You trying to fuck a werewolf?"

His laugh vibrates around the car like it's being amplified by a hundred speakers. Or maybe that's just your laugh, mixing with his. "Well, *no*, but that would be one of the many topics I've always wanted to—"

A car speeds by you so quickly it almost sends you careening off the road.

It's like nothing you've ever felt before. The car touches down like a lightning strike, and when it moves past you, it brings everything around it surging forward like a black hole. The patrol car would have flipped if you and Inoa didn't grab onto the steering wheel at the same time, pushing against the powerful current in the air.

The car spins violently. Large bits of debris smack the doors as you spiral, cracking glass and denting the exterior. It's all you can do to put your head down and hold on to the wheel, hold on to Inoa, hold on to yourself and pray to whatever gods are out there to keep you alive.

And just as suddenly as it happened, it's over.

Cacti and grass and sand have been ripped out of place and thrown into the middle of the road. It's too quiet outside, as if all the animals roaming the desert and singing their nightly songs have died. They very well might've. It's a miracle you and Inoa didn't join them.

The fallout happens quickly. You don't have to look at Inoa to know what you have to do.

He pulls his seat forward and buckles up. You throw the car into reverse. Upshift. Even as beat up as it is, the patrol car shudders back to life.

This time, there are no tendrils of smoke to guide your way. You're speeding into the night, the front lights of the car flickering madly, and the only sound you're able to distinguish is the air you're struggling to breathe.

You're not as strong a driver as Inoa, and the car that passed you has much more horsepower than a Corolla, but eventually you spot its steady bright lights ahead. Try as you might, you can't seem to get close enough to push the fucker off the road.

Beside you, Inoa pulls out his gun and throws his head and arms outside of his window. He tries to shoot out the tires. They hit—several times—but instead of ripping the rubber apart the bullets melt upon contact.

It feels like only minutes have gone by, but when you glance away from the sleek black bumper of the car you're chasing for long enough, you see the sun starting to rise. In the back of your mind, you can't help but think there's something off about it.

You're flying west down the US 50, heading back to Carson City, heading back home. You see truckers and early morning commuters—maybe you're near Eureka or Austin. They're starting to crowd the road, and the black car you're pursuing has the difficult task of trying to swerve around them to escape you. And now you have the difficult task of ensuring their safety, too.

But it's like they don't even notice you. Not when you throw on your siren, not when you slam on the horn, not when Inoa throws himself out of the window again to scream *"Watch out!"* as you and the black car zoom past, clipping mirrors, side exteriors, even one poor bastard's open car door.

The other drivers are parked, distinct lanes be damned. They stare at the sun. They're watching it rise, big and red and strangely terrible, from under the western horizon.

Which side does the sun rise from again?

At the first empty opening, you curve the patrol car sharply to the right. You speed up to try and see who's inside, but the windows are tinted. Once you get close enough, neck and neck, you swerve and smash against them. Inoa shouts something, but you can't hear it.

The black car drives on like nothing happened. It doesn't even *budge*. Seeing no other option, you hit it again.

That's when Inoa leans over you and points his gun out your window.

From this speed and the distance, there's no way the driver of the black car could escape a bullet. Inoa's never shot his gun before, never shot one in his life, he's confessed to you. And yet, here he is. Here he is in front of you, blocking your view of what's ahead, ready to shoot.

It's a heart-stopping second.

The black car's window rolls down far enough for the interior to be visible.

Ash bursts from the car. It burns your eyes and skin.

You're still trying to see into the car, but the air is suffocating and hot. Inoa retreats into his seat with another shout, clutching his face in pain.

The road is clear to you again. Just in time too.

You're about to drive directly into the sun.

You try to step on the brakes. You really do. But before your foot smashes down, the pedal isn't there anymore. The wheel isn't there anymore. The seat isn't there anymore.

"*Shit, Morri—!*"

You're not there anymore.

*

You wake up. Your head feels like it's split open. Your body hurts. Your face is pressed against something hard. You can't see a thing.

But you can hear. It's hard to make out anything specific at first, but that's okay. Whatever's making the noise keeps repeating—they're shouting from a distance, and as they get closer you think you can identify a rhythm to it.

You try to move your mouth. To hum out the rhythm. It sounds familiar, like you could maybe shape the letters and eventually make a word. You know, like they used to do in kindergarten. You try, but something fresh and nasty trickles from your gums and throat. You think you might be bleeding. It makes certain parts of your mouth hurt. A tooth or two might be about to fall out.

You're really, really tired.

More sounds flow over you, a metallic scream and then rhythmic beating. You can almost feel it vibrating against your face, that beating. No, wait, not beating. It's too refined for that. And there's no reason why *this* noise makes the thing pushing against your face move, when the *other* noise does nothing.

You still can't see anything. It's like there's a blinding light covering your eyes. Instead, you concentrate on all those beats, the sensations they're giving you, and you're humming along with the noises in a one-person cacophonous concerto. And then somehow, the world tilts back into focus. It's not beat and rhythm and song that you hear. It's footsteps running toward you. The other noise—a car screeching to a halt. The noise before that— someone shouting your name, like they're doing right now, just as they finally come into view.

"Morrison? Morrison, what—oh, Jesus *Christ*." Officer Anderson stops a few feet away from you, witnessing what truly feels like your broken and mangled body. "*Morrison*, is that you? What the fuck is going on?"

Oh, you don't know. *What a fucking piece of shit.* But your mouth still hurts, so all you do is groan pitifully into the asphalt and curse your rotten luck.

Damn, you didn't realize you'd driven so far back home. You swear to God just a second ago you were driving away from the Ely border, holding Inoa's hand, talking about your mother and your childhood and the strange, wonderful magic you used to make together. Did the time really fly by while you two were having so much fun?

Or, no, did it slip through your two clasped hands when...

Oh.

Oh, oh no.

Where *are* you right now?

Where is the *car*?

Where's *Inoa?*

You vomit. Mushy fries, your half-digested burger, and bits of protein bars as pink and puffy as flesh and sinew flow freely all around you. It mixes horribly with the blood congealing on your clothes. You really hope that blood is yours.

And apparently, so does Anderson. Despite the disgusting mess you've made of yourself, he pulls you upright onto your ass and drags you by your elbows across the asphalt, toward his patrol car. He mumbles to himself all the while: "Knew there was something wrong with you, do you hear me? Knew you were always trouble, and now *look* at you. All of this is *your* fault, I know it is, I've always known it."

You're too tired to fight him off, but you have enough strength to hold your head up.

The sun is a blazing ruby on the wrong side of the road, looming so large it can't break from the horizon. There is nothing else around it or beyond it: no road, no desert, nothing. It's eating the world.

Of course, Anderson ignores it. Instead, he unceremoniously dumps you into the back of his patrol car—where, much to your everlasting shock, is the wild girl with the multicolored hair who yelled at you yesterday.

Your throat rips open. "What the *fuck* is she doing here?" Because truly, *this* is the most outrageous thing to happen to you in the last twenty-four hours.

"That information is no longer any of your concern, you *fucking* criminal," Anderson snarls. "I'm not going to die out here with you. Not me. I deserve better than the *hell* you're about to burn in." And with that, he slams the door and begins a valiant sprint to another patrol car. If you squint just a little, you see Cooper in the driver's seat. You think he even waves before they speed away in the opposite direction.

Fucking *pricks*.

At the very least, the harbinger of your downfall has the courtesy to look just as insulted as you feel.

"I really hate cops," she says. And then she turns, as if she's seeing you for the first time. "Wow. You look like shit."

"Thanks," you say. A bit of blood trails down your chin. You swipe it away with a ripped sleeve, and soldier on to preserve your dignity. "Let me repeat myself. Why are you here? Where are your friends?"

"My colleagues and I were in the middle of escaping when that tall thuggish one caught us. It took them three hours to maneuver the traps we put out for them." For someone handcuffed to a police car seat, the girl puffs out her chest with pride.

"Congratulations to your colleagues." You snort and shake your head. "'Colleagues,' is that really what you call yourselves?"

"What's *that* supposed to mean?" she asks, the sails in her ship temporarily deflated.

"Not a damn thing. I just thought the new crop of witches would have given themselves a name that's a little less...corporate. Coven Comrades. Anarchic Alchemists. The Baddest Bitches. Something cool, is all."

It's almost funny, the way the girl's eyes go wide. You'd compare it to the blazing sun that's only getting closer, but, well, it doesn't seem appropriate.

"You're one of us," she says through a strained breath.

"Not really..." You shrug miserably. "But I'm related."

"No, no, I should have known. You were different from the others. And, like, you just came out of nowhere and fell from the *sky* just now, no wonder those cops got spooked! How far did you astral project?"

"*What* did I do now?" You're distracted. It's getting hot in the car. You're still feeling sluggish, but the compressed air is starting to burn clarity into your pained mind. You're wasting time talking about this. You have to get out of here and go home. You have to find Inoa.

Slowly, carefully, you push your body forward. You're about to reach a hand to the front console, and you rummage around until you find rough, rigged metal—handcuff keys. They steam between your shaking fingers.

"Astral projection, man. Like the sun and the moon and stars?" The girl next to you narrows her eyes, even though you're, you know, clearly in the process of saving her damn life.

"I'm not really interested in astrology, sorry."

"Are you serious?" The fact that she's being freed seems to escape the girl completely. "God, you're being so annoying right now. I didn't come here to teach but, like, where do you think your magic *comes* from?"

"I told you, I don't have any magic. My mother did."
Eventually, the girl's handcuffs fall to the floor. Your job
is finally done for the day. You gingerly open the door and
all but roll yourself to something of a standing position.

The other car door slams too. Brightly colored hair
bobs toward you. On her right, the sun looks like it's
starting to pass the spot you apparently *fell from the sky
from* a few minutes ago.

You swallow hard. "Why is the sun moving? Why is it
getting bigger like that?"

Suddenly, she looks bashful. "I don't know. It's not
supposed to. *My* colleagues didn't do that."

"Well, what's it *supposed* to be doing? What were you
trying to do?"

"What we've been trying to do is, basically, turn it
back on," she huffs. "The sun is a conduit for magic, all
right? But there hasn't been any magic on this side of
America for literal centuries. So, we wanted to fix it."

"A lot of good that did. Look at it. You turned it into a
black hole."

"It's *actually* becoming a pulsar—you know what?
Forget it." She crosses her arms and turns away. "I can't
believe you seriously don't know this. Magic users flock to
one another even when they don't know it. Did you just
avoid them all like the plague growing up?"

Your throat flares again, and you want to shake her,
but she's kind of right, isn't she? You've been avoiding shit
like this your entire life, haven't you? Like you always do.
And all these people cropped up in your life to help you
work through it after your mother died—this girl, the old
man in the bar, *Inoa*—and look what you did. You pushed
them away until it was too late. And now, everyone you've
loved, could have loved, are gone.

"I should be better at this. I should know more. I'm sorry," you say, to her and to your mother, and to your partner, and to everyone else.

Silence is the only response you get. But that's fine. You can survive silences. You can probably even survive, for all intents and purposes, the end of the world.

But you don't want to do any of it alone. You don't want to do anything at all without your partner at your side.

You turn back to the girl, a newfound life pumping strength into your veins. "So, what happens now? How do we go about fixing the sun for real?"

Shyness crosses her face again. It makes her look too young for any of this. "I don't think this is something we can do on this side. Since, like, a lot of *this* side is disappearing into that thing?"

Your mind is running ahead of you again, and you're not too sure you like what you're thinking. "Are you saying one of us needs to...what, go into the sun?"

"Technically, yes, but don't think of it as walking into the sun," she chastises. "I told you; it's a conduit. Think of it as a giant magic portal."

"So, theoretically, everything that's disappearing on this side is winding up on the other side of that thing?"

She nods.

In the nearing distance, the air crackles and whitens. The dusting of hair on your forearms starts to singe. "And do you know what's on the other side?"

The girl nods again, then shakes her head. "Yes, things end up on the other side. No, I don't know what that other side *is* or looks like. But I've heard stories."

"About what?"

"About people who used to come back and forth through it. They'd go over to recharge their magic and learn new tricks. Find lost, mystical artifacts sometimes too."

"And did they survive?"

"What do you mean?"

If your sudden strength translated into actual physical prowess, you would have rushed over and grabbed the girl in your excitement. All you manage to do is press hard against the side of the car to lean closer to her and urgently repeat yourself. "Did they survive going over? The people from your stories, did they ever make it back alive?"

At that, the girl gives an uncomfortable shrug. "I mean, they were just stories my grandmother used to tell me, all right? I don't know for sure. But I guess they always did when she told them. Yeah, they always survived."

"Right. Okay." One last thing. "What's your name, kid?"

"Philomena Stevens. You?"

"Just call me Morrison." You pull back. Your mind is racing a mile a minute, and your body is officially on fire now, and you can only partially blame it on the sun. Hell, you might even be smiling.

"So listen, Philomena," you say. "I'm going to walk into that big sun portal conduit thing. It's eating the world, and I think it ate my partner, so I'm going in to look for him. While I'm in there, I'll see what I can do to fix it from the inside."

What the fuck are you even saying? What the fuck are you even *thinking*? You smile even harder.

"You can't be serious," Philomena breathes. "You said you don't have any magic."

"But my mother did," you say. "She taught me how to heal things and find things with it her entire life. I can't think of a better use of that magic than what's going on right now. Saving the love of my life. Fixing the sun. Things like that."

She's staring at you, her eyes wide and nearly incomprehensible against the glare of the sun. "That's... ridiculous. How can you be so sure about any of this?"

"As long as I'm alive, my mother's magic did not die with her." When you lean in this time to look at her, you gently grasp her shoulder. "Go find your colleagues, Philomena. See what you can do to fix it out here. All right?"

She pauses, assesses you again. Decides. "Yeah, sure. I can do that, Morrison."

You nod at her, and then you walk around the car. Thankfully, the sun is closer. You can throw your back against the car and look up, right into this big, terrible, burning beauty you've been trying to avoid your entire life.

"Shit," you say on a ragged breath.

But you don't run away this time.

LOST/FOUND

Brooklyn Ray

Warning: mild body horror, brief mention of sexual
harassment

And the sea came to her stretched out like a friend in the night, spitting salty wishes at her feet...

There is something out there. Hollis watched moonlight skate across an empty ocean. *Look.* She listened to waves hit the shore, tasted the brittle chill of midnight as it settled on the beach. *Out there—right there.* Like this, seated on the edge of the world with her toes buried in the sand, she wondered if there were lips pressed to her ear or if the wind had tossed her hair, a simple thing masquerading as something else.

Nights like these, Hollis Griffin remembered that she'd been acquainted with a star once. *There.* The sky felt closer, blanketed around her like a scarf. *Don't close your eyes.* Days, weeks, months ago, a stranger had sat on a bench beside her, just as they sat on the sand beside her now, and days, weeks, months ago, a stranger had tilted their head, just as they tilted their head to look at her now. Days, weeks, months ago, the star had said, "I'm lost."

But tonight, Hollis spoke first. "You're not lost," she said. "You say that every time, and I never believe it. You know that, right?"

"I know, what?" Each visit was different. The first night, the star had been a rabbit with opalescent fur and round, black eyes. After that, they'd appeared as a bird. A strange, faceless woman. As nothing but unmistakable sound, their voice as familiar as a spoon on the edge of a teacup.

Hollis hugged her knees to her chest. Shifted her feet back and forth through the sand. Her aunt had always said, *Saying something untrue a second time is wasted breath. That's why it feels harder.* "That I don't believe you," she said, and cursed her aunt for being right.

The star took a new shape tonight. Not something, but some*one*. Their hands were long, as if they'd tried to replicate a boy with nothing but his skeleton as inspiration. The outline of clothes and skin punched a hole through the dark, but where there should've been fabric, flesh, detail, there was sky instead. Star nurseries spun in the hollow of their elbows. Meteors sped across their eyes. Their lips, full and quirked into a smile, blurred like a comet's tail. They were beautiful and terrifying. Hollis wondered, as she always did, if they were real.

"I think you do." They sat back on their bony hands and tipped their chin, nodding toward the sea. "Do you ever go out there?"

"Out where?" Hollis narrowed her eyes, following their gaze to the place where black met black on the horizon.

The star flicked their wrist. Their shape fractured, the movement too quick for time to understand. "Into the ocean. Do you ever go out there?"

Hollis wanted to know their name. She'd never asked before, because she'd always believed they might not be real. But they were real enough tonight, weren't they? A piece of the cosmos chipped away for her and her alone. "I have before, but I'm not a good swimmer. Can't keep my head above water for long."

"I'd like to try," they said. Moonlight glittered on their upturned nose, snagging the frayed edge of a meteorite lingering close to their mouth. Hollis watched them gather sand in their strange hands. Saw golden flecks sink into the lines of their palm and wondered how far their future spanned, how long their past stretched.

What did time mean to a star? She uncurled one arm from around her legs and pressed her fingers to their wrist. "Do you have a heartbeat?"

"Do you?" the star asked. They tipped their hand and bent their wrist, fingers light and silky, pressed to the underside of her arm. They did not move after that. The star went quiet, their chest stilled, and their eyes stayed fixed on her, wide and open.

The star had visited Hollis for days, weeks, months, but she had never touched them.

Not until tonight, when waves inched closer and the ocean insisted she do so.

"Yes," she said, too quickly, and swallowed hard. Wind caught her pastel-pink hair, and she decided to be brave. Hollis shifted onto her knees in front of them, hand still perched on theirs, and reached. The star did not move. They simply watched, mystical and unpredictable, until her hand found their cheek. Heat radiated there, thrumming like blood under thin skin, restless and uncontained. There was a whole world inside them, she thought. Something uncharted. "Are you one whole heart? Or is there a place where you keep your secrets?"

The star leaned into her hand. "You're my only secret, Hollis Griffin."

Waves crashed on beaten sand. Hollis kept her hand on their cheek for a long time, feeling skin that wasn't skin, warmth that wasn't warmth, and slowly brushed her thumb along their eyelashes.

"What's your name?" Hollis asked.

The star laid their hand over Hollis's knuckles and dragged her palm to their lips. "Zaniah," they said, whispering each syllable like a prayer against her pulse.

And the city clutched her true nature between concrete hands, cursing the ocean for convincing her to stay...

Eight rubber trees in terracotta pots lined the window of an apartment perched on Venice Boulevard. Two crooked lines split the glass, scars left behind from her late boyfriend, a mistake dressed in designer jeans. There used to be nine terracotta pots on the two-tiered shelf, but he'd snatched the smallest from the windowsill and hurled it at Hollis's blurred reflection. She'd been standing awkwardly in the galley kitchen, as she did right then, in violet lingerie, as she did right then, and he'd tried to shatter her into bits, convinced she would fall at his feet.

To his surprise, she did not break. Only cracked.

Stubborn sunlight poured across the horizon, blotting the sky with swatches of orangsicle and honey blossom and amethyst. She remembered the look on his face, that man—that boy—as he flipped his phone around and shoved it at her, expecting her to flinch.

That's you. That's you. That's you.

He'd gone on and on, a broken record set to scratch, a half-healed scab asking to be picked.

"That's me," she'd said, as she said it right then, to no one and someone in the quiet, open room.

As darkness clawed at the sunset from above, Hollis sat on a sheepskin rug in front of her broken window and hit the shutter on her camera, capturing picture after picture, movement after movement, while her body shifted into practiced poses. The delicate strap on her sheer nightgown slipped from her shoulder. Lace caught on her breast, clinging to the surgical steel pushed through her nipple. She touched her face, because touches meant something to the people who tipped her, and she spread her legs, because looking was what they paid for, and she let the colors of a day long gone wash over her, because seeing her like this, half-stripped and captured between two points, would make them believe she was containable.

Zaniah rippled into being near a mustard-yellow couch she'd paid twenty-six dollars for at a flea market. They were several things at once before they became a singular something, shifting from a winged, bipedal creature to a four-legged bird, and from a four-legged bird to a cylindrical ring, hollow in the middle, and finally to what stood before her, a person missing their personhood. Eyes blinked on their palms in tandem with the eyes on their narrow face.

"That's you," they said, and gestured to the window where Hollis's seamless reflection sat poised with her legs open, panties pushed away by one hand, phone clutched in the other.

"I'm working," she said. Lingering light shot between Zaniah's transparent bones. They turned holographic. Forged and imaginary. She caught the edge of the coffee table through their calf, saw the chipped paint on the front door beyond their back, watched something unsteady flutter in their chest, suspended there, caged and helpless.

Small text stacked on her phone followed by notifications—tip received—and generic emojis. *You're beautiful. Such a pretty girl. Wow! Can I see more? Fuck, you're like a doll. Smile for me.* She didn't look at them; she never looked at them, because they were compliments paid to a costume.

The star didn't move. They were still, as they almost always were, watching her with foam-colored eyes and a tempered smile. Nebulas exploded under their cheeks and collided on their shoulders. Blue pulsed in their knuckles. The shape of them wavered, coming and going, until they shifted into focus and became opaque. They touched a fern on the side table where a tattered copy of *Interview with the Vampire* sat atop hand-stapled zines, then stood on the tips of their too-long toes and inspected the framed taxidermy moths on the far wall.

"Zaniah," Hollis said, voice steep and sharp. She set her phone down.

The stillness shifted and her breath caught. They appeared before her, as if the air had parted and time had stopped to let them pass. Suddenly, the strange white eyes on Zaniah's face were inches from her chin, and the eyes on their palms were concealed, pressed to the sheepskin on either side of her hips. They were there, *right there*, mouth set and shoulders rounded toward their smooth head. Tonight, they hadn't perfected ears.

"Hollis," they said matter-of-factly, and waited.

She swallowed, retracting her hand from the confines of her underwear. "You don't seem lost tonight."

"You do." Their voice was a thousand whispers.

Maybe. Maybe not. Truthfully, Hollis didn't know if she'd ever been found. Her phone vibrated insistently, but she ignored it, focusing instead on the slope of Zaniah's jawline. "You sound like my ex," she murmured. Her eyes flicked from Zaniah's wide mouth to her phone seated beside them. Movement came naturally—easing her shoulders against the floor and resting her arms above her head. The star followed.

They touched their nose to the center of her left palm. "You're a remarkable liar."

"Is that what I am?" She closed her eyes, because if anything was true, that was certainly it.

Carefully, Zaniah trailed their thin fingers across her cheek, over the coarse hair on her brow, to the seamless pink line at her temple. When Hollis opened her eyes, she gazed into a pale, murky pupil ringed in high-gloss white, stitched into their lineless hand, framed in dark flesh patterned like the Milky Way rather than eyelashes. They tucked their thumb beneath her wig and pushed. A mixture of *Warm Burgundy 109, Babydoll,* and *Electric Rosebud* became an abandoned halo around Hollis's dark stubble, kept short with a black-handled razor. Her fists inevitably clenched.

Evening scaled Zaniah's skin, twisting their incandescence into humming orbs in the hollow of their hips and the dip below their upside-down collarbones. Their mouth brushed the shell of her ear. "Stars do not have the luxury of staying hidden. Neither do you."

The familiar prickle of tears jabbed at her eyes. Perhaps being seen like this, revealed, caused an avalanche in her chest, crushing everything but her heart. Maybe she'd been waiting for days, weeks, months to push her exoskeleton away like a spider and climb from the abandoned carcass, changed, new, remade. Hollis couldn't place the feeling, as if she'd become unknown and known at once. She didn't know what pushed her to do it, other than being curious of how simply Zaniah had stripped her defenses away. She didn't know why she grasped Zaniah by their sculpted face, or why she pulled their mouth to hers and tasted iron and moss and ice, or why a sob gathered in her throat when they vanished.

Hollis didn't know a damn thing.

Shadows stretched from the terracotta pots lining the windowsill. She scrubbed her hand over her shaved head and stood. Her lace gown still fell on the right side, exposing the small curve of her breast, and her phone still vibrated, making demands. She looked at her reflection in the splintered window and straightened her back, squared her shoulders, lifted her chin.

That's you, her mediocre ex had said, and shoved a picture of a person dressed in black, wearing a shirt with silver buttons, with their head shaved and their smile split into a laugh, standing under neon lights at a club with a beautiful blonde wrapped around their arm. That person had sipped cocktails made with Fireball whiskey, and stumbled into a bathroom stall with red walls, and went to their knees between pale, shaking legs as a Louis Vuitton heel found purchase on the toilet seat. That same person looked back at her from the window he'd tried to shatter.

Avalanches and exoskeletons be damned.

Hollis worked through the night. She adjusted her wig. Laughed and swooned and rubbed cayenne on her mouth to make her lips swell. Touched places on her body she rarely let others touch, donned the roles people wanted her to play—the damsel, the virgin, the schoolgirl—and tore them from herself once the livestream went dark.

The ceiling tilted. She watched, unable to sleep with the taste of a star still lingering in her mouth, and remembered how it felt to tell the truth.

A pandora moth rested on her dresser, wings pulsing blue.

And the sky told the moon to be kind, and the moon told the sun to be brave, and the sun told the storm to be gentle, because kindness and bravery and gentleness only accompanied falling the first time...

Two pumps of lavender syrup and a tablespoon of coconut sugar sweetened the organic Brazilian coffee in Hollis's dented plastic tumbler. She hung her apron on a hook next to the barista station at Bluebird Coffee and tapped on the tablet beside the pastry case. Two years ago, a psychic on the Venice boardwalk had stopped Hollis with a wrinkled hand on her wrist and told her she was a kingsnake, dying without sunlight. *A cage is no place for a wild thing like you,* the psychic had said, *even if you've built it yourself.* She hadn't known what to do with a statement like that, but exactly one day later, Bluebird had hung a Now Hiring sign in the window, and Hollis had filled out an application, and even though she didn't need the money, she took the job anyway.

"Hollis, can you cover a shift tomorrow?" Joseph, the manager, cleaned the espresso machine as he spoke.

She nodded. "I don't drive, but I'll try. Storm should pass in the night, yeah?"

"You know how people are. One drop of rain and Californians call in the cavalry. I doubt it'll be an actual *storm*, but if it you need a ride, just text me. Bluebird can cover the cost of a Lyft."

"Nine, then?"

"Yeah, nine to four."

"I'll be here."

"Thanks, I appreciate it. Remind me to give you a free cookie tomorrow. You like the weird one, right? The maple or—"

"Honey molasses!" She tossed the words over her shoulder and patted the pockets on her high-waist jeans—phone, ChapStick, credit card—before stepping into sticky spring air.

Southern California rarely saw storms like the one brewing over the ocean. The beaches had been evacuated, and local businesses were closing early; restaurants canceled their delivery options, and grocery stores ran low on overpriced bottled water. Lightning flashed. Thunder rattled the sky. The smell of wet asphalt filled the coastal air, thick and salty with June humidity. Hollis crossed her arms over her chest and studied the bruised sunset. Dark, billowing clouds brought night to Venice Beach like an uninvited guest. She pulled at the bottom of her cropped sweatshirt and took quick steps down the sidewalk.

There is something out there. Hollis's apartment was four blocks away, on the other side of the boardwalk. *Look.* She stared at her feet. Debated what kind of takeout she'd order at the Cheesecake Factory—fettuccini alfredo, fried macaroni and cheese, raviolis, a black bean and beet veggie burger. Her wig was stringy and damp, clinging to her cheeks and neck. *Out there—right there.* She gasped the moment her elbow was seized.

One time, not too long ago, a stranger had said, "Carry a knife." Her avatar was a pixilated faerie, bouncing in a chat-room designated for sex workers. "Hopefully you won't have to use it, but you never know. Some creep might recognize you."

Hollis had never used her knife. She momentarily panicked, wondering if she had a firm enough grip on the handle, and hoped the sound, a heavy click and slide, would be enough. It wasn't. Breath left her too quickly. She pressed the blade to their throat as her back hit the wall of an old sea-food restaurant with boarded windows. Hollis snared her captor in a fierce glare, daring them closer, but her expression ruptured once she noticed the subtle flicker beneath their skin. Pale eyes. The intense angles of their face and too-long fingers.

"Zaniah," she hissed, their name a relief, and dropped the knife to the base of their throat. "What the fuck are you doing? I could've..." *Could they be killed?* "You scared me, and—and I haven't seen you." Her voice wobbled. Six days ago, she'd kissed them, and six days ago, they'd disappeared, and all six days since then, she'd waited for them to come back.

"I've been practicing," they said. Their throat worked around a swallow. Tonight, the star had forged themself proper ears and sloped but moderately normal shoulders, a serene face too intricate to seem human, and dark blue bones beneath beige flesh. At first glance, Zaniah might pass as another oddity carried to the coast from Hollywood's gutters. But when they smiled, Hollis noticed their teeth, pointed where they shouldn't be, bright white against black gums.

The alley between the abandoned restaurant and a long-forgotten fishery was thin and shadowed. Hollis closed the knife and slid it into her bra, drawing unsteady breath while Zaniah shifted, plucking at long, black sleeves dangling over their wrists. Hollis had never seen them wear clothes. Denim clung to their legs, but their waist was far too smooth, as if they'd forgotten to construct a pelvis.

"I've never done this before." Zaniah's iridescent eyes flicked to Hollis's mouth.

"Do you want to?"

"I'm unsure. Humans call it a kiss, don't they? What you gave me?"

"Yes, that's what we call it."

"It frightened me and I enjoyed it," they said matter-of-factly.

Hollis stifled a laugh. For days, weeks, months she'd known them, and for days, weeks, months they'd found her, twisting their shape into something new each time. She touched the fine hair behind their ear. The color, navy deep enough to be black, dripped into their skull from each piece. For a second, she debated asking if they were real. But she had always wondered, and she would never stop wondering, and she knew wondering would not stop her from kissing them again if being kissed was what they wanted.

Rain splattered on her cheeks and their nose, dampened her sweatshirt and clung to their dolphin-smooth skin. She cupped their cheek. "Did you enjoy it because it frightened you? Or were you afraid and... And—"

"I was afraid and excited at once."

"Afraid of me?"

"Afraid of disappointing you."

"Will you kiss me again?" Hollis asked.

Zaniah gave a curt nod, but something living and startled sparked in their eyes.

Thunder split the dark sky. Hollis drew them in, slowly, carefully, until their lips touched. Water followed the seam of their mouths. Zaniah didn't bother with typical permissions or allowances. They kissed suddenly, wholly. Hollis tilted her head, closed her eyes, and contemplated the technicalities of a kiss like this. *I'm kissing a star*, Hollis thought. *A star is kissing me.* They tasted like an icy tray filled with pennies, tongue soft and flexible, breath thick on her teeth and the roof of her mouth. The typical wetness that accompanied kissing was replaced by something smooth and petal-soft, flexing and changing to match Hollis's preferences. She didn't know if Zaniah needed to breathe. If their pulse spiked or their body reacted. She couldn't tell if they were enjoying themself until she broke away and saw their eyes, paler, and their cheeks, higher and darker. Their appearance shifted, merging and bending like an old photograph taken at the wrong time, right when someone took a step. Their ears blinked in and out of existence. Their hair was gone and back again in a blink.

Hollis took their hand. Rolled her thumb over their extra knuckles. Squeezed their chilly palm. "Are you hungry?"

Zaniah tipped their head. "Hungry?"

"Do you eat?"

"I believe I can, but I never have."

Somehow, that was the least surprising thing they'd said since she'd met them. "My treat, then."

Before she could steer them from the dark alley, Zaniah set their free hand on the wall, keeping her there. "I'd quite like to kiss you again before we go."

Light flared in their chest and throat and the soft hollow of their elbows, radiating through their shirt. Hollis set her hand on each place and searched for fuzzy warmth, the kind too tempered to be true heat but enough to remind her of it. A blush, almost. She took each of their wrists and guided their hands, placing one palm on her stomach, beneath her sweatshirt, and the other on the side of her neck.

"Sometimes I like to be touched," she said.

"I've never touched anything like you, Hollis Griffin."

"You're the second person who's said that to me."

"Did the first treat you well?"

Hollis remembered her. She'd smelled sweet like peaches and harsh like tequila, but Hollis couldn't recall her name, only the look in her eyes after they left the club, fell into the back of a Lyft, climbed the stairs to Hollis's loft, and made love on the floor. She remembered her blonde hair and the piercing in her nose. She remembered her raspy voice when she said, "You're not a girl, are you?" How she'd smiled when Hollis shook her head. Hollis remembered her heels on the wood, then on the stairs as she left, chasing the last bit of night before the sun broke across the sky.

"Well enough," Hollis said.

Zaniah kissed her. They cupped her nape and smoothed their palm over her ribs, touching her reverently, entirely too slowly, and kissing her with the same fervent want they'd kissed her with before. Hollis pushed into them. She set her body against theirs to see if she might sink into a galaxy. If she might fall into them, carried out into space like debris from an abandoned ship. She didn't. Her body met theirs and thrummed, heated and wanting and held.

The sky opened. Rain hit them harder, faster, but Zaniah did not stop kissing her, and Hollis did not stop kissing them.

And the ocean called to them from a place far below. *Crash into her. Crash into her.*

"It's cheesecake."

Hollis held a forkful of red-velvet cheesecake in front of Zaniah's mouth. They sat together on the couch, Hollis with her knees touching, perched on her heels, Zaniah with their legs crossed, fingers idle in their lap. Rain streaked the cracked window, blurring their reflections while lightning cut paths across the dark sky.

They glanced from the fork to Hollis. "What does it taste like?"

"Sweet," she said. She took the bite for herself and nodded, then gathered another forkful and held it out to them. "Try it."

Zaniah was hesitant the same way pigeons were hesitant. They flicked their eyes between the cake and Hollis's face again and again, gauging whether they should dash for the food. Suddenly, they snapped their teeth around the fork. She flinched. They'd moved fast enough to blur their features, flesh turning transparent for the duration of a blink, then jolting back into place as they chewed.

"See? It's sweet," she said.

"That's what this is? Sweet?" A bit of frosting clung to the corner of their mouth.

"Do you like it?"

Zaniah nodded. "What do you like?"

Hollis swiped the frosting from their mouth and licked her thumb clean. "To eat? Lots of things."

"Being human," they said. "What do you like down here?"

The question twisted through the air like smoke. Hollis didn't understand it at first. Words were missing, filler and explanations, what Zaniah meant and how they meant it. Living a life trapped in skin she couldn't shed, in a place she couldn't leave, had always felt as profoundly simple as a sunburn. Consequences to living. A constant cycle—pain, change, heal.

Hollis had never been allowed to become something else. "The views," she confessed. "Sometimes I look out at the ocean, or up at the sky, or down at the street from my window, and I realize how far and vast and small we are. How we can be all those things at once." She set the plate on the coffee table. Lightning flashed. Seconds later, thunder rattled the sky. "What did you like about being up there?"

"Watching," Zaniah said. "Things like me were once things like you, so stars gravitate to the places you are. Sometimes past lives filter into new ones."

"Did you fall?"

"Yes." Their voice softened. "I lost my balance. One moment, I was looking at Mercury, and the next I was looking at Earth, and after that I was falling. I recognized a life chipped away from the rest of me, and then I crashed into you."

Rain hit the window. The lamp on the side table and the lights paneled above the kitchen flickered before they went out. Dim city glow leaked through the glass, illuminating the terracotta pots. Across from her, Zaniah's mismatched skeleton pulsed beneath their skin. Different shades of blue thrummed outward, darkening veins and ligaments. The hollow of their eyes and the curved notch beneath their cheeks held flecks of gold and pink and silver, galaxies suspended on their face. Hollis hadn't felt them crash into her. She hadn't heard them collide or noticed their tangled bones smash against her own. She was already a wrecked place, and she couldn't help feeling sorry for being the one Zaniah fell for.

"You were a soft landing," they said, as if they'd read her thoughts.

"I can't imagine how."

Hollis had grown into a person too complicated to fill the role society had emptied for her. *Here,* the world had said, *squeeze yourself into this box and call it home.* But she had been too jagged to fit. Sometimes she was convinced she had extra bones and two blood types and a spare set of hands. Sometimes she wondered about tearing off her skin to see if another suit waited beneath.

"Have you always known what you are, Zaniah?" she asked.

They tipped their head, dove-like and quiet, and set their palm on her cheek. "Of course not. No one ever knows what they were or are or will be. I have lived as many things. Her, she, they, he, us. But mostly, I've lived a life of longing, looking for pieces of myself scattered throughout time. I think you're one of those pieces, Hollis Griffin."

Before she could stop herself, Hollis believed them.

That was the thing about believing. Once it happened, it happened completely. It was all-consuming, a cousin to love, three steps from hate, with a depth Hollis could not define. *Believing* was a conscious and subconscious choice colliding inside someone.

Hollis hadn't believed in much. Gods felt too far, politics felt too fake, and she had never found the courage to turn inward. To believe that in some strange, fantastic way, she had always been the *more* she'd searched for in people and places.

She wanted to be told, simply, as Zaniah would tell her, so she held on to hope as they held on to her. "What makes you think that?"

Zaniah's big eyes softened. Their brow, fitted with soft hair and firefly freckles, creased, as if they hadn't expected the question. "We whisper about humans. Some of us remember what it was like to be you, just like some of you remember what it was like to be us. Don't you remember?"

"I've only ever been this," Hollis said. Her voice cracked, because she needed them to say it, to put a name to it.

"Who are you when you aren't Hollis?"

There.

Relief pooled in her chest, and something else—dread turned inside out—coiled around her throat, squeezing. "Griffin," they said, "when I'm not Hollis, I'm Griffin. Just Griffin."

"You aren't *just* anything, Griffin. You never have been."

They pushed their blushing-pink wig away, then the nylon cap, and ran their palm across their shaved head. Somehow, even though their eyes were the same shade of blue, and their fingers were still too thin, and their hips were still too wide, Griffin had escaped.

"No one will think I'm beautiful like this, Zaniah," Griffin snapped, suddenly barbed and afraid. Because money paid the rent, and Bluebird wasn't enough, and their viewers might not tip a girl who wasn't a girl or a boy who wasn't a boy, and surely they wouldn't understand the sexual appeal of a chipped-away star who'd lost their luster. "What will they call me? Who will I be to them? Nobody. Nothing, I—"

Zaniah crept closer. They dropped their hand to Griffin's chest and pushed, sending them toppling onto the couch. "They will think of you like I do," they said, voice laced with whispers, words spoken in languages she'd never heard. "They'll call you handsome, maybe. Breathtaking and startling and striking. They'll look at you and think of impossible things becoming possible. What do humans call that? Inevitable yet impossible manifestation?"

"Magic," Griffin said, breathless. They rested their palms on Zaniah's carved face. Looked backward in time, past Mars and Jupiter and Saturn, to places in the sky humans had never been, and they saw themself. "We call that magic."

"Then they'll call you magical, and it will be true."

Griffin kissed Zaniah. They tasted like starlight and frost, beginnings and endings. Zaniah pressed against them, pushing Griffin into the soft cushions, one hand on their chest, the other looped beneath them, pulling their bodies flush together.

"You found me," Griffin said, absent, lost against Zaniah's cool cheek. "You found me."

Zaniah held them as the storm passed. Their skin pulsed blue, as it had for days, weeks, months, and they told Griffin stories from way out there. How they'd sped through the cosmos, how they'd shot through the atmosphere, and fell through gravity, and landed in the sea. How when they breached for air, because air had been something they needed after that, Griffin's suntan lotion had greeted them.

"There you are, I thought," Zaniah said, and tucked their mouth against Griffin's pulse. *"I've finally found you."*

Griffin's eyes burned. They laughed, a single, bewildered *hah.*

Here we are, they thought. *Finally. Here we are.*

AWRY WITH

DANDELIONS

J.S. Fields

Chapter One

"I can do it. I can break the link between our minds."

Orin stared at the wispy phantom, the edges of her bleeding into the dark corners of the dream. Xie had to have misheard. Twenty damn years they'd visited each other every night as ghostly apparitions, and sporadically during the day. Sometimes Orin to Mette, sometimes the other way around, but the duration was always the same. Thirty seconds. No more, no less. They had collected the start of a thousand conversations but had never managed anything of real substance. The first few seconds were always disorienting. Then came the nausea. Then came the attempt at talking. Then it was over.

"Orin?"

The phantom woman pulled at the corners of her embroidered nightgown. Orin saw little lutes on the fabric, or maybe lamps. The details were always best closest to Mette's face, where Orin could make out each solitary freckle on white skin, her dark-brown eyes, and light-brown hair. Orin's eyes were the same color, but xir hair was far shorter and darker, xir skin tawny. Orin also refused to wear nightgowns. Nude was the only way to sleep.

"You don't have to ignore me." Mette stood—well, hovered—in a huff at the edge of Orin's bed, nightdress dripping shades of rose in the moonlight.

Xie swallowed bile and tried to think of something to say. The sharp edges of Mette's cheekbones and jaw began to blur. Orin felt the dream slipping away. Xir stomach continued to knot. This sounded too much like a real conversation—something they'd decided years ago was a lost cause. Thinking each other anything more than dreams caused too many problems. "Sorry. What?"

Mette put her hands on her hips and cocked her head, a pose she'd had since childhood. "I need you to come to me. In real life. Not this"—she gestured in a circle above her head—"whatever it is we get trapped in every night. I'm serious."

"Ridiculous. I don't even know where you live. I don't even know your last name." *I don't even know if you're real.*

The dream continued to blur.

"We have to stop this. I don't think I can do it alone."

"Do *what* alone?" Orin asked, exasperated.

"The party."

"What?" Her words made no sense. The dream dissolved to fragmented color. Orin blanched and leaned back. From the range of silk and embroidered cotton nightgowns xie had seen Mette wear over the years, Orin had a good idea what kind of party she would attend. It was definitely not one Orin could get into, even riding a dragon. Even riding a dragon with *lasers* on its head. Besides, that assumed Mette was even real, which Orin had never been too sure about. Recurring dreams happened. Lucid dreams happened. Some kids had imaginary friends. Orin's had just...never left. Not for lack of trying.

Mette rushed her final, disembodied words. "Three days from now. The Kingdom of Methalimus, near the Starbond Sea. South of the solar farm. Give any city wall guard you see your name, and they'll let you through. Promise me, Orin, that you'll come. *Promise me.*"

"There is no way—"

The dream broke apart.

Orin crashed back into xir body. Xir eyes flew open.

Then xie leaned over the side of the bed, and vomited.

*

"Heyyyyyy, you! Yes, you, the man in the hat with the...sculpture? Barrel? You, sir, look like a man who could use buoyancy, and do I have the product for you!" Orin held up a glass beaker filled with a thick, milky substance. "Just a bit of home processing and you could float that barrel right down a river, regardless of contents! You could mudproof a dragon's foot! You could manufacture any number of prophylactics and guaranteed no skin irritation!" Orin flapped a hand in front of xir face and released a small handful of colorful rubber sequins into the uncooperatively stale wind. "Possibilities," xie whispered loudly. "Endless."

The man in thick indigo-dyed cotton pants and shirt, bearded, bald, with a bit more orange to his skin than what was considered Earth-normal, came over and wrinkled his nose at the bag. Red and blue sequins stuck to his pant legs, which wasn't wholly unusual at the second biggest market on the continent, but occurred with far more frequency on the crafts side. However, since Orin supplied the sequins to the whole market, using them here was just good branding.

"What is it?" the man asked. His eyes flicked to Orin's face, and he frowned. "You okay? Rough couple nights?"

Orin swished xir hands from left to right, trying to pull his attention back to the plants and simultaneously trying to ward off a wave of dizziness. Thirty seconds of interaction with Mette always equated to half the night, and as much as Orin had grown accustomed to it all, just once, xie wanted a full night's sleep. Looking like a hollowed-out pumpkin did nothing for market sales.

"I have a genetic condition, and I've been up all night caring for these delightful plants so they would be in prime condition for today. Have a look."

Orin stepped to the side so he could see the full table. A three-tiered shelf consumed the back half, filled with potted dandelions that had budded but not yet bloomed. Thin, delicately spun glass tubes ran from the bottom of the pots into a trough on either side of the table, and a cloudier version of the blood dripped from the ends. The front half of the table was neatly arranged, with perfectly measured bags of dandelion blood threatening to congeal in the morning sunlight.

The man reluctantly moved his attention to the plants, poked one of the bags, and quickly drew his finger back when the substance rippled. "Is it alive?"

"Ah, no." Orin tossed the bag in xir hands at the man, who had to drop his barrel to catch it. Orin caught the barrel with a practiced smile for the practiced show. "It's a purity you'd need an HPLC to believe, and it won *seven* awards at the End Upcoming Entrepreneurial Fair last year. Normally we're sold out by this time, but we brought a double batch and don't want to take the excess home. We can cut you a deal."

The man poked the bag again and wrinkled his nose. "Latex? Chewing gum?"

Orin set the barrel down and tsked with xir hand. A few sequins still clung to xir palm, and xie brushed them onto xir wrinkled linen pants. Xie'd pick them up later for resale, and would definitely make sure they were all gone before xie fell asleep. Otherwise they'd be all Mette would talk about for a week. Sequins were much better emotion-free conversation than 'where do you live, come see me, hey maybe you're real and this isn't all a delusion.'

Orin wiped xir face with xir hands, hoping to rub the memory of Mette away too. The sale mattered. Mette did not. "Latex from *lion fern*, sir."

"The label here has it twice the price of standard latex."

Orin went behind the booth and pulled out a thick sheet of cotton paper. "This has different properties though! The rubber is *unpuncturable* if manufactured correctly! The fluff seeds have similar properties. *Plus* they stick to anything, *and* I've had customers buy the plants just for the decorative value. I've got the purity report right here. If you take a look at the graphic—"

"Pass. At that price by weight, it'd be cheaper to import plastics from Earth." He handed the bag back to Orin—more firmly than necessary—retrieved his barrel, and walked away. His heels kicked up a little too high for Orin's liking. Pssh. Man didn't know an exceptional deal when it dropped into his hands.

A woman called out from the other side of the stand. "Hey, how much for the base plants?"

Orin put the paper down, squared xir shoulders, and turned around, another wide smile on xir face. "Ah, miss, I have some lovely clippings in the back—"

The rush of the sale fell away, and Orin lost xir breath. Xir skin broke out into a sweat. A familiar feeling, like xir brain was peeling from xir skull, settled in. Rushing blood thumped in xir ears, *bum pum bum pum*. The outline of the world blurred. Xie saw a glowing tulip-red hole, long, thin cylinders of glass, and unknown faces debating design xie didn't understand. Leather-gloved hands.

"They're, uh, just give me a minute." Orin nearly collapsed onto the brick street and took deep breaths of pig-shit air. That was the stall next to xir's—the manure vendor. Excellent quality. Terrible smell, and a terrible time to visit Mette. The fantasies had a rough go of it during the day—or Orin's mind tried harder to fight them because xie wanted sales to afford a decent dinner. Xie also wanted to be a whole, independent person who didn't stumble around with headaches and nausea, and who got to sleep, *and* who could eat any food they wanted to because they still had enamel on their teeth.

Mette's hand caught something hot, and while Orin couldn't see the offending item, xie still hissed in shared pain. "Damn it, Orin!" Mette hissed. "Get out of my head."

Orin ignored Mette and tried to focus on xir potential customer. "Just a...another minute," Orin wheezed at the woman, who had already started to wander toward the pigs.

Then, just as suddenly as it came, the headache eased. The burning faded. Breath filled xir lungs and in a hop Orin was back on xir feet. Xie brushed pieces of brick and a few shards of glass from xir pants and refused to admit defeat. "Miss! Won't you come and let me show you what these plants can do? I can offer a ten percent discount! Twenty, even, if you're buying bulk!"

The woman waved xir off with that concerned smile people always got when Orin had one of xir episodes. Xir smile bled away. The thrill of the sale ebbed, leaving only the residual headache and a memory of blistered skin. Orin cursed. Xir mind always jumped to that fantasy realm at the absolute worst times. The woman and the man had been the first customers to come down this row in, four hours? Five? Half of the day had passed and xir shelves were still full. The crowds stubbornly remained slow and thin. Orin didn't need to be daydreaming about fantasy women and fire.

Xie needed sales. Now.

Ends Market ran twice per month—the space was used as a food cart plaza otherwise—and was the biggest market this side of the Starbond Sea. The only bigger one, in fact, was the one in Methalimus inside the gated city, which was likely why Orin's imagination had finally decided that was where Mette was from. Who didn't dream of selling at the Methalimus market? Of course, vending at both major markets was tightly controlled, and one had to apply through a jury selection.

Orin could hack it at End with small-batch dandelion latex. It made *really, really* good rubber (or rubber sequins), and since they didn't manufacture any petrochemicals on the planet, the sticky seeds of this variety—*Orin's* variety—were used for exterior texturing on buildings and, by at least one customer, for scrapbooking.

Those applications at Methalimus Market? There was no way, even with the mild medicinal properties of the dandelion fluff. Orin had applied the past five years in a row. Received a form rejection each time.

"Bad day, then? You want to close early and get food?" Blathnaid knocked his hand against Orin's temple while xie stared at the small cluster of people bartering for a fat piglet. Xie turned and exhaled forcibly enough to vibrate xir lips. Blathnaid stood a head taller than Orin but had the same thick musculature. His hair, though, was hellebore green—a mutation the original planetary colonists hadn't had, and that no one could adequately explain. It only occurred in those born in End. He hadn't gotten the corresponding purple-green melanin mutation at least, and his skin was a perfectly human light brown. They both wore linen clothes as neither could afford cotton, which meant they both looked perpetually wrinkled.

"Crap day. You see any big crowds at the main entry?"

"Nope. Dead as an Earth horse out there. Everyone's doing their shopping at Methalimus this cycle so they have a shot at seeing the coronation. It's in...two days, I think? Yeah."

Orin slumped into a three-legged chair, which immediately threatened to topple. "Well, there goes my food budget. Crickets it is."

"Nah, I can help." He thumped his chest pocket.

"You already pay all the rent, Blathnaid. You shouldn't have to do food too."

"Meh. I don't mind. Besides, we can always eat those dandelion leaves—"

Orin kicked him halfheartedly in the shin. Blathnaid gave a mock yelp but grinned. "Leave the *lion ferns* alone. They're the wave of the future."

"You make twice on sequins than what you do on selling raw latex. I still think you should move over to the craft section and broaden your client base."

"I hate you."

Blathnaid almost cut a retort—xie could see it in the smirk of his eyes—then opted for a different tone. "Not a lot of future if you die in the present, Orin. You have to eat." They both hadn't had to worry about eating much, not recently, but it was plenty easy to remember xir and Blathnaid's childhood as errand boys for the markets—first the small ones, then, as they got older and quicker, the big ones like End. Easy, too, to remember how people's tips didn't buy more than a meal a day, and how the roof in the barn where they were allowed to sleep leaked badly, especially in monsoon season. At least the market was airy and cool—the bamboo and oiled tarps keeping the worst of the sun and rain off, and the brick roads keeping the insects at bay. With hundreds of vendors at any given time, the stalls stacked row upon row in an endless yawn of commerce.

Aside from Blathnaid, it was the best part of Orin's life. Not that xie could have held any other kind of job. Not with Mettc in xir head.

"Yeah. Fine." Xie stood and pulled a thick, insulated box from under the display table. "Help me get the plants packed back up and we can go."

"Or, you could talk to this guy first." Blathnaid stepped back behind Orin. A young man, perhaps twenty, stood a handspan from the edge of the display. Nothing about him was extraordinary, not his walnut-bark-brown hair and skin, nor his yellow-brown eyes or fitted denim jacket that spoke of comfort but not wealth.

Orin *knew* him.

They'd never met before, xie was certain. He wasn't a former customer or patron, and he was too young to have hired xir or Blathnaid when they were younger. His clothes didn't distinguish his home country at all, but Orin knew if he smiled, xie would see his bottom teeth out of alignment. Knew he had a dimple in his chin and another on his right cheek. Knew he paid in notes and not credit, even for big orders.

"I was wondering about the plants," he said, and his voice sounded exactly like Orin knew it would. Snappy, like when you kicked a field dandelion just right and the flower head popped off.

Orin reached over and pinched Blathnaid, who swallowed his surprised squeak with a burp. Then he pinched xir back, hard enough that xir eyes watered.

"L-lion fern." Orin straightened and tried to reset. Xie knew him from Mette, but Mette wasn't real, and this man clearly was. Therefore having this reaction was unnecessary. "Sir, may I introduce lion fern, a robust new variant on an old tradition? If you'll look to your side"—xie pointed at the left bucket, half-filled with white dandelion blood—"you'll see the purest latex known to the planet. It has superior rubber potential. Great for small-batch, high-end processing, with endless uses in both the life sciences and astrobiological arts. Could I interest you in a free sample?"

"I'd like a case of the plants, please, or however many you're willing to sell me." The man reached into his jacket and pulled out a singular note, stamped with the potentate's—the current diplomatic figurehead of the northern hemisphere—face.

He paid with those a lot, write-in notes that could have any value the vendor wrote on them. Orin knew that. Xie *knew* it was coming, but seeing the note, the potentate's bored yellow eyes faded into the pink background of the cotton paper, xie still couldn't believe it.

Blathnaid's eyes bugged from their sockets, and Orin had to restrain xirself from snatching the note and running away. That kind of money was a proper house for Blathnaid and xir, with running water and electricity and a full fridge.

It was all that *plus* a ticket to Methalimus, first class. If xie wanted to believe in midnight dream women.

"Any amount you think is fair," the man said, placing the note on the display and anchoring it with the edge of a clay pot.

"Sir, we would *love* to box these plants for you. Won't you please have a seat?" Blathnaid pulled Orin's chair around and offered it to the man, who nodded his head and sat.

"Snap out of it," Blathnaid hissed as he pulled Orin back behind the tall wall of dandelions and pointed to an empty box. "If it's Mette, tell her to shove off until we get the order finished."

Orin nodded absently as xie packed vegetable foam around a pot, then slid another wrapped pot next to it in the box.

"How many do you want to give him? You have like twenty more at home, right?"

"Yeah. Give him everything." Orin stood and handed the first filled box to the man. "Did you have a vehicle around here, sir? Dragon cart, maybe?" An ox cart would have been preferable with the delicate dandelion pots, but the only mammals bigger than pigs that had survived the trip from Earth were humans. The colonists had gotten creative.

"Just around. Give me a minute and I'll be back. We can load then. And thank you." He gave a soft salute, skirted the pigs and their mud, and disappeared behind a booth selling lichen dyes.

"They'll get smashed if he takes them by dragon cart." Blathnaid shoved the last pot into a slot that was just a hair too small for it. The edge of the cardboard ripped.

"Not our problem. I just want him gone."

Blathnaid taped the corner of the box and leaned against the display. He puckered his lips to the side in a sort of funny frown. "What's going on?"

"Nothing."

"Liar. Normally I can't get you to *stop* talking. Do I have to get you drunk?"

"You can't afford to get me drunk."

"Can." Again he tapped his pocket, and pitched his voice down low. "Last gig tipped well because I'm a maaaaaster illusionist."

Orin couldn't bring xirself to smile. "I just...know him. You know?"

Blathnaid raised an eyebrow. "Sex? Sales? Robbery?" His eyes narrowed and a mischievous smile spread across his face. "Please tell me it was sex."

Orin tapped xir temple.

"Oh. Fuck."

The *thunk thunk* of rubber wheels over potholes drew both of their attentions down the brick lane. A wood cart wide enough to hold twice the stock Orin was providing jostled between the few remaining shoppers. The wood planks had a fresh coat of red stain, and the wheels were definitely new. The Komodo dragons that pulled the thing were *not*, and Orin could hear their labored breathing from half a block away.

"Weird guy," Blathnaid said with a shake of his head. "He's got Methalimus notes, *blank* Methalimus notes, yet he drives a cart with dragons that look old enough to have come over with the original settlers from Earth and are clearly not well trained. No way they'd pass inspection and get licensed for transit. And his jacket has gold thread woven into the cuffs. Did you see that? Like spider silk or something. Like he's got some awesome job but doesn't want us to *think* he has an awesome job, but is concurrently too ridiculous to realize that handing us a note like that screams 'I work for Methalimus government.'"

The cart stopped close to Orin's stall. The dragons strained against their ropes, their forked tongues licking the pig-shit smell from the air. Blathnaid began loading the cart before the man hopped from his seat. Orin pocketed the note. It was always possible he might change his mind.

"If you need more, sir, please do let me know. My contact information is stamped onto the bottom of every pot. I take electronic communications and carrier pigeon, if you prefer."

The man grabbed the last box and pushed it up against the others, in the back of the cart. He handed Blathnaid a five-mark, the usual currency, and nodded in thanks. "Will see how these go and get back to you. Put anything you think is fair on the note. The auditors check, but not closely. Thank you, mister?" He frowned, likely trying to decide where to kiss Orin. Left for women, right for men. Forehead for everyone else.

Orin pointed to xir forehead.

"Ah!" He stepped into Orin and briefly kissed Orin's hairline. He'd have had to stoop to get any lower. Orin kissed his right cheek. "I'll be in touch, Orin."

"Sir?" Orin called after him as he climbed back onto his wagon and tried to convince his dragons that the pigs were too expensive a lunch. "Your name, if I may? For customer service and to let you know about sales? Do you have a card or chip I could scan?"

The dragons started forward, and at least two ceramic pots broke in the process. Orin cringed. The man ignored it. "Sir Minjae. I'm under direct contract with Lady Lorimette. The dandelions are set to seed a few days, correct?"

Orin nodded. "Yes, sir. Their flowers are only just opening. This variety seeds in three days, sometimes a day or so faster. You can force the processes with a sharp blast of heat if you have a small acetylene torch handy. But I have seed bags if that's what you're looking for. You'll be able to plant them more quickly, or I have the raw seeds with the sticky latex still on them if you're looking for decoration?"

The man stroked one of the dandelion leaves. "She's banned magic at the ceremony, so biological it'll be. Lady wants the seeds in plant form for the coronation. She's got a dream of walking back out after the ceremony in a shower of petals, but dandelion fluff will work just as well. The heat-opening varieties are hard to find. They'll survive repotted in glass for a few days?"

The future queen didn't want magic at her coronation? Methalimus was *built* on magic. The city had a whole damn library with devoted texts. End was where you went if you wanted to avoid it, which of course just pushed it to the black market, but whatever. If the guy wanted to buy dandelions, what did xie care what he did with them? "Yeah, whatever you want to pot them in is fine. Lion ferns are robust in the short term." Xie squinted at the man. "You could also—"

The man made a shooing motion, snapped the reins, and the cart lurched down the road. The sound of cracking ceramic pots filled the air.

Orin watched the cart lurch down the street, cringing with every broken pot. "Blathnaid, did you know my lion ferns have a reputation in Methalimus? I wonder if someone bought one, cloned it, and is selling it there?" Xie frowned and felt the tips of xir ears turn red. "My strain is patented. If I get a name..."

Blathnaid put a hand on Orin's shoulder and clucked as the dragons lunged at a stall of calves. "Orin, I love you dearly, but no one cares about your dandelions outside of wanting some greenery in their house. This purchase is unusual."

Orin weighed the next words, and the likelihood of Blathnaid laughing, before speaking. The thought was ridiculous, but then again, so was having an imaginary friend you couldn't get to leave. That thought didn't slow Orin's frantically beating heart. "Do you think it's Mette?"

"Huh?"

Orin shrugged, pretending xie didn't care when in fact the prospect of Mette orchestrating the event was *terrifying*. "You know. Maybe Mette is trying to get me to Methalimus?"

Blathnaid cocked his head. "Are we taking dream woman seriously now? Did you send me a note via pigeon and then the pigeon got eaten, conveniently, by a dragon?"

"No. Yes. Think about it. Lori*mette*?" A weight dropped in Orin's stomach as xie worked through the details. Xie felt the familiar nausea rise up, though Mette's presence was nowhere near. "Lady? As in, about to go through the coronation ceremony in Methalimus to become princess under our potentate?"

"Okay." Blathnaid leaned against the booth frame. "'Coronation' is just a fancy word for a party, so this makes her rich as all get out? This would also explain how a man purchasing for the coronation knows about you and your no-name dandelion lion fern even though Methalimus and End are separated by an entire sea."

Except it didn't, because Orin had never told Mette about the market or the lion fern dandelions, or even what country xie lived in. There'd never been enough time and they had *rules*. Unspoken, sure, but they'd both learned that trying to convince people you wanted to meet the phantom in your head got you absolutely nowhere, so what was the point of tormenting each other with details? Never mind that the disorientation and nausea and the whole *floating above your own body* thing always got in the way of deeper introspection.

Orin sucked in a deep breath. Pig-shit air did wonders for grounding you in the moment.

Blathnaid poked xir in the ribs. "What are you going to do?"

Orin sat on the lowest shelf of the display and watched the cart turn around a corner at the edge of the market, and out of sight. The blank note lay crumpled in xir pocket. What had Mette said? She could fix them? Fix them at a *party* maybe?

Orin had already visited every soothsayer, herbalist-witch, illegal magician, and doctor this side of the Starbond Sea. They'd all said it was in xir head. Said that kind of magic didn't exist. Maybe this was coincidence. Or maybe it was Mette finally reaching out. Maybe she *had* found a way to disconnect them. Maybe...

No. It didn't matter one way or the other. If there was even a chance of finally getting a full night's sleep, being rid of the smell of fire and feeling of tight callouses, of the sight of old leather and scratchy wool and Mette's hovering, nightgown-clad form, of not puking every damn night...

No matter how small or silly or potentially dangerous meeting Mette might be, Orin was *in*.

Chapter Two

"You could have just sent a ticket."

Orin hovered over Mette's bed—an ash four poster with a coarse silk canopy. Mette sat just to the left of her actual body. She appeared to have fallen asleep directly after...work? Her cotton pants and shirt had dark smudges across them, and a pair of glassworkers' protective glasses perched atop her head.

She rubbed absently at the burn on her hand. Orin rubbed xir own, the memory of pain making xir wince. "Maybe don't touch hot things."

"Why are you such a grouch tonight?" Mette asked.

The five hours between the end of the market and bed had been enough time for Orin to actually consider the mechanics of traveling to a city xie had never been, to meet a woman xie had only met in dreams. It had also given Orin time to think about Mette, *really* think about her, and her station, her access to information Orin didn't have, and what attending the coronation meant for a mid-tier dandelion seller from End.

"How long have you known where I live? Why didn't you tell me where *you* lived? Did you think I was going to come to your door and rob you?!" Orin rubbed xir stomach, imitating Mette, who looked like she had just swallowed bile. Pressure was building at the base of xir skull, heralding an epic headache come morning.

"Orin, I...don't even know what you *sell*. How could I possibly know where you live? If this is about money, look, I... I'm trying to work out how I can get you passage on a ship to get to Methalimus. Please, don't be mad! I really think this will work."

Orin felt the tightness on xir skin that pointed to the end of their visit. "I still don't like how you went about all this. I mean, you could have told me."

"I've barely told you a thing, and you're already mad at me!"

Orin turned from her and the dream dissolved. Then, like every night for the past twenty-odd years, xie woke up, leaned over the side of the bed, and vomited.

*

"I can't believe you're turning down a soon-to-be queen. Financially this is a terrible decision. I just want you to know that."

Blathnaid and Orin sat on branchwood chairs in front of a pushcart fruit-juice vendor whose booth space Orin shared when the market ran, and debated. Clouds choked the blue from the sky overhead, their grey souring Orin's mood and the juice.

"She's using me," Orin retorted after swallowing a mouthful of a pineapple-rose-apple blend. "Can't you see that?"

"Do you care?" Blathnaid countered. "Okay, I mean, clearly you do, but should you?"

Orin crossed xir arms and sat back in the chair. "Up until yesterday you thought she was imaginary just as much as I did."

"Only because we didn't have any real information. Now we do. There's so much more to magic than what we see illegally in End. Mette's a lady-princess-almost-*queen*. She's probably read the whole damn magic library they have in the city center and figured this entire business out." He leaned in and clinked the rim of his glass against Orin's. "When I did errands for Fen the Magician, some of the stuff he had me fetch him... I mean, I *saw* stuff, Orin. And if your brain is linked to future royalty, no matter how figureheady she is, let's not pass up a chance to live in a house with fancy wool carpet instead of plank flooring. Think about it."

"But why now? Why after two decades? She's going to be a queen. You don't think that's a little suspicious?."

"Do *you* want to keep puking every night, and eating budget crickets twice a month when the market is low? *I* think they're pretty delicious, personally, but I know you hate those hairy little legs." He ran fingertips up Orin's arms.

"Ack! Stop it." Xie batted his hand away and scooted xir chair to the opposite end of the round table. "You and I worked for rich people long enough already. We're supposed to be going away from that, not back toward it."

Blathnaid smirked. "Yeah, but I'd do it for a pretty woman in a nightgown."

"I *never* said she was pretty."

"You didn't have to."

Orin ground xir knuckles into the side of the chair. "Just conceptualize this with me for a minute. I travel out of End, no, *we* travel out of End because I want another pair of eyes to confirm I'm not hallucinating. We travel out of End, which opted against figurehead royalty during colonization and works just fine as a free market with a handful of big farms, to Methalimus, where people got excited over titles? Are we title people? *Magic* people? Is that who we are now?"

Blathnaid raised an eyebrow. "We're *money* people. All those things usually come in tandem."

"Yeah, fine. You're not wrong." Orin looked back at the thin juice lady, debating another glass. "I'll go cash the note once the bank opens and get us both passage on the next trans-sea ship. We can afford one of the jet ones, with this thing." Xie tapped the rim of xir glass, trying to catch the vendor's attention. "Hey, miss, could I try the mangosteen?"

The woman looked up from her juicer, started to smile, then froze. The glass fell from her hands and broke on the brick road. Orin looked down the street to where she pointed. A wooden stagecoach, pulled by six heaving Komodo dragons, clipped down the road. The carriage swung wildly from side to side, knocking over shuttered stalls as it did. The fruit vendor kicked the locks off her cart's wheels and hurriedly pushed it off the road and into the sedge of a field, motioning for Orin and Blathnaid to follow.

"Come on." Orin pulled the back of Blathnaid's shirt while xir friend stood on the side of the road, mouth agape. Dragons... Orin shook xir head. A giant pain all around, and far too often penned in fields that would be better suited to wildflower cultivation. They were ornery, they looked ridiculous, and no one in End used stagecoaches. End didn't upkeep its brick roads enough.

"Blathnaid, come on." Xie jerked this time and Blathnaid fell back, hard enough to land them both on their backsides. They scootched backward as quickly as they could. The dragons continued, close enough now that Orin could see the speckling inside their pinkish mouths and throats. They were on good, leather leashes but still had a *lot* of teeth.

One of the dragons emitted a deep, throaty growl that sounded like an Earth gasoline engine. Orin's stomach did a flip. Xie could see the lead dragon was longer than xie was tall, and suddenly a dandelion field seemed like an excellent place for a dragon to be. Anywhere, really, as long as it wasn't right in xir face.

"This is how we die," Blathnaid said. Their butts hit the edge of the sedge as they continued their frantic scramble backward. The seat of Orin's pants immediately turned wet. Xie looked down to find xirself at the edge of a pile of pig droppings, as fresh smelling today as they'd been yesterday.

The driver pulled the dragons, miraculously, to a halt just as Orin thought xie could smell their metallic breath, and just as the wetness from the grass and shit finished saturating xir pants.

"What the hell?" Blathnaid tried to ease his breathing.

Orin thought xie saw the curtain on the main front window wiggle. Xie caught a flash of dark hair, and then xir stomach knotted. The throbbing started at the base of xir skull, rekindling xir early morning headache. Xie hunched over, face between xir knees, and swallowed bile.

"Tell Mette now isn't a good time!"

"Not the same," Orin managed through gritted teeth. This time the nausea came with double vision. Orin could see the inside of the stagecoach—its plain lacquer interior, the style of the molding around the window—as well as the green-brown muck beneath xir feet. The gaze inside the coach shifted, and Orin saw worn, brown leather boots that ended just above the ankle, thick, blue cotton pants, and fingers clenched in the fabric.

A slightly damp hand grasped Orin's shoulder. "Hey," Blathnaid said, his voice filled with concern. "What's wrong? Is it not Mette? Is it the smell?"

"Stagecoach," Orin managed to say as xir vision layered the multicolored grass over leather boots. "Can you help me get there?"

"I don't really think that's a good idea, Orin." This time it wasn't concern, and it wasn't gentle ribbing. Blathnaid has used that tone maybe four times in their shared lives, and every time, he'd been right.

Orin ignored him and used Blathnaid's shoulder to stand, took one quick look at xir backside, and decided to try to forget the unfortunate staining there.

"Orin," Blathnaid cautioned, a hand on xir shoulder as he stood as well.

Talking was no longer an option. If Orin opened xir mouth, only breakfast juice would come out. Instead, xie stalked to the stagecoach, grabbed the handle, and threw the door open.

Mette.

She grabbed onto Orin's shirt and hauled xir into the coach. "Get in. You too, whatever your name is, if you want. I'm sorry about this. But I need your help."

Chapter Three

Mette was real.

Orin didn't move. Couldn't move. What did one say to their dream-phantom-woman? Clearly puking on her was not an option, though still a possibility.

Mette's familiar head of brown hair was mussed instead of in its usual coils, but otherwise, she was exactly as she'd appeared in every dream Orin had ever had. And here, in person, Orin couldn't pretend the way her mouth turned down into a half frown, or the fine dusting of freckles across her right cheek, didn't make xir wish their connection was something...useful.

The stomach sickness rolled back and the headache eased, but Mette, in daylight, in the sounds and smells of the real world—Orin's brain couldn't process it all.

Real.

At least Mette seemed to be having similar issues. Orin tried to ignore her stained, torn clothes and worn boots, to focus on Mette's flushed face. Though they'd been on the road for near half an hour without speaking—an uncanny length of time to spend staring at a nighttime specter—Mette still sucked in air like she was about to drown. Blathnaid did his best to give them space, though Orin knew there was only so long he could look out the window before he'd feel compelled to speak.

The interior of the stagecoach smelled of fresh lacquer, which barely covered the smell of poop. Orin had expected more frills on the inside, but the interior was mostly flat wood, with just a bit of detail on the molding. The curtains were black linen, and the thin cushions on the benches were a coarse spun silk and looked homemade. A small plastic cooler—vintage from Earth—wedged against the wall opposite the door. On top of the cooler, strapped to the thing with a strip of brown leather, was a worn book with a library bar code up the spine.

It wasn't until after a particularly vicious pothole wherein all three of them whacked their heads on the ceiling that Mette found her voice again. "So. Hey." She rubbed her head and made an attempt to square her shoulders. Orin noticed wrinkles in the cotton across Mette's chest and midsection, and frowned. Orin and Blathnaid didn't have the best clothes in End, but what they had—when it wasn't covered in filth—was still better quality and better fitting than what Mette was wearing.

Mette filled her clothes out a bit better than either of them too, but that was beside the point.

"It's, um, good to see you. In the flesh."

"You dragged me into a stagecoach. When I didn't answer you that night, I didn't mean come and get me."

Mette paled. "I have answers, Orin. I just want you to hear me out. If you say no after, I'll pay for your passage back to the market on a fancy air jet. I promise."

Orin lifted xir left cheek from the bench. "Look at me. Look at us. You *dragged me into a stagecoach.*"

Mette crossed her arms and sat back in a humph.

They were back to this again—weird telepaths with shitty communication skills. Twenty years seemed like an eternity, in that moment. If every night they saw each other for seconds, how many hours had they spent together overall? What did xie actually know about Mette? She liked glasswork? She had fancy nightgowns?

She was going to be a queen. Right?

Orin smashed xir palms into xir temples. "Of all the weird magic in the world, I had to share my head with a freaking princess."

"A princess?" Mette's lip curled and she sat forward. "Wait, you share your mind with a princess? It's not just me?"

"Well, soon-to-be queen. Whatever you want to call yourself now."

Mette uncrossed her legs. She looked at Blathnaid first, maybe for help, but he shook his head and held up his hands. "Oh, no. I've got no pigs in this race. I'm here because Orin pays half the rent—well, *should* pay half the rent, so if xie decides we help you, we help you. If xie decides we beat you unconscious and take your stagecoach, we'll do that."

Mette looked increasingly horrified. "I'm... I work in a glass factory, Orin. It cost me three months' wages to come here."

This time Orin looked at Blathnaid. "But, you wanted me to come to the coronation, right?" Orin asked. "The coronation for Princess Lorimette. Mette. You sent that guy to buy my plants. I figured you wanted a gardener or something after you separated our brains."

Mette's mouth fell open. "Guy... Wait. No! I don't want you to be my servant! Orin, you and I are...never mind. I found a book, Orin, on this thing." She pointed first at her temple, then at Orin's. "I can separate us, but I need your help to do it because there's a lot of fire involved. It's complicated. I'm not soon-to-be Princess Lorimette, whom I have never met, by the way, although I'll grant you that our names are similar, and I never sent anyone anywhere."

"So." Blathnaid scooted closer to Orin. Orin watched him try to suppress a grin and fail miserably. Xie didn't blame him. The situation was quickly becoming absolutely ridiculous. "You stole a book; then you stole Orin. Is the stagecoach also stolen by chance?"

"Borrowed," Mette countered.

"With permission?" Orin asked.

"You know, that's really a grey area if you think about it."

"Okay, let's not." Orin rapped on the ceiling and, as xie'd hoped, the stagecoach drew to a stop. "You're not a princess. Fine. You didn't send someone to buy all my plants. Weird. Whatever. But what, exactly, did you pay for?"

Mette folded her hands in her lap and took a deep breath. "Sea passage on one of the jet boats, and the driver up front for the stagecoach. I couldn't afford jets for both, and I don't know how to run dragons."

Orin took a moment to absorb that. Jets. Dragons. *Mette.*

"Could I ask who he is?" Mette changed the topic and pointed to Blathnaid. "I didn't plan on a third, although an extra hand will help."

Blathnaid cut in before Mette could answer. "I'm Blathnaid, which is a word from Earth that means 'flower,' and I'm guessing my parents either decided it was an old family name that needed use, or wanted a girl. Doesn't matter. They died. Met Orin here when we were six, picking apples on an orchard. Orin puked on me our first night sleeping next to each other in a barn." He pointed at Mette. "Your fault, by the way. I got to hear all about xir first dream with you in it. We've been together ever since."

"Do you vomit after every dream too?" Orin asked Mette.

She nodded. "I sleep with a bucket by my bed. Sometimes I puke during the daytime ones too."

"Yeah, those are worse."

"And you...sell?" Mette asked Orin and Blathnaid. "I'm sorry, I'm still not clear on what you sell. I heard someone talking about End Market yesterday during our daytime connection, and I just, came. I had to."

Blathnaid ran a hand through his short hair, preening. "*I* am an illusionist. Mostly I do card tricks but whatever brings in the money."

"He makes rabbits disappear by mashing them into hidden pockets in hats," Orin added.

"If you give away the secret, then it isn't any fun, Orin."

"I don't think it's ever fun for the rabbits. Anyway, Blathnaid is a friend. The only friend I've got, really, because you can only puke on someone so many times before they start to ignore you."

Mette chuckled, and the edges of her eyes crinkle with her smile.

"I'm Orin. Same deal as Blathnaid, mostly. Dead parents. An aunt raised me for a few years before she died too. Now I, uh, sell lion fern blood."

Blathnaid snickered. Orin glared at him.

"What is a lion fern?" Mette asked. Her genuine interest made Orin's stomach churn again. There was no reason that Orin needed to impress her, but that information didn't seem to be reaching xir mouth.

"My own wildflower variant, bred for exceptional purity of blood, with some light analgesic properties in the fluff. In just the right soil—"

"Xie milks dandelions for low-yield latex."

Orin flushed. "What was that about secrets, Blathnaid?"

"We're not trying to make a sale! Let's finish the introductions before the dragons eat us."

They had zero percent chance of being eaten by domesticated Komodo dragons. Orin sniffed. "The blood, latex, whatever, has a lot of applications."

"Mmm," Mette hummed, smiling. "I'm sure it does. I also think this is the longest conversation we've ever had."

It was far too warm in the stagecoach.

"Your turn," Orin managed.

"Mette Wong. I have parents, both living, both of whom work in the factory. We've worked there seven generations, going back to the original colonists. I was six as well the first time, with the dream." She looked down at her leather shoes. "I used to try to convince them that Orin existed. Tales from a wide-eyed six-year-old are pretty easy to dismiss, it seems. Eventually, they had me convinced as well. Until recently."

"We got it into our heads to walk until we found you, once," Orin said. Xie knocked again on the roof of the stagecoach, and it jostled forward again. "No money for jets or carriages, of course, so we did it by foot, doing odd courier work along the way. Made it four months and halfway to the Starbond Sea before we realized we'd never be able to save up enough for passage on a boat, much less a jet."

Blathnaid laughed. "Also we wore out our shoes."

"Then we just...got older. Got fond of sleeping under roofs. Now here you are, and I know nothing about you."

Mette pursed her lips, her eyes everywhere except Orin. "I have a lot of things I want to ask you, Orin.

Thousands of things I want to tell you, but it never seemed like there was any point."

"We should have at least tried," Orin said.

Mette flushed. "We never had time!"

"Port!" the stagecoach driver called down to them. They stopped moving. The driver opened the door, and the smell of salt immediately hit their noses.

"We can talk more on the boat," Mette said, sliding from her seat and onto the boardwalk. "The spell book I *borrowed* is one of the oldest in the library. Looks like it was brought over by the original colonists. There was a whole chapter dedicated to people like us. I *can* make it work, but you have to be present and I need help with the logistics." She lowered her voice. "We could be sleeping through the night in *three days*."

Sleep sounded glorious. Magic did not. Orin looked over xir shoulder at Blathnaid, who gave a lopsided grin. "In if you are. I've never been on a boat before, and if you die doing this, what will I do with all the buckets we've amassed over the years?"

"Did I ask you along?" Orin asked Blathnaid as xie hopped from the doorway next to Mette, Blathnaid just behind.

"Technically, Mette did." He grinned wide enough to show most of his teeth.

Orin rolled xir eyes and turned to Mette. "You know I just sell dandelions, right?"

"I do now. I was hoping to use your sales pitch more than your product though."

That took Orin by surprise, and xie blinked into the noonday sun.

"I... You know, I really thought you were going to be the princess."

Mette snorted and took Orin's hand. "Well, you dream big, don't you? I can boss you around if you want. Get on the boat. I promise you won't be disappointed."

Chapter Four

"You want to use the ceremonial flame as a glory hole?"

Mette canted her head, narrowed her eyes at Orin, and sighed. The sun beat mercilessly down on the trio as they leaned against the white railing of the jet ship, whose propulsion neither Orin nor Blathnaid understood. It went fast. That was all that mattered.

Moderate waves smacked into the sides of the ship and occasionally sprayed them, which Orin didn't mind at all. It helped wash off some of the stink. They had enough money for a cabin room—there was no bank on the boat to cash in Orin's note—but Blathnaid didn't think it was fair to subject other passengers to their aroma. Orin agreed. Better on the deck anyway, where no one could hear them talking about living in each other's heads.

"No, I don't. I don't know how you could have spent as much time with me as you have and not understand how to work glass."

Orin tucked a strand of wet, salty hair behind xir ear. "I don't see you growing plants."

"It doesn't matter." She set her jaw. "I need a bigger flame than my shop can handle to work with the size tube we need, and the ceremonial flame they light for coronations is perfect. It takes up most of the plaza, and they tightly control the temperatures so they can fuss with colors, which gives me the size *and* control I need to not cook you alive when you hop inside it. If Blathnaid can work the temperature mechanism and you can distract anyone trying to stop us, I can bring the raw materials and make what we need."

"A glass tube," Orin repeated, still trying to understand Mette's plan. "What?"

"Well, a *sleeve*. It used to be called a parchment sleeve, if we're being particular, because the early versions shown in the magic book were made from thin scraped hide and set on fire. The person on the inside died, but for the person on the *outside*, it worked just fine. That's why this one will be made of glass, so in theory, Orin won't die." Her cheeks flushed. "The early colonists didn't like having their minds fused. Apparently it happened a *lot* after they first arrived, and no one knows why. But it's less common now, to the point of being almost eradicated. Genetic drift maybe."

"Okay, but we're not going to light Orin on fire, correct?" Blathnaid asked.

"No, because it's the temperature that matters, and we can get the glass as hot as the paper, and it'll just get soft instead of combusting.."

"How do I get inside a burning hot piece of glass?" Orin asked, xir voice dripping doubt. "Especially without burning myself. And how do you even make something like that in the middle of a palace?"

Mette's eyes turned apologetic. "I have the three sections made. I'll just use the ceremonial flame to bind them together, end to end. For the height, well, you're pretty short, Orin. Honestly I think a ladder would be sufficient."

"I hadn't noticed," Orin muttered and turned towards the water.

"We don't have to do this, Orin, if you don't want to."

Orin looked back. The wind had torn Mette's hair from the remains of the coils, and it whipped around her face and neck in long, frazzled strands. In the direct sun, the wear to her clothes was impossible to miss, as were the old burns on her hands and arms. Everything she wore was of good quality, like her nightgowns, but day clothes had no way of staying clean—not in a factory anyway. Or Mette just didn't care as much about her appearance as Orin did.

Year after year, day after day, they'd visited each other, lived each other's lives. Now they'd finally met, and the idea of separation, at least for Orin, had lost its shine. Xie couldn't remember life before Mette, not really. Xie couldn't seem to picture life after Mette, either.

"This is *magic,* Mette. Old magic. It doesn't make any sense to me. You really think you can do this without killing one of us?"

Mette leaned against the rail, close enough that their shoulders touched. They'd stood this close hundreds of times in the past but never in sounds and smells and touch. The back of Mette's hand brushed Orin's, and the familiar pain tickled the back of Orin's head. Xie had a flash of double vision until Mette took a step back. "I'm tired, Orin. You're a piece of my soul, but I would smother you with a pillow if I thought it would get me a full night's sleep. So no, I can't guarantee anything, but I sure would like to try."

Orin looked at her and blinked, stunned by the remark, until xie saw Mette's smile.

"It's not just our lives we could lose," Orin cautioned.

"But think of how much we could gain. I'm afraid of who we will become if we don't."

"Yeah. Yes. You're right." Orin smiled back. "Without the suffocation part though."

"Think how many more dande...lion ferns you could sell if you didn't look half-dead all the time."

Orin playfully jabbed a finger towards Mette's sternum. "Lion ferns sell themselves, friend. You can't find a better latex producer in the small plant area. Highly portable, hardy, a good source of vitamin C if you're in a bind, and... Why are you staring at me?"

"Because I feel like I've never seen you before. Not like this, anyway."

Orin didn't think. Xie stepped into Mette and kissed her, barely brushing lips that tasted like ocean salt. Mette grabbed Orin by the elbows and pulled xir closer for a single heartbeat—before a wave of double vision and nausea backhanded both of them.

They fell back from one another, on their backsides, and slid a safe distance away. Orin's heart raced, the softness of Mette's lips and the strength of her hands reminding Orin that it was a good thing they'd never tried this before. Growing close, even in the dreamscape, would have only led to heartbreak.

"I hate this," Mette murmured.

"If you're both done with the worst experiment ever, you should come over here." They'd taken Mette's cooler and book with them onto the ship, and Blathnaid finally lifted his head from the thick book, which was entitled *Old Earth Magic: Tips and Tricks*. He stuck a red felt bookmark at the spine and closed the binding. "There are some side effects listed I'm not too keen on."

"Like?" Orin stood and moved behind Blathnaid, putting as much space between xirself and Mette as possible.

"Memory loss, for one. Problems with equilibrium, speech, hand-eye coordination, and even some heartburn apparently." He stood, placed the book on his chair, and came over to the rail to the left of Mette. "I don't know enough about magic to tell you if it will work. The book is real though. I recognize the name of the author. Fen's been giving me weekend lessons for years. He used to talk about her—the author—in hushed tones. It's a real spell. You get lowered into a hot sleeve, er, something cylindrical at a certain temperature, Mette says the words in the book, and in theory, your *otherworldly connection* severs. That's specifically what this spell and the sleeve were designed to do. Random mind connections were a huge problem for the original colonists. No one wanted to live this way if they could help it."

"That doesn't give me a ton of confidence, Blathnaid," Orin said.

"You forget that we have to break into the castle courtyard during the coronation to even get access to the fire, and we have to do so with three glass tubes and whatever other tools Mette needs. Then we have to stack the things without being noticed, glue them up, however that is done, drop you into it without burning you to death, and then somehow get you back out once the whole incantation is done. The spell working won't be the miracle."

"Just the pep talk we needed." Mette strapped the book back to her plastic bin and removed three glass bottles of water, offering one to both Orin and Blathnaid. "I'm really good at what I do, you two, and glass glue isn't that hard to use. As long as Orin can keep people talking and keep selling them on not needing to check on the fire as long as xie can, I think we'll be just fine. Once we are in the courtyard, we will need five minutes, tops."

"We have to *get* to the courtyard first, and our big talker, Orin, has to go in the sleeve at some point," Blathnaid pointed out. "Who keeps the guards out then? We need a bigger distraction. Something monumental."

Mette pursed her lips and looked apologetically at Orin. "I don't know. It's a big space, and the only things in there other than the fire and us will be whatever plants they bought to sacrifice and scatter."

Blathnaid sent a sharp look at Orin. Xie leaned back against the railing and slid down to xir bottom. Plants. Lion fern. Heat.

Distraction, xie could do.

"I've got an idea," xie said, groaning. "But it's really sticky, and I don't think either of you are going to like it."

Chapter Five

People called Methalimus a castle only because stone had been used in its construction, Orin was certain. No part of it looked at all like what children's stories described. The walls were bare cinderblock with an occasional red brick facade. Oval shaped and somehow coming to a triangular point, the parts that could be considered roof were covered in wood shingles. The courtyard sat on the west side of the building, and its dividing wall was just a square of river stones stacked only a bit higher than Orin's head.

Sitting poorly on the stone wall were Orin's dandelions, all now repotted in round bottles from Mette's factory, which explained why the man who'd bought them looked so familiar. They were custom pieces, Mette had informed her, and they had gone back and forth on design for several months. The lion ferns were uniformly in full bloom, which swelled Orin with enough pride that xie could almost forget about the whole sleeve thing and burning to death and kissing Mette. Almost.

"Sorry it took so long," Mette said as she ran up next to Blathnaid and Orin. She held two round loaves of bread and three thin glass jars of juice in her hands, and handed them out. The sun only just peeked over the stone rooftops of the city of Methalimus, but people already filled the streets. The air smelled like wine and pollen, and white plumeria flowers hung across every doorway.

Orin ripped xir bread in half and offered one side to Mette, who politely shook her head and stepped back the moment Orin's hand looked like it might brush her own. "Had mine in the shop. I couldn't carry three along with the drinks."

"We appreciate both." Blathnaid took a long swig from the bottle, finished it, and placed the empty glass in a padded, cylindrical bin marked GLASS REC. "As well as the lodging and the showers."

Orin grunted in assent as xie chewed a too-big bite of potato bread. The shower had been glorious, as had been the faces of every one of the factory workers they'd had to walk past to get to them, Mette quelling questions with her glare as she led them through. Orin had offered to spend the blank note on lodging for the night, but Blathnaid had argued that there were a dozen or so better uses for the money, and Mette had offered her room at the factory. So the three had all ended up huddling on the floor on a pile of blankets because no one could agree on who should take the bed and...

They'd slept through the entire night.

They hadn't been touching, Mette and Orin, and had Blathnaid wedged between them, and for the first time in forever, Orin awoke only with the morning sunlight.

And...oh, everything just *smelled* different when you got to sleep through the night. The world seemed to have more color. Mette, too, seemed different—her eyes bright as she stumbled awake, still drunk on a solid night's sleep. The morning had seemed so full of possibilities, in that moment of waking. No need for burning glass and crashed coronations. They could just all travel together, work together, *be* together...

Orin's mood plummeted. They could travel together, work together, but they would never be able to even hold hands in friendship, not without the headaches and the puking.

"You're not having second thoughts, are you?" Mette asked, bringing Orin back to the present. "Or are the clothes too tight? You want a thick, tightly woven wool for this, trust me. I know it looks like a jumpsuit, but you don't want your clothing catching fire."

"You slept last night, didn't you?"

Mette's smile fell away. "Yes. The whole night. You too?"

"Yup."

"Spending every night close enough to touch you, and not being able to, wasn't really the solution I was looking for though."

Orin felt heat rise in xir face, saw the same mirrored on Mette's.

"We need to do this," Orin said.

Mette nodded. "I know."

Then they were back to staring.

"So the three partial sleeves?" Orin asked when xie couldn't think of what else to say. "I can draw crowds away, but can you and Blathnaid move them on your own?"

"I've got the forms and the glue in a hand cart," Mette responded. She let out a long exhale that Orin could almost feel. "As long as it doesn't tip, we're fine. What about you? Got your distraction thought through?"

Orin grinned and picked up the glass-potted dandelion that Blathnaid had just liberated from the west side of the wall. "I was born for this. The second Lady Lorimette appears, we're good to go."

*

Lady Lorimette rode an impressively large grey Komodo dragon. and *wow* did she look imposing, riding without saddle or harness. She was regal, in starched and ironed orange cotton pants and a bright-yellow linen shirt. Her hair shone a deep russet in the sun, and her skin was so dark it reflected blue highlights. She rode alone as tradition demanded, but thousands lined the sidewalks on either side of the brick and cheered or booed, depending, Orin surmised, on their political affiliation. Some of the children beat handmade drums, and in between the cheering, Orin caught snippets of normal, everyday conversation. The weather. The economy. Magic. The wind had turned mild, the clouds dispersed, although smoke from the ceremonial flames dulled the brightness of the sky. The air smelled of smoke, but it would be another hour or so before the princess walked through the ceremonial flame. The staff in charge would wait to fan it to its hottest point until right before she appeared in the courtyard.

"Time!" Blathnaid whispered into xir ear.

Orin ran.

Xie dodged around children and pets and almost lost an ankle to a dwarf Komodo someone hadn't thought to leash properly before breaking out of the crowd and into the main parade route. The dwarf Komodo made another lunge for xir ankle at the same time, and Orin tripped, landing on xir knees on the brick, pot carefully cradled in the crook of xir arm.

The princess's dragon reared. The startled Lady Lorimette lost her grip and slid backward off its body and onto the street. The dragon—exceptionally well bred— settled immediately. Lady Lorimette did not.

"Get out of the street!" she hissed. Orin heard running feet on brick. Likely the guards, who had been half dozing at their posts, approaching.

Orin opened xir eyes as wide as xie could and walked forward on xir knees. The almost-queen scowled, and in the bright sunlight, Orin caught the faintest green tinge to her eyelashes. Ah. That explained a *lot*. Green hair. Dandelions instead of magic flower petals. If one of Lady Lorimette's parents had been from End, no wonder she didn't care for magic.

And it would make Orin's task much, much easier.

Xie stood and offered Lady Lorimette xir widest, most enthusiastic smile. "I'm with the royal gardener, and, Lady, you forgot your flower! You can't forget *this* flower. It's the non-spelled organic one. You're forgetting the *message*."

Guards shouted and pleaded with the crowd to part.

"But I wasn't supposed to carry one during the procession, I didn't think." Lady Lorimette batted at the leaves that Orin thrust into her face. "Who are you?"

"This is the most important one!" Orin tried to push the pot on Lady Lorimette again as she swung a leg over the dragon's back, attempting to remount. When she still didn't take it, Orin pulled a silver badge from xir pocket with xir picture, license number, and description of xir business etched into the face.

Xie turned xir smile to a disappointed frown. "I came all the way up from End this morning to specially deliver this one. When you carry it in, it will bloom the moment you cross the threshold, not because of magic but because of breeding." Orin put xir free hand on xir hip. "The head gardener told me you wanted to make a statement. This is that statement. I'm the breeder. Here's my badge. Only the *best* breeders get badges."

One of the guards finally managed to break out, and a heavy hand fell on Orin's shoulder. The dandelion slipped forward in xir arm, and xie didn't have to manufacture xir look of panic. Xie kept xir badge out.

"Lady!" Orin and the guard said at the same time. It had only been about two minutes. Blathnaid and Mette needed at least one more before Orin joined them.

Lady Lorimette paused mid-mount and scrutinized the silver.

"You didn't read any of your letters this morning did you, Lady?" Orin asked. Stocky fingers bit into xir shoulder as the guard awaited instructions. The crowd sounded either closer, or louder. There was a growing panic on Lady Lorimette's face as well, which helped steady Orin's nerves. A little.

"No. There was too much to do and...I...must have forgotten." Lady Lorimette shooed the guard. "Let the gardener go."

Orin jerked free of the guard and thrust the pot into the lady's hands. Something scaly brushed xir calf. Damn dragons and people not following leash laws. "Don't forget *this*."

She took it, still hesitant. The guard stepped closer. If Orin didn't close the sale, xie'd spend the next decade showing Mette around xir prison cell.

"Think of the message," Orin suggested. "Organic. Free range. Natural. Magic-free." Orin raised a hand and wiggled xir fingers. "Hand-churned soil."

"It *would* be a good message," the lady drawled, rotating the pot in her hand.

"Sure would. People love hand-churned soil."

"Did my gardener say whose idea it was?"

Orin beamed. "Yours. Of course it was yours."

"Lady?" Another guard finally emerged from the crowd, taser drawn. Almost. It was *almost* time. Just a bit longer.

"No, it's fine," she said, shaking her head. She took another peek at the badge and forced a smile. "Orin was jogging my memory. Go back to your posts. You're disrupting the procession."

The first guard whistled, and both bowed but couldn't make as hasty a retreat as they'd hoped. As Orin planned, the crowd had spilled onto the street, eager to see the disturbance. Orin turned to see two dozen guards stuck amongst at least four thousand people. They tried to herd the crowd, but even with whistles and taser threatening, the crowd wasn't easy to move.

"Sorry," Orin said over the din, scrunching xir shoulders in fake apology. "I didn't mean to cause a ruckus, but you couldn't go on without your prop. I'll give you the quick rundown. This plant is my own unique cultivar. Licensed and patented. The seeds are showy *and* have healing properties. All natural. You place it on the throne when you get in and stay really still for at least five minutes while I snake a little acetylene torch around the back and flame it until it goes to seed. Very nature over magic. Very coronation."

Lady Lorimette's attention turned to the oval door to the castle. A head edged from the left side opening, and a panicked face assessed both the crowd and Lorimette's chances of making it through without her dragon clipping someone at the knees.

"Yes, I understand," she said absently. "It was a brilliant idea of mine to have these at the ceremony. It's nice to have such a dedicated workforce." Lady Lorimette leaned down and lowered her voice. "I don't suppose there is there anything you can do about the spectators?"

It had been three minutes, as best as Orin could count. Time to go. "Lady, I would *love* to help you with that! Just stay right there until I come back. Don't move. It might upset the plant with all these people. In fact, the more guards you get to come to you to help protect the lion fern, the better. I'll go round more up." Orin jumped once into the air like xie couldn't wait to do the woman's bidding, then dodged back into the crowd, running as quickly as xie could to the back courtyard entrance, the fire, and Mette.

Chapter Six

"Psssst!" Orin located the sound and looked up as xie ran along the courtyard wall to see Blathnaid leaning over the stone between several glass pots, gesturing for xir to come closer. Three guards lay unconscious in the street. Orin didn't ask questions.

"Door just a few meters down. It's unlocked. The rest of the guards are all dealing with the crowd. Nice work."

Orin coughed in the thick smoke. Visibility was limited this close to the courtyard fire, but Blathnaid already had the side door open. Orin ran in. Once inside, oppressive heat joined the smoke. The ceremonial fire spread out in a ring about ten meters in diameter, blue at the base and orange at the tips, and was constrained by a ring of grey cinderblocks. An array of glassworking gadgets cluttered the ground. Blathnaid stood at what looked like a control panel, adjusting knobs and frowning.

Just to the right of Blathnaid stood a giant, red-orange glass tube. It was twice Orin's height and maybe four times xir width. The glass was thick and green in the places where it was cooling, but red hot in others. The two glue lines were both easy to see, and sturdy looking. At least Orin wouldn't be crushed to death.

"You're late," Mette said as she tossed a thick pair of gloves onto the brick. No emotion in her words, but Orin didn't blame her. They'd already made this choice. There was no reason to dwell. "It's almost too cool to work. Hop in. I'll get the incantation started."

Orin stared at the glass monstrosity. The heat felt like it might raise welts if xie got much closer, and the opening was well above Orin's head. "How? Did we bring a ladder?"

"Got it!" Blathnaid stepped away from the controls and shook a wooden ladder from flat to tripod just in front of the sleeve. His face, already sweating, turned cherry red. "Don't cook in there, okay? I'm not going to raise your dandelions if you die. You have to live, if only for them."

"Hey! You can't be in here! Come out now." The voices came from the other side of the wall, but Blathnaid had barred the door. Still, the wall was easily scalable, although the smoke made it hard to see. They had negative time.

"Now!" Blathnaid yelled.

Mette opened the book and started to read a string of nonsense words. Orin ran to the ladder, the wood already darkening, scaled to the top, hands blistering from the heat, and stopped. Xie had a moment of doubt, a moment where xie considered what xir life would be like going forward without Mette, weighed against the opportunity to kiss her again, a moment to consider the price they were both about to pay, before xir vision doubled. The back of xir skull pounded. Xie saw through Mette's eyes as she sank to her knees in pain, still reading from the magic book.

"The plants ready?" Orin yelled down to Blathnaid.

"Got them all!" he called back up.

That was that, then.

Blisters popped on xir hands. The soles of xir shoes became sticky. Tears flooded xir eyes, and Orin jumped without looking, off the top of the ladder and into the center of the glass cylinder.

Xie landed on the hard ground, scraping already torn skin and crying out from the pain. Xie could hear Mette outside, insistently reading words in a language xie barely understood. A *clang clang crash* rang in xir ears as Blathnaid threw pot after pot at the cooling sleeve. Small glass bulbs shattered, sending the flowering dandelions first into white balls, then into ribbons of seeds. Orin moved to xir knees, biting into xir tongue so xie wouldn't scream from the heat. Xie took just a moment to admire the long, thin packs of seeds that floated on the air currents, landed, and stuck, semi-permanently, to anything in their path. They'd have been hell to see through for the coronation ceremony and were likely hell on the guards and grounds crew now, as they tried to scale the wall and choked on smoke and seeds. They were a *fantastic* distraction. Orin still had just enough space in xir mind to be a bit proud of it all.

"Out of pots!" Blathnaid yelled.

The rest of Orin's skin started to bubble. Xie heard part of the door to the courtyard break apart. Blathnaid yelled.

"...*officinale!*" Mette screamed the last word and slammed down the cover of the magic book.

The world extinguished.

Chapter Seven

For a moment, there was no light and no sound. Just pain. Blisters searing open. Tears that evaporated before they could form.

Then, like a curtain being pulled, the rest of the world flooded back in. Where there had been only orange-red, however, now the glass was thick green and cool. Sweet air blew into the sleeve, settling some of the blisters. Cooling xir skin.

Orin still heard the guards though. Xie had to move, no matter how much it hurt. Xie flexed xir forearm and popped the blisters that marred the skin. Clear fluid dripped onto the ground, and Orin clenched xir teeth and eyes against what felt like a hundred Komodo dragons, all driving their teeth in at the same moment. An acid bath would have been more comfortable.

Xie breathed deeply, trying to get past the pain, and startled in the perfumed smell of dandelion.

The heat. The flowering plants turning to seed. Right.

Orin looked up, eyes watering against the dryness, to see a snow of dandelion seeds loop down from the sky and coat xir skin and clothes—a rain of soundless cotton candy fluff. They stuck to xir ears, xir eyelashes, xir nose. On the exposed skin, blisters cooled and deflated. The seeds formed a patchwork film over the open wounds, closing them to the air. Orin stopped shaking, not knowing when xie'd begun. The world stilled.

"Orin?" Blathnaid tapped on the sleeve, panic in his words. Xie saw his deformed outline through the glass, looking more mushroom than person. "Orin! Answer me."

"Alive," xie croaked back. "Guards?"

"From what we can see, Lady Lorimette is in hysterics about the flowers going off before her arrival. Her dragon is the only thing out there that *isn't* panicking. The crowd is either delighted or terrified, and I can't tell which. A few guards broke in but left when the dandelions went off. Can you get up?"

Orin managed to stand, xir unexposed skin burned but not blistered due to the wool. There was also some...not disorientation really, but...clarity? Xir vision had definitely sharpened, and this time it wasn't due to sleep. Xie hadn't realized how many crisp edges the world had or how quiet the air was, even with all the yelling.

"I don't think I can climb out. Ladder?"

"Sure thing. Hang on." Orin saw Mette's silhouette turn and walk away, and realized, abruptly, what was going on. Orin saw only what was right in front of xir. Xie hadn't realized how much of Mette had seeped into the corners of xir vision, and how much background noise had come from Mette's own ears. And now, *now*...wow. Just *wow*.

They had done it.

Still Orin waited, unmoving. Xie heard guards and yelling, Blathnaid cursing, and Mette shouting that they needed to go. Orin stood in an island of fluff and searched for sadness, a sense of loss over this woman xie barely knew but who had shared xir mind for years, but felt...what? Hope? Joy? Maybe...anticipation?

Even after the ladder came cascading down, nearly decapitating xir in the process, even after xie climbed out of the glass tube and Mette caught xir eyes, even then, there was no double vision. No headache. No nausea. There was just Orin. Just Mette.

"Well?" Blathnaid asked after Orin jumped from the top of the tube and landed hard on the ground. He pulled Orin into a hug before Orin's hiss of pain backed him off.

"It's done."

"And you're alive."

The words seemed callous, but Orin heard the relief in them, saw Mette's hesitant approach. Xie held out xir left hand and Mette took it, and there was only air between them, and dandelion fluff, and fragments of obsolete lives. Now there was only Mette—tired, stained, shadow-eyed Mette. They could have anything they wanted now. Well, almost anything.

"You okay?" Mette asked. "It...isn't what I thought." Their hands remained tight together, Orin's fingers brushing over Mette's knuckles, but Mette didn't step any closer. She licked her lips, dry from the fire, but this time, Orin didn't move in. They were strangers now, passing acquaintances at best. They had their lives back, but they didn't have each other. And damn, Orin *wanted* that moment again, Mette's arms pulling xir in, Mette's breath mingling with her own, but it was gone. *They* were gone. Orin had lived, but there'd still been a price.

"Yes. You?"

Mette nodded.

There really wasn't anything else to say. Orin searched for words to fill in the silence, but Mette shook her head. Orin understood.

Something that looked like fireworks went off in the corner of Orin's vision. The coronation had to continue, of course, even with a problematic crowd. It bought them a few moments more. Xie stared at Mette for another breath before taking Blathnaid's hand and motioning toward the port. It did no good to keep staring. "We're going to cash that note before this scene settles and they realize what happened. I don't think we're going to go back to End. I'll write, sometime. Tell you where we are if you want to visit. If you want. No pressure."

"Maybe." Mette sighed. "Orin, do you think..."

Orin gave her hand a final squeeze, then released it. "We made the right choice. We can make another one, later, if we want, but right now, this"—xie pointed at the glass—"this was good."

Mette smiled sadly. "Yes. Yes, I know." She leaned in and pressed her lips briefly to Orin's forehead. "I'm glad I don't have to smother you with a pillow. Take care of yourself, Orin."

"You too." Orin smirked, then whispered into her ear. "Princess."

Mette grinned as Orin and Blathnaid turned and walked back through the gate and into the crowded street. There would be time to be sad, and time to celebrate. But for the first time ever, Orin could see a future. It involved sleeping through the night without pots by xir bed; it involved a full-time job where xie didn't have to worry about passing out. It involved travel. Friends. Adventure. Xir own mind. Xir own space.

And eventually, maybe, once xie and Blathnaid landed on their feet and figured out who they were, that future might involve Mette too.

At the very least it was going to involve a lot of really excellent naps.

THE FAR TOUCH

S.R. Jones

They arrived a day early, partly because Kiyah said the runes had told her it would be wise, and partly because Inatu had booked the wrong days off work.

Kah had been back on firm ground for six hours (and only out of debriefing for less than half an hour) when a harassed-looking security officer stuck their head around the changing room door, and told him that an angry old woman in an ugly car was yelling at the intercom at the front gate, demanding to see him. The woman was Kiyah, because nobody else would dare bark at armed security guards; the car belonged to Inatu, and it was very ugly indeed.

Kah did not wait. He was tired and upset, and part of him wanted badly to go to bed, but the station dormitory was uninviting at the best of times and the long halls and clean, open-plan offices were starting to make his head hurt. He was caught somewhere between agoraphobia and claustrophobia, used to living in a capsule barely big enough for him to stand in and currently desperate for both open space and the security of very close walls.

The science outpost could offer him neither: it was a modern building constructed with far too much thought for those who remained on the ground and no real consideration for somebody returning from space. It was all long white hallways and crisp blue carpets, with ceilings that were a little too high for comfort and a lot more strip lighting than was necessary. When Kah had first arrived here, he had been impressed—it oozed efficiency and ambition—but now...now it was just a winding maze of meeting rooms decorated with tasteful photographs of equipment, punctuated with the occasional austere staff room or cupboard-like kitchen where one could mix uninspired hot drinks that didn't float away when you tried to consume them. There were people here, but he did not like being around them. They did not meet his eye when they passed him, not because of who he was but because they were preoccupied with their own business. He would not have liked it any better if they had been more friendly.

Perhaps outside would be better.

He gathered the few items he thought he might need and scooped them unceremoniously into a Space Control branded shoulder bag. He had very little with him that mattered, having left behind more or less everything that he owned before coming out here. At the time, it had been a necessary sacrifice for his future. He had embraced it; now he regretted it.

He had nothing. He *felt* like nothing.

He was an astronaut stranded on an unfamiliar planet, and everything he loved was three hundred and fifty kilometres out of his reach, circling the upper atmosphere while he was forced to bend to gravity's will, and walk out of the station on his own two feet.

The sky loomed over him, and the sheer size of it almost forced him to step back into the relative safety of the station lobby. He'd been warned about this, but it had all just been theory, and he had certainly never expected it to happen to *him*.

"Everything all right?"

Behind him, the station's on-duty receptionist was leaning forward over her desk to look at him, huge black eyes wide with curiosity, as if he were a specimen rather than a person. Perhaps that was fitting; he no longer belonged here, and the creatures around him no longer felt like his kin. He gave her a thin smile and nodded. It was tempting to say something flippant, or to try and mask the truth by claiming a moment of light-headedness, but if he did then she would call the medical team and they wouldn't let him out. It was already a sketchy arrangement, mainly allowed because of past precedent. Everybody knew he left the base every year for the ritual; the fact that he had only just got back might raise some eyebrows, but so far nobody had questioned the much-loved status quo.

"I'm fine," he lied.

She did not look convinced, but smiled back at him and nodded, feigning understanding just as he was feigning confidence. He wished she would sit down again, but she didn't, so he turned his back on her and forced himself to step outside.

The air tasted gritty; there was no breeze to lift the dirt, but compared to the conditioned air of the station or the filtered air of the capsule, it was something of an experience. He sniffed it, large nostrils flexing at the top of his trunk, eyes half-closed against the glare of the sun. He put up a hand to shade his face and hurried across the yard toward the perimeter, as if the fence there might offer some protection from the vast nothingness that hung over his head.

He signed out at the little booth by the gate, and the security guard waved him out without opening the barrier, clearly worried that Kiyah might try to drive through if he did so. Kah ducked underneath it, nearly caught his bag on it as he stood, and managed to force a smile as he approached the car. He saw Inatu in the front passenger seat turn and reach over to the back to manually pop the door open. It was meant to be automatic, controlled with a button on the front dash, but the car was so old that the only part of it Inatu bothered to maintain was the engine. Even that didn't sound particularly healthy to Kah's moderately machine-literate ears, but unless the vehicle was a spacecraft he didn't feel it was his place to comment on it. He tossed his bag across the seat to the far side and slumped in next to it. Kiyah had the car in reverse almost at once, and he had to fight with the door to pull it closed as she heaved the car in an ungainly, backward circle in an attempt to get them turned around. She muttered to herself under her breath, complaining about the manners of the security team while she battled with the steering wheel.

"When did they give you your licence back?" Kah asked, once the somewhat exciting manoeuvre had been completed and he felt it was safe to distract her with talking.

"They didn't," said Inatu, and Kiyah shot them a look, which was risky given that it meant taking her eyes off the road.

"It's all private roads out here; I don't even need one," she said, which wasn't even close to true, then added "Welcome back," almost as an afterthought. Kah smiled, and it was the first real smile he'd worn since the return module had crashed down. The world might seem strange to him now, but a bumpy ride in Inatu's barely road-worthy car felt much safer than it ought to. Not physically safe (there was no doubt the whole thing was one unexpected pothole away from falling apart), but emotionally safe, because worrying about surviving the car ride was something he had done so many times before. He knew the drill as well as he knew the ones they had put him through at the station: belt up, hold on, try not to squeak every time Kiyah took a hand off the wheel. Every little lump and bump on the road seemed to be transferred right into his spine via the flattened stuffing of the back seat, but six hours ago he had been plummeting through the cloud layer. It didn't feel all that bad by comparison.

They drove in silence for the better part of an hour. Even if Kah had wanted to talk, the sound of air rushing through the open windows and the grating rattle of the car itself would have made it difficult, and he was in no mood to shout. He stared at the seat in front of him and the back of Inatu's head. Occasionally they glanced over their shoulder to smile at him from behind a large pair of sunglasses and a big sun hat made of woven straw. It was fitting attire for the journey: there was very little out here but sun and baked earth, and the wavering horizon where land and sky tried to blend themselves together in the heat. The sky was blue, fading at its highest point to a light shade of teal. Kah knew why—had studied atmospherics and light scattering among many other things—but he did not think of that right then. When his eyes dared to drift outside, all he could think was *green is the colour of life.* It was inaccurate, but it had been something he'd learned in childhood and somehow it had stuck in his mind.

Eventually the beaten dirt track met a junction that connected it to an actual highway, and Kiyah declared that she was tired and didn't want to drive any more. She stopped the car without bothering to pull off the road, and she and Inatu got out to stretch and swap places. Kah stayed put, still not 100 percent happy with being out in the open, but he knelt on the back seat and leaned his arms on the frame of the open window, watching them.

Inatu was tall and slim, wide shoulders left bare by a thin-strapped shift that came all the way down to their ankles. They wore no shoes, preferring to go barefoot whenever possible—even out here, where the road surface was so hot that they had to practically hop away onto the verge and stand in the dust. Kiyah was shorter but larger, both in girth and in presence. She loomed, even though she was the shortest of them, and her heavy shoulders sagged as if the weight of her chest were pulling them forward. She had been old for as long as Kah had known her, but even though she was grey-haired and silver-eyed with age, she was far from past it. She stood on the road with her hands on her hips, glaring defiantly at the thin line of mountains that rose above the heat-shimmer at the far end of what they could see. She was dressed as she always was, in a long skirt with tassels around the hem and a loose-fitted top with big billowy sleeves. Her shawl had been tossed casually over the back of the driver's seat, because even the hottest days of summer were not enough to part her from it.

"So what was it like?"

Kah looked across to Inatu, who had taken off their hat to fan themselves with the brim. They were chalky brown, skin tanned under their fuzzy coating of vellus. A small gem glittered on a stud high up on one nostril, catching the sunlight as Inatu scratched at their chest with their trunk. A long mane the colour of dry grass shifted past their shoulders in the hot desert breeze. Kah's was darker. He felt his colouring was overall much more subdued: he never tanned because his vellus was too thick, and his mane was mid-brown, neither dark enough nor light enough to be interesting at a passing glance.

"It was all right," he said, after considerable thought.

"Just all right?" Inatu asked. Anybody else might have sounded incredulous, but they didn't. Inatu was a strange soul at times, but had a way of being sensitive when others scoffed—something that Kiyah was doing already.

"All right?" she echoed. "They blasted you up into space, and all you can say about it was that it was '*all right*'? You're the first one of us to ever see what's up there with their own two eyes, and you can't even manage more than two words to describe it?"

Kah thought about it.

"I really can't," he said finally, and Inatu laughed, smiling at him, while Kiyah tossed her head and huffed.

"Bloody useless," she chided. "I bet when they asked you what space looked like all you could say was that it was a bit dark,"

"Oh, it was never dark," said Kah. It had been black, at least in some manner, but not in the way he had expected it to be. When the capsule's lights had been on, it looked like night outside the windows, but not the nights he had seen before, from the ground. There had always been a sense of radiance—a sense of energy of some kind, perhaps invisible to the naked eye but still tangible in some way. With the capsule lights switched off, that radiance turned blackness into an ocean, infinitely deep, peppered with glittering stars and the hazy strata of other galactic arms. It was impossible to think of such a sight as 'dark.' Dark suggested nothing was visible, but in space Kah felt he had seen more than he could ever have dreamed of. And yet, remembering it now left him feeling empty.

Inatu and Kiyah got back into the car, their positions switched, and Inatu paused before hitting the ignition. They used the rearview mirror to peer at Kah over the top of their glasses, black eyes filling the reflection so that he could see little of their expression.

"Something's bothering you," they stated. Kah said nothing, and looked away.

Kiyah nudged Inatu and pointed down the road.

"Come on—we've got places to go. He'll talk when he's ready to; you know what he's like."

And that was the thing: they did know him.

The only people who had known him longer were his parents, and frankly, he liked Kiyah and Inatu better. His mind wandered to earlier years, and the life he had had before he'd joined the Coven. There had been so many questions without answers—mysteries that could not be unravelled, even with the wealth of information he could find online or hidden away in books. His mother had described him as precocious, but on reflection he would have preferred to have been called curious. He had wanted to *know*; he just wasn't sure *what* he wanted to know. It was a difficult predicament, and Kiyah and Inatu hadn't been able to give him all the answers, although they had stood at his side and encouraged him to find them. When he'd told them he was going into space, they had been excited for him; when he'd told his parents, they had only complained about the burden it would put on them if he never came back. It had upset him so much that at the time, he'd wished that it might come to pass, just so they would suffer.

What kind of monster did that make him, he wondered, and did monsters like him really deserve to see the things that he had seen up there? His own eyes had seen sights that others would only ever know through pictures and recordings. He had sat at the capsule's main windows, lights switched off, and looked down upon a world that had never witnessed its own beauty. He had seen cities from so far away that he could eclipse them just by raising a finger and resting its tip upon the glass. He had seen the oceans, and had seen their tides rise and fall on every coast at once.

And he had seen magic. Not just felt it, or practised it, but *seen* it on a truly global scale: when the capsule drifted into the planet's shadow, it was right there, as clear as the tiny clusters of lights that marked out the metropolises and motorways packed with cars. He had looked down from on high and seen the very veins of the world, faintly blue, spreading like a spiderweb of rivers. He had always known that they were there, of course, but even in his wildest dreams he had never realised there were quite so many.

"They're going to purge the Line, you know."

Nobody had said anything for nearly ten kilometres, but Kah still had to speak up to be heard. The sound of air rushing through the old banger's open windows, and the tinny, intermittent warbling of various radio stations as the car's movements nudged the dial back and forth between two stations was almost enough to blot out everything else. He was heard, though. Inatu glanced at him in the rearview mirror, eyes wide, and Kiyah half turned in her seat to glare at him.

"You what?" she bellowed, then reached out a hand to fumble with the radio, eventually managing to force it off. "Say that again."

It sounded like a challenge, as if he were the one personally responsible, but he wasn't.

"They're going to purge it. The main line from the city, all the way down to Haredhe's main capacitor farm. They sent us the memo this morning. They say it's the only way to stop the Haredhans from restocking their missile facilities."

"It's the only way to crack the damn planet, is what it is," Kiyah snapped, and again he felt as if she were accusing him of something—accusing him of being involved, perhaps, or of not stopping it. Or was that his own guilt speaking up through her? He had tried to put in a word on the matter, but nobody wanted to hear from a witch when it came to matters of war. As an astronaut he might have had a stronger voice, but it seemed his role as the former would forever overshadow his role as the latter. Superstition overruled science, at least in the minds of people who claimed to believe in science alone.

"The Architect will never stand for it," said Inatu.

Kah shook his head.

"They've already signed off on it, apparently,"

"That's rubbish—utter rubbish!" Kiyah fumed. "They of all people should know better!"

"I know," Kah replied bitterly. "I did my best, Kiyah— I told them, you can't expect a power surge to only affect the things attached to the Line. I told them it'll rake up everything if they do it—it'll be..."

It would be devastating. He could think it, but somehow the idea of saying the words was too much. Kah slumped down in the lumpy back seat, and spent a few minutes looking at the torn fabric that was supposed to hide the metalwork of the roof. In the front, Kiyah shook her head, visibly bristling; he could see that her hair had fluffed up, lifted by her half-raised quills. Men didn't have quills, so he'd had his removed, but he could still feel them sometimes, when things made him anxious. When the news about the purge had been delivered to the debriefing room, he'd felt the follicles they had grown from tense by instinct, a mix of fear and fury which had now boiled away to tired and helpless terror.

The banger rattled on for another half kilometre before Kiyah spoke again.

"Absolute nonsense," she snapped, and the other two murmured their agreement.

"How much are they going to flush it with?" asked Inatu. Kah caught their eye in the rearview mirror.

"The memo didn't say. Enough to blow their main capacitors, though—that's the plan, anyway."

"Blow out their power grid with a surge, then sweep in like saviours and pretend they never did it, I'll bet," said Kiyah, and Kah had to admit that she was unlikely to be wrong.

"So, this is how the world ends," said Inatu after another hundred yards of scrub and dust had flashed past them. Out on the plains, Kah could see a herd of rommu wandering through the scant clumps of coarse grass. They were wild ones, he supposed, lumbering along in single file, their stooped backs heavy with stored fat, and their flat and drooping faces downturned to protect their eyes from the sun. They moved slowly, unhurried, vast back legs propelling them forward, each one using their single front limb to balance themselves as they went. They were not majestic creatures, but they were solid, and familiar, and docile.

Who will explain it to them when it happens? Kah thought. And would any of them even survive?

"They say it should be fine," he said, even though he knew damn well that it would not be. Kiyah snorted, nostrils flaring wildly in her rage.

"I dunno. If somebody pumped enough blood up your arm to blow up your heart, I don't think the rest of you would end up looking great," said Inatu. A crude analogy, maybe, but they had a point and Kah didn't see the need to argue.

"I know," he said. "I'm just telling you what they're saying."

"They're saying they're idiots," said Kiyah, and Inatu and Kah both nodded solemnly. "I can't believe—well, I *can* believe it, but I shouldn't have to—but to think the Architect has approved this? That's just...that's—"

"Incompetence?" Kah suggested, but she shook her head, spines still bristled enough to knock and rattle against the headrest.

"Arrogance," she said, as if the word had just made itself known to her. "It's just fucking arrogant, to think you can control that kind of power." She half turned in her seat again, and Kah saw that her huge, milky eyes were narrow with rage. "Curse him, I say!" she snapped. "If he wants to blow the side of the planet off, then I hope the line feeds back before it ruptures and blows the whole damn side off him too!"

Kah smiled weakly, and in the front, Inatu chuckled darkly.

"Let it be," they said, and Kah nodded.

"Let it be," he agreed.

"Let it be," Kiyah confirmed, a gave a single, forceful nod, as if to seal the deal. Kah watched her spines settle as she turned around again, righteous anger sated by their bargain, though she still looked unhappy.

*

They left the car at the place where the road petered out to nothing and unloaded the bags that Inatu and Kiyah had packed in the trunk. Kah made a valiant attempt to carry more than necessary, before Inatu came up behind him and took away the heaviest of the bags. There were no words, no apologies, just a quiet understanding that he was not as strong as he had been the year before. Kiyah carried nothing, as was her right as the eldest; she also set the pace, and they followed her out into the red baked earth, away from the last vestige of a civilised world, toward the mountains.

The sun beat down, and the passing breeze peppered them with grains of sand, sharp and stinging, battering the backs of their legs as if the weather itself was herding them onwards. A narrow path, barely more than a rommu track, was hidden among the jagged rocks that littered the lower slopes of the cliffs, but all three of them could have found it without even having to look. Muscle memory led them to it, and they were grateful for the small amount of shade the rocks obscuring it offered. Clusters of little animals scattered for cover as they slumped down to rest for a moment before tackling the hills. Inatu handed out bottles of water, and they stood around to drink in silence. Kah dared to look at the rock face looming over them, and wondered—as he did every year—if Kiyah would manage the ascent. Then he wondered if the other two were thinking the same about him this year, but he wasn't brave enough to ask.

The water was warm, and tasted of nothing but the plastic it was contained in. In the shadows around their feet, a few small lizards (being either too brave or too lazy to flee from them) looked up with dazzling orange eyes.

The upward climb was slow and uncomfortable; the path strewn with dust and gravel that could slip underfoot at any moment. At about halfway up Inatu started humming, and by three-quarters of the way Kah was ready to strangle them if they didn't stop. It was another familiar moment, another part of the ritual, in many ways, and he capitalised on his irritation to keep his feet moving up the slope. Then they came to a sharp bend, and Kiyah called out her annual warning—"Mind your step here"— and the line of rocks sheltering the path petered out. Kah paused at the bend, one hand resting on the cliff beside him, and looked out over the suddenly revealed view.

Nothing but rocks and sand and dry soil, for as far as the heat would let him see, before it melted away into the watery mirage at the horizon. The road wasn't visible on this side of the mountain, and there were no others. There were few places left unembraced by the ever-reaching arms of civilisation, and this was the biggest: he'd heard it called a wasteland, but there was no waste here that he could see, only beauty. He had looked down on it from the capsule and seen the vast stripe of the Line—largest of the lay-lines—flowing right through here, along with its network of tributaries and capillaries. At each end he had seen the clustered lights of cities, and many more besides peppered the lands where the capillaries converged, but here in the desert there were no buildings, and no power stations leeching energy out of the earth. The Line was too big to be tapped out here, and only the magnetic interference of the planet's poles made it safe to interact with at its termini.

He might never see this place again, he thought. At least, not like this. Even if the Line was purged successfully, the shock waves would tear up the plains and topple the rock formations they were currently climbing. It had been worrying him all day, but it was only now, only when he could actually see what was likely to be destroyed, that the full horror of what was being proposed began to sink in. Kiyah was right: it was arrogance, to think that science could control the kind of power that surged beneath the tranquil sea of dust and stone. Even witches as old and as powerful as Kiyah did not claim to be able to command it—only to tap into it, and trust their consciousness to the unfathomable whims of its currents and eddies.

"You coming or not?"

He looked up the path, and saw that Inatu had paused a few dozen paces ahead of him. They were smiling, but it looked brittle—not forced, just strained—and he knew with absolute clarity that they were thinking the same things he was.

"Just enjoying the view," he said. Inatu looked out over the plain as well, raising slender fingers to add an extra layer of shade to their gaze. Sunglasses, hat, and now a hand, and even with all that, they still seemed to be squinting. "Are you okay?"

"Just tired," said Inatu. "It all makes me so tired, you know?"

Kah did. He'd been back on the ground for less than a day, and he was already starting to think that returning had been a mistake. He forced his feet back into motion, and Inatu waited until he was right behind them before starting to walk again too. If the path had been wider, the two of them might have gone side by side, but there was no room. Inatu held out a hand to him, though, and he took it and squeezed it tightly. They walked in single file, hand in hand, and somehow the humming seemed less annoying to him now.

They were all exhausted by the time they reached the top of the cliff. The rest of the mountain loomed over them still, far too high to be climbed in a single day, but their journey was now over. A wide, flat ledge wound its way around the mountainside, dotted with the odd boulder that had rolled down from higher up. Opposite the top of the path, there was a deep crag that opened into a low-ceilinged cave. Manhandling the suitcases through the gap was always a struggle, but once inside there was enough space for them to sit comfortably and let themselves cool off. Kiyah took off her shawl and draped it over a nearby lump of rock; Inatu took off their hat and fanned themself with it. Kah was just glad to sit down, and leaned himself against the cool stone of the cave wall, panting lightly and wondering if they would ever come here again.

There was very little light, save for that which crawled through the narrow opening behind them, and for a short time, Kah sat staring towards the darkness at the back of the cave and dreamed quietly of space. Perhaps he actually did fall asleep, or perhaps not; the next thing he was aware of was the crackling of coals, and Inatu squatting down over a small campfire which they had lit with a portable gas match.

The shadows flickered away, revealing reddish-brown rock worn smooth by the relentless hands of time and weather. At the back of the cave there was another gap; this one artificially widened to make it easier to use, leading into a short tunnel that connected to the caverns in the mountain's heart. The network was vast, but largely unexplored even by the witches, who only sought out the second cave and in it, the pool of luminous water that collected under the faint trickle of a natural spring. All around it there grew mushrooms and other plants that lived without sunlight, and like the water, they had a kind of phosphorescence, and seemed to shift and creak as the witches approached. Around the spring, a faint line glowed a soft shade of blue like veins inside the rock: a web-like network of lay-line capillaries, flowing through the stone and infusing the water with their power.

Kiyah stepped forward first, and dipped her hand into the water. She touched her fingers to her forehead, and then to her lipless mouth. When she was finished, she gestured for Inatu to do the same, and then for Kah. He did as he was bade, feeling the hum of energy in the water when he touched it. It made all the vellus on his body stand up on end, but it was far from an unpleasant feeling. When he touched his fingers to his forehead, he silently begged the planet to forgive them; when he pressed his fingers to his mouth, he prayed for his lost sense of belonging.

"Do you think it will survive?" said Inatu, once he was finished.

Kah shook his head. He didn't need all his years of training to know what a serious earthquake would do to this cave, which had stood and dripped out its water for untold centuries. One big kick from the Line and it would all come down, buried under the remains of the mountain—or worse, the fracturing stone would release the water collected up here and let it flood into the valley, where anybody could get their hands on it. Lay-infused water wasn't bad per se, but in the hands of the uninitiated (or more likely, the downright unwary) it could do damage. The wildlife might get strange on it too, and while rommu herds were peaceful enough under normal circumstances, it was best not to get them irritated or excited.

"There are other springs," said Kiyah, putting an end to any further discussion.

Kah knew she was right, but he couldn't help but wonder if they would get the chance to go and look for them.

This could be the last time we do this, he thought.

"We should get ready," she said. "And this year we're going to do it properly—no messing about, and no silliness, understand?"

She said it every year, but Kah supposed that there was a first time for everything, even at the end of the world.

*

When the first trails of green began to creep into the highest parts of the sky, the three of them ventured out of the cave and began their final preparations. Kiyah was already naked, and set about sketching out a large circle in the dust a few paces away from the cliff edge. Inatu was busy unpacking crystals from the suitcases they had brought up from the car, leaving Kah with the very important task of brewing tea.

It felt surreal, setting up the old tin kettle over their campfire, and filling it with water from the cave pool, ferried over to where he needed it in an old plastic bottle. He had done this so many times before, but this time his fingers felt clumsy, and the lid of the kettle seemed to fight him when he tried to put it back in place. Was it loss of muscle mass, or loss of muscle memory? He couldn't remember making tea once since the previous year's celebration—not since the station had brought in the machine that dispensed drinks in the canteen. Not long after that the capsule had been launched, and up there all he had had to drink was distilled water with the option to add flavoured drops from a small selection of sachets, which were fiddly to use in zero gravity. They tasted nice but were hardly in the same league as freshly brewed tea made with lay-water.

He and Inatu undressed while the tea was cooling to a drinkable temperature. For Inatu it was easy; all they had to do was slip their shift off over their head and then put their hat back on. They were wearing nothing underneath—no underwear of any kind, as was their way. For Kah it was a much slower process, and that was what made him self-conscious about it. Jacket, vest, unzip trousers, then an awkward moment when he had to backtrack and take off his boots because the trousers wouldn't go down over them.

Inatu chuckled at him, watching his progress from the shadow of their hat.

"I can't believe they sent you into space."

"I haven't worn normal clothes for eight months."

"There's nothing normal about some of the things you wear," said Kiyah, trudging in from her work on the cliff edge. She grabbed a cup of tea and stood over them both, blowing on it irritably while she waited. Kah quickly shed his underwear and folded up his clothes to pile them up on top of Inatu's shift.

"Socks," said Inatu, and Kah bent over to yank them off, trying his best not to look embarrassed.

"Hat and glasses," said Kiyah.

Inatu gave her a mournful look.

"Do I have to?"

"You do know the sun goes away at night, don't you?"

Inatu took off the hat and tossed it lazily away across the cave. They were slower to shed the glasses, though, blinking slowly and squinting with what might have been a touch of exaggeration as they folded them in their lap.

"Did you forget your contact lenses?" Kiyah asked them, then sighed. "Fine, keep the damn glasses. I can't be bothered to go looking for your corpse if you wander off the edge."

"That might still happen," said Kah, because they were sunglasses and he felt that their use after dark was probably limited. Inatu seemed less concerned.

"At least I'll die fashionable," they said, and Kah couldn't argue with that; he had no idea about fashion, and even if he had, he was at least a season behind on the current trends. He thought about that as they gathered at the circle, and sat down at their allotted points to drink their tea. What else had he missed while he'd been in space? And even before then, when he had been training so hard to achieve that lofty dream? Years had gone by without him. People at the station talked about television programs and audio shows, or exchanged book recommendations, but unless it was a text on physics or mathematics, Kah had passed them all by. That seemed like a mistake now, like he was a soul cut adrift from some kind of collective consciousness that the rest of his species shared. He could not decide if the payoff had been worth what he had lost out on. Nobody else had seen what he had seen—had experienced the wonder of it—but what was that worth, in the grand scheme of things?

He sipped his tea, cradling the side of the mug with his trunk as well as supporting it with a hand. The ceramic was still hot, but the air was cooling fast and the heat was welcome. The tea had a strong mineral tang to it, the not-quite-metallic flavour of the lay-lines. He could feel the energy in it, the lifeblood of the world, spreading slowly out from his stomach after every sip. It was not heat, but it felt like warmth of another kind, like opening a door and stepping into a much-loved home after a long and difficult journey.

There were people who would never feel this, either through fear or ignorance. There were people who would do away with magic altogether for those exact same reasons, and those who wrote it off as archaic religious nonsense if only to save themselves from facing the truth.

Kah had worked with some of them, and met others at conventions and seminars. He had listened politely while people who considered themselves important in the world lectured him on how magic was nothing or even that it was simply science dressed up in other words. The former angered him, and the latter fascinated him, but neither was the truth as far as he understood it. Science could use the lay-lines, but it could neither explain them nor bend them to its will. Not even Kiyah could do that.

She was watching him, eyeing him thoughtfully from her seat in the dust. She held her mug so close to her chest that it was practically nestled in the long crease of her cleavage, her old arms with their loose skin not nearly wide enough to cover the lower parts of her breasts, which hung down over the swell of her belly. He could see the sagging folds of the outlet just below her sternum, that mystical gateway through which she had birthed her children, and between her crossed legs the darker, hairier fur that grew abundantly on her mons. She never trimmed it; the very idea of her straddling a mirror to attack it with clippers or scissors was an affront to everything Kah knew about her. She didn't even pluck her eyebrows, which meant they joined together in the middle whenever she frowned, as she was right now.

"Tell me what you're thinking, Child," she said, and Kah looked into his cup before answering, nervously tilting it in his hand so the blue-grey water swirled and sloshed against the edges.

When he spoke, he addressed her formally, as she had addressed him.

"Mother, I was thinking about the world, and everything that's in it, and everything that's beyond it."

"And what do you think of those things?" she asked.

Kah was quiet for a while. He turned to look at Inatu, who was holding their mug in one hand and leaning back on the other, long and lean, comfortable in their own skin in a way that most people could only dream of. They smiled at him, encouraging him, and he nodded to them and took a breath before answering.

"I think we should have gone to space sooner," he said at last. The other two were quiet, and he took it as an invitation to elaborate. "We've spent so much time exploring our own world that there's nothing left here for us to find, and I think that's caused us to fall out of love with it. We take it for granted now. People don't look around and see the wonders any more—all they see is profit, or purpose, or..." He floundered, shaking his head, feeling the empty pores where his quills had been tensing along his scalp as his temper stirred.

"Entitlement?" suggested Inatu, and it was indeed the right word.

"Yes. And now we're only just beginning to look at the stars—scientifically, I mean. It's as if every eye on the planet has finally turned upwards, and it's just a little bit too late. We're going to blow ourselves up over what? Borders and bragging rights? And everything we might have learned out there will be lost." He fell silent, his anger burning out just as fast as it had come. The ghosts of his quills settled themselves, and he looked down into his tea, feeling ashamed of himself for being part of what he had described.

"I don't know who this 'we' you're talking about is," said Inatu. "None of *us* are part of this, Child,"

"But we are, My Love," Kah replied, looking up at them sharply. "All of us—I'm not talking about individuals; I'm talking about a species that has lived on this wonderful floating rock for thousands of years, and has never once managed to be at peace with itself. We are part of that. We can dance around it or try to wash our hands of it, but everything that is in us is also in the people who are preparing to purge the Line. One and the same—we are all one and the same."

"We are a living, breathing host. The world is an organism of many parts, from the smallest plant to the greatest of animals," said Kiyah, speaking to them both. Kah nodded, but Inatu shifted a little in the dust. They leaned forward and placed their now empty mug on the fast-cooling earth between their thighs. Inatu was always immaculately trimmed at Coven gatherings, and Kah found himself wondering if they judged him for being much more lax about it.

"So it is, Mother, but that doesn't mean that every creature on the planet bears responsibility for the actions of a few," Inatu was saying. "That herd of rommu we passed—should we hold them accountable when the Line is purged? What about the insects, or the trees? Or us? I for one feel angry about it, not guilty, and if I could think of a way to stop it, then I would."

"Even rational creatures harm themselves, My Love," said Kiyah, speaking carefully, her words measured and slow.

Inatu shook their head quickly, muttering '*no, no,*' under their breath. Then, louder, they said, "I don't think the world is suicidal or depressed, Mother—but I'll say this: it may be infected. There may be a cancer growing in it. I don't know, but even if that was the case, a healthy cell isn't to blame for the damage done by a tumour."

"Healthy cells still die in the cure," Kah said quietly. The other two both turned to him, one still looking thoughtful, the other's look of irritation heightened somewhat by the large reflective lenses of their glasses.

"Speak up, Child," said Inatu, and it came out so sharply that Kah flinched away from them. For a brief and aching moment he longed for the solitude of the capsule, and the endless fathoms of dark-that-wasn't-dark. He tilted his head back and sighed at the stars, which were just starting to prick their way through the sunset as night made its final approach.

"I don't know, I just... I don't want to think of the end of the world, but sometimes curing a cancer means damaging the other cells around it. And sometimes the cancer wins anyway, no matter how hard you try. Everything has to die one day. That's just part of being alive."

The three of them fell into silence, but it was not as comfortable as it had been during their journey. Inatu prodded at their cup, tipping it back and forth with the end of one finger and making it spin in lazy circles between their knees. Kiyah did not look away from Kah, but drank the last of her tea, then scratched at her chin with the end of her trunk, before snorting out a short burst of laughter. It made her nostrils flare, and her shoulders bounce.

"I was worried space might change you, but you're just as bloody depressing as ever," she said to him. Kah smiled, and then chuckled; across from him Inatu smiled too.

"I don't know, Mother. Maybe he has changed. I'm not hearing all the questions he usually has," they said slyly. "Did the stars give you all your answers, Child?"

"No, My Love. I just have so many more now, I don't know which one to start with."

"Start with whatever one gets to your mouth first," suggested Kiyah. Kah looked at her blankly, not entirely sure what she was suggesting.

"That's a good idea, actually," said Inatu. "Come on, like meditation. Take a nice deep breath, close your eyes, clear your mind..." They demonstrated as they spoke, wiggling themselves into a more comfortable position, back straight, long arms resting easily on their knees, head tilted back a little. The last of the light was fading out of the sky, catching them in profile and touching their mane with flecks of gold. Kah copied them, but didn't close his eyes when he leaned his head back. Instead, he looked at the stars.

Stars were nothing. On a scientific level they were burning gas, some compressed under their own weight, some consuming everything around them, and some locked in gravitational dances so complicated that simulating them could confound even the most advanced computers. But on a practical level, what were they? The only one they ever interacted with was the one that was fast slipping away over the horizon, taking with it both light and warmth. The rest were mirages, after-images of galactic history, faint reminders of what had been rather than what currently was.

"How many of the stars are real?" he asked, and Inatu and Kiyah both burst out laughing. "I mean, some of them are probably gone now, but the light's only just getting here. When I was up there, I kept wondering if one day I might see a new one—only what if it wasn't new at all, but was just a ghost of one that's already died."

"You haven't asked questions like that since you really were a child," said Kiyah.

Kah smiled, remembering the days when he had chased her around after meetings, babbling out his questions while she packed up candles as folded up blankets, and scrubbed away the circles the Coven used for their rituals. There had been a lot more of them back then, but time and age and complicated life commitments had thinned their numbers, and now—for this Coven at least—it was just the three of them.

"Can't your scientist friends tell if they're still there or not?" asked Inatu. "Analyse the light coming from them, or something?"

"I don't know. Maybe. I really wanted them to help me analyse the radio wave data we were picking up out there. See if there might be some residual echo from deep space lay-lines..."

"From what now?" Inatu chuckled.

Kah looked at them, blinking away the after-images of the stars and peering into the dark to see them. Night was truly upon them now, turning everything to velvet shadows and intriguing shapes, with the sole exception of the remains of Kah's tea, which was phosphorescing gently in his mug. He downed it quickly, relishing the tremor of energy it sent through him as he swallowed. For a moment his head swam, the final drops tipping him from sober into the slightly altered state that the ritual required.

"I was thinking, our planet can't be the only one that's alive," he said, wiping his mouth with his trunk and carefully putting his mug down just outside the circle. "And then I thought, if planets are alive, then why not space itself? Space is a vacuum. A nothing with lots of bits floating in it...but then so is an atom when you look at it with the right machines. And if space *is* alive, then it should have lay-lines in it too, just like the planet does, and like we do."

"We have arteries and veins," said Kiyah.

"Yes, and they carry our energy in them just like the lay-lines do," Kah replied.

"I like the idea of that—spacey lay-lines, stretching across the universe," said Inatu dreamily. "Will they not help you look for them, Child?"

"My Love, they were just far more interested in seeing how crystals grow without gravity," Kah replied. He wanted to be bitter about it, but it was hard to focus on that now.

He felt the lay-line pulsing deep underground, because its energy was pulsing inside of him as well. The first time he had drunk the water here, he had been laid out cold for eight hours straight; he had more tolerance for it now, but it was still a powerful and heady feeling.

"I assume they still looked like crystals," said Inatu, and he told them that yes, they did.

The air was getting colder, and Kah felt his skin prickling as his vellus fluffed up to help keep him warm. This was the night of Summer, a celebration observed between the equinox and the solstice, its rituals handed down for untold generations. Warmth was at its core (even when the chosen ritual spot was anything but), and Kah could feel his thoughts drifting toward flames and fire, and the heavy heat of sunlight on a cloudless day. Most of it was memories from the car ride, but there were other images too, strange ones that seemed to intrude upon his thoughts like steam leaking through cracks in an unfastened window. Growing roots, expanding leaves, the clatter of movement with more legs than he had or gliding without any legs at all, a sensation of excitement, of recklessness and joy and anticipation. A part of him wanted to get up and run, not to go anywhere but purely for the joy of being alive and free.

Across the circle, Kiyah gave a decisive nod to nobody in particular and hunched herself over.

"It's time," she said, and put out her hands, reaching for them both.

Kah took her right hand in his left and held out his other to Inatu, who laced their fingers into his and squeezed his hand fondly. The feel of hands against his own seemed to chase away the memory of isolation, and he relaxed into it, the last of his uncertainty melting away into darkness. He exhaled slowly through his nostrils, and his breath steamed like smoke, still carrying the last few flickers of phosphorescence. Inatu did the same, then giggled at the curling patterns rising above them.

Kiyah broke the circle momentarily so she could swat Inatu's knee with the back of her hand. "Stop it, both of you! Concentrate."

"We're being dragons," said Inatu.

"You're being something, all right," said Kiyah.

Kah grinned, but managed to keep himself from sniggering. He tried to keep his mind on the present, and keep it from wandering off to the myriad of places it wanted to go. He found himself thinking of the water dripping in the empty cave, and the strata of the rocks that trapped the rare bursts of rainfall so high above sea level. He watched the last of his steaming breath fade as it rose towards the sky where he had spent so long alone and wondered if he might ever chase it back up there. He thought about the sun, hidden now but ultimately responsible for so much, including the gently spinning orb on which all things lived. Nothing could survive without the sun; creatures swarming in the darkest places beneath the oceans, or bacteria hidden in the ice sheets at the poles—even they owed their life to the sun, because it had made the world, crafting it from dust and rock and warming it until it began to breathe. But what had birthed the star? Or the galaxy it hung in?

Kah thought all these things, his breath deepening and his heartbeat slowing until it was in sync with the deep thrumming of the Line far below them. He twitched his fingers and felt both Inatu and Kiyah squeeze back in reply.

"Three as one," he breathed, and Kiyah—who should have begun the chant—let go of his hand and flicked his thigh just as she had chastised Inatu.

"Three as one," she said, and he could hear the amusement in her voice, which only made him smile even more. On his other side, Inatu gave the reply.

"And one as three," they said carefully, as if it were taking effort to make the words. He wondered what they were thinking about, and braced himself for the moment when he would find out.

"Parent, Partner, and Progeny," said Kiyah, and Inatu chuckled darkly. She sighed. "What?"

"We're a terrible Coven," they said, barely able to contain their amusement.

Kah felt a surge of something, like a shiver running up his arms, and got a split-second image of something that was not of his own mind. Laughter, absurdity. Not unkind or uncaring but abstract, observant. It came with the smell of body lotions and the chatter of lots of people talking, their voices mixed together with faint music and the clatter of passing feet. It was the shopping centre that Inatu worked at—the sounds and smells of the shop they spent so much of their time in. Kah had never been there, but he welcomed the sensations like old friends. Then Kiyah let go of his hand, and it was gone just as fast as it had come.

"We are not terrible," said Kiyah.

"*You're* not—you're actually a mother—but *we're* awful," Inatu tittered. "Kah's older than me, but he's the Progeny!"

"The Progeny is always learning," said Kiyah.

"And I'm the Partner and I've never even had sex!" Inatu continued, ignoring her and chuckling between the words.

"Because you like people," she said firmly. "Honestly, we go over this every year—*every bloody year*—and I keep telling you that if you want to swap, you can!"

"Oh no—I don't like people at all," said Kah, and that was too much even for Kiyah, who burst out laughing as well. Inatu's fingers slid out of his grip so they could clasp both hands over their mouth and giggle helplessly for a few minutes.

"You *are* both terrible," said Kiyah, "but we are not a terrible Coven. Now behave yourselves and give me your damn hands."

"Yes, Mother," said Kah, and held out his hand.

Inatu echoed him amid another attack of giggles, but managed to rein it in enough to hold out their hands as well. It took a moment for them all to settle down, and for Kah to get his breathing level again. This time he closed his eyes, hoping it would speed up the process, but all it did was show him the infinite darkness of his own eyelids, shot through with pulsing lines and flickering colours that were every bit as mysterious and fascinating as the night sky above him. It was hard not to chuckle at the comparison; he thought of worlds within worlds, from the microorganisms living on his skin to the atom-like arrangements of planets spinning around stars.

"Three as one," said Kiyah, and Kah snorted with laughter, wondering if the bacteria inside his gut ever met up in little circles to marvel at the majesty of his colon.

"And one as three," said Inatu, sounding somewhat strangled.

"Parent, Partner, and Progeny," said Kiyah, now with a note of warning in her voice.

Kah took a deep breath, trying to hold back another bout of giggles so he could answer.

"Hand in hand, for all to see."

It took longer to come than it would have done if they hadn't all been laughing, but when it did it was electric. He felt the rush of the air conditioning in the shopping centre, and the cool breeze drifting past patterned curtains in Kiyah's kitchen. He saw a dozen places at once, all layered over the inside of his eyelids: Kiyah's garden, where her grandchildren were chasing each other around the flower beds, and the ceiling of Inatu's bedroom which was plastered with stickers that they collected from protests and concerts. He saw the things they knew best:

the canteen at the hospital where Kiyah had worked for forty years, and the faces of Inatu's many friends. Houses he had never lived in melted together with views from windows, hallways in schools, books on shelves, gatherings of people talking over plates of food. His own life was there too, hidden among the less familiar. Blue carpets under cold strip-lights, the buttons of the capsule's control panels, his own reflection in glass, and the feeling of clothing brushing against a weightless body. A year of their lives mixed and rolled between them— laughter, sadness, and the endless drift of space.

They repeated the chant, all three of them together, though Kah could never tell if they were speaking out loud or merely repeating it in their minds. The bond between them felt endless, the lines between who each of them were seeming to thin almost to nothing. He was aware of the earth beneath his naked body, and the frigid air as he drew it into his lungs, but they were passing sensations as a world of others flickered through his nerves. He felt the way that Kiyah's breasts pulled at her shoulders, and the curious weight of having a womb even though his own had been removed. He felt the cramp forming in Inatu's left leg, which was tucked under their body a little more closely than was comfortable, and the tickling urge to laugh that was making their breath hitch. It was infectious. He hadn't laughed properly for so long, and it felt good. It wasn't even that anything was funny anymore, just that the world was amazing and he was genuinely glad to be a part of it.

They said the chant again, and even familiar body-senses began to be eclipsed. He felt the earth not just as a substance to sit on but as a packed conglomerate of particles, jostling one another and shifting restlessly under his weight. He felt the air, and tasted a thousand drifting aromas that it had collected on its travels. He sensed the bubbling, bustling passage of water trapped inside the mountains, each molecule fighting its way towards the crack that would release them into the cave. He felt the swell of pressure over mountain ranges, and the blissful release of rain over the lowlands. He tasted thunder, and smelled the budding charges that would soon be sheets of lightning.

When he opened his eyes, the sky was clear and full of stars.

He laughed. Not much, just a cackle, as quickly gone as the lightning he had sensed in some other part of the world. It was enough to set Inatu off, though, and he could feel through their bond that it was a tidal wave they had only just been holding back. That made him laugh again, harder this time, caught up in his friend's emotions. Somewhere in the middle of it, he picked up a surge of exasperated amusement from Kiyah. He thought he heard her talking, but it was hard to pick the words out of the brilliant jumble of feelings and thoughts rushing through his mind. He knew she was telling them both to settle down, so he tried to. He tried to breathe through the laughter, and when that failed, he pulled back a hand and clapped it over his mouth.

"Kah!"

For a dizzying half second, he was just himself again. He was sitting in the cold on top of a mountain, contained in his own skin, his thoughts entirely his own. He was looking at the long stretch of milky blue in the ink-dark sky where a distant spiral arm crossed above them, and the stars were shining brightly. In that moment he saw it with a clarity he had never had before, and marvelled at how he had never noticed what was now so obvious. There it was—a lay-line in the sky, not just a drifting bank of stars but a flowing band of energy, radiating out from the very heart of the galaxy itself. He reached out, snatching at a hand to remake the circle, knowing that he ought not to have let go but mesmerised by what his lapse in judgement had shown him. He felt fingers close to his and caught hold of them, wrapping them in his own, and felt the incoming pulse of consciousness.

"*Kah!* Hand! Now!"

But both his hands were full. He squeezed the fingers he was holding and felt a rush of unfamiliar feeling, both through his hand and in his mind. Unusual emotions rushed through him, similar enough to be familiar yet not quite as they ought to be. Images of faces that were flat and narrow, tiny button eyes in bright colours flashing past under blue skies, the sound of voices saying words he didn't know. The hand he was holding felt different, the fingers short and bare, like the hand of a child.

There was confusion—his own, and Inatu's, and somebody else's, but it did not feel like Kiyah. She was still present, but her thoughts were all delight and the kind of smug amusement that only grandparents are ever really capable of.

"Honestly, Kah, what have you done? You've broken the circle and now we're interrupting somebody else's evening," she said, and he could not answer, because he was too busy looking to his left, to the spot between them that was nothing but cliff-side and night.

In his mind, lost in the deep tangle of thoughts and emotions, he could see another face there, looking up at him. A small, naked thing, hairless but with a mane, flat-faced, trunkless, puffy around the mouth in ways he couldn't quite describe. The scientist in him could guess at what it was that he was seeing, but he could not quite believe it, nor put it into words. And then there was a thought, as clear as any he had ever felt:

I didn't want to be alone.

"You're not alone," said Kiyah, smiling warmly, eyes still closed. "None of us are ever really alone, no matter how far apart we are,"

"That wasn't me," he said. Next to him, Inatu laughed nervously and squeezed his hand. They were looking too, and perhaps they were also seeing what he was seeing.

"I know," said Kiyah. "But you'd do well to learn that too, Kah."

The spell wavered, the energy in the tea nearly spent. Kah looked down at the little creature that was with them but not, and it said words to him, and he nodded, understanding them only through the flood of emotions that they came with.

"Blessed be, friend," he said, and held on to the fading fingers until the last fleeting sensation was gone, and the thoughts inside his mind were just his own.

They sat on the cliff top in the dark, the old woman and her two young friends. For a very long time nobody spoke.

"They will be alone, though, once the Line is purged," Inatu said at last. They had drawn up their knees, and hugged them to their body against the icy chill. Kah shivered too, but it felt more like adrenaline than cold.

"It's as I said: a living organism of many parts, Kah, and no part is ever really alone," said Kiyah. She pulled herself to her feet and stretched languidly, which made her spine click. "Though," she added thoughtfully, "it might be an idea to find a better way to talk to one another. You should ask them about it after we drop you back at the base, Kah. Maybe searching for aliens will distract them from this purge nonsense."

"I doubt it," said Kah, but he dared to hope, and overhead the stars twinkled brightly in the darkness, as wonderful and as distant as they had ever been.

INK AND STARS

Alex Harrow

Warning: mild body horror, sexual content

Magic never lied.

Which would have made things far too easy, Chaz Neoma supposed. No, for this, they only had themself to blame.

"You," Chaz drawled, sprawled naked and on their back in Liam Morgenstern's bed, "are a spectacularly terrible idea."

Chaz had known that long before their needles had etched the first line of black ink into Liam's umber skin. They should've never taken this job, never mind how good the money was. Never mind how thrilling it felt to finally carve their art and magic into Liam's skin.

The thought made the ever-present hum of Weave magic flowing through Chaz's veins and its manifestations inked all over their body swell to a roar that only their hands and needles on Liam's skin could soften. And even then, part of Chaz knew the blood welling at their needles demanded something closer. Something more like lips and tongue.

Parts most definitely not outlined in the standard waivers Chaz had all clients sign.

And this was much worse than a combination of magic and desire.

Bad enough to mix tattooing with stolen goods, especially when it involved lifting a ship out from under an agent of the Allied Planetary Forces. With anyone else, this would have been one by the books: drug the pilot, disable the ship's navcom, jettison the ship's original crew off to the closest deserted moon in the ship's short-range escape pods, bag another ship jacking that'd result in a happy bidder, and secure a full account for Chaz. Knowing this ship was one of the APF's only sweetened the deal.

But this was Liam fucking Morgenstern, one of Chaz's oldest friends, and quite often, lovers. The one person whose lure Chaz had never been able to escape—the worst mistake in Chaz's life, and one they'd make over and over again, given the chance.

"Am I now?" Liam's tongue traced the sensitive skin below Chaz's navel, following a cluster of triangles tattooed there, the movement punctuated with enough teeth to make Chaz hiss and dig their fingers into Liam's tangled sheets.

The nest of soft pillows on Liam's oversized bed seemed at odds in the middle of what must've been a freight captain's utilitarian cabin once, but now was transformed into something luxurious and unabashedly frivolous in minimalism, paired with real linen and silks. Holographic fireflies twinkled in the air, illuminating Liam's tight black curls like fairy lights. Their lazy dance left shimmering contrails painted across riveted metal walls, glowing and fading to the rhythm of soft music coming from the ship's speakers set into the ceiling above.

It was exactly what Vee used to call Liam's Fuck Me Playlist, usually before she gave it one particularly exaggerated rendition at Academy Karaoke Nights, just to get a rise out of Liam.

In the middle of a cargo glider, this space was a definite reminder of the three of them. It had Liam's penchant for hedonism, the soft purples and pinks that echoed Chaz's ever-changing hair, and the fireflies were definitely Vee's touch, even though she'd never admit as much.

Gods, Liam had even named the ship SWIFT—almost certainly a fuck-you to the Old patriarchal Earth trend of naming ships after women. Bet Vee was thrilled about that. Unlike Chaz, she'd never wavered from Liam's side, no matter what the universe or the APF threw at them. Chaz used to envy her ability to stay. Now those thoughts opened a scab in the shape of Liam and Vee deep inside Chaz. Stars, Vee would punch them if she learned Chaz'd come back without telling her.

Chaz longing to tell Liam *why* they were really here, what this pretense of reconnecting with Liam for old time's sake really was, would give her good reason.

Even if right now, Chaz rather enjoyed those pretenses, even as they failed to convince themself that *pretense* was all this was.

Liam paused their exploration and rose to regard Chaz with a knowing stare. They'd always read them far too well for comfort. "Getting distracted already? I must be getting rusty."

"Just taking in the scenery." Chaz smiled through the urge to add *I missed you*. They knew better than to sharpen this moment with additional knives.

"That so?" They sucked their bottom lip between their teeth and dramatically trailed a hand down the front of their body. "Well, then let me give you a refresher. Can't have you getting lost."

A mischievous glint in Liam's eye was all the warning Chaz got before Liam leaned down and bit the soft skin along Chaz's left collarbone, *hard*, hard enough bruise. They kissed, licked, and nipped their way down, letting pleasure patch the gap the missing years had torn between them, even if only for a little while.

Stars, this wasn't how Chaz had planned to do this.

And yet...

And yet, the shards of magic Chaz had embedded into the ink forming intricate constellations on Liam's shoulder only added to the way Liam Morgenstern made Chaz's magic hum with the need.

Like Chaz, the Weave craved connection. Its shards were scattered across galaxies in a diaspora not even the history books fully recollected. Some argued Weavers had always been nomads, outliers looking for a lost home none of them truly remembered. Maybe that's why it'd always been easy for Chaz to run. Maybe it was in their nature, snaking through them deeper than the Weave did.

And yet, however long or far they ran, they always found their way back to Liam.

"Yeah," Chaz gasped, the syllable caught on a moan as Liam delved deeper. "You're the absolute worst."

"Good." Liam's silken whisper stroked the sensitive skin inside Chaz's thighs. Chaz felt their lips curve into a smile. Heard the warmth in Liam's voice, at odds with their usual commanding tone—barking sharp orders at unsuspecting cadets, making demands, taking names. "Anything else would put an awful damper on my reputation. Can't have that."

"Hmmm," Chaz hummed in languid assent, brushing a curl of purple hair out of their eyes. "That much hasn't changed, then. Still too worried about what others think of you. Thought Vee'd have set you straight about that by now. Where's she anyway? Figured I'd see her earlier."

Liam tensed. Chaz cursed themself and bit back the need to apologize, though they weren't quite sure what for. Wasn't like they were doing anything Vee didn't know about. Besides, they'd both known each other far too long to believe apologies ever truly made up for anything they'd flung at each other. They'd always let actions do the talking instead.

It might've been a blip, but the soft lighting seemed to flicker and the music cut out, as if the ship itself was somehow in tune with Liam's easy movements and something had thrown it off.

Instead of continuing on their path, Liam pushed themself up on their elbows between Chaz's legs. Dark eyes regarded Chaz through long lashes—sensuous a moment ago, and now guarded with uncertainty. Chaz had caught glimpses of that same hesitance while tattooing Liam earlier, but it had felt too raw to comment on.

"I don't know about you, but in my line of work that kind of concern is a survival trait. As is being attuned to cues." Liam sat back on their knees. "We don't need to do this right now if you're not—"

"No." Chaz placed a finger against Liam's lips. "That's not what I meant at all. I'm just..."

Falling into bed with a mark to distract them. Not telling Liam the truth about this job or how desperately Chaz wished they could stay. Just this once. Talk about hitting a new personal low.

Chaz swallowed and settled for "It's been a while, is all."

That much at least was true. It'd been three years since Chaz had last seen Liam, and still, they made every fiber of Chaz's magic sing to a tune only Liam knew by heart. It'd been too late before they'd asked Liam to take off their tight-fitted black jacket, revealing the curve of a shoulder strangely delicate on a person made of nothing but sharp angles and precisely executed orders.

Chaz's eyes remained drawn to that same spot, the place they'd spent hours relearning beneath gloved hands and the vibrations of their tattoo machine. The constellation they'd inked into Liam's skin was beautiful in its simplicity, each line imbued elegantly with the slightest shimmer of holographic fluid laced into the ink— at odds and at peace with itself, much like Liam themself. "If you're sure."

"I'm sure. Please."

Casual sex had never been something Chaz was interested in. Definitely on the gray side of asexuality, Chaz needed more than physical attraction for them to consider the intimate vulnerability of sex. But Liam— sensual, deeply sexual Liam, whose body was their very own kind of love language, one they shared liberally and with great abandon—was an exception. They'd never pushed Chaz. Never crossed any boundaries Chaz hadn't explicitly opened to them. Liam had understood that intimacy took time and trust for Chaz, and they never rushed them. Never went further than Chaz was willing to go. Always left them an out. Even when it had meant Chaz walking away. For both theirs and Liam's sake.

"Okay. Let's put that to the test then. Just tell me when, yeah?"

Chaz barely got a tight nod in before Liam captured Chaz's mouth in a bruising kiss. Chaz remembered comparing Liam's kisses to a sport once. A sport whose rules and execution Liam had studied to perfection. And like any star athlete, Liam wasn't shy about showing off their skills, with Chaz a more than willing participant.

"Okay?" Liam checked once they let Chaz come back up for air.

"Stars, yes."

Liam's grin kindled a fire deep in Chaz's chest. "Good. How about this?"

Chaz wanted to tell them to stop talking. Stop anything but their slow progress down Chaz's body, each bite, nip, and kiss interspersed with just enough pauses to allow Chaz to tell them to stop if they needed to.

Except stopping was the last thing on Chaz's mind, no matter the consequences.

Three years without Liam, and Chaz was right back where they'd broken off, the mingling scent of blood, fresh ink, and witch hazel ointment still lingering in the air quarters. Tangled with the very last person Chaz should get themself involved with.

Not when they had both broken this off years ago, their promises to stay in touch scattered like stardust.

Not when Liam's uniform and position stood for everything Chaz had crossed galaxies to get away from.

Not when Chaz was here on a deadline.

Given the types of bidders they'd taken on lately, that term was rather literal. Which meant they'd need Liam distracted and as far away from the line of fire as possible. Chaz may hate themself for it, but when it came down to it, they were caught between fucking and betraying Liam for the sake of a con or letting that same con result in Liam getting killed. Two terrible options, but only one Chaz was willing to live with.

And so, Chaz allowed themself to lie back, hands tangled in Liam's loose curls, each gasped "yes" and "more" rewarded with appreciative sounds and smiles against the fine hair between Chaz's thighs, where Liam proceeded to slowly, methodically, take Chaz apart with their tongue, fingers, and breath.

*

"Hey," Liam said some time later, their bodies hot and sticky against the mess they'd made of the sheets. "SWIFT to Neoma. You still with me?"

Chaz must've nodded off because it didn't sound like this was the first time Liam had tried to get their attention. They were about to ask what the Swift was; then the reference clicked and what came out instead was "Does Vee know you named a ship after her?"

And just like that, Chaz realized they'd said something very, very wrong.

All traces of lazy fluidity evaporated from Liam's body. "All right," they said with a flatness that raised goose bumps on Chaz's sweat-slick skin. "Let's do this."

Before Chaz could get another word in edge-wise or ask Liam why the hell they'd reacted like Chaz'd punched them, Liam pushed away. The harsh lines of their shoulders suddenly formed an impenetrable barrier, locking Chaz out as effectively as a door shut in their face.

Chaz's heart fluttered, then sank into the indentation Liam's body left. They rose from the bed and crossed the room, dragging Chaz's heart with them only for it to sink deeper, like a skipping stone that lacked the momentum needed to clear rippling waters.

"Liam, what—"

"Please. Don't." All sensuality bled from Liam's voice. Their Agent Face, a term penned back when they'd both been young and naive enough to joke about such things, hardened his expression.

"Now that the pleasantries are over, let's talk about why you're really here."

Chaz closed their eyes. Made themself inhale and exhale slowly. Forced their muscles to unclench and resisted the urge to clutch the silken sheets, as if the fabric was some flimsy stand-in for the wall that had suddenly manifested between them and Liam in the space of poorly timed words.

Chaz knew better than to defend themself or play ignorant. All that would do is send Liam into a tailspin. Chaz would be lucky if they only ended up in the SWIFT's brig, with a one-way ticket to an Allied Planetary Forces holding cell.

"Okay," Chaz said. Swinging their legs over the side of Liam's bed, they rose as dignified as one could, stark naked, and freshly fucked—in more than one way. "Can we at least get dressed first?"

Liam snorted. There was no humor in the sound. "What, you decide now's the time to remember who you are?"

Chaz clenched their teeth and let the insult roll off without a response. Given the circumstances, this wasn't scratching the surface of all the things Liam could have hurled at them.

Liam nodded stiffly and jerked their chin at the trail of clothing they'd left in their haste to get each other undressed. "And don't even think about going for that stun-blade. If I even see a trickle of magic—" Their hand hovered over their own blaster.

"Wouldn't dream of it." Chaz winced and only allowed themself to mourn the absence of anything soft holding Liam's sharp edges together. They deserved as much. Worse, probably, given how willingly they'd betrayed the person who had stood shoulder to shoulder with them longer than anyone else ever had.

Getting dressed gave them a few precious moments to brace for the oncoming storm. Compared to Liam's set of all-black combat fatigues, Chaz's loose, ripped jeans, a gray chest binder, and their favorite synth-leather jacket made for a poor excuse for armor. As they'd covered themself in a collection of several galaxies' worth of tattoo designs and spent years growing comfortable in their own flesh, Chaz had given up trying to hide their body under too many layers. Still, the urge to place anything they could between them and Liam became an itch that pulsed in time with the magic beneath their skin.

Inhale. Exhale.

Chaz squared their narrow shoulders and faced Liam head-on. "Who told you?" And, because Chaz was desperate for any ally and this was fixing to be a no-win scenario already, "And where's Vee? She usually wouldn't leave your side—"

Liam's stricken expression made the words go dry in the back of their throat. Liam looked gray, their full lips narrowed into a tight line. It was as if Chaz had pulled a knife and stuck them right through the ribs.

"Liam?" Chaz took a tentative step, then stopped. Part of them ached to touch Liam, to keep the pieces of their suddenly cracked facade from falling apart completely. Another wanted to put as much distance between them and Liam as the small space permitted. Liam looked ready to punch them. Even years later, Chaz's muscles still remembered every single sparring match they'd ever lost to Liam. "What is it? What happened? Is Vee—"

Overhead, one of the ship's speakers crackled loud enough to make Chaz flinch.

"You need to come with me," Liam said, voice toneless and distant. "Now."

Despite the ship's central heating, the flat edge to Liam's words made Chaz shiver and draw their jacket more tightly around themself. "All right"—and because of Chaz's masochistic mood—"just tell me when."

Stars, thinking about Liam naked and between Chaz's legs did not help matters. At all.

Liam's tight black fatigues managed to accentuate every tight muscle along their torso and upper arms. Which brought memories of those same arms pinning Chaz against the wall of an already narrow supply closet during their Academy Days.

"Just walk, Neoma." Liam's growl yanked Chaz back to the present. Ushered them down the corridor Chaz remembered, only fleetingly, from their earlier stumble into Liam's room. The SWIFT's shape was inspired by a stingray, an Old Earth species of maritime life Chaz had often been asked to tattoo on people from various corners of the universe.

Thanks to its AI autopilot setting, the SWIFT didn't technically need a crew to safely navigate it through the black—a convenience Chaz had initially appreciated. Running into any members of Liam's APF squad would have put quite a damper on their tête-à-tête.

So, why couldn't Chaz shake the prickly feeling they were being watched? They scanned for cameras overhead, but the ones in plain sight were dark—operational sometime during the previous century.

As Liam directed them past the ship's small cargo hold and down a hatch that, if Chaz's knowledge of the small craft they were hired to steal didn't fall short, would take them to the ship's power supply and engine room, Chaz couldn't help but suspect that being alone with someone as dangerous as Liam Morgenstern didn't exactly boost their chances of coming out unscathed.

One, Liam had the home advantage. Quite literally, as they seemed to know every corner of the ship much more intimately than Chaz would have expected.

And two, something about the ship pinged a deep-seated, deeply superstitious part of Chaz's outer-rim upbringing. *Spaceships could have souls.* They'd always believed that the idea was bullshit superstition.

Until now.

Maybe it *was* a bullshit superstition. Maybe it was Chaz's nerves, frayed tatters after their reintroduction to Liam Morgenstern's hot and cold. Maybe crackling speakers and flickering lights were evidence of how no one should've sent Chaz on this run to secure anything more than an outdated rust bucket in the first place. But one thing kept pinging them, deeper than even the current of their magic. Something that responded to Liam as if the last three years had been but a blink of an eye.

No, this ship wasn't a failed mission. This ship... wanted something from Chaz and their magic. It tugged on them, sending pulses that curled like tiny claws into their mind, their muscles, pulling them further and further inward. It was as easy, as terrifying—and as ridiculous—as that.

Descending further and further into the SWIFT's bowels felt like climbing into the maw of a dragon, waiting to bite down and devour them. It also felt like answering an unspoken. *Closer. Keep coming.*

Dents and scrapes from long years of intergalactic warfare were etched into the ship's narrowing walls, and certainly didn't help disillusion Chaz. Neither did the erratic overhead lights that cut out just in time for Chaz to almost lose their footing. They walked along a corridor of jagged teeth, some broken and dull, where the ship must've taken too many close hits.

"I really hope you're not getting me all the way down here just to throw me out of the next airlock," Chaz said, if only to fill the emptiness around Liam's stony silence.

The only answer they got was the scraping of the air filtration system. Chaz sighed, hating how Liam's presence at their back—even menacing—made their skin itch with the need to wrap their magic around Liam. To tighten the invisible tether between Chaz and the flecks of magic embedded into the star chart inked on Liam's shoulder.

Fuck. This was exactly why Chaz never inked anyone they knew. When magic was involved, the process of tattooing was as intimate as sex—more than, in some ways. As a Weaver, Chaz's art became a unique outlet for their magic's intrinsic need to spread, connect, *live*. A tap from the metaphysical to the physical, with Chaz merely the conduit to facilitate the flow of one into another. Their art became a way to propagate their magic, to keep it alive by scattering it through entire galaxies, drop by drop.

With Chaz's usual clients, it worked exactly like that. Chaz purposefully didn't stay long in any given space. As a result, most of their clients remained nameless faces who signed the appropriate waivers and didn't form a personal connection with Chaz—other than the sessions it took to bring their design to life. Which was where their reputation for minimalist tattoos came from—small enough to finish in one sitting, usually, yet showcased enough detail and skill to keep word-of-mouth traveling ahead of them. Which secured full books and happy shop owners who never failed to offer Chaz exclusive, and short-lived, guest spots.

Until a job came along that Chaz couldn't refuse. Because try as they might, part of them had never fully escaped Liam Morgenstern. Now they were going to pay the price for thinking they could have another shot at what they used to have.

Serves me right for being a stars-be-damned idealistic idiot.

Liam stopped them in front of a heavy steel door to the left of the SWIFT's engine room.

Liam stepped in front of them, their rigid back effectively blocking Chaz's view from a biometrics scanner coded to Liam's features. It was much more thorough than the advanced scanners Chaz had come across in their cat-burgling years. Impressive. The scanner took its time, waving back and forth across Liam's face.

"What are you hiding? The Allied Forces' Crown Jewels?" Chaz asked.

Of all the reactions they'd anticipated from Liam, the flash of abject grief that streaked their face was not it.

"Frankly, I would take whatever the APF throws at me over this any day." A mirthless grin slashed Liam's face like an open wound. "Then again, I suppose, that's exactly what this is."

"Um. You going to let me in on what's going on or—"

The words shriveled in the back of Chaz's throat as the door slid open.

"Wh—what...?" Chaz staggered back, their eyes fixed on the horror in front of them. "Liam? What the hell is this?"

"Not what," Liam said quietly. "Who. You said you wanted to know where Vee was."

Chaz blinked. Swallowed against the threat of bile rising in their throat.

Before they could say anything else, or their brain could fully process what—no, *who*—made up the SWIFT's power source, the lights flickered and a disembodied voice—too much like Vee Swift—said, "Hey, Chaz. I've missed you."

*

"Vee?" The name scraped their mouth. Before they could catch themself, they staggered toward a cryo-tank in the center of the room. The body inside floated, submerged in greenish-blue liquid, tethered by a tangle of tubes normally used to provide readouts on temperature and vitals while in stasis. Except there were no vitals readouts here. The analytical part of Chaz's brain kicked in. There wasn't enough undamaged surface tissue remaining to get a stable readout. This wasn't a life-saving measure. This was death suspended in false hope.

"What happened?" It took Chaz a moment to recognize the hollow question as their own.

"I died," Vee's voice said through the ship's comm.

Two words. Spoken entirely too matter-of-factly for Chaz to process while staring at Vee Swift's lifeless body— the ravaged husk left of it, burned nearly beyond recognition. The urge to argue, to deny this wasn't Vee, that it couldn't be, rose inside Chaz like a geyser, threatening to bubble to the surface. Then Chaz spotted the jagged remains of the tattoo they'd inked on Swift's shoulder, the design similar to, and in the exact place as, the one they'd put on Liam.

It didn't make any sense. None of this did.

Chaz stared at Liam who stood perfectly still in the entrance to the small room, regarding the cryo-tank with a faraway look.

"The APF sent us into an ambush," Liam said, each word inflectionless and mechanical. "They knew we wouldn't make it out in one piece. The mission was meant to be a recon. We didn't see the explosives until we were already in too deep. Vee—" Liam cleared their throat. "Vee went in to retrieve the systems core and try to disable the countdown. When she realized it was too late to get out on time, she triggered the blast doors to seal herself in and—" Liam closed their eyes.

"It's all right, love," Swift's eerie voice soothed through the ship's speakers. It sounded so damn real, and made the hairs at the back of Chaz's neck stand on end.

Liam shook their head, the curtain of their long black hair obscuring their face. "They called it acceptable losses in the debrief. The bastards just wrote you off like you were nothing, like you weren't—"

Yeah, Chaz thought. *That's just like the stars-be-damned Allied Planetary Forces. Playing their numbers game without any regard of who's at the losing end of it.*

They ached to reach out to Liam, to slip their hand into Liam's, to anchor them, because right now, they looked one crack away from shattering. But Chaz knew better than to try and touch Liam when they held themself like this, like someone bracing for a blow. Like they could block all their hurt with perfect posture.

Chaz thought the years between them would've cautioned against this: desperately wanting Liam to let them in. By now they should've known better.

"So what happened next?" Chaz asked, even though part of them hated using directness to deflect. Better to let slumbering dragons lie. Chaz was too exhausted to even call themself a coward for that.

At their side, Liam clenched and unclenched their fists, refusing to meet Chaz's eyes. "I found a Weaver."

Four words tipped Chaz's world. They shook their head. It didn't help. Their surroundings came unmoored, like the ship around them hurtled through an asteroid belt, dodging space trash with the gravity turned off.

"No." Chaz's voice rang hollow. Detached. "It's not possible."

Chaz had barely spoken before they noticed there was something wrong with the glass encasing the cryo-tank. At first it had looked smooth, if slightly distorted by the bubbles in the cryogenic fluid, just like any other standard-issue tank. Chaz had been so focused on the body floating inside, they'd missed the finely carved designs inlaid in the entirety of the tank's enclosure. The lines were faint in their delicacy. Nearly unrecognizable. Except Chaz had studied the language they formed longer than they'd been able to read the standard alphabet. They'd been sneaking them into their art for years before they figured out ways to layer them into the ink they put on people's skin, infusing each of their clients with their own unique sliver of magic, and thus keeping it alive across galaxies.

Someone had etched star runes into Vee's cryo-tank. The truth was etched into the glass right in front of them. The same runes that made Chaz's skin itch with restless magic, just in a different handwriting.

Liam had found another Weaver.

What was worse, the Allied Planetary Forces had gotten *their* hands on another Weaver.

After Chaz had spent most of their life searching for others, crossing entire star systems where Weavers were nothing but myth—stories told at bedtime, and in some parts, stories nightmares were made of. At some point Chaz had lost faith that people like them still existed. And now they stared at the proof they'd been looking for.

They weren't the last one. There was another. Maybe more.

Chaz's breath hitched, crashing against the prison of their ribs, suddenly too constricting to let in enough air.

"How?" The word emerged raspy, as if dragged across sandpaper.

"It was coincidence, really. The APF picked him up on a routine sweep months ago. Held him without charges while they investigated a kidnapping case he had some tenuous connection to." Liam shrugged. Shifted uncomfortably. "You know how it goes. They just kept coming up with new reasons to hang on to him. Transferred him to solitary when he became combative. Declared him unstable and a risk to himself and others when they found the runes he'd carved all over his cell with a spoon, his fingernails, whatever he could get his hands on."

Chaz squeezed their eyes closed, forced their hands to unclench before their knuckles cracked, or worse, before they lashed at Liam for being so fucking casual about the fate of a person. *A Weaver.* Someone who could've easily been Chaz if they hadn't cut their losses and ran from anything hinting at an APF uniform.

But Liam just kept talking, their voice flat and inflectionless. "That's how I found him. After Vee—" They shook their head, as if saying what had happened out loud made it too real. As if anything could be more real than the truth inscribed all over that tank, resonating in Vee's digitized voice filtered through the ship's speakers.

"Liam." Stars, she sounded exactly like Vee. Like she'd perfected Liam's mental spirals and knew when they needed something other than touch to ground them.

Liam's shoulders relaxed marginally in response. "I offered him his freedom in exchange for bringing Vee back."

"And made him do something Weaving was never meant for," Chaz finished through gritted teeth. "Stars, Liam. What have you done?"

"What I had to."

"Did you, really?" Chaz looked at the ship's comm output lining its ceiling, because it somehow felt better—anything felt better—than talking to Vee's impossibly still body. "And what about you? Are you okay with this?" The question sounded ridiculous spoken out loud, but Chaz wasn't going to stand there and pretend Vee didn't exist, in whatever form it might be.

"Well, I died, so. Not like I was exactly blessed with an overabundance of options here." Vee's desert-dry tone was playful, even in a situation like this.

Chaz would've laughed if they hadn't been so busy trying to keep a hold on the rapidly unwinding threads around them.

"So, yeah, I like living," Vee said, and Chaz swore they heard a shrug in her voice. "And if it's tethered to a ship's AI, like some cyber-gearhead's wet dream... Guess it could have been worse."

Which, of course, was the precise moment the SWIFT's proximity detectors set off in flashes and high-pitched warning shrieks throughout the ship's hull.

"Speaking of," Vee said casually, as if the ship's warning sensors weren't blaring all around them. "Guess the cavalry finally caught on. Took them long enough. They're slow without you, L."

Chaz tried to untangle the unspooling threads Liam and Vee had dropped on them. But they didn't have time. They didn't have the room to process, and life wasn't built on neatness. Every thought screeched to a rapid halt. "The cavalry. Wait—the gods-be-damned APF is tailing us? How in the black—" They swiveled to face Liam. "Are you going to tell me what the fuck is going on here?"

"Oh," Vee said, her voice suddenly small. "You haven't told them."

"Told me *what*?" Chaz almost had to shout the last word over the arrhythmic blaring of the ship's warning system, alerting them to the approach of three of the APF's fighters.

Liam pinched the bridge of their nose. Despite the flashing lights, the tic didn't disguise the shakiness in their fingers or the way they pointedly refused to look at Chaz, until they visibly drew themself together, their face sliding into cocky self-assuredness—an expression specifically designed to keep everyone at arm's length. "Right. When I said I wanted to know why you were really here, I lied. I knew about your contract to steal the SWIFT and sell her to your highest bidder." Their dark gaze pinned to Chaz. "Which happens to be me. Oh, and I saved you the hassle of stealing her for me. That bit, I managed all by myself."

"Well," Vee supplied, "I guess you could say I helped. A little."

Chaz nodded, the movement mechanical, a vain attempt to buy time. To remind themself to exhale before asking the question they already knew the answer to, but had to ask anyway, if for nothing else than to hear the answer from Liam's own lips. "What do you need me for then?"

Liam's laugh was a dry, lifeless thing. They knew what they were about to ask of Chaz was the thing they'd spent the last three years running from. And yet, Liam said it anyway.

"I need a Weaver."

*

Back in the Academy, when Chaz's anxiety had been at its worst, Liam had spent an entire night sitting in silence with them, not touching them, just being there through the quakes of a particularly bad panic attack. Chaz didn't remember how long it had taken for their heart and lungs to stop clenching, the rest of their body eventually following behind, but at the end of that long, sleepless night, Liam had left them with a promise.

Chaz's secret was safe with them.

Liam would never use it against them, and Liam would never take advantage of it.

Chaz wouldn't let them start now. They squared their shoulders. Lifted their chin. Forced their muscles to relax. "You know, all you needed to do was ask."

"I couldn't." Liam's smile should have softened their face, but it was a tight hairline crack through typically masked composure. They usually managed better than this. But then again, Chaz supposed, this was far from usual. "Not without letting the Allied Forces in on...everything."

In on you. On Vee. Stars.

Chaz wished they could pretend they didn't get it. But they'd been to the Academy. They knew how the APF operated. Just like they knew the Allied Planetary Forces were the closest thing to family Liam had ever had. And now they were putting that on the line. All for a slim chance to bring a woman they loved back from the dead and to patch things—or more?—with Chaz. Given the circumstances, both seemed pathetically unlikely.

"Then don't," Chaz said, and turned to the runes woven into Vee's tank. "Let me try and figure this out. Buy me time. Pretend you're still their hotshot star agent."

Liam stared at them. "Who says that's not *exactly* who I am?"

Chaz met their gaze. Liam tracked their nod toward Vee's tank. "Pretty sure this tells me all I need to know." And stars, they hoped they were right, because if they weren't and this was an elaborate APF trap set to ensnare one of the galaxy's last remaining Weavers... Chaz swallowed hard. Looked from Liam to the ceiling then to Vee's tank, and let their heart grow heavier than it already was.

Honestly, at this point, Chaz would've gone with them willingly, for no other reason than being too damn tired to run anymore.

"Just keep them busy—don't let them look at us too closely."

"Yeah. You've got it. Just." Liam turned and let out a huff, a sharp-edged, stifled sob. "Just fix her. Please."

*

A little more than ten minutes later, Swift said, "You can't fix me, can you?"

Liam had checked in with them a second time, their voice notably strained. The incoming messages from the APF fighters circling had become more and more forceful—spouting docking prerogatives and thinly laced threats about opening fire should the SWIFT continue to desist. Either Liam wasn't as convincing as they thought they were or the APF had caught on to them. With their luck, it was probably a mix of both.

"Just hold them off a little while longer," Chaz had replied through clenched teeth, fighting to keep a hold on their focus, lest the tenuous threads they'd woven between the magic layered over Vee's tank and the patterns inked into their skin slipped out of their reach.

They realized they'd been wrong when they'd compared this magic to a different handwriting. This was a different dialect: symbols hinting at an entirely different alphabet. Where Chaz's own Weaving always had a loose tug on their surroundings, a tether from one being's core to the next—pieces of it scattered across galaxies, hidden beneath layers of ink to create a fragile, but far-reaching web—this was much, *much* more condensed. Chaz's magic felt diluted in comparison. As if they'd run long and far enough to lose their connection.

And yet, every new symbol they deciphered, every new thread they plucked and interwove with their own, made their bones sing with the promise of power, the promise of a home they once believed was nothing but superstition. A way for Weavers to explain centuries of persecution and diaspora to the far-flung reaches of space. But this, more than any text or fable, made Chaz think that maybe, just maybe, this legendary place where Weave originated from, where there were no borders and divisions, just magic and the art of exploring it, might actually be real.

Chaz had given up the search for other Weavers years ago, convinced that the only way to keep the shredded remnants of their magic alive was to weave threads of it into the ink they put on their clients' bodies. It had been all but instinctual, a reflex tugging at each fiber of their being.

It wasn't until now that Chaz realized what a pale imitation of the real thing their tattoos had been. That what they'd been trying to do was weave a map across galaxies. A map that had brought them here, aboard a stolen vessel, tethered to the essence of a dead agent, and the last stop for another who had run out of options.

Chaz had never believed in fate or predestination.

The universe didn't work like that.

But Chaz *did* believe in taking a hint.

"Chaz?" Vee asked again. Her voice held an edge. It hadn't been the first time she'd tried to get their attention.

"No," they finally said, allowing themself to exhale carefully, focusing on clutching the magical strands that spanned around them. "I can't fix you, Vee. I'm sorry."

The ship dimmed, as if Vee pulled on the systems to make herself smaller. "Well. You tried."

Chaz shook their head, the movement tight and controlled. "No, sorry, I'm not saying this right. It's just a lot. This magic—" They closed their eyes, tried to dim the brightness of the Weave all around them. The Weave attached to every part of the room, a web of lightning radiating outward from Vee's tank, connected to the ceiling fibers, the riveted metal walls, the cracks in the floor, breaking it down into smaller and smaller particles, each irrevocably interconnected and alive. "If it was just a tether to tie you to this world even though—"

"Even though I'm dead."

"Yeah." Sweat prickled the back of Chaz's neck. Their binder tightened around their chest like a vise. "Except you're also *not*. Not completely. With your body in stasis and with the magic inscribed in the tank... It's a map, Vee. And I think it'll lead us to others like me. Other Weavers. And with them..." Chaz refused to lie to Vee. She deserved better than that. Besides, she'd never been the kind of person who'd take any bullshit. "I can't bring you back, but they might be able to. If there are more."

"And if this map of yours isn't a trap or just some giant fuck-you to me and the rest of the Allied Forces who imprisoned this guy for nothing other than existing," Liam finished the thought, suddenly at Chaz's side. Or rather, standing slightly above them, because at some point, Chaz had slid to the floor, their back leaning against the tank, the glass cool against their neck and the side of their face. Worry pinched Liam's expression. "You okay? Do you need—"

Chaz waved them away. "Fine." Liam inclined their head, though they both knew Chaz was lying. "I can tug on the Weave to cloak us, probably long enough to get out of the APF's perimeter. Just need you to be sure, because ''

"Because it means we're running," Liam said. Simplicity came and went, holding the words tight.

"Yeah, because we sure as shit weren't running before." Stars, if spaceships could snort in derision, Vee just might manage it. "Like we have another choice."

Chaz decided not to point it out, but technically *they did*, because really, it was Liam who had the choice to turn them over to the Allied Forces of Planets. With enough groveling and toeing the line, Liam might be reinstated, but it still left Vee dead—her tank to become an artifact the APF's data and encryption unit would pick apart. Same with whatever they'd scavenge of Chaz's magic.

"There is no other choice," Liam said, voicing aloud what they'd all been thinking. "We run. But we run toward a chance." Liam glanced at Chaz and held out their hand, posture fixed, resolved. Ready to take on whatever the universe threw their way. And then some, maybe. "You sure you're ready for this?"

It was a simple question, but Chaz knew Liam was asking for more than Chaz's magic. They were asking Chaz to run with them instead of from them. To stop chasing after their dying magic alone. To trust them, both Vee and Liam, to keep them safe, keep them flying, and keep their magic alive.

Some space triad they were.

It'd taken Chaz this long, three fucking years, to realize how much they'd missed them, facing down the Allied Forces and all.

Chaz grinned and took Liam's hand. Their magic merged with Liam's, locking a connection from the fresh ink on Liam's skin, to the remains of Vee's, and the rest of the ship. "Just tell me when."

HOROLOGIUM

Emmett Nahil

The chip tower had been shorting out for the better part of an hour. Mechanical bits pinged in the holding dock, away from the gyrating center of the intrafuse: tiny screws and metallic pieces rained down like earth-hail from the flayed core. Coeie wasn't particularly keen on chip repair as a general rule, but what must be done simply must be done. Gathering up their tools in one kit, they parsed what they needed: chip lodger in their left hand, portable vocarecorder in their right.

Flicking the heavy copper switch, they felt ship's internal cable system whirring and kicking up.

"TOLTEK THREE, REPORTING."

The baritone, clanging voice of the ship's comm system thrummed from some hidden place underneath Coeie's feet, echoing up through the notched floor paneling.

"Yeah, Toltek, command here."

"CONTINUED REPORT, CODE 4182. IMMEDIATE CHIP DOCK UNLOAD IN PROGR—"

"Shit, *shit, shitshitshit—*"

Fingers skittering down the still-shuddering chip command dock, Coeie felt a pressure headache starting high in their temples. The chip tower spewed, not only tiny gears and pins, but whole chips to boot, the plastic-bound bits of electronics shooting from their normal holding spaces and clattering against the metal floor.

The chip tower wasn't the most critical piece of engineering on the ship—that fine honor was designated to the basement-bound server banks and the airlock—but it was the most irritating. It controlled all the nonessentials, lights, comms, sample logs, and most of the transmissions, back to base. The nanny that minded Coeie's every move. Sorted among the dozens of polished, plastic chips were thousands of annoying, insignificant details painting a picture of everything that had happened on the ship for whoever knew how to read them. Older officers in the department mentioned ghosts inhabiting the vessel—springing up sometimes, right at the end of a long star-rotation—from within the consoles. Some even said that hidden deep within the code were shadows of what had yet to occur.

But this wasn't the end of a long rotation, and Coeie wasn't an older officer, and they weren't inclined to believe superstition. Not by a long shot.

*

The chips still clattered to the floor in waves, layers upon layers of the tiny lacquered bits tinkling to the metal ship deck.

They scrambled, long limbs flailing, trying and failing to catch the chips as they came down.

"Toltek, halt chip dock unload, *immediately*." Miraculously, Toltek listened. Risky as halting an action mid-command was, Coeie was prepared to take the chance. Maybe if they were lucky, they'd avoid losing light and sound barriers around the ship. Blackout conditions with nothing standing between the ship and the infinite danger of space was a sure way to fall into space-madness, and they certainly didn't have the time to deal with that kind of paperwork.

*

"TICK-TOCK."

"...Come again?"
But Toltek had fallen silent. If they didn't know better, they could have sworn the ship was saying its own name. The ship's grating baritone voice echoed throughout the command room. No other words came to clarify.

*

Coeie couldn't halt the shudder crawling its way down their spine, as if someone had cracked an egg over their head. The last of the fallen chips lay in clusters around their rubber-soled utility boots, and they bent to begin to pick through the pieces. They had never been more cognizant of the fact that they were the only administrating officer on the ship, that they had denied a copilot in favor of a solo harvest mission. That the Horologium Supercluster was over 700 million light years from home. From their planet, and the academy base office, and from the rest of the officers and any other help they could give. The knowledge of solitude rang through them like a funerary bell. Like a lone voice calling to prayer in the night, or like a ship deciding to speak into the darkness of its own volition.

*

Picking up the pieces was drudge work, nothing they weren't used to. The other downside of running a solo harvest was the simple fact that they had to do absolutely *everything* themselves.

No stone could be left unturned if the meal-vac decided to spit out empty casings instead of sausage, or if all the daily report logs were corrupting as soon as they were made, or if the windows decided to leak water for no reason one day. The harvesting was the easy part, mostly comprised of trips to the operations bay, and sticking their hands blindly in the claw grips used to collect promising-looking space rock. It was everything else that was hard. Not that Coeie was afraid of a little hard work, so to speak. Academy training had made sure that they were good with their hands, and their nervous personality made sure they kept enough spare tools and parts in their kit to fix pieces of the ship as they inevitably failed and glitched into oblivion.

After all, Coeie was only required to collect one multi-ton harvest rock a day, which left more than enough time to putter around the decks, asking Toltek questions and tinkering with the ship. From what they'd heard around base, other pilots liked to collect as many asteroid bits as their claw-hands could carry, hoping for a promotion, a bonus, or at least a pat on the head from a managing officer. The rocks this side of the supercluster were doubtlessly carrying thousands of intriguing elements, but Coeie's directive was, singly, concerned with gold.

None of the supervising expedition managers were willing to part with the notion that there were more valuable things in space, no matter how many times Coeie had tried to explain it to them. That if they could just collect a *few* samples, just a side trip here or there, nothing too far afield, it would all pay off in the end.

They'd know more, and wasn't that valuable? *Of course not*, the supervising expedition managers had said; they were an explorer-miner, and that was just how it had to be for the time being. Until base decided their scientific mind would best be used parsing plant samples on the other side of the star system, this was their reality. Relegated out amongst the less interesting stars and asteroids.

"Toltek, I'd like coordinates."

"CURRENT COORDINATE TRIANGULATION: 1.5 BILLION TETCHROMETERS STARBOARD CENTAURUS B, 2.5 BILLION TETCHROMETERS AFT MEGANON F."

Coeie barely held back a groan, raking their fingers over their curly, tightly buzzed hair, and scratched the back of their neck. For the seventh time in the past three days, the ship had begun to list away from the interior of the Horologium, where the ore clustering was supposed to be at its densest. Their patience was already stretched near the breaking point after the sixth course correction a few hours ago.

This floating, nuclear-powered disaster had been pitched to them by corporate mission control as a nearly automatic vessel—one barely needed to touch the controls to direct it. Point 'n' shoot away, no need to fuss with the knobs and buttons comprising the control panel and undersized handscreens. All updated hardware on a vintage frame, no need to worry about faulty automation...that was, until the automation started to do just that. They should have listened to their father and gone to flight school.

He would never have settled for being just some cross-galaxy picker, sniffing out rocks to grab. Coeie had watched him build a ship engine from scrap, organizing the parts neatly beside him on his workbench. The memory of the earthy, slick grease smell that stuck to his hands and shirt tugged at the pit of their stomach. He'd wanted Coeie to go into flight training, like most parents did. Reliable schedules, running shuttles for a while after school, and eventually, maybe, moving up into the army corps. The thought of running flights for the military had made them gag, even if it shouldn't have. Someone eternally barking orders at them struck them as no way to live.

Their last argument about it had occurred right before Coeie was scheduled to head off to the company base. It had hung heavy inside their chest, dulling bit by bit with the passage of days, weeks, and then months, leaving the impotent throb of guilt behind.

"Piece of *crap* ship," Coeie spat in lieu of a more openly derogatory curse, heading back from the engineering bay to the control room.

The room wasn't their favorite in the vessel, but the view almost made up for it. Almost. Windows cut holes out into the most-likely-infinite blackness of space, sparked up at irregular intervals with reflections from a nearby solar flare. The light drew their eye to the multitude of asteroids in this part of the galaxy, all striped with gold mineral veins like captive zebras with the world's worst camouflage.

It was no better for their sanity that the knobs for the controls moved on their own when the ship was on autopilot. The image of the control tower flashed in their mind's eye, the pile of chips leaping to their deaths as

Coeie stood there, unable to do anything but shout into the void, to the ship itself, for it to stop, *pretty* please.

The control tower had listened, and ceased spewing the chips as soon as they'd activated the voice command. They were grateful the speaker couldn't register the exhausted desperation they were sure was permeating their voice.

Something about the ceased command seemed impermanent, like the ship was simply waiting until Coeie walked out of the room, deciding whether or not to obey.

*

They'd been shaking off that prickling, ominous, feeling for almost two weeks now. The idea that the ship was holding its breath around Coeie, waiting for an opportune moment to inhale and move around like the living thing it really was. They supposed it was only right to call it by its given name, and endeavored to call the interface Toltek as much as possible, and to keep their negative comments about the speed and general durability of the handscreens to a minimum. Their father had warned them about getting attached to things that could break. What he didn't know wouldn't hurt him, Coeie supposed. But this week, as they entered the outer reaches of the supercluster, everything had begun to go sideways.

"TICK-TOCK."

Coeie whipped around at the sudden voice, as if there would be a clear source of the words other than Toltek, speaking out of turn. Just the ship command voice center, deciding to speak a non-command phrase, completely unprompted. They shuddered hard, peering from corner to corner, scanning the room. Nothing out of the ordinary jumped forth, just the same hexagonal room, well organized with wall-to-wall paneling in a dull shade of beige. Controls sitting in organized rows of knobs and buttons, just as before, dully shining underneath the artificial strip lights above their head.

Coeie had never known just what was inside the panels. They'd never seen the innards, even before takeoff. The entirety of the wiring was cut off, invisible. Only the fiddly little dials and switches remained. Maddeningly simple on the outside, when one knew the true complexity of the machine.

What was worse, upon reflection, was that Toltek was *in* there. Whatever motherboard generated that harsh baritone lived inside those panels. Or in the walls. Or somewhere within the body of the ship itself, buried deep.

*

The screwdriver seemed to jump to their hand from the emergency technical kit, kept tucked away in a miniscule compartment under the side panels. Front-facing boards came off easy, once they were able to pry out the thinly welded rivets keeping them in place. The edge of their pocket knife came in handy for that, letting crumbs of cheap alloy dust their lap. Taking the grates and dividers out next was trickier work, as they partitioned off wires and various connective joints which held the handscreens steady above. They lowered each piece gingerly, not willing to shatter the thick, reinforced glass framing each one. Wires came next, a veritable thicket of them, in dusty-looking primary tones.

Coeie parted them with the back of the screwdriver, a horrible, tense knot building in their stomach as they did.

The hole they'd created had enough space for their head and most of their narrow shoulders, and they peered into the wiring. Apprehension coiled in their gut.

A small, animal part of them wanted to flinch back, to hammer shut the compartment with as much alacrity as they could muster.

"Toltek's somewhere in there," they muttered to themselves, setting their jaw firmly and thrusting themselves back into the darkness.

*

Initially, blackness reigned. They blinked once, twice, if only to make sure their eyes were open at all.

"...Toltek?"

Snaking a hand upward past the wiring, they parted a slightly larger hole for themselves, eyes acclimating to the dark. Outlines became clearer and clearer. Pinpricks of light cast outward like miniscule lighthouses onto an open ocean. But the back of the compartment had begun to illuminate too. Coeie made out details, specificities of the circuitry within—

It was glowing.

The interior of the ship was *glowing*.

It was almost nothing at first glance, but the realization made them gasp, pushing their head backward and—

Pain. Sharp and insistent and tingling all at once, at the back of their head, generating a crackling noise behind their exposed scalp. Electric turquoise spots danced across their vision, rapidly expanding to cover everything.

Springing sideways, they fell out of the compartment, rolling back onto the command room floor.

"Ah, *shit*! Shit..."

*

When their vision returned, there was a person standing over them.

Tall, taller than Coeie by a good bit, wearing a shimmering, endless duster, under which they sported a pristine set of tux and tails. A finely groomed, jet-black mustache framed their darkly lipsticked mouth, which was curved upward in a generous, toothy smile.

Their own mouth fell open, and they dumbly scrambled backward, sending their electronic handiwork skittering out from underneath them.

"Who the hell are—"

"Ah. I'm known as the It, friend! A pleasure to make your acquaintance." They bowed, with an antiquated flourish that sent their coat fluttering.

The intruder's feet should have crushed the metal shavings, screws, and bits underneath them, but the parts had passed straight through their highly polished, heeled dress shoes.

Coeie blinked hard, not for the first time today, and tried to close their mouth in the most subtle way possible.

"I'm not awake, am I."

"Of course you aren't, friend." They loosed a sparkling, full-throated laugh. "I couldn't visit if you were still awake."

"But I—" They were suddenly aware of the cold, hard press of the console parts under their hands. "This doesn't feel like a dream."

The It sighed, looking disappointed. "Well, that's what I always try telling people." They huffed a sigh, looking like someone who'd just lost a coin toss. "You scientific types tend to take it so much easier if you think you're dreaming."

"I'm sorry?"

"*Scientific types*, friend."

"No, no, I got that, but...what do you mean, 'always try'?"

"Irrelevant, friend."

"Did Toltek let you in?!"

It laid a single, gloved finger to their lips, rouged, glistening smile curling upward for the second time.

"Additionally irrelevant to the situation in which we find ourselves." The It gestured broadly around the half-deconstructed control room.

Cocic was incredibly aware of their near-perfect isolation. They stood as fast as their aching head would allow, their fist vise-like around the screwdriver.

"What do you want?"

"If you'll be so kind, friend, do allow me to show you something. Time is short, and we have much to do."

But before Coeie could get out a word in protest, the It spirited the screwdriver out of their palm, and entwined their fingers deftly.

"Hey—"

"Your trust would do wonders in expediting this process, my friend."

No sooner had Cocic opened their mouth to respond than the It snapped, loud and solid, directly next to Coeie's ear. The ship was gone in a perfect instant, replaced by a darkened street. They staggered backward, nearly tripping over a cobblestone that hadn't been there a moment ago, only to be steadied by a smooth, gloved hand on their shoulder.

"Easy now, friend! Astral jump can be a tricky thing when you're new to it, but as aforementioned, we don't have gads of time."

The It swung to Coeie's front, placing both hands on their shoulders, looking them dead in the eye.

"I *like* this dimension, after all. And you've never been, so steady yourself, friend."

Coeie's senses finally took in the scene around them. The smell was horrible, but glittering gas streetlights reflected off of the sludge lining the curbs and gutters. Couples and groups of friends rolled easily down the street, music bleeding out of every other doorway.

Has she got you know what, yes, she has got, you know what... That certain, that certain party... Has she got, I forgot—

Jazz music. Floating into the air and sinking into everything around them. This was a scene hundreds of years old, and Coeie couldn't help but reach out to brush their fingertips against the worn brick city walls.

"Now, now. No time for that." The It swept them up, directing them toward an intricately padlocked wooden door. It would almost have been unassuming if the It hadn't pushed them right in its direction.

*

A burly gentleman with a watchman's stance in a short coat melted from the shadowed doorway to open the doors, and the hot, acrid smell of open liquor bottles wafted forth. When asked for an entry code, the It cupped a hand to the side of his jaw and whispered a few gentle words into the bouncer's ear, who waved them through an open hallway.

"Sit, my friend. Please." The It slid out a worn rattan chair, next to a round, slightly less worn table. Coeie gazed in a wide arc around the room.

"This is...early years. Back on Earth?" The audience was sizable and positively glittering with *style*. There was a veritable panoply of humanity; individuals of all shapes and sizes wearing suits, dresses, antiquated men's dress shirts with fringed skirts, jewel-toned lipstick under finely polished mustaches. The It fit right in; Coeie couldn't help but feel distinctly underdressed for whatever occasion this was. They picked at a loose thread at the edge of their jumpsuit sleeve.

"Too right. Don't worry; no one notices you." The It settled into a chair next to them, stretching their long, elegant legs out in front of them. They lazily waved a hand, and a waiter appeared next to them in a matter of moments. "Two Manhattans please. In a pinch, pal."

The It waved him away with a wink, and the waiter blushed high in his cheeks as he scurried off to a well-outfitted bar at the far end of the club.

The stage in front of them was not expansive, but it was beautiful. A dusty backdrop framed a painted set: meticulously rendered clouds hung low, and the worn wooden floorboards were cottoned with fluffy clouds spangled with sequins sewn into the material. The floor lights tempered, the slight crackling of their incandescent bulbs audible even at the distance at which Coeie and the It found themselves, sending dots of light shining out before the stage.

Sweeping over with a tray, the waiter deposited a pair of cherry-colored drinks in front of the two with no small flourish, still blushing under the It's gaze.

"What do you see, friend?" the It asked. Coeie raised an eyebrow at the It, and they shot them a sparkling grin in return. "Humor my interest."

"I see lots of people. I see a stage. Is this where you're from?"

"These are my people, and yours. Well, your ancestors, at least."

Oh.

The implication dawned on Coeie all at once, as if all the lights in the club had been cranked on at once.

"This is a gay club?!"

"There you are, my friend. No need for such surprise on the matter."

"But I thought—"

"Hush, friend. The show is about to start." The It smiled around the rim of their cocktail glass as the lights dimmed and the glitter lining stage sparkled.

*

"That was *amazing*, and the fans she had, and the costume changes in the middle?!"

"I know, my friend."

"And the *music* was—"

"Incredible, I know."

The two had spilled onto the street with the majority of the other club-goers, and the It was currently trailing behind Coeie as they meandered down a partially lit side street. They stopped at a corner, underneath a streetlight.

"But...why?" Coeie tripped to a stop, the inertia of the two Manhattans coming to rest in the pit of their stomach.

"The why isn't for me to say, my dear friend." The It gazed down at them, lipstick and tuxedo still flawless and crisp in the streetlight's cast shadow. "I've been charged with bringing you...ah, how to say it. A little bit of perspective, I suppose."

Coeie met their gaze, half-blinded by the light haloing the It's figure.

"You might want to prepare yourself, friend."

"Hold on, for wh—"

"Tick-tock."

Without another word, the It reached down, drawing Coeie's eyes closed with two delicate thumbs.

*

They woke with an audible, choking gasp, to the cold sterility of the command center floor.

"What the *fuck.*"

They rolled to sit, cross-legged, body sore, mouth cotton-dry, and utterly alone. They hadn't been asleep, that was for damn well sure. The It had told them so, and the evening had none of the fuzziness of a recollected dream.

Coeie looked down at their gray, standard-issue uniform and felt a flat, mournful hollowness surfacing where the drinks had been. The scattered bits from the interior of the ship's command panel were still strewn about, and they shook their head. This was foolish. Astral-jump technology was still years from completion, and the fact remained that there was absolutely no way someone out there had perfected simultaneous time-dimensional jumps for two people. If the It was even a person. If they had even been there at all.

Shaking their head, they began to painstakingly gather the small pieces of console. They must've missed their daily log and—

Toltek.

Besides the company-mandated logs Coeie made, Toltek would inevitably record security footage of various rooms related to mining operations. The command center would certainly count as one of those.

"Toltek. Query."

"YES, TOLTEK RESPONDING."

"Location of all command room security logs."

"LOCATION...SEARCHING."

Toltek was absolutely, unequivocally, *definitely* not programmed to avoid a line of questioning, especially from an administrator.

"LOCATION: UNMOORED."

"Unmoored? Are you positive?"

Only rogue programming was unmoored. Code that had been corrupted beyond Toltek's internal self-repair procedures was isolated, cut off from the rest of the system, and, it was expected, contained in advance of administrative termination.

"AFFIRMATIVE; ALL LOGS UNMOORED."

"*Damn.*"

*

The ship's server stacks were in the basement. It wasn't a basement in the traditional sense, but a dingy, lower hold that hadn't been remodeled. It wasn't that Coeie was *scared* of it, per se. They just didn't necessarily enjoy the sensation of being cut off from the rest of the ship. Toltek usually managed the stacks internally, but voice-responsive command didn't extend belowdecks.

The lower hold door slid open with a muted *shhk*, and the motion sensors took notice, lights flickering to life one at a time. With a slight hum, low-slung halogen lamps illuminated the stacks, shining on the rows of dull titanium servers, encased in the protective wire caging that slung each one a few inches off of the ground. No vibrations to disturb them that way, and when Coeie needed to preserve energy, they could turn off gravitation for a while with no dire consequences to the guts of the ship's computation system.

Still. Creepy, all the same, how much they looked like hanging tombstones.

No, Toltek meant laborious manual entry for all commands while in the basement. The light swayed overhead with the subtle to-and-fro of the starship, and the servers rocked gently in place. After making their way to the panel, they tapped at the start key. The only marker designating its connection to the rest of the ship being the handscreen, which stuttered to life with a flickering glow. Making contact, they typed in the first command, keys clattering quietly as all old-Earth tech did. It would have been comforting if the command had been the only thing to appear on the screen.

```
:ENTER/SECURITYLOG/LOCATION/COMMCENT
ER
     LOCATION/UNMOORED:
:ENTER/CODEUNLOCK
```

```
    LOCATION/UNMOORED:
:ENTER/ADMINPIN4219
    LOCATION/INACCESSIBLE:
:ENTER/ADMINOVERRIDE
    LOCATION/INACCESSIBLE:
:ENTER/ADMINOVERRIDE
COMMAND//TICTOCK:
```

Coeie jerked away from the keypad, as if they'd received an electric shock. Fear rose, bile-like in their throat, choking them. Turning fast, they scanned the stacks, hands propping them against the command station. The light overhead swayed with the same gentle regularity, casting stark shadows into the corners of the basement. There had to be something wrong with the ship's software. There must be a bug, or some kind of virus that had infected Toltek, or some interfering command panel, or—

They couldn't calm their heartbeat, and fuzzy black dots began to swim in front of their eyes. Between hard breaths, they called out to the shadows.

"Toltek? Query?"

Silence reigned.

"Query?!"

Coeie turned back to the command panel.

```
COMMAND//TICKTOCK, TICKTOCK:
```

Their breath caught, and everything fell into darkness.

*

"Hey. You."

Coeie shifted back into some form of consciousness. This was...new. Their brain usually didn't address them so directly.

"You, *Coeie Mazarran*. I know you're awake in there." Their thoughts usually didn't take an aggressive tone with them either.

They'd found themselves lying down...again. Coeie registered the slight hum of the ship's engines against their ear, which they supposed was pressed to the basement floor...the basement where they'd gotten that bizarre command message.

Panic flooded them as soon as the memory did. They sat upright, eyes snapping open. A complete mirror image stared back at them, wearing a distinctly annoyed expression, arms akimbo. They loosed a scream, scampering as far away from their doppelgänger as they could, before knocking against a server.

"What—*who*—"

"There they are! Good evening, sleepyhead."

Coeie just barely restrained another scream, clapping a hand over their mouth in anticipation and pressing down hard to tamp down any escaping sound. They seemed completely identical, from the rumpled jumpsuit to the long limbs, to the spatulate, dark fingers resting against its—their hips. This was wrong, wrong, wrong, *wrong*, and the animalian, guttural part of Coeie's brain was thundering out that they needed to run, right now, as fast as their legs could carry them.

"Yes, it's me, but also sort of you! Spooky, right?" The doppelgänger shrugged lackadaisically, scratching the side of Coeie's—its face. "The It's lucky. I don't get to pick what I wind up looking like."

Coeie's eyes darted to its feet, and, sure enough, part of the doppelgänger's leg passed through the edge of a server. Their brain bellowed louder for them to run, *run right now, because you don't belong with this...thing*. If the doppelgänger could follow them here, somehow, they surely would be able to give chase. Exhausting all alternatives, Coeie forced themself to speak.

"You're the same as the It?"

"Well, I sort of resent the comparison. I don't have nearly the same flair for the dramatic. I think it's middle-child syndrome in action."

"S-sure."

"You can call me the They."

Coeie lunged forward, fist first, but the They dodged easily to the side. Coeie stumbled forward, head aching dully. Bad aim, and worse planning.

"Uncalled for. You could have just asked. And stupid of you, you really knocked your head after that panic attack."

"What the *hell* is happening on my ship!?"

"Easy, tiger. Nothing bad, for you at least." The They extended a hand to tentatively pat Coeie on the shoulder. They could feel the doppelgänger's hand warm and solidify as it made contact, and they couldn't restrain a full-body shudder and the change.

"For me? Is that supposed to be *comforting*?!"

"Well...I mean, no. Not really. Do you wanna get out of this basement?"

They balked. "Why should I let you into the rest of the ship?" Coeie scowled back at the They, crossing their arms over their chest.

"I thought you were supposed to be smart. You seriously think if I can materialize down here, I can't materialize up there? I've got your fingerprints and everything."

"That's...horrifying."

"Yeah! Life is horrifying! But you know what's more horrifying? This basement." And as if to prove a point, they flung an arm in the direction of the automated doors. "Corporeal beings first."

Coeie backed around the They, eyes tracking the doppelgänger as they backed through the doors and into the light of the lift. The They followed, a vaguely bemused expression playing around Coeie's features.

"You're a projection of me."

"Yep."

"With my own...voice?"

"You got it."

The They's bald admission that they were some kind of holographic, demi-material figure made Coeie felt less bad about staring. They couldn't find a single detail out of place, from the tone and texture of their deep-brown skin to the small silver earrings they wore. Even their boots were the same melded latex tread and stiff velcro straps, scuffed in the exact same pattern as their own.

"You done?"

"Almost." The lift's smooth ascent continued.

"Well, finish up quick; we've got work to do. People to see."

"People?"

The lift surely should have stopped by now; it was only a couple of decks between the basement and the command center.

"*People.*" The They grinned, black-brown eyes reflecting Coeie's own. "Hold on now."

The lift shot upward for half a moment, surging toward the stars with unprecedented velocity. Coeie's stomach dropped, and before they could feel the effects of the surge, the lift screeched to a halt.

The automatic doors rolled open to reveal Coeie's bedroom door. Where the rest of the craft used to be, a doorway had appeared outside the lift doors. Coeie spun around to question the They, mouth agape. But the They was gone, the inside of the lift as empty as it had been when Coeie had first descended into the basement. The small, doubtful voice inside their head whispered that it wouldn't be so simple to rid themselves of the doppelgänger.

Gingerly, they touched the wooden paneling on the door, fingertips brushing the brass doorknob. Cool to the touch, and just as rough and solid as the real thing. Their mind began to spin, questions circling.

How had the They been able to mirror their appearance, the look of their childhood bedroom door? They hadn't thought about their bedroom in months, years, even. Since going into the company, and since their argument, they'd only messaged their father occasionally, every once in a while asking some general question about the neighborhood. They hadn't given him reason to linger. They certainly hadn't given much thought to going home.

From where Coeie stood, just inside the lift doors, they realized the low, nearly imperceptible hum of the ship's motors and generators had dimmed to almost nothing. As Coeie cautiously stepped out of the lift, the doors slid shut with a soft *whunk* behind them. They opened the mirage-bedroom door a crack, leaning in to peer through the sliver-like opening.

Sunlight.

The light was streaming in through the doorway, from the two corner windows, between the mottled green curtains hanging over their bed. Upon which, funnily enough, the They sat. The room was silent, save for the noise of cicadas outside, which leaked in through one of the open windows.

"Where is this?"

"Where is—*oh*, don't be stupid." The They turned to face them, wearing a dry look they could just *tell* was identical to one they wore when frustrated about tech malfunctions.

"I mean, is this real? Did you make it? Is this some kind of...I dunno, mirage?"

"Mirage would sort of be outside the realm of my capabilities. Huh, would be cool though. I've gotta try it sometime." The They turned from their seat on Coeie's old indigo comforter and peered out the window. "No, we all deal in space. And time."

The room was exactly as they'd kept it, right up until the time they'd left for the base. They'd assumed that their dad would have sold it, or transformed it into an elaborately organized storage closet. The They rose from their prior position on the bed to stalk around the room, pulling open drawers, poking at the books on their squat bookshelf at the foot of the bed.

"Hey, what are you—"

"I just look like you; I don't know that much about you." They touched at the spines, walking their identical fingers along the titles. "Asimov, huh? He got a few things wrong, didn't he?"

"Don't." Coeie swiped the book from the They's hands. "That's mine."

"What's mine is yours, right?" The They laughed, showing Coeie's teeth. Hands up in surrender, they backed away from the bookcase. "Sorry, bad joke. Do you wanna see the rest?" They gestured toward the door with their chin.

As they'd ventured from the bedroom, Coeie half expected to see the rest of the ship rematerialize, and for their old bedroom to shimmer out of sight behind them. But the They hadn't lied; the house was just the same as when Coeie had left it three years ago. As they made their way downstairs to the kitchen, they spied a familiar figure puttered around the table.

"When you said people..."

"You can't talk to him. I promise. He won't be able to see you."

"Bullshit. Dad? Dad!"

The They hadn't lied, again. The two of them were as good as ghosts to him. Coeie tried to speak, to yell, to throw dishes to get his attention. As soon as they'd picked up a plate to throw, an identical one popped into being, right in its place. When the dishes hit the wall, they made no sound.

A rolling tidal wave of loneliness overtook them as they looked over at their father, gray-streaked braids tied neatly behind him, scribbling a to-do list over the counter. That ache of homesickness hadn't reared its head in years, not since they'd first arrived at the academy. Their father had waved them off as they'd hauled their suitcase to the dorm rooms. They were an only child, and used to loneliness, but this feeling of fearful newness cut to their core.

"I want to go home."

"Home? But we've just got here."

"No, I mean—" To their surprise, Coeie felt the pinpricks of tears welling up. "I want to go home. I don't want to be out in the Horologium anymore."

"But you can't. You've been *contracted*, haven't you?" The look on the They's face twisted into a sad sort of grin. They cocked their head, palms outstretched. "Didn't you want to escape everyone else but yourself?"

"I didn't; I just wanted—"

"Wanted, what? Isolation? To forget yourself?" The They advanced on Coeie, cutting off their view of their father. Coeie attempted to push the They aside, palms flat against their shoulders. Trying desperately to muscle them away. Equally matched, the They didn't budge.

"You think you can just *run* from other people?"

"*Stop* it! I want to go home, I want to go home, *I want to go home—*"

A downward swing of their fist, meant for the They's shoulder, met nothing, and then they were falling forward, momentum carrying them into pure darkness. Wind whistled past their ears, and instinctively, they squeezed their eyes shut, bracing for impact.

Impossibly, the voice of the They filled their ears, even as they fell.

"No one is meant to be alone."

The impact of Coeie's landing smacked their head against the floor, and they faded into unconsciousness.

*

Their head hurt. Specifically, their head *throbbed* from a sizable bump on their forehead, where their skull had physically smacked against the floor from...wherever they'd fallen from. The They had gone, replaced by the ship's usual low hum.

"Toltek?"

"T-TOLTE-K. THREE-E. REPORTING."

Toltek's audio program was slurred and glitched, the syllables oddly distorted. Coeie shook their head, trying to dissipate fuzziness.

"Prep bio-scan, to log."

"P-PREPPING."

They had to know if they were concussed, or dreaming, or otherwise delusional. The They had some kind of intimate knowledge of their life, and if whatever it was had been able to replicate their physical form completely, who knew what else they'd be capable of. What was worse, the two beings had undoubtedly known each other, been in *league* with each other in some capacity. How they had known each other, they could barely begin to speculate at. Both seemed ethereal, more than human. Not divorced from their human-ness, but just...slanted away from it.

Coeie had heard about alien encounters in the outer galaxies: stories of abduction, of folks sucked out of their spaceships onto alien vessels. It was growing more and more common. They had to admit, they'd never heard of aliens that could replicate your body, or transport you to a location created solely from memory.

"B-BIO SCAN: ACTIVE."

Toltek's voice still glitched, but right on cue, they were haloed in a fluorescent ring that commenced the work of scanning their entire body.

"RESULT: EXTREMITY LIMBS INTACT, GENDER INCONCLUSIVE, MINOR INJURY IN U-UP-PER PARIETAL CORTE-TEX."

No surprises there. Binary astronauts didn't have to deal with this 'inconclusive' nonsense, among other things. They ambled off of the command center, the results of the scan confirming the signs their pounding head was giving off.

*

If the visitors were going to kill them, they would have done it by now. Of that Coeie could be certain. If they were here to hijack the ship, or take their harvest, they could have done it, and left Coeie on some distant planet, displaced from their current time and place entirely. It would surely have been no effort to them. The thought, as comforting as it should have been, still sent chills running up and down Coeie's spine.

Risking a log, they called out into the air.

"Toltek, log."

"A-AFFIRMATIVE. VOICE TRANSCRIPTION: STARTING IN THREE...TWO...ONE."

"All right. Solo log from Coeie Mazarran, going on one and a half years in orbit. Journal report, uh. General status update." They coughed, suddenly self-conscious of sounding foolish to anyone who would listen. Their superiors received all entries; they were logged and put away for review somewhere at home base.

"I've...been experiencing phenomenological intrusions? Impossible to distinguish if intrusions are organic or inorganic, involving...illusion of physical and temporal transport."

Best to leave out that these intrusions were taking humanoid form.

*

The bits from the console were still scattered about the floor, like so much dismal confetti.

A blaze of light shone through the porthole window. In a flash of who-knows-what, the nearest star, visible from the outside of the ship, grew brighter and brighter, blazing with what had, a few moments ago, been an unremarkable constancy. Coeie slid a foot back, one hand shielding their eyes from the light, the other extended sideways, fingers hunting for a solid surface to brace themselves against. Toltek blared a long screeching note of protest, its voice melting into a garbled slur of warnings as the light grew and grew.

This was it. This was how they were going to die, at the hands of a star in motion, or an asteroid, or—

The starlight, blazing as bright it was, steadied at a constant level just shy of blinding.

"Tick-tock, Coeie."

Lowering a hand, Coeie squinted into the light, eyes half-watering from the strain.

"Am I dead?"

"Oh, certainly not."

"Are you here to kill me?"

"Quite the opposite."

"What, then?"

"To recall you to life, dear."

"But I'm already—"

"I know. You are certainly breathing and respirating and walking around. Alive? I'm not so sure." The being sighed. "You may call me the Xie."

A cold trickle of fear struck at the core of Coeie's being. The Xie's body was near-formless in the bright light, and they couldn't make out any face through the brilliant glow.

"I'm not quite there right now. But I've come to show you something new."

Coeie sank to their knees, wavering in place, eyes welling for the second time. They let themself scrub at the corners of their eyes, hands falling uselessly to their sides. "Why?"

"I can't tell you why. Only to show you a future that could come to pass."

They laid a well-worn palm against Coeie's brow, and a sensation like dripping egg yolk ran from the place where their hand rested, chilling them from the outside in. A flickering unreality clicked to life behind their eyes, like a neon sign being turned on inside a corner store.

They were behind the control panel again, fully reconstructed and seamless. They were flicking switches, reading the monitors, checking the ship's progress until, suddenly, they were not. Coeie rode along, a passenger in their own body, as they walked to the mine hold. The gold was kept, of course, walled off, away from the curious fingers of those who harvested. Coeie was not to be trusted with the product, of course. In self-defense, however, there always was a simple, effective button, that, to save the pilot, allowed them to eject the cargo. The button was protected by a heavy, red-tinted plastic case, and Coeie was helpless to stop themself as they watched their fist smash the flimsy plastic to pieces, pressing down hard on the button. A deafening alarm sounded. No automated voice announced the action as the cargo tore from the basement hold and out into the stars once again.

With a high, whirring, panicked scream, Toltek melted away with the starlight, and would speak no word in protest as Coeie wordlessly dumped the cargo. They knew, without a hint of doubt, that the logs Toltek had stored would be wiped, utterly and completely. Upon ejecting the harvest, they walked to the mid-deck, took a sharp right turn that led to a long, empty hallway, ending in a matte-gray porthole door, secured by a sizeable hatch.

The escape pods were through that door, attached to the bottom of the ship like ticks on a dog. They had, apparently, gathered supplies and some tools, because when Coeie's body opened the trap door to the pods, they dropped in supplies they didn't remember picking up. They had shed their standard-issue shoes, in favor of the black leather boots they'd worn to the ship's launch all those many months ago, and Coeie watched the black shoes, stiff with disuse, dangle over the hatch, slowly lowering to meet with the floor of the tiny vessel. Down, down, down went the rest of Coeie's body, snaking easily into the pod's bucket seat. Clear, unobstructed windows comprised the snout of the vessel, and Coeie could barely see their own reflection for the astral glare. Stars glimmered back into the pod, infinite in variety.

"Please don't worry about this part." The Xie's voice slithered between Coeie's ears easily, comfortably. Like water stuck in their ear after a shower, the voice sloshed back and forth, muting other sounds.

"I'll help push you off."

With no further ceremony, Coeie looked up to see the porthole closed. The Xie, true to their word, had noiselessly and invisibly snapped the latches holding the pods into an all-clear position. Coeie clicked seatbelt buckles and secured their harness, adjusted the various dials, turned a few switches, and tucked their bags between their legs. Sick rose in their throat, along with a creeping sense of urgent fear. Reaching out with their thoughts, they touched the Xie.

Where am I—where are we going? This isn't real; why are you showing me?

"Because you wanted someplace where you will not have to be alone." The voice still traveled through their mind, clear as a bell. Coeie suddenly felt a foreign, but not entirely unwelcome, sense of calm sweeping over them, trickling from their hairline where the Xie had pressed a hand to their forehead.

They'd never wanted to be alone. Not like this, not out here. Not constantly watched and monitored by Toltek. Not grubbing in half-empty asteroid belts for gold to send back. Not sure when they'd be able to afford to see their father again. Not like this.

Coeie watched their body make the necessary preparations and was in the process of settling into the seat, adjusting the vents and making sure the locks on the hatch were secured. The pod couldn't have been longer than four meters in length, and the thick reinforced glass shield was crystalline in the starlight. Smooth plastic molding coated the inside, with hard, new metal insulating the outside. The pod was built for escape, surely, but also for protection. They nestled in the seat, seeing their own hands rest on the joystick and side controls with a practiced ease.

Will you stay with me?

"I'm showing you where to go. Don't worry. We all will."

All—

"None of us are made to go alone." The voice shifted, and now the light was, decidedly, residing somewhere behind their right ear. "The It, the They, and I... We're simply shepherds to some. Ghosts to others."

Past, present, and future, then.

The feeling of something suspiciously close to a grin dawned on them, in their mind's eye.

"The It wasn't joking; you're sharp."

The Xie wasn't behind them. More like around, about them in the all-encompassing sense. Keeping their word. The pod shuddered to life, tiny engines sputtering and building to a steady roar. Coeie hadn't felt a living, rumbling vessel underneath them in what felt like an age. The satisfied hum filled their stomach and warmed them from the inside out.

"If this is what you choose, I'll guide you."

You're giving me a choice?

"Of course. You needed help and we three heard you." They could sense the Xie sigh inwardly. "But of course, you could go back to Toltek. I *could* restore the ship, bring back all those crumbs of gold."

The wide expanse of the universe wrapped around the windscreen. Comets glimmered, the nearest stars glowed with a burning constancy, and the dark chunks of ejected mineral mindlessly flowed about the ship, buffeted by solar currents and unseen gravitation, bumping and crashing into one another at random. The midnight-dark of the surrounding sky was clustered with distant galaxies, with asteroids they hadn't seen yet, and with thousands upon millions of miles of open sky.

It looked suspiciously, seductively, like the wide expanse of freedom.

Smoldering and antiquated, the ship hovered just above the pod, half-crumpled from the force of the Xie's entry. It was silent, the cargo hatch hovering open like a fish's gaping mouth, jagged harvesting teeth idle and still as death.

I've made my decision.

"Welcome back."

The Xie's voice sounded even more sonorous outside of the fuzzy confines of illusion. They lifted their palm from Coeie's head delicately, stepping back a little. The Xie's glow was still achingly bright, and Coeie's knees still ached, but they rose on wobbly legs, wiping sweat from their brow.

"There are more of you. You have to be guiding me *to* somewhere, or something."

The Xie smiled, a full-mouthed, beatific smile, still managed to shine despite their constant shimmering light.

"Show me."

And when the Xie extended an improbably human hand to them and led them down the hall to the escape pod, Coeie took it firmly.

They did not bother looking back.

DEATH MARKED

Sara Codair

Warning: violence, mention of murder

Enzi chased glimpses of pale purple and white silk through a rainbow of party guests. People spun, stomped, and moved to a blend of strings and beats blaring through speakers attached to overhead drones. Every time Enzi snared their sister in a quick look, someone flailed into their line of sight, and when the dancers whirled away, Ulsa was gone. Tailing professional spies was easier than trying to keep track of their estranged sister at a party, but at least Ulsa hadn't spotted them yet.

Circling a small space free of dancers, Enzi tried to get their bearing. Straight ahead, the statue of the Goddess loomed over the open-air ballroom. To their left, they could barely make out the fountain in the middle of the dance floor: a ring of purple stone glistening with colored light. A spout of water shot up from it, raining mist on anyone who got too close.

Enzi took a deep breath. They unclasped their painfully knotted hands behind their back. They needed to relax. This was supposed to be their night off, a chance to just be Enzi, former heir to Sector 17 and the Flaming Flower Land Holding, and not a chief security officer from the Lunar Guard. It was time to celebrate their sister's twenty-first birthday, her official crossing from adolescence to adulthood. It was their chance to finally talk to Ulsa and seek her forgiveness.

Their heart sped when they saw their sister's face. Her champagne hair fanned around her rosy cheeks as she spun by the fountain. Her dress flared as she twirled, like she hadn't a care in the world. Her relaxed smile would vanish if she saw Enzi here, but they couldn't ignore each other forever. Enzi's heart ached when they thought of missed late-night conversations, of how long it had been since they had a good debate about the Goddess. How they didn't even know the names of the two girls Ulsa danced with.

Enzi took a step toward her, their feet weighed down by guilt. They inhaled slowly and sneezed as perfume tickled their nose. Two more steps and they were back in the crowd, watching her, waiting for the right time to make their presence known. They sneezed again.

The deeper Enzi got on the dance floor, the worse the smell became. Civilians were obsessed with Earth memorabilia, and that included fragrances developed to smell like terrestrial flowers: roses, lilacs, and lilies. No one really knew if those scents were accurate. It had been five hundred years since the Goddess had terraformed this rocky moon and plopped a handful of humans on it, assuming she had been a goddess to begin with. For all Enzi knew, she might have used now-forgotten tech to create atmospheres and seed the moon with human-friendly flora that thrived in the Drogan Moon's alternating fortnights of light and dark. But that was an argument for another night. With their sister, maybe.

This evening was the last day of a dark fortnight. Perhaps it would also be the last day of their familial estrangement. When Ulsa whirled away from the fountain, Enzi stepped behind two men swaying close together. Over the shoulder of person wearing a sleek, black dress, Enzi saw Ulsa skip toward the north end of the dance floor. Enzi kept their distance, using the partiers as a shield for as long as possible. They paused at the edge of a huddled group, pressed close, smiling around champagne flutes, and watched Ulsa wipe sweat off her forehead.

A burly man in a pink sequined toga spun into Enzi. His elbow slammed into their chest, knocking the wind from them as effectively as getting whacked by the tail of a dragon bot would. They stumbled backward. Before they recovered, the stone edge of the Goddess statue sent pain through their ribs and shoulders. They ignored it, lurching to their feet, instinctively ready to charge.

"I am so sorry!" Color drained from the man's flushed face. "I was too caught up in the song. I didn't see you."

"It's okay. No harm was done." Enzi forced their shoulders to relax and their fists to unclench. The purple liquid from the man's cocktail glass beaded on Enzi's black suit, wet the collar of their deep-blue shirt, and trickled under their tank top that doubled as a binder and light armor.

"Do you need a napkin?"

"No. Please, go back to the party." Enzi took a step toward the fifty-foot likeness of the Goddess. Enzi's back throbbed and their neck ached as they looked up, taking in the Goddess's short, spikey hair, glowing the same red-orange as the leaves and shrubs in the royal garden. Her stone smile appeared forced, but the long-dead artist who had sculpted her had managed to capture a glint of mischief in her eyes—as if she was amusedly aware of something no one else was.

As children, Enzi and Ulsa had spent hours at the foot of this statue, trying to figure out the Goddess's secrets.

As children, Enzi and Ulsa had been inseparable.

Enzi had doubted the Goddess was a magical being, even when the unexplainable had stared them in the face the night they'd saved their sister's life and lost her friendship.

Three years ago, they had followed their sister's screams to a secret tunnel that led to the castle. When they found Ulsa failing to defend herself against a group of assassins, Enzi hadn't hesitated to break the Goddess's Law and stab a man with a hunting knife. The Goddess forbade killers from ruling, but that was the last thing on Enzi's mind when they were fighting for their sister's life.

Later, when the assailants were dead and the black skull had appeared on Enzi's wrist, they'd tried to find some explanation for it, other than magic, but they failed every time.

Enzi hadn't wanted to be Death Marked. They hadn't wanted to give up their right to rule Sector 17. They'd just wanted to save their younger sister's life.

*

A service bot wheeled up to Enzi as they skulked toward the garden where cocktail hour was taking place. Each of the bot's five arms held a tray topped with an assortment of fizzy drinks. Enzi reached for the green one, craving the bite of sour apple, hoping the alcohol might quiet their racing thoughts. Their fingers closed around the cool glass stem, but they reluctantly left it on the tray. If they got a chance to talk to Ulsa, they wanted to be sober.

The crunching and swishing of a gown snagged Enzi's attention. Their aunt Eldotch walked toward them in a frilly yellow dress. Her puffy white sleeves billowed like icing on a cupcake. "You're not *actually* a guest tonight."

Enzi frowned. "Of course I am."

Eldotch arched her graying eyebrows. "Guests are invited. Ulsa said she didn't invite you."

"Mother invited me." Enzi crossed their arms, hoping Eldotch didn't notice how tightly they squeezed their biceps.

"Your sister doesn't want you here, not after you dropped heirship on her lap with no warning."

Enzi snorted. "Is that what she said happened?"

Eldotch ran a hand over her frizzy red-and-gray braid. "Yes. She said not only did you make your choice without first consulting her, but you left to join the guard the next day without saying goodbye."

Enzi chewed their lip, silencing the true story. Only Ulsa, their parents, and a few trusted palace guards knew that the skull on their wrist had appeared before Enzi had ever made their first official kill for the guard. They'd pretended leaving was a choice, because the truth would've been too great an embarrassment for their parents to shoulder.

"I assume there is more to the story." Eldotch narrowed her icy blue eyes.

Enzi squinted back.

Like Enzi, a kill mark had robbed Eldotch of her right to rule. She had been young when it had happened. A man had tried to abduct her, and in a struggle to get free, she'd pushed him off a cliff. For anyone else, the crime would've been forgivable, but when it came to those meant to rule, the Goddess was inflexible.

Eldotch hadn't joined the guard like Enzi. She'd clung to a political career, eventually convincing her sister to appoint her as Sector 17's delegate to the Lunar Council, where she became chairperson of the council's budget committee. This was a position that was typically held by the sector's heir. Now that Ulsa was of age, she could take it from Eldotch at any time.

"Sometimes there is more. Other times, there is less, because the person who told the story made it out to be far more dramatic than it was," said Enzi.

"Ulsa does have a knack for dramatics." Eldtoch's pursed lips relaxed into a smile that once upon a time would've tempted Enzi to lower their guard. But after more than two and a half years of covert missions and several months as an officer, Enzi had no trouble spotting false sincerity.

Enzi mimicked Eldotch's patronizing smile. "Are you enjoying the party?"

"It's all right, but if your sister hadn't insisted on paying the decorators and cooks such exorbitant fees, there would've been room in the budget for more elegant décor. Her ceremonial platform is more plain than yours was."

Enzi held their chin high. "Both Ulsa and Goddess care more about the people than the superficial adornments on her altar. The ceremony is as it should be. I hope you enjoy it."

Enzi turned their back on their aunt and walked away. If they were still heir, they would've planned this party with their sister. There would be no ceremonial platform where Ulsa was named heir. It would've merely been a birthday party, as ordinary as anything royal celebration was capable of being.

*

Enzi could name two dozen relatives munching crackers around the hedges, but they didn't see Ulsa. They stepped around a cousin who had a beard to their belly and a hooped gown, past a more distant cousin in a sleek burgundy tuxedo, and around an elderly person wearing crimson robes. Their stomach grumbled as they looked at two towers of cheese and crackers that flanked a three-foot tall statue of the Goddess. Her eyes were luminescent purple gems that squinted at Enzi. Her lips were pursed tight together.

Stop procrastinating. Find your sister. Speak with her. Keep her safe.

Enzi jumped back and shook their head as whispered words seeped into their mind. Had they taken that drink from the serving bot, they certainly would've dropped it. They'd roamed this garden for twenty-four years, and the Goddess had never spoken to them. Their hands clenched into fists and their throat constricted. They were cold, as if the simulated heat from drones that lit the area had somehow missed them. One hand clutched the mark on their wrist while their mind struggled to explain what others might readily accept as magic or miracle.

"She's by the punch bowl now," said a deep, musical voice.

Enzi jumped, but they released their wrist and their shoulders relaxed. Dressed to look like a party guest, Sergeant Reemins wore a silk tunic the same deep green as his eyes and lipstick. Black leggings and practical yet polished leather boots covered his legs. He appeared unarmed, but Enzi knew each boot concealed a compact stun baton, and his clunky star-shaped rings could be used to control two dozen armed drones.

"Thank you." Enzi wanted to hug him, but instead, they straightened their shoulders and nodded. Maybe the Goddess hadn't spoken to them. Maybe their earpiece had picked up a garbled transmission from Reemins's comm. "Any sign of trouble?"

"So far, we've confiscated two mouse drones armed with darts. I've sent them to the lab for analysis, but they smelled like Neuro 12."

"Good work." Enzi touched their wrist with bare fingers, wishing they'd worn devices like his. It would've made it easier to follow Ulsa. "Anything else I should know about?"

Reemins bit his lower lip and glanced at the statue.

"Spit it out," said Enzi.

He stared over Enzi's shoulder. "The fact that none of these bots were detected on the way in, combined with where they were intercepted, suggests that they were here before the party started, placed by someone who had access to the plans in advance."

Enzi tilted their head. "That doesn't narrow anything down. Mother provides her staff with fair pay, but it doesn't mean they won't sell information for the right price, and most of the people who want my sister dead have the money to pay it. What are you really trying to say?"

Reemins sighed. "Just go talk to her and get it over with."

Enzi frowned. "I've been trying to, but she isn't easy to catch."

Reemins arched his eyebrows. "If you were undercover and she was a target, you would've caught her twenty minutes ago."

Enzi stared at their reflection in their polished boots, pale skin and cold blue eyes. Reemins was right.

His face softened. "You've been talking about contacting her since you traded fieldwork for administration."

"I'm worried about her."

"If so, you can protect her better up close."

Enzi nodded. "If it goes poorly, which it most certainly will, I'll be distracted."

"Which is why you took the night off. Let me and my crew do our job. We'll keep her safe, don't worry," said Reemins.

"I know." But Enzi *did* worry. Ulsa had outright refused to have a human or bot bodyguard accompany her throughout the party and ceremony, and there were a lot of people here who felt threatened by Ulsa's liberal politics. They didn't want her replacing Eldotch on the council, and they didn't want her to one day rule the sector. "Keep me updated."

Enzi tapped the star stud in their right earlobe that doubled as a comm unit and dove back into the crowd. When Enzi got to the punch bowl, Ulsa was sipping bubbly liquid out of a glass flute. She shared their same cool blue eyes. Her strapless gown was purple silk with white swirling through it like drifting snow, and her curly hair cascaded over bare white shoulders. The lady to her right had short brown hair and a heart-shaped face, her cheeks flushed pink, lips curved in a relaxed smile. The woman on Enzi's left had brown skin and an elegant face framed with a halo of black curls. Her deep-purple tuxedo was fitted to accentuate curves—the exact opposite of what Enzi's was designed to do.

Enzi lurked behind a tower of hors d'oeuvres: roasted vegetables bathed in spice, meats wrapped in flakey pastry, and little tarts filled with fruit and cheese. Their stomach rumbled.

Ulsa's laugh was music drowning out the beats from the dance floor. Her smile and sharp gaze made her companions grin. One swooned as she took her hand and kissed it. Enzi had spent the past hour trying to find Ulsa, but now? Enzi snatched a croissant off the tower and shoved it in their mouth, savoring melted cheese and buttery pastry. They watched as they snacked, taking in each easy movement and charmed smile.

Ulsa looked happy. Maybe Enzi didn't need to talk to her yet. They took another pastry off of the rack and froze with it halfway to their mouth. Ulsa's eyes snared them. She stayed poised with her back straight, watching Enzi for two breaths, then stepped away from her companions and stormed toward them. Enzi knew Ulsa's fake smile as well as her clenched fists and blistered cheeks. She grabbed their arm and, with gritted teeth, said, "If I wanted you here, I would've sent you an invitation."

"Ulsa, I miss you," said Enzi, letting her pull them around the punch fountain, further away from the dancing food, into an alcove where red-leaved hedges encircled a fishpond.

Angry tears pooled in Ulsa's eyes. "You've ruined enough already. Leave before you make it worse."

Enzi took a deep breath. "You didn't even know I was here until a couple minutes ago. How could I have ruined anything?"

Ulsa's fuchsia lips curled into a snarl. "You know what I mean."

Enzi buried their hands in their pockets. "It's been three years."

"And in those three years, nothing in my life has been how I planned it, because of *you*." She shoved their sleeve up and pointed at the black skull on Enzi's right wrist, the one that had appeared the first time they'd killed someone. "Because of this."

"I saved your life." Enzi's hand curled into a tight fist.

Ulsa squeezed Enzi's wrist harder. "Yes, and I would've been grateful if you had stopped there."

Enzi yanked their hand away and stuffed it back in their pocket. "Either I killed them, or they killed us."

Ulsa stood up on her toes, nose to nose with Enzi. "Are you sure about that? There was absolutely no way you could've knocked them out and dragged them to the damned intero-bot?"

Enzi stepped back. "I was outnumbered—I'd only studied martial arts recreationally. You were unconscious. I did what I had to."

Ulsa's alcohol infused breath burned Enzi's nose. "Did you? Or did you make a choice so you could get what *you* wanted?"

"And what is it you think I wanted?" Enzi asked.

"Adventures in the guard?" Ulsa whispered, backing away. "A life?"

"I gave up the life I wanted so you could live," said Enzi, but Ulsa was already gone.

Enzi lumbered out of the alcove while Ulsa's words crawled over their skin like fire ants. Could they have subdued those men with nonlethal methods? Was being chief security officer of Sector 17's Lunar Guard Division more of a "life" than being an heir—eventually a monarch—would've been? Both jobs were time-consuming. Both put someone in charge of other people. The biggest difference was violence. While one job required more verbal sparring, the other was prone to explosions and knife fights. In one position, murder was forbidden. In the other, it was a tool sometimes used to ensure the security of the seventeen sectors.

Ulsa would not approve of how often Enzi had used that tool.

They wandered around people and snack displays, barely hearing words and music. Some tried to wave them over, but they didn't want to make small talk with relatives they only saw a few times a year. They relished the quiet as they left the gardens, emerging on a lawn filled with long tables. A few palace staff members were inspecting cutlery and napkins as drones set the tables.

Enzi walked until they came to an area where platforms were stacked like bleachers, all facing the stage the ceremony would take place on. Their skin itched with spectral nerves. Two statues of the Goddess, both adorned with red and purple flowers and surrounded by white candles, scowled down at them. They struggled to remember if the statue's expression had always looked so disapproving.

In the past, Enzi resisted the idea that the spirit of a being who could shape a barren moon into an oasis for human refugees still lingered around her creation, too weak to fully manifest but strong enough to motivate humans to obey. Some people believed Her energy held the atmosphere in place and nourished the plants. They feared her, afraid she'd take her life force back and kill everyone on the moon if they broke Her laws.

The music became soft ambiance. Laughter and conversation was a distant din. Across from the stage, Reemins and his crew milled around the guest seating, making sure there were no drones or explosives hidden beneath chairs or behind pillars.

Enzi padded over until they stood behind him. "Did you check the stage yet?"

Reemins startled. "Yes, it was clear." He turned and studied Enzi's face. "You talked to Ulsa."

Enzi nodded. "She hates me just as much as she did three years ago. I shouldn't be here."

Reemins clipped his scanner to his belt. "Do you still want to fix things with her?"

"Of course."

"Then you are exactly where you belong."

"I haven't felt so lost or incompetent since my first day of basic." Enzi stared past Reemins's shoulder, gaze cemented on the scowling statue. Lace patterns were craved into a gown that covered the purple stone body. Each finger on her hands was well defined. She wore a filigree tiara on her head. The other iteration of the goddess had a chiseled pair of overalls and a flat-ended hammer in one hand. They narrowed their eyes. Today, it resembled a ball-pen hammer more than a sledge. "Reemins, scan that statue again."

Frowning, he unclipped the scanner and pointed it at the statue. The screen lit up red. "Bot detected."

Beetle-like wings unfurled from a bot. It shot toward the space between Enzi and Reemins. In one fluid motion, Enzi slid a tiny blaster from their sleeve and squeezed the trigger. Purple fire consumed the bot as it sunk to the ground, a harmless pile of metal.

"You brought a weapon to my party?"

Enzi spun around. Their sister stood on the platform behind them, toeing at the ground where Reemins collected the melted bot.

"I saved your life. *Again.*" Enzi glanced over their shoulder. "Reemins, order another sweep the party. If there are any more around, I want them caught."

"Yes, Xir." Reemins nodded and spoke hurriedly his comm.

Enzi met Ulsa's eyes.

Ulsa's deep frown reminded Enzi of the day they'd accidentally cartwheeled into her glass pony collection. She'd worn that same sour look as the cleaning bot sucked up glittering shards. "Mother said you were on leave for a few days. That you were here because you wouldn't miss this whether I wanted you here or not. But you're working, aren't you? You're undercover, pretending you want to be friends again. "

Enzi took a deep breath. "I *am* on leave, but when Reemins told me you refused to have an actual bodyguard, I brought a blaster, just in case."

Ulsa took a step back. "So, you decided to disregard my wishes and *become* my bodyguard?"

"Ulsa, I care about you. I don't want to lose you any more than I already have."

"If you cared, you wouldn't have left in the first place." Silk rippled behind Ulsa like boat wake as she stormed away.

"I left because I thought it was what was best for our family," Enzi shouted.

Ulsa paused. Enzi held their breath, hoping Ulsa would turn around, but she shook her head and ran back toward the party.

*

Three gongs vibrated from every overhead drone, signaling to guests that the official ceremony would be starting soon. People streamed away from food and dance to the platforms. Flashing lights stilled as people took their designated seats. For Enzi, this was between their parents and Eldotch on a platform directly in front of the ceremonial stage.

Mother's red hair was coiled on top of their head. Her cheeks were covered in freckles, and her lipstick was a bold aquamarine that matched her tunic. Enzi's father wore a tuxedo, the same shimmering gray as his hair and eyes. His blocky jaw was clean-shaven, but he had a thin mustache growing above his lip. He frowned as he looked at Enzi. "I take it your conversation with Ulsa didn't go well?"

"That's the understatement of the day." Eldotch's dress crinkled as she sat beside Enzi.

Mother glared at her sister, then reached over Father and squeezed Enzi's arm. "You're here. That's what matters."

"She doesn't want me here," muttered Enzi.

Mother folded her hands on her lap and straightened her shoulders. "She does. She just doesn't want to admit it."

Eldotch arched her brows. "She looks about as happy to see Enzi as she would coming face-to-face with a dragon bot."

Mother shook her head. "That's part of not wanting to admit it. Ulsa can hold a grudge, but she lets go quickly when given reason to."

"I hope you're right." Enzi stared at the statues. Their glares had somehow morphed to smug smiles.

A string quartet played. Ulsa walked out onto the platform, which was laden with white candles and flowers the colors of fire and night. She possessed the chilling beauty of a winter storm as she lit wicks and made vows— the same vows Enzi would never get the chance to make. Truthfully, they had been a mess the day they were supposed to make those same vows. Their parents hadn't wanted the public to know a group of insurgents had nearly infiltrated the castle—stopped because their eldest child killed them—so they let the party go on as planned. Guests assumed it had been nerves when they'd seen Enzi ignore their food at dinner. Chalked their behavior up to anxiety when they'd lurked behind bushes instead of socializing. Enzi had climbed onto the platform and stood between the Goddess statues as their sister stood now. Their stomach had roiled and their body had shaken hard enough to prevent any candle lighting at all.

Everyone had watched in silence while Enzi struggled to breath. When they'd finally found the courage to speak, they hadn't sworn to selflessly serve the people as their leader. Instead, Enzi had announced they were relinquishing their position as heir to Section 17, to the Flaming Flower Land Holdings, and joining the Lunar Guard.

Enzi would never forget how the audience had gasped and dissolved into whispers. Ulsa had fled to her room as soon as she could without causing a scene, and Enzi had fled to the darkest corner of garden where they stifled their sobbing, alone and unguarded.

Ulsa hadn't come out to say goodbye when Enzi had left the next morning. She'd acted like Enzi had had a choice. At first, Enzi had hated her for it, but as time went on, they just missed her, their best friend. After every success, Enzi wanted to tell Ulsa about it. When something went wrong, they'd craved Ulsa's comforting optimism.

Enzi chose to forgive Ulsa, but they feared Ulsa would never make that choice for them.

*

Tears stung Enzi's eyes as they watched Ulsa light the candles. Her lips were pulled into a soft smile, but sadness tinged her eyes. "Dear friends and family, thank you for attending my Coming of Age Ceremony. It is with great pleasure to announce my first act as heir to Sector 17 and the Flaming Flower Land Holdings—I will travel to the capital and represent our lands' interest in the Lunar Court of the Seventeen Holdings, so that my dear aunt Eldotch may finally retire and spend her remaining days on her estate with her grandchildren and great-grandchildren. I will hold this position until it is time for me rule Sector 17.

"While I am in the courts, I will do everything I can to encourage other sectors to adopt tax and labor policies similar to ours. Poverty in Sector 17 has declined by 50 percent in the past decade, but we are still a long way from economic equality."

Applause thundered from most of the audience, but Enzi noticed too many people frowning while half-heartedly clapping. Enzi glanced at their aunt. An unnerving smirk rested on her face as she watched Ulsa. Eldotch had made it clear she didn't want Ulsa spreading liberal ideology further into the seventeen sectors. Her smile, wicked as it was, sent Enzi's nerves alight beneath their skin.

They glanced at their sister. Ulsa's jaw clenched and her lips pursed. She blinked away tears, hands white-knuckled and clenched hard. She looked as if she had proclaimed a death sentence for herself. Enzi bowed their head. They should've been the one replacing Eldotch in the courts. They could've tried, even if the results would've been futile. In the end, joining the guard had been the only way to truly relinquish their heirship without the truth getting out.

Maybe Ulsa didn't understand that. Maybe she would've rather risked embarrassment undermining Mother's authority if it meant Enzi staying. Maybe Ulsa wasn't angry that Enzi had forfeited heirship. Maybe she was angry because Enzi hadn't fought for a chance to stay.

*

A live band played soft acoustic music while the party guests sat at rectangular tables. Enzi sat beside their parents and Eldotch at a smaller table with a white tablecloth, a stark difference to the colorful, rainbow-stained cloths adorning the others.

Ulsa sunk into the seat between Mother and Father and glowered at Enzi. "I can't get away from you, can I?"

Enzi tried on a smile. "We're siblings. You're stuck with me."

A breeze rustled Enzi's short bangs as a drone lowered a covered platter onto the table in front of them. The platter glowed purple as the drone pulled the lid away, revealing roast lizard resting on a bed of rice and vegetables.

Ulsa stabbed her lizard with a fork. "So, Enzi, tell me how life has been in the Lunar Guard."

"I've almost died a few times," Enzi blurted. They made eye contact with their sister, wanting to convince her that life after relinquishing heirship hadn't been a walk in the park. "I have more scars than I can count, but I've also made friends more loyal than I imagined possible."

"You did choose a dreadful profession." Aunt Eldotch turned away from Enzi and glared at Ulsa. "I burned myself on the stove once while my cook was on *vacation*. I can't image how laser burns must feel."

"Goddess forbid your poor cook got to take a few days off." Ulsa sawed the tail off of her lizard. Her brows furrowed. "No one is going to die if *she* takes a break, but the Lunar Guard is the most important yet understaffed organization on the Drogan Moon. Still, even a CSO like Enzi should get a fortnight paid leave every year, which they're squandering by crashing my party."

Enzi's shoulders slumped. They pushed back from the table, wondering if they should leave now that the ceremony was over. Maybe this wasn't the right time to fix things with Ulsa.

Mother's hand closed around Enzi's wrist. "I invited Enzi. They're not crashing."

Ulsa rolled her eyes as she chewed. Enzi pursed their lips. A warm, savory scent rose from the roasted reptile on their plate. All six of its legs were still attached. Its emerald tail curled around its body. The cook had removed its head and replaced its guts with sourdough stuffing.

Eldotch swallowed a mouthful of rice. "Enzi risks their life every day to protect this sector. They need a little time off. A cook's job is far less strenuous. I don't know why I must allow mine to spend a week lazing around a lake."

Cooks weren't exactly hard to find. Last time Enzi had hired a cook for the guard barracks, they'd had dozens of applicants. "Why not have two cooks and make sure they take vacation on different days?"

"I can hardly afford one cook with my sister's ridiculous minimum wage." Eldotch pointed her fork at Mother.

Enzi's hands twitched toward Eldotch's arm, but they resisted the urge to seize her wrist.

Ulsa huffed. "The only ridiculous thing about minimum wage is that it still isn't enough to support a family in some areas."

Enzi took a deep breath. Instead of dwelling on imagined threats from their aunt, they needed to defend Ulsa's policy. "We pay our civilian cooks twenty royals an hour because fifteen still isn't enough to live off in the capital. Your budget is much bigger than ours."

"Perhaps the guard should invest more in updating its combat suits instead of squandering it on cooks." Eldotch speared a chunk of lizard meat with her fork.

Enzi grit their teeth. "The Goddess made those suits. They're powered by her energy crystals and have worked just fine for centuries. The working class, on the other hand, has struggled for decades."

"You were wearing one when you almost died last year," Ulsa blurted through a mouthful of meat. Her eyes were wide. She chewed so hard Enzi worried she'd bite her tongue. "Eldotch said your suit malfunctioned and almost cooked you alive."

Enzi froze with their fork halfway to their mouth. "How do you know about that?"

Ulsa looked at her aunt. "She told me after she read the report."

"That report was classified." Enzi's hands tightened around their utensils as they glared at Eldotch. The combat suits rarely had issues, but last year, a glitch in the programming had almost killed Enzi. It would have made the guard look vulnerable if the public found out.

Eldotch smirked. "Sector 17 paid for your medical bills and for the attempts to repair the suit, so I had access to the full report. You may not have cared enough to contact Ulsa, but she cared enough to inquire about you from time to time. I thought she deserved to know."

Enzi closed their eyes. A nervous smile twitched on their face.

"Ulsa was always asking Eldotch for updates about you." Mother's voice was as soft as a late-summer rain.

Silence hung over the group like fog clung to lakes in the morning, but the din of conversation from other tables grew louder. Enzi cut into their lizard. They should say something. Ulsa must have known that Enzi had tried to contact her, at first,. But she had refused to answer Enzi's calls, which had hurt more than getting shot. So Enzi had stopped trying.

They had been angry. They had tried to forget.

But when they were halfway across the moon and saw the daughter of a landholder pay for the meal of a homeless child, they thought of their sister.

When they met an heir who was in hiding because he had wanted to provide free health care for his people, they thought of Ulsa. Enzi believed she would have been proud of them for helping oust his corrupt, Death Marked father from the throne, assuming she didn't hear too many details about how Enzi had made it happen.

Even little things, like fire flowers and the simplest Goddess temples, made Enzi wish that Ulsa was beside them.

Enzi didn't know how to explain how they felt. They didn't know how to admit that they'd been angry—that their anger would've made things worse. So, they shoveled food into their mouth like they were in the mess hall at the barracks, even though at the other tables, people took tiny bites, chewing them with their lips shut tight, not speaking until they swallowed.

Dishes clanked and wings buzzed as bots cleared plates and replaced them with slices of yellow cake, half covered with white frosting and glittering sprinkles. Ulsa slowly cut into hers.

Enzi took a deep breath. "How have things been for you?"

"Busy." Ulsa nibbled a bite, more frosting than cake. "I've spent most of the days shadowing Mother, learning how to do all the paperwork properly, distribute food to the poor, moderate disputes, and collect taxes. I'd love to marry one day, but with all the work I've been doing, there has been almost no time for courtship."

Enzi cringed. Had they still been heir, Ulsa would have all the time in the world to flirt with the ladies, take them on epic dates, and entertain them with history lectures. "I'm sorry."

"I don't know about *courtship*. You've found plenty of time for Lilly and Kelsey." A smile bloomed on Mother's face. "Half the palace staff is placing bets on whether you'll marry one or both of them."

Ulsa blushed.

Enzi leaned forward, catching their sister's eyes. "The two people you were with by the punch bowl?"

"There'd be worse fates than marrying those two." Ulsa sighed. Her grimace faded to a grin. "Okay, fine, I was thinking about proposing in a couple months at the Orbit Ball if I have enough free time to plan something elaborate."

Enzi grinned. "How long have you been seeing them?"

The creases in Ulsa's forehead mirrored the ripples her fork made in her cake's frosting. "Since a few months after you left. They both worked in the gardens, and I'd spent a lot of time moping around there. They helped a lot. But every time someone gave me a hard time about courting people from the 'working class,' I wished you were there to defend me."

"I wish I was too." Enzi's throat tightened, but they forced more words out. "There are so many things I've wanted to tell you, but I didn't think you'd answer if I called."

Ulsa pressed her lips together in something that was almost a smile. "I probably wouldn't have, but I might have hated you less if you hadn't stopped trying."

"I'm here now," said Enzi.

"Would you be if people weren't trying to kill me?"

As Enzi opened their mouth to say yes, a gray blur raced from one table and under the one beside them. Fear stabbed Enzi's chest. The table was too long to go around, so Enzi leapt onto it. Plates and cutlery crunched. Glasses shattered. Another leap and Enzi landed on their feet between Mother, Ulsa, and a cacophony of questions.

The gray mouse drone darted out from another table, flying straight toward Ulsa.

Enzi pulled their blaster from their sleeve and squeezed the trigger. The little mouse juked away from the purple bolt. Cursing, Enzi stepped between Ulsa and the mouse and fired again, melting it before the projectile could release. *How many of these damned things are there?*

"Is that a no?" Ulsa's hands clenched around her fork as Mother and Father crushed her with a hug.

Enzi's hands shook as they tapped their comm. "Reemins, I shot one of those mouse drones at the head table."

"On my way." Reemins's voice was loud and clear in the comm.

Enzi's chest sagged as they exhaled.

"Thank you, Enzi." Father let go of Ulsa as Reemins and four guards rushed from the shrubs separating the dining area from the dance floor, all clad in the Lunar Guard's violet dress uniform. They stood around Ulsa and her parents until another two led a containment bot, a black metal rectangle on wheels, toward the drone's smoking remnants.

Enzi turned back to their sister. "Ulsa, I—"

Ulsa pushed through the crowd of gaping party guests.

Enzi rushed after her. "Where are you going?"

Ulsa charged down the aisle between rows of long tables. Heads turned and mouths whispered as she passed, but no one moved. Enzi jogged after her, glad most of the two hundred and forty-three guests were all seated and not providing obstacles Ulsa could use to lose them.

When the tables ended, Ulsa sprinted into the garden, weaving between bushes and the empty stands that had held hors d'oeuvres earlier. She was much easier to follow now that people weren't crowding the jumble of hedges, shrubberies, and fountains. She didn't slow until she was at the castle's east entrance—the one that led into the Goddess Chapel.

She leaned against shimmering stonewall, huffing and puffing. "You're not even out of breath."

"I run twice a day." Enzi leaned on the wall beside Ulsa. "Talk to me."

Ulsa closed her eyes and grit her teeth.

A menagerie of bushes cut to look like Earth animals stretched in front of Enzi while drones shone light on and around the bushes, scanning for hidden threats. The lawn where dinner had been set glowed. String music and the louder pieces of conversation buzzed. The Goddess towered over all of it, looking as smug as ever.

Does she know what pain her law is causing my family?

"I'm sorry," Ulsa squeaked. "I should be grateful you've saved me again."

"But you're not."

Ulsa rolled her head toward Enzi and opened her eyes. "Enzi, I can't do this. Even helping Mother stresses me out. I feel sick to my stomach. What happens when she dies? When I have to take over? What if I mess up and start a war?"

Enzi wanted to tell Ulsa that she would make a fantastic ruler when the time came, but they suspected she was sick of hearing it. "Mother is healthy. Unless someone kills her, you have decades to learn how to cope."

"I've doubled my med dosages since you left, and I barely have time to see my therapist." Tears trailed Ulsa's face, washing away remnants of stubborn makeup. Her hands clutched the folds of her gown. "It would've been easier if you'd at least been here to help. If you hadn't dropped this burden on me *and* left me to carry it alone."

Guilt pressed on Enzi like an ocean. They reached out and took Ulsa's soft hand. "If I could go back and change things, I'd still save your life, but I wouldn't have chosen to work in intelligence. I'd have requested a role that would've let me stay close enough to visit."

A blackbird perched on the edge of a bush, plucking a purple berry off a branch covered in red leaves. It swallowed its prize and leapt onto another, only to be chased away by a larger bird. The bigger bird, clad in feathers the same fiery red as the bush, screeched at the smaller one before feasting on berries. Even things like that, the birds and Ulsa's confession and this sprawling party, made Enzi miss being home.

Enzi thumbed wetness from Ulsa's cheek. "In the highly unlikely event you do screw up and start a war, I've got you covered in that department."

Ulsa rolled her eyes. "Let me guess. You'll win it for me, defeating my enemies with spectacular explosions."

Enzi shook their head. "Blowing things up is always a last resort."

"But say I did cause a war, maybe because policies go too far and the right revolts. How would you win it?"

Enzi stared into their sister's eyes. "I wouldn't."

"What do you mean?" Ulsa's hand fumbled for Enzi's.

They grinned. "When was the last time there was an actual war between sectors?"

Ulsa stared at the Goddess, as if the answer was written on her forehead. "Centuries, but there was almost one last year between Sectors 9 and 11 because Hirian found out Balder was Death Marked and he wouldn't abdicate his throne."

Enzi arched her eyebrows. "And what happened?"

"Balder got drunk and fell down the stairs, and his son, who'd been missing for years, came home. He implemented a universal health care policy, but he also modeled new labor laws off of Mother's." Ulsa pushed off the wall and turned, face-to-face with Enzi. "He didn't fall, did he?"

Enzi shook their head.

Ulsa's eyes widened. "There was a bill for you traveling to Sector 11 during that fortnight. Sometimes I forget the guard does as many assassinations as it prevents."

Enzi shrugged. "We stop wars before they happen. I

promise you won't start one on my watch."

Each sector had a division in the Lunar Guard, but most rulers ignored the fact that their division didn't answer to them, funding aside. First and foremost, the guard's job was to prevent war from breaking out on the Drogan Moon. Sometimes, that meant assassinating toxic rulers who clung to power no matter how the Goddess marked them.

Enzi gazed at the sky. Thousands of stars twinkled. Enzi imagined invisible lines connecting them to form lions and spoons, scorpions and maidens.

"Do you miss the fieldwork?" asked Ulsa.

"No." The answer was out of Enzi's mouth before they'd fully processed the question, but it was true. "Is it weird that I enjoy the paperwork?"

A smile broke through the misery plastered on Ulsa's face. Giggles bubbled over her lips. "You definitely would've made a better ruler than I."

Enzi shook their head. "I'm as good an administrator as I am a spy, but a person who can so easily justify murder has no place ruling a sector."

Ulsa stepped away. "Would you murder me if that is what it took to keep the peace?"

Enzi frowned. They clasped their hands behind their back. "Murder missions aren't part of my job description anymore."

Ulsa showed her palms, like she was about to fend off an attack. "No, but you order them, don't you?"

"Of horrible people who violate the Goddess's laws. If you stirred things up so much that we had to remove you, I'd fake your death and set you up with a false identity in some rural area on the warm side. Probably in whichever town had the prettiest girls."

Ulsa's smile returned. "That doesn't sound so bad."

"No, but it's unlikely. You piss off old aristocrats like Eldotch, but the people love you." Troublesome aristocrats could be assassinated or disappeared, but it was a lot harder to put down a rebellion. Even if Ulsa weren't Enzi's sister, she was the last person they'd want to remove from power.

Her smile grew. "The people are the one perk of this job. While I'm on the council, I can make a difference on the whole moon, not just the sector. And when Mother passes, I can continue her work."

"I'll help you as much as I legally can." Enzi reached a hand out to their sister.

"I'd like that." Ulsa squeezed Enzi's fingers.

Enzi smiled, but their heart was still beating fast. Ulsa's words implied her reign of silence was over, but would she like who Enzi had become?

*

Enzi should've been light with relief, but their chest was tight and their heart refused to slow. *Does a killer belong in the good graces of an heir, even if that heir is their sister?*

Ulsa, on the other hand, was a dam that had finally burst. By the time they got back to the dance floor, Enzi had learned all about the foods Kelsey and Lilly liked, how they never wanted to stop working with plants, and their plans for producing heirs. It seemed Ulsa had already asked the two women to marry her, and that the proposal, which had to be extravagant, was a mere formality.

The dancing had resumed. Synthetic beats made it hard to hear Ulsa. The flashing lights blurred with moving bodies, and the crowd resembled one giant organism. Lilly and Kelsey stood at the edge of the chaos, glaring at

Enzi.

"Maybe I should talk to them before I introduce you." Ulsa chewed her lip, looking back and forth between Enzi and her girlfriends.

Enzi winked. "I won't be far away."

As Ulsa walked off, almost skipping, Reemins stepped out of the shadows and stood beside Enzi. "She looks happy."

"I made her laugh." Not too far in front of Enzi, Kelsey frowned and Lily smiled while Ulsa spoke to them. Their words were swallowed by the music.

"Then why do you look like a cadet who just saw their first corpse?"

Lily and Ulsa hugged, but Kelsey stood back, frowning at the ground.

Enzi's fists clenched and unclenched at their side. "She reminded me of who I am."

Reemins cocked his head. "And who, exactly, are you?"

"A monster. A killer who loves paperwork."

Reemins laughed. "Killing doesn't make you a monster. But the paperwork? That is pure evil."

Lily and Ulsa looped their arms around Kelsey and led her onto the dance floor. Enzi sighed. "Did you find any more bots?"

Reemins nodded. "We did, but it was in the castle kitchens, hidden in a secret compartment within a cupboard. We're questioning those who have access."

Enzi took a step toward the dance floor. Ulsa's shimmering outfit was a beacon twirling through a haze of strobes and dancers. "You're authorized to use whatever means necessary to discover the culprit. This isn't just about saving my sister, but preserving a useful politician."

Reemins slunk back into the shadows, and Enzi edged closer to their sister. They gagged on the stench of sweat and perfume, weaving through jumping and gyrating bodies. But Ulsa and her girlfriends weren't there.

When Enzi emerged near the garden area, a few people milled around cupcake displays and beverage stations.

Enzi jumped as a strong hand squeezed her shoulder.

"I think you're getting through to her," said Mother.

Enzi let out a tense breath. Mother smiled at them. "When did you see her?"

"Just a minute ago at the tea station." Mother set her hands on the top of Enzi's arms and turned them. Over her shoulder, they caught glimpses of their sister in a heated debate with Kelsey. "Ulsa said she hopes you have enough leave to attend the Orbit Ball as a guest and help her plan a sneaky proposal."

"I think I can manage that." Enzi smiled, chiding themself for panicking about Ulsa being out of sight. Only two of the drones had escaped notice of security, and everyone was on higher alert now. If Reemins was following protocol, there would be both human and bot eyes on Ulsa for the rest of the party.

"I hope you visit more, now that you don't have Ulsa as an excuse to avoid home." Mother winked. "You should also try talking to some guests other than me, your father, Ulsa, and Eldotch."

Enzi nodded. "Did Eldotch fight you about giving Ulsa her job?"

Mother frowned. "No. Why would she?"

"Because she hates everything Ulsa stands for."

Mother shook her head. "That's true, but at the end of the day, her role in the courts is only a job. She's more than a decade older than me and ready to retire."

"She didn't try to convince you to appoint anyone else?"

"No. Stubborn as she can be, she knows it's not her place to."

"I'm just surprised," said Enzi.

Mother shrugged. "Maybe you don't know her as well as you think."

That was exactly what Enzi was worried about, but not for the same reason as Mother.

After using their comm to check in with Reemins, Enzi let Mother lead them around the party. They mingled with cousins, great aunts, and members of landholding families. As they listened to talk of happy employees, of shrinking coffers, of thriving crops, and gossip about who was courting whom, Enzi couldn't help but store away bits of information. Things they could use to gauge how likely these people might be to want Ulsa dead. But while some people hinted at certain grievances, Enzi realized they didn't gain anything by removing Ulsa from the picture. But if Mother and Eldotch were to die, and Ulsa never had children, succession would move back to Eldotch's line even though Eldotch herself couldn't rule.

Enzi's comm buzzed. They tapped their ear to answer.

It was Reemins. "Enzi? There is something I need to show you."

Enzi excused themself from the conversation and found Reemins in a circle of shrubs surrounding a fishpond. "I found these in the castle security feeds."

He projected an image of two people wearing baggy

black prep-cook smocks, handing off a box to one another. It looked benign. The next image was one of the boys talking to someone else, handing them something obscured by their sleeve. The third was the holder of said mystery item talking to Eldotch's cook.

Enzi frowned. "What, exactly, is this supposed to prove?"

"We think the box shown there was the same one we found in the hidden compartment of the flour cabinet. Alone, it's not enough to hold up in court. We're trying to locate the people in the photo and isolate a DNA sample from the box. But right now? I'm just saying keep an eye on your aunt."

Enzi nodded, wondering if they would view this series of images with any seriousness had they not already been suspicious of Eldotch. Enzi used Reemins's feed to locate Ulsa. His rings projected an image of her strolling into the castle arm in arm with Kelsey and Lilly. The door shut before the drone could follow her inside. Enzi's guts twisted. They followed the path from Reemins's feed and ran toward the girls.

"They probably want some time alone," Reemins said, padding to a halt beside them. "And even if Eldotch *is* behind this, do you think she would do anything herself?"

That was probably true, but Enzi couldn't help feeling suspicious—as if their sister was running into a trap. When they passed a statue of the Goddess, and saw its hand raised with a finger pointing at the castle, they ran faster.

The sounds of the party faded to a barely noticeable lull as Enzi sprinted past dancers, lights, flowers, and shrubs, and slipped into the chapel. They slowed over the stone floor, catching a glimpse at the statue whose arm waved toward the next door. Enzi pushed through it, emerging into a hallway with plush red carpet. Paintings of the dead glared at them from wood-paneled walls. Enzi ghosted by, eyes fixated on the end of the hall.

Peering around a corner where two halls met, Enzi saw Eldotch walking back from an indoor restroom, off-limits to most guests besides the royal family.

Ulsa appeared in the other hallway, walking toward Eldotch, laughing and stumbling with Kelsey and Lilly. Eldotch waved. Smiled and talked. Enzi watched, back pressed to a wall, loosening their blaster in its hidden holster. They weren't surprised to see movement in the shadows by a statue. A mouse drone turned toward Ulsa. Enzi wasn't at the right angle.

"Ulsa, I was just looking for you!" Enzi ran out of the hall. The mouse's back opened as Enzi slipped between her and the mouse. The dart released as Enzi's hand closed on the trigger.

Ulsa and the girls jumped back. Eldotch's face flicked from a wrinkled scowl to wide eyes and raised brows. "That's the second one that got past your forces tonight!"

Ulsa swallowed hard and pointed at Enzi's tie. "You're hit."

A little white needle stuck into their shirt. They hadn't felt it prick their skin, but that didn't mean it hadn't.

Ulsa reached.

"Don't touch it. The whole thing could be laced would poison." Enzi wanted to take a deep breath, but didn't dare let their chest expand lest it hit the dart. They breathed shallowly and gingerly touched their comm, whispering for Reemins to come with a med bot and containment tech.

"Is it touching yours?" Ulsa ripped a strip of fabric off

of her dress as Kelsey pulled a cloth from her tuxedo pocket.

"I don't think so. It can wait until Reemins gets here."

Tears streamed down Ulsa's cheeks. "That dart was meant for me. You didn't hesitate to get between us."

Enzi wasn't sure if it was emotion or poison making their throat feel squeezed tight and hot. "You're my sister. You're my best friend."

"I've been horrible to you. I've held a grudge when I should've been grateful." Ulsa's fingers tore at the sides of their silky gown.

Enzi's fingers twitched toward Ulsa. They wanted to hug her. They didn't dare move. "I didn't exactly make an effort to talk things over. I ran when I should've fought to stay by your side."

"Enzi, are you okay?" Reemins charged into the hallway with two drones and three guards.

It only took seconds for the drone to remove the dart and scan Enzi, confirming the needle hadn't penetrated their armored tank top. As soon as the bot was clear, Ulsa threw her bony arms around Enzi and crushed them with a hug. "I'm so sorry."

"Me too." Enzi squeezed her back, trying not to sneeze as they inhaled her lilac perfume.

Flaxen hair half covered their face, but it didn't obstruct their view of Eldotch, who slowly backed down the hall. Enzi narrowed their eyes and bared their teeth. *I know it was you.*

"I hope you catch who did it." Kelsey's soft voice drew Enzi's attention away from their aunt.

"I will." Enzi smirked as they let go of their sister.

Ulsa brushed off her dress and wiped tears off her red

cheeks. "I never formally introduced you. Enzi, this is Kelsey and Lilly. Both use she and her pronouns." Ulsa pointed at Enzi. "This is my sister, Enzi, who uses they and them pronouns."

"Thank you for saving her life," said Kelsey, and shook Ulsa's hand.

Enzi smiled. "She's probably in danger because of something I did."

Ulsa shook her head. "I only lived to be in danger *now* because you saved me last time someone tried to kill me. This isn't your fault."

*

With the party guests gone and the music off, Enzi could finally hear the song of insects and birds singing away the final minutes of the dark fortnight. Red fish glided through a stone pond, occasionally creating splashes as they leapt to snatch bugs. Ulsa sat beside Enzi. They both watched fins swish through the water.

Ulsa put their hand over Enzi's. "Do you really think it was Eldotch?"

Enzi pressed their lips together. "She has motive, but the evidence connecting her is shaky at best. I can't prove it yet, but my gut tells me she is responsible."

Ulsa closed her eyes and sucked in a deep breath. "I was going to live with her...and shadow her for a few months before she fully retired. When she moved back to her country estate, Kelsey and Lilly were going to join me in the delegate residence."

Enzi squeezed Ulsa's hand as the impending sunrise leached darkness from the sky. "I wouldn't recommend that. When are you supposed to leave?"

Ulsa's cool eyes met theirs. "In three days. I'm sure I

could use my status to get some kind of living quarters in the capital, but it might take longer to find something I'd actually like. And while I can afford it, I'd rather not waste unnecessary funds on housing."

Enzi squinted as light pierced the horizon. "Are you saying you want me to somehow get Eldotch out in three days?"

A smirk crept across Ulsa's face, glowing in the first rays of a new day. "Your house has a few bedrooms, doesn't it?"

Enzi tilted their head. Fear and hope rose in their chest like the ball of fire creeping into the sky. "Are you asking if you can stay with me?"

"Can I? We'd probably be too busy to see much of each other, but it might give us a chance to catch up."

"It's three bedrooms, but it's small and simple compared to the castle." Enzi stood, giving into the urge to move while trying to picture what it would be like to live with their sister again. "I have routines that might seem weird to you."

"I don't have to come if you don't want me to." Ulsa sat, still and quiet, while Enzi paced around the pond. The water looked red now, reflecting the color of the changing sky.

Enzi sunk against the wall in front of Ulsa. "It probably is one of the safer places you could stay until the guard catches whoever wants you dead."

Ulsa beamed. "Is that a yes?"

Enzi nodded. Lightness inflated their chest while they watched the sunrise with their sister. By the time the sky had lightened to a pale purple, they felt like they could float away. They had their sister back, and had no intention of losing her again anytime soon.

WEAVE THE DARK, WEAVE THE LIGHT

Anna Zabo

The waxing moon hung high above Pittsburgh, bright and silver, illuminating nearby clouds crossing the night sky. Ari added their own ephemeral puff to PPG Plaza's chilly air. They'd already paid the fee and had a wristband to get onto the ice rink. All that was left was to lace their skates.

Had Theo and Bess joined Ari, no doubt they'd tease them for being a fire witch on ice. That was bullshit. Opposite elements attracted each other, and Ari enjoyed the chaos invoked between the two. They loved ice skating and swimming. The darkness of night. All the things they shouldn't. Rebellion was as close to Ari as the amber they wore against their skin and the citrine in the pocket of their red wool coat.

Colored lights from the spires of the glass castle surrounding the plaza cast a rainbow on the skaters. A lit tree in the center of the rink glittered, and upbeat Christmas tunes thrummed in the air, despite it being mid-November.

Ari glanced up, but between the lights and the bright moon, no stars hung in the sky—at least none they could see. The stars watched, though. They always did, regardless of the moon or the lights or the season.

That knowledge was as frosty as the breath in Ari's lungs as they hit the ice, shaking away the thought. The night felt perilous, like the edge of a cliff.

Unfortunately, the surface of the rink was utter *crap*, full of snow, nicks, and gouges. They'd expected nothing less. Even with resurfacing, the small rink became scraped up minutes after the Zamboni chugged back into its lair.

Didn't matter. As long as they kept moving and tried nothing fancy, their skates would take them where they wanted—around and around until all that existed was the tinny music, the scrape of blades, and the fire Ari'd come to collect. Oh, their element was with them, long ribbons of fiery red, orange, and blue, but the heart in their magic was missing. The *passion*.

Ari hadn't felt whole since Samhain. They'd opened themself that day, and chaos had entered. Loneliness. Lack of desire. Which was apropos, in a way. They'd always had a tenuous connection to their magic and their element, and no one could explain why Ari's magic stuttered and fizzled even when they filled themself with as much fire as they could manage.

Bess had chided them—gently. "If you choose a path..."

They *had*. But no one else in their circle believed chaos was a proper path.

Tonight, to get away, Ari'd donned brilliant gold tights under their long black skirt, wrapped themself in a retro Joy Division sweatshirt, taken their skates, and slipped away from the apartment they shared with Theo.

There was magic in the laughter here, in the delighted shrieks of kids and the embarrassed, happy yelps of teens clinging to the walls of the rink. Power lurked in grins of those who could spin, skate backward, and weave through the crowd.

Life. Delight. Happiness. Ari wrapped that warmth into their soul, a little spell to carry their hope through winter. Something to warm their heart when everything else was emptiness tinged with frustration.

Fire and water could be many things; the ice beneath their blades was proof enough of that. But fiery rage and anger weren't what Ari needed to chase away the void that had formed in their soul. Little spells worked—mostly. Larger spells fell flat. Life grated and itched. Ari found themself alone in a circle full of friends and an office full of coworkers.

Bess had told them to be specific with their spell, and they'd *tried*. They wanted a connection. Something less ephemeral than the occasional hookup. They had their friends and their job, but neither of those warmed their soul.

So much for opening themself up to the universe. The void between the stars had poured right in.

In front of Ari, another skater wobbled and fell. They leapt over tangled legs. Landing, however, sent Ari careering out of control until a gloved hand settled on their arm and a hard body steadied theirs.

"Careful." Amusement filled that voice. Power and danger.

Every piece of Ari's magic turned toward the stranger who'd caught them. Elemental energy clashed and wove around them—Ari's fire and something deadlier, tempting, and powerful.

The stranger was tall. A black knit hat covered light hair, and black leather gloves rested against Ari's coat. Inhumanly blue eyes caught theirs. A midnight peacoat was paired with a bright white scarf that glittered like diamonds. Those features could have been masculine, or not. There was something otherworldly, something terrifying and wonderful about that face. Light and cold. Darkness. Eternity.

Ari blinked, but the effect didn't vanish. "Thanks."

"Nice jump." Whoever they were let go. Still, Ari felt the pull of the other's magic, like gravity.

Passion bloomed in Ari's bones, the first they'd felt in months. The need to touch, taste, and share was almost painful in intensity.

The skater glided away and was lost in the crowd before Ari could voice a second thanks.

Shit.

Ari skated after them.

Despite the tiny size of the rink, Ari couldn't spot the person who'd caught them. There were black knit caps and leather gloves galore on tall strangers, but none wore a scarf full of light or had eyes as old as the universe.

Ari shivered. Not from cold—that never touched them—nor from fear, but from nearly extinct fervor sparking to life. This was intrigue and danger. Theo would've said to be careful. Bess would've cautioned against having anything to do with that particular stranger.

But Ari had a heart of knives and a soul of fire. Of course they'd follow.

A few more loops gave Ari time to settle, to whisper a charm, to trace symbols in their mind, and to collect wisps of fire. Then they stepped off the frozen water, thanked it for its presence and time, took their skates off, hoisted the carrying bag on their shoulder, and headed toward the Point.

In theory, Point State Park closed at sunset, but it was also a pathway, part of the city, and this time of year, it was lit with LED trees and giant snowflakes on poles. Part of an old star fort was marked by a zigzagging path across a lawn. Ari walked under the bridge that sped an interstate over land, then water. Nature lurked beyond. Trees and shrubs. Native plants. A piece of wild at the edge of a city, bound by water.

Dried leaves scratched across concrete walkways, blown into tree beds. Some animal rustled in the underbrush. Ari strode past a tree made of lights strung like a maypole, made their way around the silent and drained water fountain, and came to a stop. They stared at the confluence of the rivers, their skates at their feet.

So much water. But fire too, in the passing trains across the river, in car engines on the interstate, and in boats slipping through the rivers.

Ari found their memory, the fine cord of emotion, that odd element, and used it to will the stranger back to them.

"Youth," that same voice said from behind, "is bold and reckless."

Ari's heart stuttered. "But you came." They turned enough to catch the brightness of the scarf. "And I'm not *that* young."

"I came." Agreement, and amusement, as well. The stranger stepped next to Ari, and cold fire curled around Ari's legs. "And you *are* that young if you're summoning *me*, little fire witch."

This time, Ari turned to regard the stranger's profile in the dim light. The hair that peeked out from their winter hat was as gray as the moon, and their scarf glittered like nothing had a right to do. Something magical dwelt inside this being. A flame that wouldn't burn—it would cause you not to exist.

Too much power swam inside and around them, an element Ari didn't understand but *tasted*. They should have been terrified. Instead, they craved the knowledge in those eyes and that skin under their fingers.

Ari swallowed. "You're not human."

"You knew I wasn't human the moment I touched you."

Ari had, but this wasn't any elemental being they'd heard about, that was for certain. Not fae, nor phoenix— the fire was the wrong type for that. Chilling white-blue, rather than blazing red, violet, and yellow. "What do I call you?" they murmured.

Those eyes locked on theirs. "My name's Jonathan Aster."

Aster like the bright flowers of late summer, the last color before the frost. "Pronoun?"

A twitch in Jonathan's lips. "*He* feels the most correct at the moment."

Ari filed away that tidbit and gazed out at the black water of the rivers that reflected the bright lights from the shores, the bridges, and the hills. They kept their name behind their lips.

Jonathan laughed. "It's only polite to gift me your name, seeing as you have mine."

Ari bristled and watched silver clouds slide across the sky. "It's Ari Zydik. And they."

Jonathan nodded. "Yes." As if it were an affirmation, as if he'd known their name already, as if he'd always known Ari.

What are *you?* This question remained on their tongue, though barely.

"What spells will you cast when you get home?" Jonathan slipped closer to the river, then turned, blocking the view. Ari had to study his face. "What will you make from the sparks you collected?"

"Is that any of your business?" Ari snapped.

A chuckle was the reply.

Jonathan was stunning in a delicate way. Strong lines. High cheekbones. Teeth as white as his scarf. His skin was darker than Ari's pale complexion. Even in the moonlight, the golden hue was evident. Sun-touched, but that still didn't seem like a fitting description.

Not an angel. Not a demon. Ari'd never met either, but Jonathan's energy was wrong for what had been described in the books they'd read. He was light *and* dark. There was a sense of eternity, but not timelessness. "You're old."

"Very." He stalked forward. "Very old."

"But you'll die." A sliver of space separated them. Ari watched blue eyes dance like the heart of the hottest flame.

"Eventually. But not for a long time." Soft words, a thin stream of smoke in the night air.

Energy whipped around Ari. They snatched it and drew it closer, devouring it.

Jonathan lifted his hand—but not in aggression. "You should ask before you take." His leather-clad fingers hovered near Ari's shoulder. "May I?"

They nodded, unsure of what Jonathan was asking, but so very sure they wanted whatever was being offered.

His palm cupped Ari's shoulder, and elemental energy slammed into them. Not fire—no, nothing so simple. This was a lick of lightning or the arc of a transformer, but colder. The depth of space.

The heart of the universe throbbed in Jonathan, a distant bell reverberating through the bones of the earth and the moon. Ari sucked the energy into their soul, wrapping themself around the wild, *untamable* joy.

Jonathan's lips parted in a feral parody of a smile. "Oh, little witch, you are something different."

Ari placed their hand on Jonathan's midnight peacoat and slipped two fingers between the buttons. "I'm hardly little." Hardly young or inexperienced. What would it be like to have this man under them? Bound? What would his skin taste like under lips and tongue? To linger in bed and talk about the mysteries of the universe?

Jonathan's laugh, sharp and biting, clouded the air. "Dangerous."

"You or me?"

"Me. You're merely reckless."

"Am I?" Ari pushed their fingers further into the coat, stroking the warm fabric that lay over muscle and bone.

"You have no idea what you're playing with." He removed his hand and took a step back, out of reach.

Ari brushed their thumb against their lips, tasting lingering warmth. "Not fire. You're not that."

"Certainly not *that*." Jonathan's scarf glittered in the moonlight, as did his eyes.

The latter blazed for a second, and Ari sucked in a breath, feeling that strange, cold brightness twine and burn within them. Ancient. Older than the world. "Starlight." The word fell from their lips. Of *course*. Aster. Star.

The playfulness on Jonathan's lips fell away.

"Plasma, then." Something Ari shouldn't have been able to draw or keep or even touch. And yet, they felt the strands inside them, as much as they could hold.

Reckless? Maybe. Dangerous? Most certainly. Even if Jonathan hadn't realized that.

"I should add brave to your list of descriptors," he murmured.

Ari stepped forward and touched the buttons of Jonathan's coat. "Why are you here?"

"Some secrets you have to earn, Ari."

They stood together for silent moments. Curiosity warred with frustration and slipped into lust. What would it be like to fuck a star? *This* star? To strip Jonathan of his clothes, tie him down, and take him apart? To verbally spar with him for hours? To be known physically and mentally by something so powerful? "And how does one earn your secrets, Jonathan?"

He unlooped the scarf from around his neck and draped it around Ari's, holding on to the ends. "Weave me a spell."

The fabric was shockingly warm against Ari's skin, or maybe that was their blush rising. Spells for another required a connection that didn't exist yet between them and Jonathan. Ari breathed out fear and drew in strength. "What sort of spell? Protection? Empowerment? Love?"

Jonathan tugged the scarf before letting the ends go. The motion brought Ari closer. "Your choice, fire witch." He paused. "Though I don't think anyone can spell someone into love."

"It's an alignment of intent. I can *help* with that, in the case of love. But if one party isn't interested..." They shrugged, dug into their pocket for the citrine they always carried, and handed it to Jonathan. Once again, when they touched, energy sparked. Ari pulled more into them.

"All magic is intent." Jonathan closed his fingers around the citrine before bringing it to his lips and kissing the stone. "It'll be interesting to see what you do with yours."

Ari wanted that mouth open in surprise and ecstasy, wanted to see Jonathan gasping in need. They wanted to know Jonathan—and wanted to be known in return.

"I had no idea humans could channel plasma. It's not an element anyone talks about."

"You, I believe, can do whatever you want." Jonathan tucked the stone into the pocket of his coat. "It might be a human trait, but I suspect that's peculiar to you." His smile was knife sharp. "I suppose we'll see."

"We'll meet again?" Those words were a blade pressed to Ari's throat, all thrill and adrenaline. They lifted their chin. Another chance to uncover Jonathan and unfold themself.

Maybe he understood, because he whispered into Ari's ear, "Most certainly."

"Good." Jonathan's neck was right there. If they turned, they could press their lips to Jonathan's skin. "I want to taste you."

This close, his laugh was like the rumble of distant thunder. "It's written into your every move."

Jonathan smelled of winter, rose, and the press of thorns. "I don't know anything about you." And he knew nothing of them. Oh, but they wanted that. Wanted to turn Jonathan inside out. Wanted to inhale his element as if it were air.

"You have my name, and you know what I am. The rest that you long for? You can find out."

"At what price?" There was always one with beings like this.

"I've told you." Johnathan straightened, but remained a breath apart. "Though I should ask you. What do you want, Ari Zydik? What price must I pay to know *you*?"

I don't know. But it was the word "control" that slipped from their lips. Both were true.

Jonathan's eyes glittered like the lights on the river. "That's quite the price."

Their laugh scratched across the empty park. "I know." Too much to ask.

A breeze teased the edges of Jonathan's hair, and he was as still and heavy as the hours before dawn. Ari held their breath.

Finally, Jonathan's lips curled up. "Take your taste," he murmured. "I'll consider your price."

They pressed their lips to Jonathan's neck, licking the skin there, and tasted mint and peril.

In the next moment, Jonathan closed his gloved hand around Ari's throat. Not hard, and not for long. Then he was walking around the silent, yawing fountain. "Enjoy the rest of your evening, Ari."

They could've followed, but heat rooted Ari to the ground. They watched Jonathan, who wasn't human at all, climb a set of stairs, walk past the Christmas tree, and across the moonlit lawn until he vanished.

Even then, Jonathan burned bright in Ari's mind and soul. They stood for a time, then collected their skate bag and trudged from the park, full of energy, lust, and trepidation.

It was a very long bus ride home.

*

Morning came way the fuck too early, pulling Ari from dreams of lips, light, and thrusting. Their phone chirped with birdsongs and soft music, and it took three tries to grab the damn thing and shut it off. They stared at slivers of morning stretched across the ceiling, still achingly hard, their heart beating against their ribs and the phantom taste of Jonathan lingering in their mouth.

What remained of the dream drifted away faster than they could pull it back. Only the hollow ache in their soul, the memory of Jonathan, and their stiff dick remained. They'd never been good at lucid dreaming nor at remembering their dreams.

"There's too much fire in you," Chole had said. She wove air and earth and practically lived in her dreams. The spells she'd given Ari hadn't helped. Strange that their inability would stem from fire, since Matty wove fire, but he'd never had issues remembering his dreams. None of their circle did, but Ari.

Another reminder of how, even in the middle of their circle, they were alone. "I want to belong," they'd told Theo before Samhain, when they'd both been working on their spells.

Theo had peered back if they'd grown three heads. "But you do."

They'd not mentioned that again, to anyone.

Last night, they'd tasted a star.

Fuck. Ari struggled out of their heavy nest of blankets. They still hummed with the energy they'd sipped from Jonathan, even after casting last night. Scattered about were sigils drawn on pages and crystals holding fire and light. Still, Ari's blood burned and sparked, and Jonathan's strange blue eyes, pale hair, and golden skin lingered in their thoughts. His scent clung to their nostrils.

Weave me a spell.

Wasn't so simple. When they'd returned home, they'd lit incense, cleared the space, and focused on setting down spell after spell while Jonathan's element was fresh inside them. Protection. Empowerment. One for sparking creativity. Even a love potion. Everything had turned flat, as spells had before. Yes, there was energy in the sigils and crystals but not *intent*, not power. The spells would never work as they should. Ari'd have to bleed the magic out of them later.

They had no idea what Jonathan wanted. Hell, they weren't sure what they wanted.

A connection. Understanding.

Ari shook away those thoughts. Sex and control were ideas they could wrap their mind around. Lust was an old friend. Everything else sounded perilously close to something they had no framework for, no way to navigate.

Didn't help that they'd tripped over Theo's black sneakers and Bess's purple heels last night, and now dreaded leaving their room. Ari liked Bess a lot—she'd encouraged needed grounding in their circle. Bess had focused the group and brought order.

They chafed at order, though. Some structure was fine, but on their own terms, not enforced by others. Bess tended to mother Ari, even though they were all about the same age and had been studying magic for similar amounts of time.

Ari darted into the bathroom and showered, then dove back into their room to change, hoping they'd escape before either Bess or Theo woke up. No such luck. Bess lingered in the bedroom doorway, wrapped in a robe, her long braids stark black lines against red silk.

Of course she noticed Jonathan's scarf in Ari's hand, shimmering like starlight even as morning sun streamed through the hallway window.

"Where'd you get that, baby doll?" Her gaze flicked from the scarf and pinned Ari with a *look*.

"Not your baby doll," Ari drawled before heading to the living room. "And a guy gave it to me last night."

"That's no ordinary scarf, love." Bess followed.

"No shit." Ari drew the scarf around their neck and pulled on their coat. They let the *love* go. It was better than *doll* any day.

Bess planted a hand on her hip. "So, what did you give this *guy* in return for that, hmm?" The way her tone changed, Ari knew she was asking: *who did you fuck for that scarf?*

Ari laughed. Yeah, they wanted Jonathan, wanted to push him down and have their every way with him. But sex for a scarf, even one wrapped in magic? Please.

Not on the first night, anyway.

"I gave him a piece of citrine." They paused. "And the promise of a spell." They'd started a dance with Jonathan that Ari didn't understand, but felt the rhythm nonetheless.

Bess stepped closer. "Oh, Ari." There was worry in her voice. Honest, actual worry. "What *kind* of spell?"

"Look, I gotta get to work. I don't have time to play twenty questions." Maybe they were as reckless as Jonathan said.

"What, spell, *what*?" Theo echoed sleepily as he stepped into the living room. His eyes locked onto Ari, and he straightened, all weariness vanishing. "Whoa, Ari." Theo's brown eyes were wide and fearful. "That's not fire in you. What the *fuck*?"

That was a drawback to living with Theo—he was an earth witch who could work water as well, but unlike Ari, Theo saw more than just his own elements—he saw them *all*, including Jonathan's, it seemed. *Definitely* time to leave. "It's nothing. It's *fine*. I'm fine. I'm gonna be late." Ari grabbed their backpack and ran out of the apartment.

They took the stairs rather than wait for the elevator. They couldn't handle the look in Theo's eyes, or the one in Bess's.

They both cared about Ari—that was mutual—but Ari didn't know if the *family* thing worked. They'd never be able to convince their circle that Jonathan wasn't dangerous, especially since Jonathan was *terrifying*. Might as well be a demon, but he *wasn't*. He was a deep part of existence, an ancient spark of energy.

Weave me a spell.

Why would a star need a witch's spell? And how the hell was Ari going to create one when they didn't know what Jonathan needed?

Despite the mention of love spells, they were sure romance wasn't what Jonathan wanted. And besides, Ari didn't love easily. Sex was fun and uncomplicated. Friendships were foundational. Romantic love was...*messy*. Ari had enough chaos in their life. Sex, though...that might be a singular focus they needed in order to weave magic. Granted, with their kinks, that particular avenue involved tying Jonathan up, and they suspected the answer to the price they'd set would be no.

Ari slung their bag onto their back. The walk and wait at the bus stop wasn't long, and no one seemed to notice anything more odd about Ari than normal. They were wearing black tights and a long navy skirt, a crisp white button-down, and a brilliant red bow tie that peeked from their coat. Combat boots rounded out the outfit. There might be snow later, and no way were they risking good shoes to crap weather. Besides, they liked the boots—all that black leather.

Squirrel Hill was pretty laid-back, but they'd probably get some looks later in the commute, especially since they'd skipped shaving. Whatever. They knew who they were.

When the bus came, Ari snagged a window seat.

Businesses, houses, and streets blurred past. Ari pulled Jonathan's scarf tighter around their neck, catching the faint smell of him—peppermint and smoke. *Impossible*. Still, Ari buried their nose in the fabric.

They didn't pay attention to the other passengers until someone sat next to them and a rush of cold fire wrapped around their limbs. Ari whipped their gaze from the window and found Jonathan's razor smile. "Hello, Ari."

"How—" Ari snapped their mouth shut and swallowed. Not the smartest question. They had Jonathan's scarf and he had Ari's citrine. "I have work today."

Without his hat, his hair was silver-gray. His skin was warm, in tone and touch, when he patted Ari's thigh with an ungloved hand. "I know. But you've been in my thoughts and in my head, and I was curious to see you."

"Curious to see me," Ari repeated. They drank in the sight of Jonathan and the warmth of his body. "You could've gotten my number, you know. Texted. Asked me out for coffee."

Jonathan—the fucking elemental star—looked at his hands. "Yes. But your cell number's not a piece of you." He drew the citrine from his coat pocket and turned it over in his fingers. "This is."

Ari curled their hands into the scarf, wishing they were curled in Jonathan's hair. "But you can't use that to ask me out for coffee."

Jonathan focused entirely on Ari. "It's not coffee I want."

Desire ripped through Ari. They grasped the scarf, the licks of element coming off of Jonathan, and pulled both close to themself.

Jonathan's eyes flickered, as if in pleasure. "Maybe you *are* dangerous, little witch."

"Oh, I am." Sitting next to Jonathan chased away the worries and the doubts of the morning. This felt *right*. They'd ponder *why* later. "There's a price for more." Despite being wicked and honed, Ari had also been hot and sharp most of their life.

"So you've named." Thoughtfulness in the set of his mouth. "Control is a heady thing, and I'm your equal, Ari."

Equal. Ari turned that unfathomable piece of knowledge over in their head, and wanted to dispute it, but Jonathan spoke it as fact. "Wouldn't be all the time," they said. "Just—in certain situations."

A slow nod. "Not over coffee, I expect."

Ari laughed. Couldn't help it. They *liked* Jonathan, in that moment. Trepidation clung to Ari—Jonathan wasn't human and he wore power like a second skin—but he was also intriguing and smiled like sunlight.

"I'll pay your price," he said, just like that.

Ari exhaled, and yes, control took his mind into the clouds. There were so many ways this could go wrong. They leaned close to his beautiful face and whispered, "My stop is coming up, so here's what's going to happen." They pressed a hand over the citrine, palm touching Jonathan's where it could. "You're going to find me after work, treat me to a lovely dinner like the gentleman you are; then I'm going to take you home, tie you up, and fuck you like the monster I am."

Jonathan's feral smile returned, and he moved his lips close to Ari's. "Reckless."

"You can say no." They wanted to lean in and kiss him, but their stop was next.

"You know I won't," Jonathan said. "Your offer is interesting."

Ari couldn't help a grin of their own. They reached back and hit the strip to signal the bus stop. "It's not an offer, Jonathan."

"Ah." If anything, his smile deepened.

They bumped his legs. "Time for me to go."

He nodded and tucked the citrine back in his pocket before standing. Ari slid into the aisle, but not before Jonathan brushed a hand down Ari's back. "I want my spell, though."

"You'll get it. I don't break promises." They caught Jonathan's hand and squeezed. "Any of them." They let go and headed to the front of the bus. Didn't look back when they stepped off. Jonathan might be there—or might not. They had no idea how this elemental existed in the world, except that, somehow, Jonathan was real and solid to Ari.

So, they were going to do exactly what they said they would. Maybe more time with Jonathan would unlock the spell he was so desperate for Ari to weave.

*

Just after five, Ari walked out of the office. They hadn't expected Jonathan to be waiting in the lobby. Same peacoat, same pale hair, golden skin, and tantalizing smile. He turned the citrine over in his hand, and his bright blue eyes burned straight through Ari.

The pack of coworkers they'd left with broke apart, with choruses of "Good night" and "See you Monday." Ari murmured some kind of response, their being entirely focused on Jonathan.

"Ari." He said their name like a prayer, as if there was no one else in the lobby. He held out his arm, as if they were on a *date*. "Shall we?"

"This isn't about romance, Jonathan." Still, they took his arm.

"Oh, I'm aware." Together they pushed through the doors into the evening.

"What do you think this is?"

Jonathan guided them through the streets of Pittsburgh, the air blustery, dry, and harsh, hinting at the winter to come. "A beginning."

They shook their head. That had been last night. They had prices and promises between them. "We've already started."

That sharp smile again. "A continuation, then. A discovery." He paused at the door to Meat & Potatoes. "Does this qualify as a lovely dinner?"

Very much so. Ari'd managed to eat at the small restaurant once before, but that was only because there'd been an opening at the bar. "If they can seat us."

They stood under the portico of Theater Square, out of the lash of wind that cut down Penn Avenue. "Oh, we have a reservation." And fuck if Jonathan's grin didn't turn Ari inside out with the need to kiss him into submission. He propped opened the door for Ari.

They entered and didn't ask how Jonathan had managed a near-impossible feat on a morning's notice. A discovery, indeed. There was so much Ari wanted to understand. So much they feared to ask, both of Jonathan and for themself.

Jonathan followed, and as he'd assured, there was a reservation for two under his name. They settled into their table.

Ari pulled a little of Jonathan's element and wove it into a simple spell, lessening the chance of being overheard. Maybe it was possessive of them, but they didn't want to share this night with anyone else. Ari skimmed the menu, but their mind kept wandering to unasked questions. "Do you exist in this world?"

Jonathan stilled, the menu motionless in his hands. "We're here, Ari. Right now. This isn't a dream."

Of course it wasn't a dream. "That's not what I'm asking." Ari tore their gaze from Jonathan and read the menu again. "When I'm not here, what do you do? Where do you go?"

Jonathan laid his menu down. "Ah. I understand. Yes, I exist in this world and time. When I'm not with you, I'm still here. People see me." He folded his hands on top of the menu and curved his mouth into a smile. "As to what I do, I own a used bookstore."

"Isn't that a little cliché?"

Ari was growing fond of Jonathan's laugh. "Perhaps, but people like me tend to gravitate toward antique items. Or collections. Or"—he waved a hand—"oddities."

Information twined in Ari's skull. "Are you telling me bookstores and antique shops are all run by magical beings?"

"Not all, surely." His smile didn't diminish.

"I—"

Before they could get their question out, the waiter arrived to take their order. Ari had no idea what they wanted, but one good thing about this place was that they couldn't go wrong with anything on the menu. Ari stabbed at a random dish and rattled the name off.

"I'll have the same." Jonathan handed his menu over, then tilted his head. "Wine?"

"Not tonight." They wanted a clear head, especially for later. "Water is fine for us."

The waiter took the menus, then retreated, leaving Ari caught by the intense desire to put the proud, powerful man before them on his knees. "Why me?"

"You called *me*, Ari. Not the other way around."

"You found me at the rink."

"You were looking for me."

"I was looking—" They'd been looking for passion. For the spark that had been missing from their life. Searching to understand their magic, for a sense of belonging. "But you've been in Pittsburgh for years, I suspect."

"Yes." He dropped his hands to his lap. "As have you."

"Since college." They'd gotten their degree, then stayed, even though they could have found a job elsewhere. Something about this town, its hills, rivers, and bridges had wormed its way into Ari's soul. "I felt compelled to stay."

"Life is strange and magical."

Every amazing moment in Ari's life had been. Even meeting Theo and Bess. Some moments had been fraught. Some dangerous. But always infused with magic and power. "What do you want with me?"

Jonathan lowered his gaze, his smile demure. If he'd planned to reply, it was lost as two glasses filled with water were set in front of them.

There was attraction, one neither of them could deny or ignore. Hell, Jonathan's element practically wrapped itself around Ari unbidden. They pulled and wove it in a way they'd never been able to with fire. Maybe *this* was what being a strong witch was like, this ability to tap into energy and use it—make it part of themself.

They pondered while they waited for their meal, and then while reveling in the taste of their flat iron steak. The lull that fell between them wasn't uncomfortable, especially not when Ari shifted to nudge their leg against Jonathan's.

"I'm going to answer your question with one of my own," Jonathan said. "Why do you want me, Ari?"

So many reasons. The most obvious being simple lust for a stunningly beautiful person. The need to tame someone powerful. However, neither of those hit the core of the truth. "Because I want to understand what you are." Ari set down their fork. "Will you answer my original question?"

He sobered into a seriousness that twisted Ari's bones and set every part of them alight. "What I want with you is *you*. Because you hunt answers, Ari Zydik. Beyond the need to control, aside from the myriad ways our bodies could come together. You seek more from me alongside those, and that's rare. That's a taste *I* want."

"Others have had you."

A shrug. "I *am* old." The grin returned. "*You* are not anyone else, though. I want you, in whatever way you wish to have me."

"Good." Very good. That gave them something to focus on other than the zing of awareness and yearning in their marrow. Lust was knowable, something they could temper and work.

Jonathan chuckled. "Would you like to hear about my rather normal life?"

Ari wanted to take Jonathan home, stretch him out, and see how much he could endure of Ari's flogger. But to know Jonathan was a desire that lay deep in Ari, more than sex or pain or pleasure. "Sure."

True to what Jonathan said, his life was mostly normal. His store carried a variety of books, and also specialized in antiquarian volumes he had a knack for finding. "I have good luck."

"Like finding me?"

Jonathan shook his head. "That was your doing, my sweet witch."

"Like managing reservations on a Friday night at a place that's usually booked out weeks in advance?"

That impish grin returned, and he sipped his water.

"The things I want to do to you," Ari murmured. The questions they needed to ask, the answers they wanted to find.

"Yes. Please."

Weave me a spell. Those words from last night hung like a challenge in their mind, sounded like the crack of a whip and the murmur of candleflame. Ari flagged down the waiter to ask for the check. Once their dishes had been cleared and Jonathan had paid, they strolled into the night. The air was sharp and crisp, and the moonlight turned Jonathan's hair silver.

Something in Ari's chest unwound. They'd called this man, this being to them. Jonathan was a sudden calm in the middle of the storm that had been Ari's life. "Does it bother you that I want to tie you up?"

"No." He peered at the sky as they walked, arm in arm, to Ari's bus stop. "Not at all. And you want to do far more than tie me up, Ari."

Much more. They pulled Jonathan to a halt. "May I kiss you?"

"Of course." Need lay in that confirmation.

Ari took the lapels of his peacoat and pulled Jonathan to them. His lips were cool, but everything else burned when they deepened that kiss into something wanton and painful. A moan escaped Jonathan, and Ari drank the sound down. When they pulled back, Jonathan's expression was equal parts ravaged and wanting.

He licked his lips. "You should definitely take me home, tie me up, and fuck me."

This time, it was Ari who laughed, dark joy ringing into the night. He pulled Jonathan back into a walk, one quicker than before. If they were lucky, they'd catch the next bus. If not, Ari would spend the next half hour kissing Jonathan's lovely mouth.

Either option was acceptable.

*

They made it into Ari's apartment and to their room in a blur of touches, tastes, and motion, the pull between them finally overwhelming them both. Jonathan's energy exploded in Ari's mind and magic. They consumed Jonathan's mouth the same way they sucked down his element, folding both into their soul.

Jonathan tasted of the night and darkness and joy. Of a light Ari didn't understand and an energy they couldn't get enough of. Jonathan was wonder and danger. He felt like *home*.

They pushed Jonathan against the wall by their bedroom door, kicking the latter closed with their foot. "I need you naked. Now."

Beneath Jonathan's bronze skin lay a blush that darkened everything, from the look in those starlit eyes to the word that tumbled from his kiss-bruised lips. "Yes."

He made short work of undressing, peeling off clothing to reveal silken flesh stretched over muscle. The hair that dotted his chest and curled around his cock was the same pale gray Ari had caught under moonlight at the skating rink, beneath a furiously simple black cap.

He was magnificent and unworldly. Godlike. "Get on your knees."

Jonathan knelt, his gaze never leaving theirs. Energy whipped between them, lifting Ari's hair, rustling their skirt. It burned their veins. They wanted to devour every burst, then thrust it back into Jonathan. "Do you have a safeword?"

Jonathan blinked. "There's nothing you can do that will harm me."

Ari combed their fingers through Jonathan's hair, then tightened their grip until Jonathan winced. "I don't want to harm you; I want to *hurt* you, but not beyond what you're willing to bear. If not for yourself, then have one for me so I know you consent." They pulled Jonathan's head back, until his proud throat was exposed, and his body taut against Ari's.

"Then Cygnus," he whispered. "Let it be Cygnus."

The swan. The constellation. When Ari let go, Jonathan gave a little groan. "You can be as rough as you'd like."

That was a dangerous thing to say. Ari hiked up their skirt and pulled down their tights. They stroked themself, watching Jonathan's hungry face. "Do you want me, Jonathan?" Their voice was rough and sharp, betraying desperation.

"Ari." His reply was a rumble. "You know I do."

Ari grasped Jonathan's chin and guided their cock into his willing, hot mouth. They both moaned, Jonathan's vibrating all around Ari. They thrust slowly at first, then with more force, their fingers twisted hard into Jonathan's hair.

His hands climbed Ari's legs.

"No. Behind your back, Jonathan. Surrender yourself to me."

That whimper was the most powerful sound Ari'd ever heard. The moment a being full of power and eternity yielded to Ari's will.

Energy shifted, twined, and flooded the room. Ari nearly came right there, thrusting deep into Jonathan's throat. Instead, they pulled out and stepped back. Both their breaths were gulps, and Ari's voice cracked as if they'd been the one on their knees. "Ever been cuffed and flogged, Jonathan?"

He shook his head. Behind those exquisite features, Ari spied excitement and fear. That only whetted their appetite. They pulled him to his feet and hauled him to their four-poster bed.

Yes, it was large. Yes, it occupied most of the room and had been hell to move. It also had hooks and rope hanging in perfect places, ready to be tied. "Stand here. Don't move."

"Yes, Ari." Jonathan's chest heaved.

Ari stripped their shirt on the way to their dresser and discarded their tights and shoes. They kept the skirt on. Took only a moment to find the cuffs and their favorite flogger before they returned to Jonathan. "Give me your wrists."

He obeyed sweetly, and Ari nearly groaned as they buckled the leather cuffs on. Lazy tendrils of Jonathan's element wrapped around Ari in return. "Don't get smart."

"Wouldn't dream of it." The snap in Jonathan's voice said otherwise.

They turned Jonathan around, then tied him to the bed, limbs stretched wide. Ari drew their hands down

Jonathan's arms and back, then bit his shoulder, hard enough to garner them a gasp and a tremble. They reached around and stroked Jonathan's dick and bit a matching bruise into Jonathan's other shoulder.

"Please."

Ari nodded. "Soon."

Ari wasn't sure what Jonathan was begging for—pain, pleasure, or that spell. They dropped to their knees to cuff Jonathan's ankles, leaving Jonathan stretched between the pillars of Ari's bed, before nipping one of Jonathan's ass cheeks. He yanked on the ropes.

"Behave," they whispered against Jonathan's thigh.

"You don't want me to."

That was true. Ari wanted snark and mouth and all the power Jonathan could offer. They wanted to consume him, beat him, fuck him, and give him everything he wanted.

Weave me a spell.

A groan escaped Ari. They picked up their flogger and went to work, slowly. Gently, even. But as Jonathan twisted, shuttered, and moaned, they hit harder and faster. Under their blows, Jonathan's back reddened and welts appeared. Leather cut into golden flesh and bright red points blossomed.

Broken skin. Blood. Jonathan's energy streamed out of him with each moan, and Ari sucked it down as if they could hold the whole universe in their soul. With each stroke of the flogger, Jonathan cried out, raw and guttural. No way Theo and Bess didn't hear. Or their neighbors. Ari didn't care. They laid into Jonathan until they didn't think he could take much more—until Ari knew that *they* couldn't take more.

When they stopped, silence engulfed the room, disrupted by harsh breathing. Energy swarmed—so much power, Ari was drunk with it. Jonathan hung his head. All that held him from falling were the cuffs around his wrists.

Ari set the flogger on the bed and slid their hands up Jonathan's sides, his skin warm and damp with sweat. "You're exquisite, Jonathan. Beautiful."

"Thank you." His words were rough and full of tears. "Thank you for this."

Ari's emotions swirled like the energy in the room, looping and bobbing and tying themselves into knots. Their throat tightened too much to speak, so they kissed his back and ran teeth over the wounds they'd made, tasting sweat and blood. Ari stroked Jonathan as he shuddered and moaned, soaked in his essence, took their combined energy, and pushed it back into Jonathan's brightness. Then they unhooked the cuffs from the frame and lowered Jonathan to the bed, gathering his wrists at the small of his back. "I'm leaving your ankles cuffed."

"Yes, Ari."

"I'm going to fuck you, Jonathan. Like I want. Like I think you need." They leaned down over that prone body and pressed their cock into the cleft of Jonathan's ass with only the cloth of their skirt between. "Hard and deep, until I come inside you. Tell me I can."

"Yes." Jonathan squirmed, and the friction and the heat were perfect. "Good." His voice was stronger. "I want you. I need—"

Ari yanked Jonathan's hair and took his mouth in a sloppy brutal kiss that had him—had them both—trembling. When Ari broke away, he kissed Jonathan's cheek. "You taste divine. Your blood. Your tears. Your soul."

A faint smile graced his lips.

Ari pushed off and fetched the lube. Prepping Jonathan was a delight, from smacking his ass to sliding fingers into him while he moaned and panted and cursed.

"Oh, now you have a mouth." They hiked up their skirt and pressed the head of their cock against Jonathan's hole.

"You weren't teasing me when you were beating me. Now—"

Ari pushed inside. Whatever Jonathan had planned to say vanished into a soft, long cry of pleasure that echoed in Ari's chest.

As with flogging, Ari started slowly, giving them both time to adjust to the other before they picked up speed. Ari held Jonathan's wrists in one hand, and the nails of their other dug into his hip. Under them, Jonathan became a gasping, moaning mess. Ari pulled starlight from Jonathan, swallowed it, then pushed it back into him with every hard snap of their hips. Maybe they were both glowing. A little lost, a little dazed.

This was magic: Ari taking Jonathan and Jonathan opening himself for it. They were a witch, and Jonathan was their element—a living, breathing, embodiment of power.

Right now, that embodiment had welts on his back and was riding Ari's cock. "You really wanted this, didn't you?" A strange thought, especially when voiced. Jonathan could've had whomever he wanted, yet Ari was the one controlling his pliant, submissive body.

Something part laugh but mostly moan poured out of Jonathan. "Don't you dare stop."

Ari smacked his ass. Fucked him harder, pushed him closer, until the only sounds tumbling from Jonathan's smart mouth were deep cries.

Ari didn't stop. They relished Jonathan's release, cries turned to gasps, then whimpers. They let go of Jonathan's wrists, grabbed his hair, and yanked. "I'm not done with you yet."

"Good, please..." It was a breathless reply that stabbed into Ari.

Please.

Weave me a spell.

They had no idea what Jonathan wanted, but they gave him all they could—their body, the energy they'd collected, and every piece of pleasure and pain they could coax from both their bodies. On and on until Ari was shouting out their own release, burying themself inside Jonathan, and slamming more element than they should've been able to hold into the heart of the star underneath them.

Apparently, sex with Jonathan was like dying and being reborn into a powerful creature. Even afterward, when Ari should have been spent and light with fatigue, they buzzed with awareness.

Jonathan, however, was a happy lump of well-fucked man. Ari freed his legs, cleaned him up, and coaxed him under the covers.

"Please say you're joining me," he murmured.

There was something sweet about that plaintive request. Ari kissed him on the cheek. "It's my bed. I'm gonna sleep in it." They stripped off their skirt. "Gotta clean me up, too."

"Ah." A sleepy, happy sound.

No motion or lights lit the rest of the apartment, save the tiny night-light in the bathroom. If Theo and Bess were home, they'd gone to bed too. Ari had no idea what time it was, and didn't care. At all. They cleaned themself up, then returned to curl up with Jonathan.

They crawled into bed, looped their arms around him, and pulled him close. "I hope you enjoyed that."

"Oh, little witch, you have no idea."

Ari snorted. "Not so little."

Jonathan Aster—an actual damn star—*giggled*. "That's *very* true."

"Go to sleep, Jonathan."

He did. And after a long time spent listening to Jonathan breathe, wondering if the buzz still dancing inside them was permanent, Ari did, as well.

*

The weight of Bess's and Theo's gazes was almost a physical presence as Ari moved around the kitchen. Before Ari'd ventured from their room, Jonathan, in a murmur that was all sleep and haze, had said he wouldn't mind some coffee. Apparently, elementals could have sex and kink hangovers just like anyone else. But his smile had been bright and his mouth pliant when Ari'd kissed him. They'd have fucked Jonathan awake, but they were nursing their own haze from the night before, and the tangled buzz mixed with their spinning mind meant conversation was a better plan than sex.

They wanted to understand what had happened and pick through the moments in peace. Spend time with Jonathan. Ask the questions flying around their head.

The *last* thing Ari wanted was to engage with Bess and Theo. Maybe later—but not now.

Ari broke the silence by grinding coffee beans. After they poured the grounds into the maker and started the pot, they turned around to face Theo and Bess.

Bess opened her mouth as if to speak, but flattened her lips instead. She shook her head. Theo cleared his throat. "You—Ari, you brought an elemental—a fucking lightning elemental or something—home. He could've burned down the house!"

"I know what he is. And he wouldn't."

"You don't know that." Theo's tone took on the scolding quality Ari disliked.

"I do, though." They leaned against the counter, letting the edge bite into their hands. The discomfort cleared their head a little. Every nerve felt stretched and pinched. They wanted coffee and Jonathan; was that too much to ask?

Bess loosened her arms from across her chest. "We're concerned, that's all."

"You always are." The coffee pot gurgled and sputtered. Theo and Bess meant well, they truly *did*, but Ari was so damn tired of it. They poured two mugs of coffee and hefted them. "I'm fine. The house is fine. I'll talk to you later, okay?" They didn't wait for an answer.

Back in their room, Jonathan lounged in bed, seemingly fragile and indestructible, hair a disaster, torso lined with marks and shadowed bruises. His posture was almost demure, but his eyes were delighted flames. Ari handed him a mug, then settled on the bed next to him. "Theo thinks you're a lightning elemental and you're going to burn down the house."

Jonathan huffed a laugh before sipping his coffee.

"Are there lightning elementals?"

"First, define what you mean by elemental."

Ari gazed into their coffee. "Everyone says the fae are elementals. Water, air, earth."

"Fire?"

"You know there aren't fire fae." They gripped their mug tighter. "I never understood that. It makes no *sense*."

Then again, neither did Jonathan existing. The lack of knowledge, the confusion in Ari twisted like a knife in their gut.

Jonathan's soft touch pulled them out of their thoughts. "There are beings you might call lightning elementals, but they're nothing like me, or the fae, or anything you might also use that word to describe."

Maybe it was the aftermath of the night before, or the energy still swirling in the room, but Ari's emotions stretched and tumbled. Ari might be sharp and dangerous in their own way, but they were mortal and ignorant in so many others. "There's nothing about that in the books I've read. No one's ever told me about stars or lightning or why there are no damn fire fae." Ari hated the sound of their voice, tight and cracking, even as frustration tightened their lungs and stole breath. "Or what the hell I am." A mediocre fire witch who'd somehow called a star to them. That was as impossible as all the rest.

A clink of ceramic on wood, then Jonathan's arms were around Ari, drawing them back against his warm chest. "You're lovely, that's what you are."

Ari snorted. "If you're trying to woo me, that's going to fail."

"Is it?" They could almost feel Jonathan's smile against their skin.

They'd asked the universe for a connection, and Jonathan had appeared, bright and shining into their life. They wanted this to last and last.

Ari whispered the first dangerous question. "Will you teach me what I want to know?"

"There's a price." Jonathan's hot breath made Ari shiver.

"There always is." They drew Jonathan's arm up so they could lick and nip at a bruise they'd placed there last night.

Jonathan shuddered, and his voice dripped with the edge of a moan. "Everything goes two ways, Ari. Magic. Sex. Answers. Come home with me tonight."

Ari turned in Jonathan's arms so they could claim his mouth. Once they'd kissed Jonathan into a writhing mess, they answered, "I can do that."

His smile was a spell of its own. "Good."

*

That night, Ari packed a bag and rode the T with Jonathan to his South Hill's home. "Tomorrow," Jonathan said, "if you'd like, we can visit my shop."

"I still find it strange that you have a shop. And a job. And a home." They ran their hand along his thigh. "All normal things."

He caught their hand and laced his fingers between theirs. "Even the fae exist in this world. Some are hidden, yes, but when you live for long enough you get—bored."

"Am I a cure for your *boredom*?" They raised an eyebrow.

Jonathan pressed the stop request strip. "Being alive is a cure for my boredom. You, my dear, are a wonderful, unexpected delight."

Jonathan's energy twined inside them, coiling like a snake. Ice and fire. So many questions Ari needed to ask, so much they wanted to know.

Jonathan stood. "This is my stop."

Together they made their way out of the train onto the platform. The night was cold and clear, with few stars peeking out from the moonlight sky. Ari's breath clouded the air as they peered into the night. "Can you see yourself up there? You're not in two places at the same time, are you?"

Jonathan glanced up. "When it's dark enough, yes. But I'm not in two places." He waved his free hand at the sky. "When you look at the stars, you're looking backward in time. This is now." He gestured to the street beyond the train platform. "I'm right here with you."

With them. That was terrifying. "This still isn't a romance."

"Does it need to be?" Jonathan hadn't unlaced his fingers from theirs.

Ari turned the question over in their mind as Jonathan led them into a residential area.

Another dangerous question slipped past their lips. "What do you want this to be?"

Jonathan slowed to a stop. Breath still smoked into the night, and Ari resisted slipping their hand into Jonathan's coat. There was light in his eyes, sparkling and gentle. Ari ached standing near him.

He brushed his fingers against their cheek. "You lead, Ari. I'll follow. Whatever you wish."

"So, I get to wish upon you?"

A dark smile. "You get to do many, *many* things upon me."

"Then we should go to your house, so I can do that." Lovely things. Wicked things. Things that would make Jonathan moan and scream. Magic things. They'd devour Jonathan's energy and thrust it back into him. Make him bleed.

Weave me a spell.

The streets were quiet but for the distant sound of cars and the deep thrum of gas furnaces cooling homes.

Ari sensed the fire there, warm and inviting, even as Jonathan's cold flame tangled around their legs. "I called you."

"And I came."

"I should have called sooner."

A bright cloud of air came with Jonathan's laugh. "Perhaps. But we have time."

Did they? Jonathan had time. He could look into the past and see himself in the sky. Ari guessed Jonathan's future was as seemingly endless. But their life—that was another story. Though, right now, they were young and here *with* Jonathan.

A turn down a street, then half a block. "Here we are."

Jonathan's home wasn't big, but it was brick and light shown from the windows where the blinds hadn't been pulled down. The ubiquitous hum of heating rumbled from the house, a hint of fire seeping out.

Took only a moment for Jonathan to unlock the front door and usher Ari inside. The space was warm, both from the heated air and the rich wood that accented every room. "This is—cozy." They hadn't expected that.

"The house was built in the '40s," Jonathan said, "but it has lovely Art Deco touches from the '30s. Adds to the charm." There was pride in his voice as he took Ari's coat and the scarf he'd given them, and hung both in the closet. "Let me show you around."

Unlike the mad scramble into Ari's apartment, this was settled and quiet, though desire lurked deep in Ari's soul. The need to be naked again with Jonathan. To touch and tease and kiss and bite and scratch—and to cuddle.

Calm mixed with their growing passion.

Jonathan had bookshelves filled to the brim. Artwork from simple to breathtaking. He also had dishes in the sink and junk mail. Bills. A computer and a TV. Old DVDs in the corner. Ari flipped through a few titles.

"Mostly, I stream now." Jonathan scratched the back of his head.

Everything was so—mundane. "This feels like home." Even more than their own apartment did. An unbidden, heady thought.

Every time Jonathan touched them, everything turned wondrous and dangerous, and this was no exception—a caress between the shoulders, meant to sooth. Ari turned to and pulled Jonathan into a kiss, one deep, full of exploration, and bent on subjection. Under Ari's palms, he trembled.

Such a simple thing. They pulled back. "You could kill me."

He stroked their cheek. "No, I can't," he whispered, painfully almost. "You're stronger than you know."

That's where this terror came from. Ari closed their eyes and leaned against him. Strong arms wrapped around them. All was crystal and light, like the selenite on their altar or the shimmer in Jonathan's scarf. He and this damn house fit Ari in a way nothing ever had. The cosmos looked back when Ari peered at Jonathan. *They* were the one who should be afraid.

And they *were*. So terrified that they could only move forward. "You gonna show me your bedroom?"

A chuckle. "Yes. Though the bed is far less...practical than yours."

"I'm sure I can find a way to tie you down." Ari let Jonathan's warmth and element flow into them. Pushed it back into Jonathan.

A sigh and another tremble. "I have no doubt. No doubt at all."

Weave me a spell.

Ari unwrapped themself from Jonathan. "What do you want?"

"Whatever you're willing to give. Or take."

That didn't help at all. "Let's see this bedroom of yours."

Jonathan led them upstairs, and yes, the bed was less practical for tying someone up, but Ari managed. In the end, Jonathan cried out their name like an invocation as Ari wove a very different kind of magic into him, one born of blood and sobs.

Afterward, Jonathan held Ari and murmured absently, as tears welled in Ari's eyes. "Tell me about stars."

Jonathan did, with words that made sense and ones that didn't, and then whispered truths in a language Ari didn't know. About loneliness and eternity. Falling to earth. The song of the universe that still echoed in Jonathan's ears. Ari shuddered and listened. Cold fire wrapped into their marrow, and *that* at least they understood. Jonathan was here, now. And so was Ari.

It had been two days since the ice rink. The moon hadn't even become full. Ari wanted whatever this was to last for the rest of their life, except their life would snuff out fast in the long exhale of Jonathan's.

They knew of no spell that would fix that.

*

Jonathan's bookstore reflected him. The shop brimmed with the old and new, light and darkness, and held his sense of passion and cold fire. Ari touched the leather-clad spine of a tome and soaked in all that was Jonathan, just as they had the previous night and this morning.

The starlight. The eternity. The joy. "This shop is beautiful."

Jonathan's smile was everything. "Thank you. I'm glad you like it."

They stood close, like lovers, near a door marked STAFF in the back of the shop. Jonathan's employee, Lillian, was at the checkout counter with a customer. Murmured conversation was as soothing as the leather under Ari's fingertips and the bruise peeking from beneath Jonathan's coat collar. "Do you need to work today?"

He hesitated before answering. "I usually work on Sundays, to catch up on paperwork and help Lil out. But I don't have to."

Ari closed the distance, slid their hands inside his coat, and pressed into the violet mark they'd left behind. Jonathan closed his eyes and exhaled. "I don't want to interrupt your life any more than I have."

"Please interrupt my life, Ari." He opened his eyes. "I have no desire to chase you away."

But there needed to be space. Ari'd always longed for both companionship and solitude. Spaces between to think and ponder. Right now, they didn't want to leave, but space could be opened here too. "I could read while you worked." They stroked his collarbone.

"That would be... It would be lovely to have you here."

So, after they stole a lingering kiss, Ari stayed. A quick perusal of the store, and they found an old action-adventure book to read. They settled into one of the comfortable chairs scattered around, and tucked their legs up, their long blue skirt keeping them warm from the occasional rush of cold air when the front door opened.

Jonathan flitted between the back room and the front counter, his occasional laugh a counterpoint to the general quiet of the store. Hours passed. Jonathan would stop by, and Ari would pull him down for a kiss and revel in the sweet taste of submission and sharp bite of starlight.

Some customers eyed Ari with curiosity—but not hostility—though they did overhear a murmured question and then Jonathan's clear response. "Oh, they're with me."

Yes, and no. Jonathan was with *them*, but that would undoubtedly be lost on most people. Ari glanced away from their book and stared unfocused at the shelves across from them. A thought twisted and swooped in the back of their mind—but they couldn't form the words to tease it out. It was all emotion and longing. Somehow, Jonathan was *theirs*. They didn't fucking care that it had only been three days.

Ari reached out and tugged on the strands of Jonathan's energy swirling between them. A moment later he walked around a bookcase into the aisle, concern marring his expression. "Are you all right?"

No. "Yes." *No*. Ari closed the book, unfolded their legs, and stood. "No." They still hadn't processed all that had happened, what they'd learned, and all Jonathan had whispered to them last night.

Jonathan held out a hand, in offering. Ari took it, pulled him to them, and wrapped their arms around him. "You're overwhelming."

A huff of breath hit their ear. "You too, my witch."

Ari held him tighter. "You're not chasing me away, but I need to go home. Alone."

"I know," Jonathan murmured. "Space. Time. Both are needed to build a relationship."

Ari opened a gap between them. "Jonathan—"

Bright fucking smile that took all of their willpower not to kiss away. "Not a romance. I know. But there are all kinds of relationships, Ari."

True and *true*. Didn't ease their desire to stay, nor the need to flee. Jonathan helped them into their coat and tugged at the starlight scarf around their neck. "This looks good on you."

"I still owe you a spell." They hadn't meant to say that.

"There's time, Ari. There's time."

Ari believed Jonathan then, but that wore off when they got to the T station. Their life was a blink, a moment to Jonathan. His was eternity in theirs.

Later, Ari watched shadows shift and move across the ceiling of their bedroom. Jonathan's scarf glowed softly on the chair they'd thrown it over, and the elements they could see and touch slithered through the room like forgotten memories.

Jonathan was *theirs*. That was the spell they'd been casting all this time. The one they'd begun at Samhain.

Weave me a spell.

"Did you know what you were asking for when you asked me that?"

The room didn't answer, but the scarf twinkled brighter.

*

Ari waited before setting their plan in motion. The moon became full, then waned, then waxed again, and Midwinter loomed—the darkest day, the longest night.

In between, Ari's life meshed with Jonathan's and his with theirs. Jonathan answered questions and pointed out the hidden mysteries of Pittsburgh. Their spells became stronger. Focused.

And they worked. Even Bess and Theo had accepted that Ari had found a balance—and that Jonathan hadn't burned the apartment down—not that they spent much time there. Many nights, Ari would find Jonathan waiting in the lobby of their office building. Sometimes, they'd go to dinner. Other times, they went ice skating. Most times, Ari fucked Jonathan. Or tied him up. Or both. But when they became so overwhelmed by Jonathan, when they'd taken too much, he'd hold Ari and whisper reassurances.

There was so *much* of Jonathan, of the light and darkness. Of submission, his need, his desire. All things Ari wanted to take and take and give back in spades.

They were human, though. Jonathan wasn't. The welts and bruises and broken skin Ari left behind faded fast, *so* fast. Yet the impact lingered in Ari for much longer.

Still, Jonathan *fit* with Ari, so much so that Ari brought Jonathan to Thanksgiving dinner. Their circle-mate, Matty, upon meeting Jonathan, looked him up and down and rolled his eyes. "Of course someone like you would fall out of the sky for fricking Ari Zydik. They have all the luck." Then he'd sat down and included Jonathan in their circle. "You've got an altar or something, or do you just exist as a giant glowing thing?"

There'd been silence for a moment; then Jonathan had plopped himself on the floor next to Matty. "I'm, in fact, a giant glowing thing. But I also have an altar."

That was true. After the second night Ari'd spent at Jonathan's, they'd explored the house, with his blessing. In a small room full of art and books and plants stood an altar not too different from the one in their own room. "You ever afraid your candles will burn your books?"

"No." Jonathan had appeared behind them and wrapped his arms around Ari. Warm. Soothing, especially here. A candle had flamed to life on the altar. "We're alike, you and me. I can play with fire too."

"A magnifying glass and a sunny day."

He'd brushed his mouth along Ari's neck. "Something like that."

Ari had turned around and backed Jonathan against a wall, then set about harnessing his energy in an entirely different way.

*

Midwinter evening, Jonathan was waiting for them in the lobby of their office after work. He held out his arm as he so often did. "Shall we?"

Ari snorted, but took his arm anyway. As always. "It's Midwinter."

"Mmmm. A day for death, rebirth, and sacrifice." Jonathan's smile made Ari feel like tripping over the edge of a knife. "What does your heart want on this night?"

Ari exhaled breath like fire into the chilled night air. Possession. Domination. Someone who understood them. Held them. Let them be. "Let's go to your house." They were close to Gateway station.

They took the T to the familiar stop and walked the familiar blocks to Jonathan's home. Like always, Jonathan hung Ari's coat and scarf in the closet alongside his own, and like always, Ari climbed the stairs to the second floor. They stopped at the threshold of Jonathan's study and gazed at the altar.

Jonathan's energy wrapped around Ari before his arms did. They covered his hands with their own and leaned against him. "Do you have chalk and salt?"

They'd never *felt* Jonathan go still like he sometimes did, that inhuman moment. For an instant, he was as hard as a statue. Maybe his heart stopped beating. Then air rushed by their ear, and his weight slumped against theirs. "Yes, of course." Then words they'd heard on the first night. "Weave me a spell."

That fire—all the fire they'd collected—sparked in Ari, born of earth and what they'd taken again and again from Jonathan. They moved like flame too, spinning in Jonathan's arms, grappling him down until his hair was in their hands. He knelt at Ari's feet a moment later.

Shock, fight, then sweet surrender. The barest hint of a groan.

"I'll weave you a collar." The words poured from Ari like starlight and night—cold and eternal. "Keep you. Own you. Use you. Be with you."

Those beautiful eyes mirrored the fire Ari wove. Jonathan bent his body toward them. "Yes."

They pulled Jonathan's head back, exposing his throat. The sheer joy in his face nearly undid Ari. "Is that what you want? To be bound to me?"

"Please." His word was a promise.

Sparks danced along Ari's skin. They loosened their hold on Jonathan's hair. "I'm mortal." Ephemeral.

When Jonathan met his gaze, his eyes were nebulas. "You wouldn't be. Not after." He brushed his fingers against Ari's. "Take me. Keep me. Bind me, fire witch. I'll be by your side for as long as you wish."

This was a gift and a curse. One that they'd had been given that first night, part of a spell Ari'd been weaving since then. Terrible things flowed through Ari. Wonderful things too. "Why?"

Jonathan's brilliant smile flashed. "You saw me. Called me. You understand the spaces between." He paused. "And you *care*."

"I care," Ari echoed. They *did* care for Jonathan. Deeply. There was power there, such energy waiting to be held in their hands. The absolute joy of hearing Jonathan cry and beg and weep. Tasting his skin and blood. Thrusting into his pliant body. Trust lay in Ari too. The willingness to give Jonathan what he desired, what he *needed*. "You care too."

Jonathan's chuckle was a deep vibration Ari felt in their bones. "Very much so. Finish weaving me into you, Ari Zydik. Claim me as your own."

They carded their fingers through Jonathan's silver hair. "Get chalk and salt, and a knife. Lose the clothes."

Jonathan's energy whipped around the room until Ari gathered it, calmed it, and drew him in. That came as naturally as breathing, taking what Jonathan gave. Controlling the power. As Ari tugged on Jonathan's hair again, realization cut through, shifting their life into singular clarity. "I've never been a fire witch. It's a fluke that I can manipulate fire."

Jonathan's sigh wasn't an answer, but the truth hung between them, as bright as Jonathan himself.

Ari spoke it into being. "I'm a *star* witch."

"Take me. Use me, Ari." Jonathan spoke softly. "I'll get you what you need."

They let go. "It'll be painful."

His smile glinted like a blade. "I know."

And it was, for both of them. Jonathan was Ari's altar; they were the sacrifice. Naked and glorious, they fought and fucked until Ari tamed Jonathan in a circle of chalk and salt. Took him and used him as he'd demanded, then wove them both together with blood, tears, and starlight. In the end, they lay tangled together on the hard floor of Jonathan's office, the copper smell of blood mixing with the scent of wax and sandalwood. Ari didn't need to open their eyes to know exactly where Jonathan was, how he looked, where tears dotted his face.

"I'm sorry you've been so lonely." Jonathan's sweet voice touched their soul.

Ari shifted and open their eyes, alone no more. "I wove you a spell. All this time, I wove *you*."

"You did. In every way I hoped you might."

"Have you always been this much of a manipulative bastard?" Ari pushed a bloodstained lock of hair away from Jonathan's eyes.

There was the grin they were so very fond of. "Yes."

Powerful. Bright. Strong. *Theirs.* "What now?"

"Now? You break your circle, my witch, and we take a shower. After that? The future is yours."

"Ours," they said.

"This isn't about romance, Ari," he murmured.

No, it wasn't. But Jonathan was theirs, and they were his, so it didn't really matter. They reached out with their foot and broke the circle.

About the Authors

ZIGGY SCHUTZ is a young queer writer living on the west coast of Canada. She writes mainly young adult fantasy, always full of the kinds of characters that a younger her was so desperate to find.

When not writing, she can be found in classrooms teaching kids about queer history, or in dark theatres and even darker haunted houses. Because of that, By Candlelight may or may not be inspired by a true story.

Website: www.ziggyschutz.wordpress.com

Facebook: www.facebook.com/ziggyschutz

Twitter: @ziggytschutz

Tumblr: www.ziggyschutz.tumblr.com

Part time, **PAIGE S. ALLEN** is many things: a queer black femme, a pop culture critic, a freelance writer, and a very tired Millennial doing the whole Quarter-Life Crisis thing. Full time, Paige is a lover of comic books, the entire horror genre, and very cheesy romances – and the queerer all these forms of media are, the better.

Website: www.paigesallen.com

Twitter: @goodbye_duppy

BROOKLYN RAY is a tea connoisseur and an occult junkie. She writes queer speculative fiction layered with magic, rituals and found families.

Twitter: @BrookieRayWrite

Tumblr: www.brooklyn--ray.tumblr.com

J.S. FIELDS is a scientist who has perhaps spent too much time around organic solvents. They enjoy roller derby, woodturning, making chain mail by hand, and cultivating fungi in the backs of minivans. Nonbinary, and always up for a Twitter chat.

Website: www.chlorociboria.com

Twitter: @galactoglucoman

S R JONES is a writer of science fiction and fantasy. Born in London, he was raised on the Welsh borders and is now more or less settled in the Midlands. He currently shares his living space with four corn snakes, to whom he reads all his work prior to publication. So far, none of the snakes have left any reviews, so it's impossible to know whether or not they appreciate this. S R Jones began his transition in his early 20s, and is an outspoken member of the trans community.

Website: www.AegisImmemorial.com

Facebook: www.facebook.com/AegisImmemorial

Twitter: @AegisImmemorial

ALEX HARROW is a genderqueer, pansexual, and demisexual author of queer science fiction and fantasy. Alex' pronouns are they/them.

When not writing diversity with a chance of explosions, Alex is a high school English teacher, waging epic battles against comma splices, misused apostrophes, and anyone under the delusion that the singular 'they' is grammatically incorrect.

A German immigrant, Alex has always been drawn to language and stories. They began to write when they realized that the best guarantee to see more books with queer characters was to create them. Alex cares deeply about social justice and wants to see diverse characters, including LGBTQ+ protagonists, in more than the stereotypical coming out story.

Alex currently lives in Salt Lake City, Utah with their equally geeky wife, outnumbered by three adorable feline overlords, and what could not possibly be too many books.

Website: www.alexharrow.com

Facebook: www.facebook.com/alexharrowsff

Twitter: @AlexHarrowSFF

Instagram: www.instagram.com/alexharrowsff

Pinterest: www.pinterest.com/AlexHarrowSFF

EMMETT NAHIL is a queer writer, artist, and game producer, interested in intersectional activism, diverse representation for other queer Middle Easterners, and bringing more nuanced work to all kinds of weird literature. He writes creative fiction and has been known to favor horror, sci-fi, urban/modern fantasy, and trans-inclusive feminist speculative fiction.

Website: www.emmettnahil.com

Twitter: @_emnays

Instagram: www.instagram.com/_emnay

Pinterest: www.pinterest.com/13enahil

SARA CODAIR lives in a world of words, writing fiction in every free moment, teaching writing at a community college and binge-reading fantasy novels. When not lost in words, Sara can often be found hiking, swimming, or gardening. Find Sara's words in Alternative Truths, Helios Quarterly, and Secrets of the Goat People, at www.saracodair.com

Facebook: www.facebook.com/SaraCodair1

Twitter: @shatteredsmooth

Instagram: www.instagram.com/shatteredsmooth

Pinterest: www.pinterest.com/shatteredsmooth

ANNA ZABO writes contemporary and paranormal romance for all colors of the rainbow. They live and work in Pittsburgh, Pennsylvania.

Anna has an MFA in Writing Popular Fiction from Seton Hill University, where they fell in with a roving band of romance writers and never looked back. They also have a BA in Creative Writing from Carnegie Mellon University. They can be easily plied with coffee and hockey tickets.

Website: www.annazabo.com

Facebook: www.facebook.com/AnnaZabo

Twitter: @amergina

Instagram: www.instagram.com/amergina